Stewart Sinclair,
Private Eye

Stewart Sinclair, Private Eye

Elizabeth Greenwood

authorHOUSE®

AuthorHouse™
1663 Liberty Drive
Bloomington, IN 47403
www.authorhouse.com
Phone: 1-800-839-8640

First published by AuthorHouse   12/21/2011

ISBN: 978-1-4567-8849-0 (sc)
ISBN: 978-1-4567-8850-6 (ebk)

Printed in the United States of America

FICTION by
ELIZABETH GREENWOOD

Utopia 2000 (1994)
Loftycross (1995)
Collected Short Stories and Four Novellas (2006)
Out of This World, a Space Romance (2009)
Sophie's Friends and Other Stories (2011)

OTHER WORKS

Nietzsche, Redeemer of Chance (1998)
Sigmud Freud and the Decline of The Judeo-Christian Culture (2008)

POETRY

Pebbles on a Beach (2011)

To my father Joseph John Greenwood Tilley
who introduced me to Sherlock Holmes
in grateful memory

CONTENTS

THE PEACOCKS
OF TARSHISH

The Peacocks of Tarshish

'Once in three years came the navy of Tarshish, bringing gold and silver, ivory and apes, and peacocks.' (1, Kings, 10;22)

Imbued with the sense of purpose which he associated with his newly-acquired profession as a private eye, Stewart Sinclair cast about in his mind for a principle which would reflect it, and he found it in none other but Sherlock Holmes who, working as he did for the love of the art rather than the acquirement of wealth, demanded of an investigation that it should 'tend towards the unusual and even the fantastic'. A more felicitous concordance of aims Sinclair could not have wished for being both untried and optimistic about his prospects as befitted a young man with high expectations both from himself and the standards set by the profession. Overtly, all along, friends and relatives had proved supportive, and any apprehension or doubt that was expressed by his father was ascribed to the negativity created by the afflictions of age; so, when he was approached by Stephen Oldfield, of Oldfield and Baxter, a good old-fashioned firm of solicitors, *pater dixit*, with a view to carrying out a private investigation of an unusual character, Sinclair could not believe his luck. Being the sensible young man that he was, however, he did not allow this stroke of good fortune to go to his head and his first question to Stephen Oldfield was:

'Why me?'

'Well', replied the senior partner of Oldfield and Baxter, 'we reckoned that a mature detective with years of practice behind him, and retirement not far off, would not bother to tackle a case requiring the enthusiasm and optimism of extreme youth.'

The logic behind the reply was flawless; they were in need of a dummy and they had chosen him out of necessity as statistics showed that the profession was far from being overcrowded with novices.

The solicitor's client was a lady whose identity he was not at liberty to disclose, as the enquiry had to be conducted under the seal of secrecy for reasons which might possibly involve matters of national security the private eye would not be requested to investigate.

'Tending towards the unusual', muttered Stewart.

'What was that? I thought I heard you say something . . .'

'Oh, nothing; just quoting Sherlock Holmes to myself. Sorry.'

The lady had a niece, her dead sister's only child, who had become infatuated . . .

'Please, note the word as belonging to the lady's personal vocabulary,' whispered Mr. Oldfield.

'As would befit someone of her rank and position?'

'Yes . . .'

'I thought as much', remarked Sinclair, glad to have an opportunity to display his worldliness when it came to the vagaries of language.

'Infatuated with a much older man,' continued Mr. Oldfield, 'who, mark my words, is about to receive a shipment of peacocks from Tarshish!'

'The fantastic!', exclaimed Stewart, 'the investigation tends towards the unusual and even the fantastic!'

'What did you say?'

'I said 'Fantastic!'

'I take it this enquiry is up your street, Mr. Sinclair, since you demonstrate such unrestrained enthusiasm?'

'Absolutely! I could not wish for anything more congenial.'

'Aren't you being a little hasty and foolhardy? I mean 'Fools rush in . . .''

'Where angels fear to tread'? Maybe; maybe not. If I crack it, Mr. Oldfield, I'll be known for the rest of my life as the sleuth who solved the mystery of the peacocks of Tarshish! That I presume is the object your client has in mind; to find out exactly what they represent since her niece is involved?'

'Precisely.'

Mr. Oldfield leant across his desk and looked at Sinclair over the top of his spectacles.

`Mr. Sinclair, while it is refreshing to see so much zeal in a young man as untested as yourself, do you not think that it would be proper for a person of my calling to advise a little restraint?'

`Oh, definitely! The case bristles with difficulties, and, there is also the possibility that your client may not be very flush.'

`I'm glad you see my point. And you're not daunted?'

It was Stewart's turn to lean across the desk.

`Confidentially, Mr. Oldfield, between you and I, how many budding detectives with a classical education have you interviewed before me?'

`To be honest, none. I mean, who nowadays goes in for a classical education? It defies common sense! The young like to swim with the flow.'

`Exactly! Oh, please, don't think I am being presumptuous, but as a classical student I picked a thing or two which qualify me perfectly for this assignment. To give you an example : Peacocks, of the genus *Pavo*, a native of India. Tarshish, in the days of King Solomon, who had a strong navy and was immensely rich, a city near Cadiz in Spain. The sea of Tarshish in antiquity was the Mediterranean . . . Does that not convey something to you, Mr. Oldfield?'

`The straits of Gibraltar! Gib! Of course! With Tangiers on the other side! This case has ramifications abroad! Elementary, my dear Watson!'

`No offence meant, Mr. Oldfield, but I think the boot is on the other foot, and it's going to cost you. I mean your client is about to send two innocent abroad to tread on potential minefields.'

`Two! There are two of you? I thought you operated alone? I've got your card here `Stewart Sinclair, private eye. Fully qualified. No enquiry too small.'

`Not in this case. Think, just for a minute. The shipments of peacocks, whatever that means, arrive somewhere in the region of Gibraltar; but that's only the port of entry for the merchandise, which presumably comes from India which knew nothing of partition in antiquity, so we ought to throw in Pakistan for good measure, and possibly Afghanistan as well in the present political climate. God only knows where the shipments go after that. Israel? The Israeli secret services have a high reputation; they don't give up that easily. Besides, the Mediterranean is vast; we may need deep-sea diving equipment.'

`How much?', asked Mr. Oldfield, exasperated.

5

'Four grands to start with, two for my assistant and two for myself,—cash. On second thought, make it five in case we get robbed in the souks in Tangiers.'

'You drive a hard bargain, young man As you pointed out, this is the chance of a lifetime, not to mention the love of the art . . .'

'I am not Sherlock Holmes, Mr. Oldfield. He had independent means. Besides, I personally wouldn't like to let a lady down for the lack of a few pounds; people might say the spirit of chivalry is dead in England.'

Stewart Sinclair had not walked round the corner of the imposing building where Messrs. Oldfield and Baxter had their offices when the exuberant mood which he had experienced in the senior solicitor's presence began to wane, and the further he went the more displeased he became about his performance. He had given way to a regrettable mood of euphoria, and by the time he reached his own premises, all he was left with was a sense of self-betrayal, induced by the admission of impetuosity on the one hand, and the practical problem with which it had landed him on the other. It had been rash of him to mention an assistant when he could barely afford to pay the rent for the office space into which he had just moved; yet, the nature of the enquiry being what it was it demanded some form of support, even in a menial capacity . . . Where to look for such a factotum was the question; and what criteria would guide his choice in the event of finding suitable candidates? A medical student, to emulate Sherlock Holmes who needed a doctor to validate the diagnostic based on the evidence found at the crime scene? But nowadays forensic science was too well-established to warrant resorting to such a ploy; and what mental attributes would he require from the person? If not obtuseness, at least slowness of mind, as Holmes himself had done in Watson's case? So as to focus all the attention on his own powers? 'Noblesse oblige'? The thought of Holmes's condescending attitude towards poor Watson whose devotion to his patients was unstinting sent a ripple of unrest through Sinclair's heart; the act was too hard to follow; he would have to turn. to another profession for an understudy. And what better person to consult for advice than his own father who would be somewhat surprised to hear that the interview with Oldfield and Baxter had gone well, and his son was in business.

`Don't go on barking up the wrong tree; forget about medical students. Go for a budding archaeologist. Take my word for it.' That was the pater's advice and the pragmatism of his reply took Stewart's breath away. It was incredible how the old man, when it matters, still had the ability to come up with a philosophical proposition which turned out to be an ace. An archaeological student, of course! Why hadn't he thought of it? It was so, so obvious!.

`And where would one find such a paragon?', Stewart asked out of spite for having been outwitted by the old man.

`The British School of Archaeology in Athens would be a likely place . . .'

`For Christ's sake, dad! Do we have to drag Greece into this? It's bad enough with Tarshish. I know Tintin went looking for the enchanted isle in the remotest corner of Britain, but I am no longer a fan of his.'

`Pity, that was a really good book, I mean for the young at heart . . . Anyway, don't worry. I have the name of a professor who teaches there jotted down somewhere. He's on the advisory committee for the Olympic games and comes over frequently. He'll suggest someone.'

`Well, if his memory of names is as good as yours, dad . . .'

`We used to go sight-seeing together all over Europe with a group of hikers. His name began with a P . . . Paterson, that's it. Henry Paterson. Nice bloke, very erudite.'

`An e-mail is a must, Dad. with a name and address. Time is of the essence.'

`I know, son; you're raring to go.'

A crumpled piece of paper in *The Musgrave Ritual*, an urgent telegram in *The Copper Beeches*, an advertisement in `The Times' in *The Solitary Cyclist*, those had been the means of communication which propelled Sherlock Holmes into each new case to his entire satisfaction. They seemed exceedingly slow by comparison with the electronic mail in use in the modern era, yet they had got the great man into the thick of it in no time at all, and made his electrifying presence felt; so Stewart Sinclair hoped would be the case for him when word came from his father's old friend; he would not have allowed himself to be put off by fortuitous delays. And so it was that after a time which appeared neither short nor long, for he kept his spirits up, he found himself one evening walking with a spring in his step towards a sailors' club in London Dockland where a student who planned to take up Archaeology had found temporary employment as an entertainer.

As he walked into the place, which was rather cramped, a geisha girl standing by herself on the stage was bowing to the audience amid thunderous applause, and the clamour suddenly brought Stewart back down to earth,—he had forgotten to mention the obvious; he was looking for a male assistant, not a female one. However, having waited so long, and come that far, he decided that perhaps in the circumstances, in view of the urgency of the case, he had better go ahead with the interview.

Entering somewhat subdued into a makeshift cubicle made up of cardboard boxes at the back of the stage, he watched the geisha girl remove her make-up in front of a triple mirror and noticed to his satisfaction that she did not look unduly feminine. She had fine, well-defined features and when she took off her wig, her short haircut finished to give her the Puckish look made fashionable by Shakespearean actresses. It was not until she removed her kimono that he realized why 'she' had been recommended as a possible 'Watson' to his 'Sherlock' as a double act.

'Christ! You could have fooled me!', he cried, when the student finally stood in his underpants.

'Good, isn't it?' the boy asked. 'The men love it!'

'Lucrative?', asked Stewart.

'Not really . . .'

'But great fun? Undoubtedly, you enjoy it, or you wouldn't be doing it. Tell me I'm wrong.'

'Who's asking?'

'Oh, sorry! Stewart Sinclair, private eye. What shall I call you? Madame Butterfly?'

'There's no need to get vulgar. The name's Sebastian.'

'Good heavens! What next?'

'I am not a sado-masochist or transvestite or whatever else you'd like to call me. Just a student on a gap year, trying to earn an honest bob or two, and I don't do drugs either.'

'I almost wish your name had been Flora as the *danseuse* who performed at The Allegro in Conan Doyle's story *The Noble Bachelor,* Sebastian . . .'

'What do you want?'

'Actually, I am looking for a male personal assistant, not a male impersonator.'

'In what line?'

'Detective work.'

'And what makes you think I would make a likely candidate for the job?'

'Apart from the name, which is a real perk, you possess three phenomenal merits. One, you can wear costume to advantage. Two, as a budding archaeologist you obviously have an immense capacity for taking pains when it comes to stripping bare ancient sites of interest without disturbing the evidence (please, no double entendre!) And, last but not least, you enjoy what you do, and there is nothing that I appreciate more than zest in an assistant. Look at the time you take to put on your Geisha make-up for such a brief appearance, so late at night, for so little profit! A labour of love.'

'In other words, you're offering me the job as your Watson!'

'Elementary, my dear boy! I commend your quick-witted spirit of repartee.'

'What's in it for me? The Geisha act is popular and I do quite well here on some nights.'

Stewart tiptoed to the far side of the cubicle and sharply pulling aside the curtains, he uncovered a group of about half a dozen lascar-looking sailors, who had been eaves-dropping.

'Ah!', he exclaimed, 'I thought as much. Away, you sea-faring Peeping Toms!'

As soon as they had slunk away, Stewart turned to face Sebastian and whispered :

'A thousand pounds now on account; but that's not the half of it.'

'No?'

'No. When we've solved the case, there will be fame and glory to boot for both of us.'

'What case?'

'The case of the peacocks of Tarshish. But don't get too excited; they may not be exotic drag queens if you're thinking of getting tips from them about make-up. They may not be birds at all. Ah! Ah!'

'I don't care much for people who laugh at their own jokes.'

'Don't you? What about your Geisha act? That's got to be the most pathetic act of self-mockery I have ever seen, and all for filthy lucre.'

'Oh, God! Not another one of those sanctimonious saviours of the world!'

'No; just an inquisitive investigator of human motives. Since I can't trust my own, I am tempted to try and unmask those that make other people tick. Now, that is a proposition for a vocational archaeologist. What about it?'

Sebastian pondered for a while.

'How good are your hunches, I mean as occupational hazards? As I said, I make quite a good living here . . .'

'That's a risk you have to take. Surely, as an archaeologist, you can't hope to hit the jackpot every time you investigate a new site.'

Sebastian nodded his head in assent.

'True, but to tell you the truth what worries me more than anything else is by what name you intend to call me since you consider Sebastian detrimental to the quest.'

'Yes, it's too ambiguous. I'd like something more simple and direct.'

'Like what? Surely not Watson?'

'No, it's too condescending; something like Chum, Mate, Pal or Buddy . . .'

'All right; call me Buddy.'

'I was afraid of that. In the spirit of fellowship . . . All right, but don't push it too hard or I'll ditch you in some Legionnaires' lavatories in the East, for you to investigate what toiletries they used. Be at my house, near Regents Park, as soon as you have packed here, and don't breathe a word to anyone about your plans for the future. Here is the address. We're leaving for Liverpool at first lights.'

'Liverpool! I thought the case was exotic!'

'Never be deceived by the obvious ; it could be the moonshine we're accustomed to.'

'What shall I call you?', asked Sebastian, feeling suddenly dispirited.

'Sinclair. What else?'

It had not been an auspicious beginning to what was supposed to be a working partnership. All the doubts and uncertainties about the case which had afflicted him from the moment he had walked out of the offices of Messrs Oldfield and Baxter on account of its very strange nature were returning to pursue him with a vengeance, the intensity of which seemed to grow by the minute. Cocaine, (a seven per cent solution), morphine and laudanum were the tranquillisers that Sherlock Holmes had recourse to in stressful situations, and Stewart wished his father had never enlightened him about drugs that 'tickled' and eventually 'rotted' the liver, so he could have obtained some much-needed relief from his anxieties. However, the fact that he could by some benevolent quirk of the imagination associate Sebastian, the geisha girl, with Flora, the *danseuse* who performed at 'the Allegro' in *The Noble Bachelor*, that very fact was in itself immensely therapeutic in the sense that in relation to himself,—the noble bachelor—, Flora being described as 'a dear little thing, but exceedingly hot-headed', acted as an obscure preventive, forewarning against too close an association with Sebastian, which might prove detrimental to the case in the end. Besides, among all the quotations of Sherlock's on women, there were quite a few which might also apply to the niece of Mr. Oldfield's affluent and well-connected client, especially the old Persian saying quoted by Holmes in *A case of Identity* about the danger 'for whoso snatches a delusion from a woman' equivalent to that of taking a tiger cub from its mother, except that in this case chances were the animals in question were likely to be less ferocious, being peacocks. Apart from all these psychological considerations, he would have to watch Sebastian with the money, though what the connection was between the two at this stage of his tentatively heuristic enquiry, he had not got a clue. It was just one of those haphazard ramifications of the details of the case between themselves that kept a good sleuth afloat in an on-going enquiry when the adrenalin stopped flowing; or so he hoped, being new to the job. Sebastian was obviously addicted to exhibiting himself in lavish exotic garb; the Geisha outfits which he donned every night to the delight of patrons down in the Dockyard district of London were of the expensive kind. Two possible propositions arose from the observation, based on the name Sebastian. Either he wore them to experience a kind of narcissistic pleasure when he gazed at the delightful mirror image of himself before appearing on stage, or in the true spirit of a martyr, he felt a sado-masochistic satisfaction at exhibiting himself that way before louts. In either case, the question was, Would he in the long run react like a female tiger when deprived of the delusion and suddenly go haywire?

What disheartened Stewart more then anything else was the amount of flattery which he had had to lavish on Sebastian in order to get him to accept the job. Was the discovery of the truth worth such dismal cajolery, ever? Was he Stewart Sinclair in the right job, when what should have appeared a mere formality in an interview brought about such distaste and heart searching? And what about his admiration for Sherlock Holmes? Let's face it, Conan Doyle's hero, the darling of a by-gone era, was far from being an attractive human being. With so little going for him, his only title to fame was as the father of forensic evidence. But the struggle between evidence which could in some cases be planted and knowledge by revelation was one which had preoccupied mankind for millennia. In this particular case of the Peacocks of Tarshish, Stewart had a hunch that the exposure of something previously disguised or concealed, summed up as Revelation, would win the day; that, in fact, there would be no material evidence of any kind to evince in support of the existence of such shipments, except one of an intangible nature, i.e. the disclosure of facts made by a person or persons unknown with him, Stewart Sinclair, as the receptacle and transmitting agent of such a revelation. And he found the insight comforting.

One glance at Sebastian the next morning finished to disperse the phantoms of the previous night. The boy was decently dressed in a pair of blue jeans and he wore a clean T-shirt. The heels of his cowboy boots were on the high side, but not to an objectionable degree. There was no sign in his attire of the flamboyance which had made his act such a hit the night before. The boy obviously knew the difference between real life and phantasy, where one stopped and the other one began. Last but not least, the travel bag that he carried did not look over full.

'Left the Geisha gear behind?'

'Yes, another chap at the Club has got it.'

'A locum?' asked Stewart, suddenly worried.

'Sort of. In case I decide to chuck the job. For all I know, you could be abducting me for some sinister purpose. You never did get round to showing me your credentials last night. One can't be too careful these days.'

'He who hath ears, let him hear; and he who hath eyes, let him see.' It sounds as though the Jehovah Witnesses call round at the Sailors' club.'

'Yes, they do. It's all grist to the mill. I like to keep an open mind.'

'Good for you! Now to the point. A shipment of peacocks may be arriving in Liverpool. It could be a trap, a trick to side-track us while the goods, whatever they are, are unloaded somewhere else. As it so happens, the lady in question, the aunt whose niece has become infatuated with a man old enough to be her father, lives in West Kirby, a suburb of Liverpool, and Messrs. Oldfield and Baxter also have a small office in

West Kirby. Your job will be to keep the niece under surveillance, that is if she is still visible.'

'What do you mean?'

'The aunt may keep her temporarily under lock and key. Remember, women are capable of kidnapping; in fact, they are the ideal persons to commit such crimes.'

'Few people suspect them?'

'Correct.'

'And what about the niece locking up the aunt to be able to go to the docks for the delivery?'

'Equally possible, my dear Watson! Mr. Oldfield will provide us with photographs of both ladies. Now, the aunt has been advised not to try and stop her niece from going to the docks; she is our only lead. Now, whether she will comply or not, your guess is as good as mine; with women one never knows; they are unpredictable.'

'And what about the man, the one who is expecting a shipment of Peacocks?'

'Ah, that's another kettle of fish or should I say fowl! All we know about him is that he used to train and handle sniffer dogs for the Army. He's tall and looks his age, but his bearing is still impressive. Obviously, if the goods materialize, he'll be there to take delivery of them. He may even have a dog with him to avoid rousing suspicion in the girl who thinks the sun shines out of him.'

'Some men tend to become bitter in their old age if things don't go their way' remarked Sebastian, 'and they take it out on women.'

'According to the aunt, the girl is very gullible and vulnerable. She is idealistic and casts herself in the role of a sister of mercy whenever a loser comes along with a sob-story. In short, she is the type of girl some men prey on; and my sixth sense tells me that this one could be particularly cunning compared to the more benign ones she consorted with in the past.'

'You mean, they were not imposing?'

'You've hit the nail on the head, buddy!'

Looking at the photographs of the client's niece, Sebastian thought the girl looked more substantial than the psychological profile drawn by the boss had suggested. She had a square face with rather strong features. Her hair style was plain, with none of the silly wisps and curly strands made popular by the fashion of the day, and the top she wore, without frills or jewellery, indicated a preference for a classic style of clothes. In other words, she came across as a good sort, one could have an impromptu game of tennis with for lack of a steady partner.

From the spot where the boss had left him, high above Mole C, he commanded a superb view of the quayside where a huge crowd stood waiting for the ship to dock. There was something odd about the scene down below. With so many people standing close together, friends and relatives of servicemen returning from a turn of duty in Northern Ireland, a restless rumour made up of various sounds, where excited voices mingled with the fidgeting of bodies standing close together, should have risen in the air and reached him to indicate the excitement created by a sense of anticipation on such occasions. Instead of which the silence was eerie and the mood sombre; and the stir which should by all accounts have greeted the actual docking of the ship did not occur. Mesmerized, Sebastian watched the men disembark in silence to clasp their loved ones with a distressing kind of lethargy as though there was no emotional power left in their embrace. And before he realized it, they had all slunk away; only a few lonely stragglers stood on the quay, not knowing which way to turn, till they too disappeared. It was then that looking towards the exit, he saw the girl in the photograph go up to a tall, elderly man who was standing near the gates. Stunned by what he was seeing, he scrambled down from his lookout station above the wharf to get a closer look, and then unable to contain his excitement, he rushed into the car where Sinclair was waiting for a radio contact.

`Guess what! He never went on board to get delivery of the peacocks, whatever they are!'

`I know! He was on the quayside all the time. I told you to keep your binoculars trained on the wharf. Exactly what did you see on Mole C?'

`I saw the girl in the photograph go up to a very tall man who was marching up and down on the quayside inside the gates. He had a dog with him. The dog got quite excited when he saw the girl, which led me to believe . . .'

`Never mind that. What kind of a dog?'

`A white and tan Springer Spaniel.'

`Are you sure about the breed?'

`Positive.'

`A sniffer dog?'

'He looked too subdued to be a sniffer dog. I mean, sniffer dogs are always lively.'

'Go on.'

'The girl started playing with the dog. The man checked the dog several times to make him sit still, then he tied him up to a bollard. Then he started marching past the girl; it looked as though he was instructing her about something, or lecturing to her; she seemed cowed into submission, like a child by an overbearing adult,—quite different from what she looks like on the photograph, I mean, where she appears quite a gutsy type of girl. There was something surreal about the whole thing, like a scene in slow motion in an old-fashioned movie. I noticed his shoes, how highly-polished they were; they shone in the sun as he marched up and down in front of the girl; they were immaculate. He wore a long coat, like an officer's coat, and that combined with his bearing gave him a forbidding presence as he paraded up and down; it was really weird.'

'You mean he behaved like a sergeant-major, drilling the men, while kitted out as an officer?'

'That's it! You've hit the nail on the head!'

'Kind of stuff you're not unfamiliar with, hey,? Behaving like a trollop while dressed as a lady. I did say you had a lot going for you as a budding detective.'

'What now?'

'Well, they're no longer there, are they? They've slipped the net. As far as the aunt is concerned, we've drawn a blank; she knows her niece is infatuated with this man. We've failed. But not quite.'

'Ah, ah, the great maestro has a gut feeling; or, is it a stirring of the brain cells?'

'You may gibe, Buddy, but your Japanese masquerades are not the only cryptic messages sent out on the air to a captive audience . . .'

'No?'

'No. There are others, of a less obvious anatomical nature. Let's say that my sixth sense tells me that the man in question has already taken a delivery of the awaited shipment of peacocks, and that is why he behaved as he did on the quayside.'

'You mean we were too late?'

'That is not what I am saying. To be specific, it is likely that he is expecting yet another shipment, and that he will not make a move to involve the niece in a big way until he has received it.'

'Oh, my God!'

''Yes, well you might throw your arms up in the air, and that is why the old solicitor was so forthcoming with the money. It's likely to be a long process. The aunt knows her niece only too well; she's witnessed a lot over the years seeing the girls' parents chose to close their eyes in order to go with the flow; which is socially correct nowadays, like buying an insurance as security for permisiveness. The aunt is probably someone who enjoys psychic powers, a bit of a clairvoyant . . .'

'Oh, no, not spiritualism, please!'

'No; I meant psychological insights. Some people do have them, and we sleuths ought to pay more attention to them when it comes to motives especially when the latter are to do with consumerism, a form of advanced and sophisticated cannibalism, except one is feeding ad lib from an open global manger, that's all.'

'You mean the aunt fears for her niece's safety? Though I must say I fail to see the peacocks of Tarshish as edible birds, like guinea fowls . . .'

'Feared, Buddy, past tense; it's already too late. She is about to be swallowed, hook, line and sinker, and the aunt cares for her psychological welfare very, very much . . .'

'What are we waiting for, then?'

'The next shipment of peacocks, what else?'

'Isn't that taking an awful risk? She looks such a nice girl . . .'

'There's no telling', replied Sinclair with a far-away look. 'Sometimes, it takes an excess of shipments to precipitate the crisis.'

'Maybe the aunt's fears are unfounded; maybe, the girl's got her head well screwed on her shoulders, and she'll see through the man's ulterior motives, whatever they are.'

'You do not know women, young man; they're all one hundred per cent vanity. Take your Geisha girl as an example. When you don her apparel, what drives you but vanity, the vanity of self-love, the desire to seduce in order to gratify it? In your case, it's play acting; for others, it is the real thing.'

In order to remain vigilant while awaiting developments, Stewart decided that they would remain in situ, camping in the van disguised as telephone engineers, though the thought of sharing a rubber water butt as a tub with Sebastian did not appeal to him very much. The boy had untidy habits. He was wont of leaving nail parings lying about in unsuitable places and allowing soiled clothing to bulge out of carrier bags instead of keeping them confined to a tin trunk at the back of the van. As far as he remembered, no masochistic instinct had dictated his choice of an assistant in the first place, if the word 'choice' came into it at all, seeing Sebastian had been the only candidate. No doubt about it, he had to make the best of a bad job, forgetting the luxurious amenities some famous detectives had enjoyed in posh country mansions, not to mention the sophisticated female company that always adorned week-end house parties while somebody or other was being murdered for legitimate reasons, usually to do with 'filthy lucre', rather than cryptic ones like the Peacocks of Tarshish, the ambiguity of which as a clue was undoubtedly due to the pursuit of predatory egomania, a kind of rat race, when no one was safe in the 'secret chambers of their imagery', though they claimed immunity therein. And here, at that stage in his retrospective soliloquy, Stewart Sinclair wondered what reputation, if any, he would acquire among all those famous detectives of the past. Would he be acclaimed as the first modern investigator with a flair for unravelling the mysteries of the human psyche as valid clues and criminal motives at a crucial point in its history, when the evidence for committing acts of aggression and conquest had become scientifically correct and invisible, leaving no place for fanciful speculation in criminology? It was a big question; but for him, there was no doubt that all the principles of criminal investigation of the old school had become largely obsolete; the ladder up which detectives religiously climbed up to investigate criminal offences had to be put away. It had become obsolete and practically useless because reprehensible acts of aggression against the other person were now as discreet and frequent as the sending of Telecommunication satellites into orbit, leaving no place for traditional speculations in criminology based on values of an antiquated ethical nature.

Thinking about Sebastian, Stewart had other reasons beside personal hygiene to feel unhappy about the boy. Despite sharing all his own thoughts about the case with him, he found him largely irresponsive to its questions and as a result. unable to express a well-balanced opinion of the case. Of course, as an archaeological student, he would not theoretically at that stage in his training be required to make final statements about any of the artifacts that he had so far dug up; that would be deemed premature. But Stewart could not help wondering whether that circumspection, which was legitimate in an archaeological student, was not in the case of a budding detective something of a hindrance, and he could not help calling into question the wisdom behind his father's advice to give preference to an archaeological student rather than a medical one when it came to choosing an assistant. There was a vast difference between describing the symptoms of a patient in a hospital bed and the broken fragments of pots and pans, the remains of which had lain buried deep down in the earth for millennia. Sebastian seemed to be almost entirely concerned with aspects of the case which were not central to it. The niece for some obscure reason engaged most of his attention. It was odd considering his sexual orientation, unless there was a morbid transference at the bottom of it, and he saw himself as the object of desire of the man whom he had seen indoctrinating the girl on the quay of Mole C; in which case, the enquiry became one in which he, Sebastian, became a coveted, exotic prize, just as he had been briefly as a Geisha girl on the stage of that low-down sailors' club in the docks of London. It was highly possible. A case within a case? Sherlock Holmes had never had to unravel such imbroglios, though he had often been unknowingly on the verge of quite a few, in a different era.

Three days into the camping arrangement, there was a message from Mr. Oldfield's client which said :'He's on the move again'. The wording was so dramatic in its stark simplicity that they scrambled up to a messy, befuddled start at break of day to take up action station within a safe distance from the house. The sense of commotion at that time in that quiet suburb of Liverpool was unimaginable. The man whom they had both seen on Mole C was helping the girl to carry a lot of loose clothing into the boot of his car. There were shorts, Bikinis, sandals, sun hats, and underwater gear like wet suits and guns and flippers; it seemed as though the lot had been put together hurriedly, at a moment's notice. The man had a grim determined look on his face, as though he were engaging in a major operation.

'They're off somewhere warm', whispered Stewart.

'Sunny Spain!', cried out Sebastian, 'but where's the dog?'

'He's gone to Afghanistan, don't you see, to sniff out road bombs. It's because the dog is fully trained that the man can afford to go on holiday, and possibly take delivery of another shipment of peacocks as well, sharing the cost with the girl, like a gentleman. They'll put the car on the ferry bound for Bilbao. There's not a minute to lose. We must fly to Gib and hire a car there.'

'Hang on! There's something I don't understand.'

'What's that, slow coach?'

'The girl doesn't look excited . . .'

'Neither does he for that matter. Well, maybe, he spent the night indoctrinating her. Remember the way he behaved on the quay, marching up and down in front of her as though she were a moron from an under-developed country? She may be a hard nut to crack.'

'It's a wonder she goes along with it . . . not at all what you would imagine from such a vivacious type of girl.'

'Ah, the man's a stern knight. That's what a shipment of peacocks does for you. Some girls like it that way. They only escape from their fathers to fall under the dominion of another type of sanctimonious bully. The aunt knows that, and that's why she is so worried about her niece.'

'Look! There's the aunt at the window peering through the curtains!'

'What else can she do?'

Sebastian had made a profound remark about the niece. It was a fact that she looked remote, disconnected from the action as though she were a character in a play with no real interest in the script. In a way, Sebastian noticing it was odd since he was in all other aspects inobservant, but in another way it was not odd at all; he was merely substituting himself with her as a female when he impersonated the Japanese courtesan, whatever her name was, on the stage at the sailors' club. It was transference pure and simple, except that had he been in the niece's shoes, he would have behaved in exactly the opposite way, showing excitement at the prospect of an impromptu jaunt in the sun in the company of an impressive and forceful character.

Feeling suddenly guilty about concealing secret thoughts from his assistant, Stewart carried on musing aloud :

'You're right. The girl does not look particularly enamoured of the idea of a holiday in sunny Spain, as you call it. It could be that the constant lecturing, or rather brainwashing that she is subjected to under the guise of a pleasant, easy-going relationship with a man old enough to be her father who is trying to humour her up, is beginning to take its toll. Trouble is, she may be unsure about what she wants, a father figure or a lover (not that he fits the part being the epitome of the stern knight) and that is the worst possible scenario because the trump cards are all in the other hand.'

Stewart paused for a while, and then he said, lowering his voice :

'As regards the man, the way he looked this morning, when he came out of the house with the client's niece, may be ascribed to the problems attached to the delivery of the shipments of peacocks, which are of such concern to the aunt. It may be that originally the shipments arrived from Afghanistan, via Gibraltar, and then were shipped over to Ireland first before being dispatched to Liverpool, the port of entry in England. It's possible . . .'

'Anything is possible', remarked Sebastian with a far-away look on his face.

'Quite so', replied Sinclair.

'If that were so', Sinclair continued, ignoring the interruption to his analysis of the case, 'If that were so, there would be a hiatus of an awkward nature; a sense of impotence and temporary deflation of the all-conquering male martial ego. Imagine the modern equivalent of Perseus, the Greek mythological hero, who had no money and owned no horses, being checked as he flew towards Andromeda, a naked woman, except for certain jewels, tied to a rock,—his sense of frustration. He may be self—deceived or simply deceived by appearances. Maybe the bejewelled, naked Andromeda is not waiting to be rescued. Maybe, she fancies herself as a sex goddess, like a lot of other plain, down-to-earth girls nowadays who have to work for a living and dream of being air-lifted from the nine-to-five rat race for a fling with a romantic figure of sorts. Who knows? What's the stern knight to do, imprisoned in his rigid armour? He has had other ideas implanted in his head; he's been conditioned, some would say brainwashed, by the powers that be; he needs a shipment of peacocks to refurbish his esteemed self-image in order to carry the day, or else failure will stare him in the face, and old soldiers never die'

'My God, Sinclair, do I have to put up with all this mythological mumbo-jumbo?'

'You'd be foolish not to. You see, the ancient Greeks knew about 'the magic eye of perception '. It is not given to every private eye to have it. Consider yourself privileged. Besides, you'd lie if you didn't admit to some coincidental factors in my diagnosis with your own mental state. You know all about deprivation;. You'd give anything at times to have your Geisha outfit back, stored away somewhere in the rear of the vehicle, so you could have a quick fix by wearing it whenever you felt at a low ebb. Come on. own up!'

'Oh, I won't deny it; what you say is very true, but I don't make a song and dance about it'

'Ah, you've hit the nail on the head, Buddy! You're neither tall, nor stern-looking nor dyspeptic. The other bloke is. Everything is multiplied by a factor of size and disposition and circumstance, like the administration of certain stimulants and narcotics. Remember Sherlock Holmes and his different strengths of cocaine according to whether his brain was active or not?'

'Yes; the man was an exhibitionist, a bully and an intellectual snob.'

'Maybe, but it stood him in good stead and since you pay me obliquely the compliment of being like him, let me remind you of one of his fundamental principles.'

'What's that, in God's name?'

'He said : 'It is a capital mistake to theorize before you have all the evidence.' You may ask yourself what amount of evidence we have so far collected and if it seems slight to you, this may be ascribed to your inexperience and lack of any real flair for the job, for when I cast a backward glance on past events, including those of the morning, I am personally satisfied that the evidence they provided is substantial enough to encourage me to pursue a certain line of enquiry, as from now, regarding the shipment of peacocks from Tarshish.'

'Good for you!'

Sinclair paused for minute, wondering what to do in order to humour up the boy who seemed dispirited.

'By the way, have you by any chance read a comedy by Aristophanes called *The Birds*?'

'No, Tintin's adventures were more my style. He came to Britain, you know, looking for the Enchanted Isle in the outer Hebrides.'

'Pity . . .'

'Why? Are there peacocks in the play?'

'No, that's the interesting thing about it. The most attractive bird as far as appearance is concerned is the Hoopoe; the smartest one is the cock for obvious reasons; he rules the roost and Aristophanes makes much of his attributes.'

'Meaning?'

'Oh, nothing; just one of those observations one makes *en passant* ; what comes, I suppose, from having had a classical education.'

As he spoke, Stewart felt more and more unsure of his ground; he had the uncomfortable feeling that he kept rambling on for the sake of keeping his countenance. He did not really know where all that oratory was leading up to.

What exactly were the peacocks of Tarshish? How did the expression come about.? He had first heard of it in the office of Messrs. Oldfield and Baxter as having come out of the mouth of their client in relation to a man with whom her niece had struck up a relationship. God only knew how or where the client had acquired the expression, and fool that he was, in the first flush of the ignorant enthusiasm of youth, he had plunged headlong into the unknown without any secure premise, led astray by his overwhelming admiration for a famous detective who had operated in Victorian times!

As he sat in the van, abashed, in the company of an absent-minded assistant who did not seem too anxious to suggest a prompt start in pursuit of the suspect, he thought he had better pull himself together. He had received a handsome sum of money in advance for the job, and it would have been dishonest on his part not to try and do something to earn it.

'Well, what are you waiting for? They are gone! They've left!" he said abruptly to try and instil new fire into the boy.

'You're the boss. You' re the captain!'

'I was just thinking . . .'

'God preserve us!'

'that it was all very well for Sherlock Holmes to issue a warning against theorizing before one has gathered all the evidence; but there is also such a thing as having hunches, presentiments and premonitions, and the courage to act on them. You can picture the case of Revelation against Evidence, can't you, with the two of them facing each other in court, like two characters in a medieval play. All I have to go by is the aunt's disclosure about the peacocks of Tarshish. The woman has always remained not anonymous but aloof. Do you remember what I said to you, as we kept up the surveillance on Mole C, about the aunt enjoying psychic powers; being a bit of a clairvoyant? Seeing things other people can't see . . .'

'Vaguely.'

'Well, she would represent Revelation as a character in one of those Morality plays I've just mentioned.'

'If you say so . . .'

'Must you always be so negative?' Sinclair asked, incensed by the boy's attitude, 'Can't you believe in something real for a change?'

'For crying out loud, Sinclair! You're the one that's delving into the unreal, the paranormal and the supernatural. Get real!'

'Yes, I am because that is all I have to go by as evidence, scanty though it is.'

'All right. Point taken.'

Sebastian's good grace was far from being generous, but Sinclair felt that he had nevertheless made some progress towards establishing the validity of his approach and perhaps even aroused the boy's interest anew.

'So, I am prepared to gamble everything on Revelation, and to pit my brains against cracking the enigma of the shipments of the peacocks of Tarshish. What do I; I mean, do we, stand to lose? You've put the Geisha outfit into moth balls, and I am just starting out as a private eye; I'd say it's worth the spin. What do you say, Buddy?

'Yes, all right, but please no more highfalutin speeches; I've had my bellyful of them.'

'Ah, now I know why you're smitten by the niece! You have been struck by her imperviousness to the stern knight's homilies. You bond with her, don't you? She's caught between the devil and the deep blue sea,—the aunt on one side and the stern knight on the other, all tugging at her soul. You've known similar dilemmas. You feel sorry for her, don't you? Actually, so do I; and, to be honest, I think there is an old-fashioned streak of chivalry in my character of the kind that was not unknown to Holmes.'

If there was something about Sinclair that impressed Sebastian despite their differences, it was his absolute honesty. The man seemed to be possessed by what could only be called zeal in his quest to uncover the truth, and maybe in deciding to cast his lot with Revelation rather than Evidence as the twin face of reality, he would find his reward.

When they arrived in Gibraltar, the weather was overcast and Sebastian's hope of spending some time watching the monkeys' antics was dashed; the rock was covered in mist and the monkeys were sulking. Gibraltar being in the Sterling area, cash was no problem thanks to Messrs. Oldfield and Baxter's generosity back home, and they soon found themselves crossing the border into Spain in a hired Ford saloon. As they headed west past Algeciras through Andalousia, Sinclair explained his strategy.

'There is no point in going to Bilbao, we'll wait for them outside Cadiz. In case you wonder, Why Cadiz, that's because the aunt mentioned

Tarshish, which in the days of King Solomon was a city also called Tartessus near Cadiz . . .'

'Do you mean to say, we're looking for a ghost town?'

'I wouldn't think so, not for a minute. As I've said before on several previous occasions not only is the aunt psychic, but she is also a well-read woman, a bible reader who like a lot of other intelligent people read the old testament as a history book which also contains a hidden philosophy.'

'I thought we weren't going to get any more highfaluting speeches . . .', remarked Sebastian, looking out of the window.

'I'll ignore that last remark and ascribe it to the fact that a staple diet of Paellas and Spanish omelettes from roadhouses does not agree with your delicate stomach. To resume, taking all that into consideration, I am convinced that such a highly intelligent and cultured woman has in one single quotation from the Bible encapsulated a mine of information. In other words, she has presented us with a cryptic message which simply needs decoding. Get it?'

'Frankly, no.'

'You don't see the symbolic relevance of it all? About the shipments of peacocks from Tarshish in the days of King Solomon, who was immensely rich and had an eclectic taste in women?'

Sinclair stopped the car.

'All right, I'll tell you; just this once. Only eight and a half miles away lies the continent of Africa . . .'

'What's that supposed to mean?'

'Nothing in particular at this moment in time. Just make a note of it as a possible premise for future reference; it is important to keep an open mind. If nothing is what it seems, that's because we allow ourselves to be hoodwinked by external reality. I personally see it as a kind of cipher the code of which has been lost and needs to be recovered. Please, bear in mind that Cadiz is a military port on the isle of Leon. In Nelson's days, Cadiz was one of the marine cities of the world, the wealthiest port of Western Europe, famed sine the days of ancient Rome for its dancing girls. You might be inspired with new ideas for your act at the Sailors' Club. It was five hundred years under Moorish occupation; that's a very long time compared with say Paris under the Nazis by modern reckoning.'

Sinclair stopped and shook his head for a few minutes. 'Do you remember the case of Revelation versus Evidence?', he asked with an anxious look on his face.

'How could I forget it! Picturesque, vivid, original! A real, mind-blowing eye-opener!'

'There is no need to resort to sarcasm just because you feel out of your depths. I am quite a reasonable kind of fellow; all I ask for is a little more attention to issues of importance. To proceed :—Mr. Oldfield's client, the aunt, conjured up an amalgam of symbolical concepts when, quoting from the Bible she mentioned the shipment of peacocks from Tarshish in connection with the individual under whose questionable influence her niece had fallen, much to her chagrin. It was her way as the sensitive, percipient person that she is of revealing the psychological nature of the enquiry that lay ahead.'

'You mean, a lead?'

'Several leads; please note I used the word amalgam. The peacocks of Tarshish is the name she gave to a syndrome which may be recurrent; 'once in three years', says the first Book of Kings, chapter 10, verse 22, taking into account the time that delivery by sea took in those days; it might be three weeks, or even three days in our time.'

'Something like the blues? I have those occasionally, when the pressure gets too much . . .'

'So do a lot of people, but they don't necessarily have to receive a shipment of male birds which are imposing and magnificent, emblematic since Antiquity of the most ostentatious display and vain-glory.'

As he spoke, Sinclair noticed a change in Sebastian' countenance, as though the boy had at last perceived a glimmer of light light.

'Hallelujha!', he cried, 'we're getting there!'

'It's all very well for you to gibe. You're used to that kind of abracadabra.'

'For crying out loud! Think of all the mysterious messages you send out to a bunch of dim-witted sailors when you perform your Geisha act at the Club; they're in no wise capable of receiving any of them, let alone interpret them.'

By then, cutting across country, they had by-passed the cape of Trafalgar. The name had not elicited any comment from Sebastian.

'Nelson not one of your heroes?'

'He's every schoolboy's hero. Why would I be any different? Hero-worship is part of a juvenile process one outgrows.'

'Quite. Some well-minded people think Nelson did not say 'Kiss me, Hardy' but 'Lift me, Hardy' because his back had been broken by a cannon ball. Anyway, Hardy did not kiss Nelson on the mouth but on the forehead as a mark of piety and respect, in the manner people were prompted to in those days . . .'

As they were about to enter the isle of Leon, on the approach to the town, they saw an estate car that looked familiar parked on the roadside near the entrance of what appeared to be a hacienda. There being no one at the gate to admit potential visitors, they assumed entry was obtained by electronic means.

'Look, there's the suspect! He's got out of the car to request admission; the girl's not with him. My god, what can have happened to her?'

'Nothing; nothing at all. As we speak, she is probably acquiring a tan on a near-by beach You, yourself, thought that she was a 'gutsy' girl, able to take all that in her stride. And, if the man is, as I think he is, in need of a shipment of peacocks—the reason why he is here—then she is her own agent, and immune from dexterous allusions of the kind that resonate in the night.'

As soon as the suspect had driven out of sight down a long drive which seemed to stretch ahead for miles, they parked their own vehicle under a clump of trees and proceeded across rugged terrain, finally reaching a promontory which they had to climb in order to get their bearings, having first made sure that there was nobody about. What they saw stretched out below them in the distance when they got to the top just took their breath away.

There were battalions of men in combat suits marching up and down being put through their paces by fanatic non-commissioned officers, but the strange thing was many of those men looked like grotesque dummies, lying disembowelled here and there like sacks of sawdust, unstained by blood.

'My God, an Al Quaida training camp!', exclaimed Sebastian, 'right under our very eyes!'

'They wouldn't dare, not in broad daylight!'

'Well, remember what you told me? 'only eight and a half miles away lies the continent of Africa',—a stepping-stone from here. Cadiz? 'A military port, five hundred years under Moorish occupation' . . . What better place?'

'Hang on!' cried Sinclair, challenged by his assistant's sudden flush of memory, 'Where's the minaret? There is no sign of one on the site, nor is there a steeple, for that matter. Q.E.D., this is not an Al Quaida training camp nor is it some sort of Christian outfit for the training of Crusaders, like the Knight Templars. This is something else. And shall I tell you what? I've got the uncomfortable feeling that I've been here before.'

'A déjà vu?', asked Sebastian.

'Many people share the same feeling when they first come here', said a voice behind them, 'but it soon wears off.'

The speaker wore the habit of a friar, but he was not tonsured; it looked as though he wore a uniform, like many of the men in the camp below.

'Stewart Sinclair, private eye, and this is my assistant, Sebastian', said Sinclair, pulling out his ID card, 'and who might I be speaking to?'

'My name's Ignatius.'

'Any relation of Ignatius of Loyola, the founder of the Jesuits, the author of *Spiritual Exercises*?', asked Sinclair, anxious to establish some bona fide stature in such precarious circumstances, when they might be accused of trespassing.

'Only by spiritual affiliation of a kind, Mr. Sinclair.'

'Except, if my eyes do not deceive me, and what I see is true, the exercises in which those people down below are engaging with such fanatical zeal cannot exactly be called 'spiritual' ones, can they? Not in the ordinary sense of the word.'

'That's because you have no inkling into their purpose which is a salvationist one, though to you it may look suspect. Would you be here, if it didn't?'.

'Excuse me butting in, Sir' said Sebastian, thinking it was high time he rescued the boss from the deep metaphysical waters into which he had so heedlessly plunged.

'What is it, Sebastian?'

'I thought we were here to apprehend the suspect. There he is over there, Sir, engaged in a suspicious activity, drilling a lot of men in uniform.'

'So he is! My word, he has sharpened up a lot since we last had him in our sights in Liverpool, outside our client's house, last week. He looked down at mouth then.'

'Maybe he's glad he's got shot of the girl, Sir.'

'Sebastian, I'll have you keep your remarks to yourself. Father Ignatius is in authority here; he does not have to put up with inane comments.'

27

`Oh, please, Mr. Sinclair, do not be too hard on the boy. I find his comments quite refreshing and even pertinent. Out of the mouths of babes!'

`Really, Father? And how might that be?'

`The girl may have proved impervious to his benevolent insinuations, and that in the long run made inroads on his morale . . .'

`You mean `manipulations', don't you? The man's commensal.'

`We're non-judgmental here, Mr. Sinclair. Our task is to give people the help they need, when they need it, and more importantly how they need it.'

`Well, judging by the change in the suspect down below, I would say you succeed. What would you say, Sebastian?'

`I'd say, with your permission, Sir, that the suspect has taken delivery of the shipment of peacocks from Tarshish he was badly in need of; there's no doubt at all about that in my mind. I mean, look at the way he is drilling those poor beggars who are no better off than himself,—pumped up like a peacock, bawling out orders to have them wheeling round like robots at his command.'

`Elementary?', asked Sinclair with a twinkle in his eye.

`Oh, definitely! It sticks out a mile. All your hunches were right; there's the evidence before you. What more would any detective want?'

`One thing though bothers me', said Sinclair, `and here perhaps Father Ignatius can enlighten me.'

`I'll be glad to', replied the friar, who had stood by silently.

`It's the problem of diminished responsibility. `In all things one must consider the end'; it's the morality of a fable by Æsop I was impressed by as a child.'

`Mr. Sinclair has had a classical education, Father', Sebastian promptly explained by way of an apology for his boss's digression.

`In the case of the uplift of the suspect, or for that matter anyone like him who stands in need of a shipment of peacocks, and comes here to get it, is that question about the need to consider the end ever addressed? I mean, your organization recycles them into society with all their military attitudes not only confirmed but reinforced by the receipt of a shipment of peacocks. There is no possibility for them to accede to a renewal of life through an educated perception of the cause of their maladjustment. When they are released unregenerate after a stint here, as far as they are concerned sanctions are still applicable to `conduct to the prejudice of good order and military discipline' in the free-wheeling outside world ; I am quoting from Army Act 40. It is appalling, because such persons can do so much harm to unsuspecting vulnerable people especially females, who are gullible and easily impressed by their upright military bearing. It is a well-known, biological fact that women as a whole like to be dominated to feel entirely feminine.'

'I never said we were a religious organization, engaged in the recycling of souls, Mr. Sinclair', said the friar. 'We trust to chance as a redeemer.'

'And the devil take the hindmost?'

'There are always casualties one way or the other.'

'That is why it is important in all things to consider the end, as Æsop recommended. He was no court jester, I assure you. And here we shall let the matter rest. No, do not call for help; we are quite capable of finding our way out. Good day!'

As they started to wend their way back to the gate, Sebastian looked over his shoulder.

'Do you think the man was armed under that garb?'

'It's possible, but he meant no harm.'

'He was a charlatan, though . . .'

'Oh, I don't think so, not for a minute. He meant every word he said, but that does not mean to say he wasn't an impostor, someone pretending to knowledge; there are many of those nowadays who sadly go about spreading false enlightenment. It has happened before at other times in history, you know, such as the brief golden age of the Roman Empire under Hadrian, who was a paternal autocrat and a stern disciplinarian; he is said to have marched twenty thousand miles in full military gear . . . It makes me wonder whether some form of benign dictatorship, such as that of the advertising media in our time, which have our best interests at heart no doubt, is not likely to produce false enlightenment about a lot of things But that, I am sure, is not anything that would have kept Sherlock awake at night.'

Sebastian thought he detected a tone of discouragement in Sinclair's voice.

'Well, what now?', he asked as they climbed into the car.

'Your guess is as good as mine. There is not very much that we can do, except wait and see. A lot will depend on how the girl will react to the man's cajolement now he has been reinvigorated by the peacock treatment. I don't somehow think Messrs. Oldfield and Baxter will keep us indefinitely in fund, and I feel sorry for the aunt.'

'So do I . . . She cares, doesn't she?'

'She had every reason to be worried about that shipment of peacocks . . . I know what Sherlock would do in such a case . . .'

'Reach for the bottle?'

'Oh, no, he was a select drinker ;—ask for cocaine. I have no such recourse. I suppose in your case, in a way, the Geisha impersonation acted as an anaesthetic.'

'If you say so, Holmes. You must come and see it sometime.'

FINIS

THE LOST CITY

The Lost City

In the case of The Peacocks of Tarshish, Sinclair realized that he had voiced a great deal of moral indignation during the course of it, but he had in so doing overlooked one thing of primordial importance, the suspect's motives in relation to the client's niece; he had had no inkling into them and no proof whatsoever that his psychological insights such as they were rested on anything tangible. In some aspects, the suspect's behaviour in the presence of the would-be victim was consistent; he went from being stern, gaunt and cheerless, in Stewart's opinion, to being dogmatic and energetic in a debonair fashion ; and having witnessed the amazing change in the man's physiognomy after he had received the invidious shipment of peacocks from Tarshish, one could only infer that the pressure, or charm, that he exerted on the poor girl would be more effective than ever before through his having been boosted up by the Peacock treatment; she would be likely to be completely subjugated by him and more responsive than ever to his every suggestion, right or wrong, to the detriment of the aunt. It was highly possible that the man only had his own best interest at heart, and that he had to promote it in the only way he knew. through appealing to the girl's pity. That was the ultimate erotic phantasy for educated girls of independent means who could now distribute their largesse outside parental control. Arouse pity in such a woman's heart, and you're made; the female of the species will go to any length to make it up to you to feel good about herself. However, if one were inclined to think of the benefit as the result of the modern economic system, one would be wrong; it had happened before, many a time, in ancient cultures, the one nearest to our era being the age of Chivalry with its ultimate sex symbols, Queen Guinevere and her pathetic champion, Lancelot du lac, who through self-pity could wheedle favours out of the girl he'd wronged in order to advance his cause. The client's niece belonged to a class who enjoyed the privilege of money; the stern knight had no money, and the only privileges he had were those he conferred upon himself, courtesy of the armed forces' glorious ethos, which was made much of by the media to gild the pill of the ideological war of attrition against the Talibans, unpopular with the British public and just as unsuccessful as it had been in Victorian times, despite the support of an international task force.

The very idea of not being able to ascribe some sort of logical premeditated motivation to the suspect was unbearable. Having been regimented as a school leaver (some would say brainwashed), the latter was not himself in a position to throw any light in the matter; furthermore, having received the Peacock treatment, he was not likely to be the sort that would indulge in self-reproach of the useful kind. The situation had been rendered more frustrating by the fact that Messrs. Oldfield and Baxter had ruled out surveillance as being onerous, and too much of an additional financial burden on the aunt, So the villain of the piece was loose at large, enjoying a kind of immunity which could only increase his vain-glory and encourage him to grow ever more confident in his power to exert an influence on the girl to his advantage in the long run.

Sadly, Sinclair reckoned that the whole business had been, not a waste of time, but a professional failure, and he would have to do better next time.

Fortunately, an investigation came to his notice through a friend in the Royal Geographical Society which promised to be right up his street, and he thought he would contact his ex-assistant Sebastian Barnard with a view of enlisting his help once more. The boy had made such progress, starting as a hindrance in the case of the Peacocks of Tarshish to finish as an ally and a crony. in which Stewart felt he could confide.

Such a step had been made easy by the invitation that Sebastian had issued when they parted at the end of the Peacock enquiry. The Sailors' Club still operated on the same old premises in the docks and it still looked as ramshackle as ever, but then how to keep ordinary seamen under control when they were off duty was a task that no club doorman in his right mind was prepared to consider, let alone execute, for the sake of keeping the premises in pristine condition.

Having sat through the whole performance of the Geisha act, Sinclair waited until the audience quietened down to make his way to Sebastian's dressing-room. Although the reception had been less riotous than the first time, when Sinclair had sought out Sebastian on his father's advice, still the enthusiasm shown by the audience recommended a cautious approach. When he got to the cubby-hole which served as dressing-room, Sebastian had almost finished to remove his peerless make-up for which he used only the best Japanese cosmetics to obtain a flawless finish.

'Long time no see', said Sinclair in a nonchalant attempt to imitate one of the Chinese spectators.

Sebastian gave him a sidelong look through the long eyelashes of the courtesan.

'In need of help again?', he asked. 'Why is it you always turn to me, Sinclair?'

'Always, did you say? We've only just got started.'

'Oh, yeah?', Sebastian chided, 'and what makes you so sure?'

'Well, for one thing, the attendance here to-night was about one third of what it was the first time I called on you . . .'

'Nothing escapes your lynx eye, Sinclair. It is a fact that the men are getting bored with my Geisha act; attendance is falling.'

'I said you should investigate the dancing girls of Cadiz while you had the chance.'

'I know; don't rub it in. I felt out of my depths, being in your company.'

'Now you are going to tell me that I give you an inferiority complex? It won't wash, Buddy.'

'Give me another good reason why I should drop everything to follow you.'

'Lack of money, low spirits, boredom with the humdrum routine here, the instinct of self-preservation. Do you need to feel that bad at your age?'

'I can see you're desperate . . .'

'No, just raring to go. The Peacock case left a bad taste in my mouth; it was a shoddy affair. I aspire to do better.'

'Meaning?'

'Do you remember what you said to me in the car when we were on our way to Cadiz, on the isle of Leon about Tintin going to the outer Hebrides—the end of the world—in search of the Enchanted Isle?'

'I do; he was one of my heroes.'

'It was an extreme adventure, wasn't it? Comparable to walking on the moon with Milou . . .'

'Yes, it was.'

'I'm glad you agree with me. Well, the new job entails a similar type of journey which should also be of benefit to you as a future archaeologist. I have it all written down. Take the brief home, think about it, and I'll pick you up first thing the day after to-morrow ; no hemming and hawing, and no ifs and buts.'

'All right., but no moralizing; it'll be your downfall as a detective And now, shove off; I want to strip and shower.'

'Don't worry. I know how you feel. I have a lot of friends in the Muslim community. Not that I would ever want to convert to Islam, but I understand their concerns.'

Although Stewart did not appreciate Sebastian's gloomy prediction about his propensity to moralizing, he had to concede that it was improper in a detective. Strictly speaking, the task of the detective consisted in gathering material, not immaterial, evidence. All the same, in the case of the Peacocks of Tarshish, the profane feeling still haunted him that he had not gone far enough in his delineation of the suspect's psychological profile. The man invited harsher, more pessimistic comments. Was it because he was so cheerless in his assertive way and that gave him a kind of sinister aura? Sinclair even wondered whether that was not what constituted the secret of the fascination which he exerted on the girl as she hanged on his lips, waiting for him to say something warm and human. It seemed as though the man had been voided of the genuine and spontaneous feelings that make for rewarding relationships, and was just a robot which only obeyed emotions that had been implanted by a disciplinary force greater than himself to which he was in thrall and felt indebted in a sado-masochistic way. Perhaps, curiosity was what kept the girl going for the suspect was indeed a strange character,—controlling and controlled.

Still, Sebastian had touched upon a sore spot, and one which called for attention. To detect was indeed to uncover material, not immaterial, evidence of guilt. A confusion between the two would make the job of the detective unsound because it would establish a parallel between it and that of the witch doctor, who believed in the omnipotence of thoughts, blurring the dividing-line between the natural and the supernatural, the physical and the mental, as if the detective could wishfully through a kind of secret influence transmute the potentially innocent image of the suspect, allowed him by the Law, into a guilty one, offering facts based on intangible evidence as concrete proofs of guilt in order to make an arrest, i.e. remove for good somebody who is obnoxious from a group of people . . . When one started thinking about it, there was not much difference between a detective's position in society circle and the magician's. Both men depended on their own strength to meet the difficulties and dangers that they were likely to encounter in the discharge of their functions. Both intruded on the even tempo of life in a community, sometimes with disastrous results. There was malice aforethought to deal with on occasion. Like the magician, the detective believed in an established system on which he could rely and which he ccould manipulate for his own end. Both the detective and the magician had as their objective to procure an arrest,—to stop the evil course of whoever was upsetting anybody else. Whether the magician achieved that by sticking a pin through the heart of a wax doll or the detective by pulling out a gun, the end result was identical metaphorically speaking; an evildoer had been removed.

By now, through reading the brief he had been given, Sebastian would have become acquainted with the details of the next case, and in particular with its location in Central Africa. Inevitably, at some stage in their enquiries, circumstances would bring them into contact with African magic and its practitioners. Television reporters and foreign correspondents in recent times had investigated the rites of magic which were still performed in Central Africa. Many of their interviews had been conducted under the cover of darkness for fear of retaliation from secret clans and their devotees, for Africa had been the birthplace of magic and still felt protective of its privileges as the mother of lofty religious beliefs inherited from Magic, such as those upheld by the Egyptians since the early dynasties. Anybody acquainted with *The Book of The Dead* of the dynastic Egyptians would certify to the sway such magical beliefs held for millenia over all the people of Egypt, from the Pharaoh—the man who sat at the top of the stairs—to the humblest stonemason who carved the pyramids. Any likely encounters with the legacies of African magic, which had initially intimated the existence of powerful invisible forces, would probably revive and acerbate the issues raised by his natural propensity to moralize that Sebastian considered dangerous in a professional detective. The boy would be even more concerned if he heard at the start that the boss, the captain, had had a dream about Sherlock Holmes as Stanley meeting Dr. Watson as Dr. Livingstone, the indomitable Scottish missionary, and pronouncing the immortal words 'Dr. Livingstone, I presume?' from which he had woken up, disturbed by the infantile symbolism of the dream contents. He would have to watch his inner self when in Africa in order to avoid falling into the trap of perverting whatever tangible evidence fell under the scrutiny of his senses through transferring it into a metaphysical context. And that would prove extremely difficult since, unbeknown to Sebastian, the African job was all about the interpretation of strange events which challenged elucidation through common sense.

When Stewart picked up Sebastian outside his lodgings in Whitechapel, he thought the young man looked dejected.

'Why the long face, Barnard? You look as though you're off to an execution.'

'Oh, it's Barnard now, is it? Not 'Buddy' as previously agreed?', asked Sebastian, throwing his bag on the back seat.

'What are you complaining about? Barnard starts with a 'B' like Buddy; besides, it sounds more respectable.'

'Oh! We've got to sound respectable now. That's a new one on me.'

'Come on, don't sound like an inverted snob. We're off to Africa, dear boy, and equatorial Africa at that. The eyes of Burton, Speke, Gordon of Khartoum, Stanley and Dr. Livingstone are on us. Forget Tintin and his mountains of the moon. This is big, Barnard, very big. You've read the brief?'

'I've read the brief. We're off to investigate strange goings-on in the heart of darkest Africa . . . Since when do you palm yourself off as a specialist of African affairs? I thought you were a classical scholar?'

'There is no contradiction here. Let me tell you that about 460 BCE, a Greek historian whose name was Herodotus ascended the Nile as far as the first cataract at Assuan, and that in the first century of the Christian era, the Roman emperor Nero sent an expedition led by two centurions into Nubia, now called the Sudan, to elucidate the mystery of the sources of the Nile, which had fascinated Julius Caesar before him It is a mystery that has occupied the best minds in the world for centuries, you know, like *Revelation* by the apostle John, Jesus' beloved disciple. Even Conan Doyle had a crack at that, not that it would recommend it to you . . .'

'So, in a way, you misled me about the real nature of the enquiry, just because you were too lazy to look around for a more congenial assistant. I thought there was something shady about the brief.'

'Yes and no. Better the devil you know than the devil you don't. Come on, cheer up! I'll tell you more about it at London Airport.'

With hours to wait for their flight, they settled down in a quiet corner of the cafeteria with coffee and croissants. Pulling a map out of his briefcase, Stewart pointed to an area in equatorial Africa.

'This is the itinerary of our journey:—from Zanzibar to Kampala in the south of Uganda and on to Masindi in the north, in an area which stretches roughly between Lake Victoria and Lake Albert. We jet into Kampala but for the rest of the journey, we may have to hang around bus stations and railway yards for connections and make use of steamers too. Don't expect many mud huts, but you will see lots of European houses and churches and endless rows of banana plantations as well as mango groves. Did you know that there are as many varieties of bananas and mangoes as there are of potatoes?'

'No, I didn't.'

'Regarding the case we have to look into, as you've probably gathered from the brief I gave you, it is extremely intricate. Broadly speaking, what it entails is like investigating in the present a projection of the past into the future.'

'If you'll excuse my obtuseness, it sounded like a lot of mumbo-jumbo when I read the brief . . . .'

'I'm glad you've raised the issue of witchcraft', said Sinclair, folding away the map.

'Who wouldn't going away to Africa? There are enough Television programmes to alert people's minds to its continued influence.'

'You watch those sorts of programmes?'

'Yes. Why not? It's interesting stuff.'

'Good for you! Well, let me tell you that we may have to suffer the bane of witchcraft because inevitably we will antagonize a lot of people when we start ferreting around for clues.'

'You mean, they'll use unconventional methods to discourage us?'

'I wouldn't put it past them.'

'You don't believe in the goodness of the noble savage, then?'

'I don't believe in the innate goodness of any man, full stop.'

Sebastian pondered for a while.

'What about the source of the Nile?' he asked, pouring himself another cup of coffee.

'What about it?'

'Won't you want to see it, I mean as a classical scholar, while you have the chance?'

'My dear boy', Sinclair replied with a smile, 'as we speak it is probably flowing under a row of brick bungalows (Bengal-lows, ah, ah!) in a typical colonial town called Jinja. This is the age of the nuclear reactor, Barnard, the ultimate civilization. You know, the ancient Egyptians are often blamed for not using their stupendous architectural skills to build dams across the Nile to harvest its waters instead of monumental temples to their gods; perhaps they had their priorities right. They put their own spiritual welfare first. By the way, this reminds me of something.'

'What's that?', asked Sebastian, who was beginning to feel in a more mellow mood.

'I forgot to explain why we were stopping in Zanzibar for a couple of days.'

'I did wonder about that. It is such a long way away from our destination.'

'The area we are going to a few miles inland from Lake Victoria, apart from suggesting the vales of paradise of the dynastic Egyptians. resembles Zanzibar. It is lush and colourful with flowering shrubs and tropical birds like the magnificent crested cranes. Zanzibar has a similar atmosphere ; it will help us to acclimatize ourselves.'

'You've done your homework well, Sinclair.'

When they landed in Zanzibar, a strange fever seemed to take possession of Sinclair. Sebastian, who had been bowled over from the air by the incredibly blue colour of the Indian ocean as it lapped white coral reefs in slow motion down below, had just one desire,—to go sight-seeing, but Sinclair was not in a receptive mood

'Come on, slow coach; this is no time to mooch around. I promised Charlie Davenport that I would call on him the minute we touched down.'

'Who the hell is Charlie Davenport? His name is not mentioned in the brief . . .

'Charlie works at the British Consulate; he's an old friend of mine.'

'Let me hazard a guess; you were at school together. It's the old school tie brigade, isn't it? As the French say 'plus ça change, plus ç'est la même chose'.

'Since when were we blessed with the gift of tongues?'

'Since childhood. I went to school at the French Lycée in London. My parents, who were quite clued-up, thought the world had turned global.'

'Good for them! Any Swahili? Pity; that would have made you really dexterous. Still, I can only congratulate myself on having a really efficient sixth sense for picking you as an assistant.'

When they got to the consulate, Charlie Davenport was not there; he had left a note to say he was waiting for them at the Internet café round the corner. Sinclair was not impressed. There they were having just landed to carry out a secret mission and straightaway they were thrust into the glare of the public eye, and a potentially evil one, and by a consular official who should have had their welfare at heart.

'What's the big idea, Charlie, meeting us here of all places? I know you had quite a reputation at school for playing practical jokes, but isn't this going a bit too far?'

'Not at all ; I am being pragmatic. This is not a matter that falls under the agency of the Foreign Service.'

'You might have chosen a less public place . . .'

'You mean like the Mosque or the local harem? There's safety in numbers; besides, nowadays the Internet draws almost as many men to its dens than either the Mosque or the brothel.'

'Point taken. By the way, Charlie, this is my assistant, Sebastian Barnard; he is studying Archaeology.'

'Splendid! You couldn't have done better in view of the nature of the enquiry. Shall we sit here and pretend we are waiting for a screen to become vacant? Sebastian, you keep a sharp look-out. We must walk out of here before a screen becomes available and we're caught napping, which would send out the wrong signals.'

Charlie Davenport bent over the table and motioned them over to him.

'As you know, I have a friend in Kampala, an elderly man who is an anthropologist of some repute. How he obtained the information he holds, I have not the foggiest notion. Obviously, he has his sources having worked in Uganda for a very long time. All I can say is that he is a man of the utmost integrity, not one of those charlatans with half-baked notions one meets nowadays in so many walks of life . . .'

'We came across one of those outside Cadiz in our last case,' Sebastian butted in.

'Please, don't interrupt Charlie', groaned Sinclair. 'It's bad manners.'

'As I was saying, you can trust him implicitly as a man of science and a social historian. Now, he claims to have discovered a secret organization which on the face of it deals in human trafficking . . .'

'Children?', asked Stewart.

'No, adults only, at least primarily, so it is possible that eventually there may be children involved somewhere along the line.'

'That sounds like a long on-going investigation,'

'I wouldn't like to say. The outfit would have its headquarters somewhere between Lake Victoria and Lake Albert in the old kingdom of Buganda. as indicated in my initial letter to you.'

'A lost world which is being reactivated in the nuclear age, with ramifications in Europe . . . White flesh tastier?', asked Sinclair with a far-away look on his face. 'People in Europe have recently been tried for ritual murders and cannibalism.'

'Your guess is as good as mine. Now, I want you to go back to the Consulate; you need to be officially accounted for. My secretary will take care of the paper work. I'll go out first; you follow me.'

'I think we have to go anyway`, remarked Sebastian. 'It looks as though a screen is about to become available over there.'

Back at the consulate, things went very smoothly, thanks to the efficiency of Charlie's secretary, a buxom wench with considerable attributes, at least as far as Sinclair was concerned. Charlie insisted on seeing them out himself.

'You'll find everything you need to know about Professor Murray in this envelope. One last word of caution. Don't hang around too long in Zanzibar.; it's always been a dodgy place. Keep away from the bazaars; they will try and sell you rhinoceros horn as an aphrodisiac; the trade is illegal. Well, good luck and Godspeed!'

As soon as they got out into the sultry air, Sinclair mopped up his brow.

'My God, those guys in the Foreign Service know how to take the heat! Did you notice Charlie's secretary's breasts? The hanging gardens of Babylon! I couldn't take my eyes off them. He must be one of a special breed.'

'You mean father-to-son with transmitted traits?'

'Yes, colonial ones, like arrogance, self-esteem and a taste for debauchery . . . Charlie has done very well for himself. His wife is a stunner.'

`She winks an eye?'

`She's above all that. Her beauty alone elevates her. She's an icon.'

`It sounds as though you're a worshipper.'

`So are a lot of people. End of story.'

Soon they found themselves immersed in a scene made familiar by Television programs in which multi-national crowds are seen mingling with beasts of burden and man-powered vehicles in the busy trading quarters of African towns. Anxious to get away from the overpowering smell of spices which mingled with that of sweat and animal droppings, they got on a motor launch and crossed the straits which separate the island from the mainland, eager to make contact with the African continent, especially as they had missed the opportunity to do so when they were in Gibraltar. The journey across took just under two hours as compared with the fifteen-minutes by air, and they felt their spirits which had been undermined by the steamy atmosphere in the town restored by it. However, no sooner had they stepped ashore and seen the African scrub reaching away into the far distance without any hill to break its wild sweep that they were cowed by the sense of its elemental power as terra incognita and promptly sought a return passage to the island. Safe in the air the next day on the flight to Kampala, they could afford to laugh about it, though not without a vexing sense of inadequacy. Once in the interior, on the job, they would have to try and do better.

They had not left the runway behind at Kampala for long when Sebastian was bowled over by the region. It was exactly as Sinclair had described it. With the vegetation every bit as lush and exuberant, and the climate as hot and damp, it did indeed resemble Zanzibar, and Sinclair had been right in thinking they could acclimatize on the island before travelling to that part of Uganda which to a man with his erudition evoked the Elysean Fields of the ancient Egyptians. Sebastian was so bowled over by the place that he suggested they spent the day appreciating the local colour rather than continue their onward journey overland to Masindi. But professor Murray had other ideas.

When he heard that the two detectives whose pay was coming out of his own pocket were not proceeding at once to his place near Lake Albert, ostensibly to give themselves time to recover from jet lag, he chartered an aeroplane and airlifted them from the scrub.

Sinclair was not surprised. According to the data supplied by Charlie Davenport. the professor had obtained subsidies for his new venture from several royal societies and trusts as well as the Foreign Office. Personal friends had also made financial contributions to guarantee an eventual shortfall. It was even rumoured by evil-minded people that the anthropologist would dip his hand into his daughter's dowry should circumstances demand it. rather than fail. The man was therefore not prepared to allow two nondescript detectives from Europe to spend time at his expense footling around the shores of Lake Victoria at night in the forlorn hope of catching a glimpse of an hippopotamus. That just was not on. What did surprise Sinclair somewhat was Sebastian's reaction to having had his expectations thwarted by Professor Murray; as soon as he saw the electric power station on the bank of the Nile from the air at Masindi, he took an instant dislike to the place, and began muttering to himself about the spirits of the Nile crying out in agony against such ruthless forms of aggression; what with that and Jinja, it wouldn't be a wonder if it all came home to roost, much to the amusement of Professor Murray, whose face assumed an expression of sardonic contempt which did not escape Sinclair.

'That's what comes from reading *Tintin au Congo* ', said Sinclair, casting a friendly look in Sebastian's direction to try and soothe him.

'Ah, a fan of the Belgian wonder-boy!', exclaimed Professor Murray. 'I wonder how many people in Belgium at the time of the blacks' rebellion fifty years ago realized how close their fellow countrymen in the Belgian Congo came to having their throats slit by natives while waiting to be evacuated,—men, women and children. Their colonial paternalism had been an example to the world. I tell you, it was touch-and-go. I know; I was there. I had joined my father who ran a mission in a village on the upper Congo river that flows north to the Atlantic. I remember it well; out came the drums and the war paint. The only legacy of the paternal rule of the white man in the Congo is the armoured vehicle which helps the Congolese in the Democratic Republic to exterminate one another according to some ineradicable ancestral impulse.'

They had obviously got off to a bad start. To make matters worse, a terrific thunder storm broke over the lake during the night and both Sinclair and Sebastian were so terrified by its intensity that they fled from their beds in search of reassurance, but no one in the household was about to pacify them, and in the end, after having sought shelter uselessly in diverse nooks and crannies, they retreated to their bedroom exhausted.

Professor Murray was not the kind to waste time on civilities. Next morning. at breakfast, not a word was breathed by anyone in his household about the storm; the man obviously ruled the roost not so much with a rod of iron as with a cryptic code of conduct. The immaculately groomed females moved and spoke with a kind of suave genteelness which was bliss to watch,—not a hair, not a word, out of place, and presumably not a feeling either. They were all in perfect harmony with the economy of matter, such as it was presented to them. And at that junction Sinclair reflected while munching a piece of toast that he had stumbled accidentally on something worth noting despite his somewhat humble situation as a private eye flanked by a less than average assistant, who was impulsive as well as unguarded in his speech; and that he ought to make a mental note of it for future reference.

After breakfast, the females of the household disappeared with the discreet elegance of gazelles sniffing danger on the early morning breeze.

'Now, boys, let's get down to brass tacks', said the professor who seemed to have been energized by a copious English breakfast 'You don't mind if I call you boys, do you?'

'Not at all, Sir', replied Sinclair, 'not that we wish to dispense with formalities. In our profession, they count for a lot; in fact, you might say they are essential to the investigative process.'

'Oh! And why is that?'

Sinclair hazarded a benign smile.

'It's elementary, really. To keep the process on going in a civil manner.'

'Fair enough', replied Professor Murray, 'Where would you have me begin?'

'Begin at the beginning and end at the end, please, Sir.'

The pragmatism of the reply shook Sinclair himself, but not so Sebastian who had the greatest faith in the boss's ability to refract bombast and perhaps even return it to the sender, boomerang-like.

'Very well', said Professor Murray, 'but this begs the question, How much do you know about the case, or more precisely how much did Charlie Davenport tell you about the case?'

'Enough to get me to fly to Africa . . .'

'You didn't think it was too big for you to tackle? I mean, what do you know about Africa?'

'Sinclair's a classical scholar, Sir', Sebastian blurted out; having taken an instant dislike to Professor Murray when he appeared out of the African sky to abduct them from the vales of paradise; he just could not help himself.

'Really, young man, and how do you think the knowledge of dead languages can help him in this part of the world?'

'Everything is grist to the mill for a private investigator', retorted Sinclair, who was beginning to lose his patience. 'Professor, I am not one for wasting either my breath, or your money. Before we go any further, there is a standard procedure which has to be observed. I need you to draw up a list of all the members of your household, domestics included; of all the visitors who came to the house in the past six months, of all the suppliers of commodities who call on a regular basis. of all the vehicles you own and the technicians who carry out maintenance work on them. When you have supplied me with those, we will pick up the threads where we left off, before you began digressing'.

'What, now?'

'Yes, immediately. You have a secretary, haven't you?'

'My daughter acts as my secretary.'

'Get her.'

'She's probably gone to the local market with my wife . . .'

'Recall her. In the meantime, my assistant and I will take a morning stroll through the grounds; they look magnificent.'

'My God, Sinclair!', exclaimed Sebastian as soon as they had got out of earshot, 'I never knew you had it in you to stand up to the man.'

'I didn't want him to think he could trifle with us, just because we hadn't come out of Scotland Yard.'

'Do you think he was trying to intimidate us?'

'I don't know . . . A missionary's son, he may have been indoctrinated as a younster in the Belgian Congo, or frightened by the sound of war drums in the vicinity of the mission house, or by the savagery of Arab traders who murdered the whites who deprived them of African slaves. Africa has always been a place of bitter conflict one way or the other.'

'Why do you think he complied so readily with your request for information?'

'I don't know; expediency, I suppose.'

'He's a queer fish, isn't he?'

'Yes. At the moment, he has to consider his options very carefully. If he dismisses us, he runs the risk of upsetting Charlie Davenport who recommended us and was instrumental to his getting a subsidy from the Foreign office. The reason why I suggested a walk round the grounds was to give us a chance to locate the trash cans and have a look inside. One of the questions he has to answer concerns the number of visitors who stayed at the house during the past six months. During breakfast, I happened to notice a gift box of groceries from Fortnum and Mason on the sideboard in the breakfast room. If we find wrapping paper in the bins and he answers the question in the negative, we'll know . . .'

'He's lying!', exclaimed Sebastian.

'No, not lying, Sebastian, telling an untruth. Please, try and moderate your language. Come to think of it, if my memory serves me right, Sherlock Holmes was not in the habit of searching for clues through bundles collected by rag-and-bone men in his time, was he?'

'I wouldn't know about that; you're the expert.'

They were wending their way slowly back to the house past beautiful green lawns lined with jacaranda trees when they espied two garbage bins by the side of what looked like a large incinerator.

'There goes your evidence, Sherlock ; reduced to ashes. Now is the time to remember the maxim you so often quoted to me in Spain when I was suffering from an overdose of Paella.'

'What was that?'

'Never let the atmosphere round a case get you down.'

As they came in full view of the house, Professor Murray's daughter was engaged in the process of putting away papers in her father's filing cabinet. She looked up at the two detectives and then went out to join her mother who was sitting in the verandah. Before reaching the spot in the drive where the car had been parked in a hurry, the mother turned round and raised an arm as if to call someone, but the daughter hurried her into the front seat and drove off, flat out.

'It looked as though the mother wanted to say something', remarked Sebastian.

'Maybe she had forgotten her coat indoors, and she wanted to retrieve it. but the daughter thought it was getting rather late for market. Come on, let's tackle the old boy. This reminds me about the procedure . . .'

'What procedure?'

'The mode in which I want to conduct the proceedings in this case.'

'`What's special about it? It's a case like any other case, isn't it?'

'Not to my mind . . .'

'You mean there's something fishy about it?'

'Let's say it calls for unusual tactics, contrary to the usual practice, you know, about a person being innocent until proved guilty.'

'You mean, they're all guilty until proved innocent,—all of them? Charlie Davenport included?'

'Yes.'

'My God, Sinclair, was has come over you? Why this pessimism?'

'As a phantasmagoric story it's just a little too pat. Anyway, when we go in there, don't pull out the old notebook; just keep your eyes and ears open and let me do the talking.'

'Ah, there you are! Enjoyed your constitutional? More exciting than Clapham Common, eh? Here's your questionnaire.'

'Thank you, Professor,' said Sinclair, folding the paper and slipping it inside his breast pocket.

'Won't you sit down?'

'No, thanks; we're in the habit of standing when on a job.'

'It stimulates the 'little grey cells', eh? As Poirot is wont to say . . .'

'I don't know about that . . . Those prints round your study, Professor, they look pretty gruesome. Do they recall a local event of some historical importance?'

'Yes, indeed, they do. They illustrate the battle of Masindi which broke out not far from here on June the 8th, 1872 and lasted just an hour and a quarter. The caption below each one of them says it all, especially the one which shows vultures in their hundreds settling down over the African dead lying in the thick grass decimated by the fire power of Baker, the British explorer, whose mission was to abolish slavery by eradicating all resistance to white rule by local potentates, who just lived to flaunt their authority over their subjects, and did not want to see it challenged by white men for the purpose of saving their own people from slavery. His victory did not bring Baker any real advantage.'

'No?', asked Sinclair.

'No, if you look closely at the print below, you'll see the natives who survived the massacre hiding under cover of long grass to harass Baker and his men, who, in the end had to retreat to a trader's station on the Nile. Ironical, isn't it?'

'Yes, very. But then, the anti-slavery movement in the United Kingdom was very strong at the time; Baker had to keep going. Professor Murray, what little information we have about this case, we hold from a consular officer and may broadly be called hearsay of an extraneous kind to the type of bureaucratic business such people conduct daily as a matter of course; what we need is information straight from the horse's mouth. If I understand rightly, and I stand to be corrected, you claim to have discovered a secret society, a kind of parallel world, with headquarters in Uganda, where people who have absconded from Europe live as an advanced civilization. Do you mean a modern mecca like Las Vegas, or Brazilia, or Dubai?'

'No, not quite. Some of the people who live there have been listed as 'missing' in Europe.'

'Kidnapped as children?'

'No, there are no missing children there.'

'Have you been in touch with Interpol to be in a position to assert that?'

'No. I just know it for a fact. I've been an anthropologist all my life. I know a lost world when I see one.'

Sinclair paused pensively for a while.

'Since we have been called upon to assist in this case, all the way from Europe, would it be presumptuous on my part to infer that our role here is to provide some form of protection for you from persons unknown? Is your life in danger? Are you being threatened? Have you received anonymous letters? Do you suspect you are being stalked?'

'Let's say that as an anthropologist, the very inquisitive nature of my studies involves a great deal of snooping which some people may feel resentful about. It was Charlie who thought a bodyguard might be a good thing to have if I were on the trail of something really big.'

'And are you? Such as human trafficking, like the slave trade in the nineteenth century?'

'I might be.'

'Children were involved in that, you know . . .'

Sinclair pondered for a while.

'Your daughter works for you?'

'Yes, she edits all my notes; I couldn't manage without her out here.'

'I see. Has she got a boy friend?'

'My daughter is very popular with the white male community . . .'

'I meant a steady relationship with anyone?'

'You know how it is nowadays. Relationships crop up all the time, when and how it suits; those young people have a very down-to-earth attitude to such matters. They don't agonize.'

Sinclair walked away from Professor Murray's desk and took a few steps round the room, looking at the prints on the walls.

'Professor, if, as I understand it, our job here is purely to provide you with a bodyguard, I would appreciate it if you were on the level with us at all times.'

'But, of course, my dear chap, that goes without saying!'

'I'm glad we see eye to eye. Is there anything in what we have just discussed which might loosely be termed as 'loopholes'?'

'Not that I am aware of; it all seems quite straightforward.'

'Jolly good! I think that is all we need to know at this stage. We'll toddle along now and proceed with some routine investigations of our own relating to security. My assistant will let you have a verbatim report of our first interview.'

'May I just remind you that we dine at eight, on the dot? My wife is very keen to stick to customary times.'

'Very well, Sir. See you to-night at eight.'

Back in the grounds they took hurried steps towards the old Jeep that Professor Murray had put at their disposal and drove off in the direction of the town. Sebastian felt indignant and once in the vehicle he wasted no time in venting his feelings.

'A verbatim report from your assistant, without notes! You have got a nerve, Sinclair, Why, you told me not to pull out the old note-book!'

'Don't worry about it; the place was bugged.'

'You can't be serious!'

'I am, dead serious; behind the prints of the battle of Massindi between Baker of the Nile and the king of Bunyoro at the time of the slave trade.'

'Christ!'

'Please, don't use that name as a swear word; I happen to be a fan of Jesus of Nazareth, one of the greatest religious philosophers of all times.'

'Sorry, I didn't know. I thought you were a non-believer. And where are we off to, now?'

'To the market-place, on the trail of Mrs. Murray and her daughter.'

'What on earth for? You're not going to tell me that they are on your suspects' list too?'

'I told you, they're all guilty until proved innocent. Did you not notice how circumspect the professor was when it came to his daughter's relationships? He said she was very popular with the male white community.'

'Might she be involved with a coloured man?'

'Why not? The expression 'a touch of the old tar-brush' has long been banned from the vernacular, except perhaps in Professor Murray's private world.'

'But Mrs. Murray! She wouldn't say 'Boo' to a goose; neither would her sister or her niece . . .'

'She does look rather meek and mild, I must say, but then somebody might be leaning on her, who knows?'

'What are all her relatives doing here anyway?'

'Oh, I don't know; just getting a break from the Scottish climate, I presume.'

Sebastian kept silent for a while and then he said :

'There was something I didn't understand during the interview; it's the remark Professor Murray made about Clapham Common. It was meant to be funny; that much I do know.'

'The common had a bad name in the good old days. It was the meeting-place of junkies and homosexuals, or 'queers' as they were called then. You're not exactly oozing with virility, are you? No offence meant, and Professor Murray may have drawn the wrong conclusion about our relationship. He may even be homophobic, who knows? You do look rather effeminate, not that it bothers me in my job. I might have ended up with a female assistant for all I know.'

'Then, putting two and two together, Professor Murray would seem to have rather a lot of old-fashioned prejudices?'

'Bull's eye, Barnard! You're learning! Murray definitely has a chip on his shoulder.'

'Do you think he knows about the Geisha act? Did you happen to tell Charlie about it casually when you mentioned me?'

'No! Why should I? I just said you were studying Archaeology. I don't know what Charlie knows, what the Professor knows, what any of them know. They're all guilty of knowing something I don't know and that's not fair. Like the daughter being involved with a black fundamentalist with links to Al Quaida. Remember Uganda supplies nationalist troops to the peace-keeping task force in Afghanistan which may not go down well with more radical extremists. Professor Murray strikes me as having mixed feelings about Equatorial Africa due to his father having been a missionary in the Belgian Congo. Remember how sarcastic he was about the. Democratic Republic of Congo when we first met him?'

'Tintin met a missionary in *Tintin au Congo*.'

'I wish you'd stop mentioning Tintin; it doesn't do us any favours. The lad was suffering from an inflated juvenile ego, wasn't he? Claiming his exclusive reportage was sought after by the highest bidders in the international press; and that canny dog of his, always appearing at the right moment to rescue him from the brink of disaster, he wasn't devoid of canine snobbery either . . . Don't you think it was all a bit excessive?'

'Maybe, but it did inspire boys to aim high and aspire to be achievers.'

'I wouldn't call the Geisha drag act an exalted performance, would you?'

'No, but who knows what amazing pots and pans I may dig up one day from some obscure archaeological site . . .'

'I wish it would be soon, Barnard; this case does not portend any good.'

Looking for Mrs. Murray and her daughter through the crowds in the market place, a long way away from the parking lot, was like searching for not one but two needles in a haystack. Every time they thought they had spotted their heads bobbing up above the surge, they vanished from sight as haphazardly as they had appeared. Enquiring at random about the English ladies from various stall-holders they managed to obtain confirmation that the latter had indeed made purchases that morning, and that one particular trader at the far end of the market place might be in a better position to give them further information; they always spent a lot of time there chatting to him.

'Did the man wink an eye when he mentioned the trader the ladies were friendly with, or was it my imagination?', asked Sinclair.

But Sebastian was in no position to answer; he had been too busy looking at the amazingly colourful women's outfits on sale in the market.

By the time they reached the stall, the space was empty; the props had been removed and the old boy who was sweeping away the last traces of garbage spoke no English.

'Damn it, Barnard! I wish you'd concentrate on the job. Quick, back to the house. I need to ask the professor more questions.'

When the hair-raising trip was over, they arrived at the house to find it deserted. In the grounds, an elderly gardener was keeping an eye on the sprinklers which kept the lawns in beautiful trim. After the bustle of the market-place, the place exuded a serene calm reminiscent of the English countryside; one might have been anywhere at home, in the southern counties. Sinclair slumped down on a rustic seat and removing his tie invited Sebastian to sit down. No sooner had he done so that the old boy who was manning the sprinklers disappeared and soon after returned carrying a tray with a jug and glasses which he set down at the far end of the bench before retrieving his watchful stance by the sprinklers.

'Colonial bliss at its best, Barnard; you'll never know anything better. People killed and risked being killed for it. Can you wonder? Think of the advantages the exploration and conquest of Africa procured for them, each according to their own fancies, which ranged from the wildly erotic to the sublime and mystical, compared to which our own particular brand of endeavour seems piddling. Well, what can we do about it? Nothing at the moment, except engage in a much needed post-mortem; and, please, do try and keep your mind focused on the object of the exercise rather than the wonderfully colourful outfits of African women we saw in the market earlier on.'

'To err is human', replied Sebastian with a far-away look in his eyes.

'If you say so . . . Let's start with Charlie Davenport whose initiative initiated the whole thing,—the reason why we're here. When we met Charlie in the flesh in Kampala, he handed me an envelope, saying, and I quote 'You'll find everything you need to know about Professor Murray in this envelope.' Right?'

'Right', replied Sebastian.

'But when I opened the envelope and became acquainted with its contents, I found that the letter disclosed nothing more than the information Charlie had acquainted me with formerly in an e-mail. Usual diplomatic reserve, I suppose. Remember, it was Charlie who was instrumental in obtaining a subsidy from the Foreign Office for the old boy's new venture in Uganda. Now Murray says he hired our services because Charlie suggested he should have a bodyguard if he were on the trail of something big and potentially contentious. Now, you could ascribe Charlie's solicitude for Murray' s safety to a humanitarian concern for an ex-pat, fellow European, and an elderly one at that, as befits a consular officer anywhere abroad. Or, looking at it cynically, as a way of keeping Murray tagged through us for whatever reason. Now, the ten million dollar question is, Did Charlie have a long term, vested interest in suggesting us as a couple of untried, unskilled private eyes rather than some more experienced ones from a well-known agency? Of course, coming from

Charlie, a consular officer, a recommendation for a particular detective would carry enormous weight with Murray; the old boy would plumb for it, unreservedly.'

`Charlie's guilty of influencing Professor Murray, then?'

`Not so fast. How do we know the professor is telling the truth when he claims it was Charlie who suggested he should have a bodyguard? Perhaps Charlie never suggested such a thing.'

`The professor made it up; he's guilty of lying.'

`Again, I say `not so fast'. We flew out of Europe on the information given me by Charlie, a member of Her Majesty's Foreign Service, regarding the nature of the case,—information which he claimed he held directly from Professor Murray, `a man of the greatest integrity, a man of science and a social historian' blaa, blaa. blaa. So, we've had to take everything on trust from two personae gratae working in the same area of Africa without the possibility of testing the veracity of the facts they attested independently by checking them out one against the other. In reality, Charlie never specified in what capacity the services of a detective were required in this case.'

`They're both guilty!'

`Oh, stop behaving like a dummy, Barnard! You're just aping a character in *Murder on the Orient Express*. To go back to what I was saying, Charlie knew Professor Murray would take everything he said about us on trust, and vice-versa we would take everything he said about Professor Murray as gospel truth, and never query anything.'

`So much for the old school tie system, I don't think it's anything to be proud of.'

`I'll ignore that, Barnard. What we need to do now is to consider the role played by the females of the household. I don't think it is as compliant as would appear at first glance, on the face of it. The daughter probably has a *penchant* for native men; she certainly did not rush out of her room on the night of the storm for the opportunity to comfort us both, did she?, which was a pity considering she is quite shapely.'

`True.'

`Ah, here comes the professor! He looks fagged. We'll interview him right here, in the garden, away from the bugging devices in the house. Get the old note-book out and keep your wits about—dummy.'

The professor paid no attention to them and walked straight up the front steps.

'Professor Murray! Hullo, there! We'd like a word, please, Sir.'

'In my study', the professor replied curtly.

'I'm afraid that will not be possible, Professor; the place is bugged. We're not novices at this game.'

The professor sighed, shrugged his shoulders and staring at his feet retrieved his steps.

'Please sit down, Sir, and have a glass of water; you look as though you could do with one.'

The professor signalled to the gardener to come over and ordered a bottle of Indian Tonic water with lemon zest.

'Professor, I'll be honest with you and come straight to the point. My colleague and I are somewhat disconcerted. As we understand it, we are here at your expense to serve as your bodyguard; yet, this morning you went out without us. One of the first questions I asked you (you are, after all, our host) earlier on to-day was, Are you being stalked? because if you are, you cannot leave this house without our knowledge. I take your point about anthropologists being likely to rub native people the wrong way through the inquisitiveness of their researching, which may reveal the most barbarous instincts of men behind the practices of certain ancient cultures, but as occasional occupational hazards such occurrences would not bring about catastrophic consequences; at worst a sorcerer somewhere would stick a pin through an effigy of yourself, and you would not feel as much as a prick. I can only suggest one of the two following alternatives ;—either you are being stalked by jokers, out for a lark, and your safety is not at risk, or you have indeed in the course of your anthropological research stumbled on something big, with global ramifications, as you hinted earlier on this morning after breakfast, in which case you cannot go out without permanent cover. It would be preposterous to pretend that the arrival of two detectives from Europe in a mixed community such as this one would pass unnoticed. Your occupation is a bland one, compared to a lot of others in modern Uganda, and speculations must be rife as to why someone like you should give hospitality to two investigators. My assistant and I have no intention of setting off carrying easels and boxes of water-colours to sit around the shores of Lake Albert, pretending to be tourists on holiday, neither do we wish to go stalking wild animals in the bush, or bird watching. We need to get on with the job or return home. I would hate to call you a time-waster, Professor Murray. The way you airlifted us outside Kampala led me to believe you meant business, urgent business.'

Professor Murray looked up at Sebastian who stood pen poised in the air, ready to take down a ground-breaking statement.

'Well, at least my response was appropriate, as befits our mechanical times, not through using some rudimentary tool, like pen and paper. Where is your tape recorder, young man?'

'Professor Murray, we are licensed to carry arms; let's not confuse the issue', intervened Sinclair. 'From now on, expect to catch a glimpse of us every time you look over your shoulder; but let me warn you; this could be a dangerous game, giving your enemies, whoever they are, the advantage. Your investigative skills as an anthropologist are primitive and pathetic as such compared with theirs, which are state-of-the-art and possibly even beyond. Charlie Davenport worked that out pretty fast, I'd say, and he saw where his duty lay in the interest of the Foreign Service; Charlie's no fool.'

At that precise moment, the sound of tyres was heard grinding to a halt on the gravel path leading to the back door. The old gardener left his stance by the sprinklers and lumbered up in the direction of the house to help Mrs. Murray and her daughter unload their purchases. He must have said something to them, for they both looked up as Sinclair appeared, out of breath, having pelted all the way, and stared at him for a few seconds before resuming their task. Feeling he was intruding in a somewhat cavalier fashion, he wandered off a little way in the direction of the garbage bins, but before he could get very far, the daughter had got back into the car, and was driving out of the property with her foot flat down on the accelerator. Running back to the house, he got there in time to see Mrs. Murray disappear indoors, followed by the old boy carrying the shopping.

'Your daughter not working for you to-day?', he asked the professor, who was striding energetically towards the house to join his wife.

'No, not to-day.'

'The arrangement is quite flexible, then?'

'Yes, quite flexible. You know how it is nowadays; children have rights, and know their rights, and lacking the sensibility to understand the limits of those rights, abuse them without compunction.'

'I'd like to see her bedroom, if Mrs. Sinclair doesn't object.'

'What now?'

'Yes, this minute, with my colleague.'

'I'll go and find out.'

As soon as Sinclair had motioned him over, Sebastian gave vent to indignation. 'You have got a nerve using bullying tactics on a famous anthropologist like Professor Murray as though he were a common garden criminal!', said Sebastian, as soon as Sinclair had motioned him over to his side.

'You're peeved because of the remark he made about the note-book, aren't you? Actually, come to think of it, a tape-recorder might not be a bad thing to have.'

'Maybe . . . What's the big idea behind taking a look at the daughter's bedroom? So you can sneak in there at night without knocking over the furniture?'

'We may both have to slink in one day, in case of a showdown.'

'What kind of a showdown?'

'I don't know; a showdown of sorts; I don't trust any of them. Period.'

Presently, the old retainer came back with a message from the lady of the house to say it was perfectly in order for them to take a look at the daughter's bedroom. Entering the place, they found all the ladies having tea with Professor Murray in the verandah while the old boy, who seemed to know the drill to perfection, promptly checked with Mrs. Murray that she had everything to hand and could officiate in the proper manner while he showed the detectives the way to the daughter's bedroom.

'The Masindi tea-party!', muttered Sinclair.

The bedroom turned out to be empty; there was not a stick of furniture left in it; only an old straw hat hanging on the back of the door indicated that a female had once occupied the now vacant space.

'I wonder how long it's been empty', muttered Sebastian. 'It's such a waste of space'

'Your guess is as good as mine, but I'm prepared to take a bet that it got vacated quite a long time ago, probably to coincide with the daughter reaching the age of consent, or maybe even earlier.'

'Would you, by any chance, be thinking about the incident in the market earlier this morning when a hint was made about the daughter being keen on one of the stall-holders, a great looking African guy?'

'I was, indeed, Barnard; top marks for your intuitive response. This would connect well with the Professor's lament about the young nowadays knowing their rights and abusing them . . . I feel sorry for him and his wife; they're about as stranded in our world as the African tribes whose ancient way of life he investigates. The girl must have a strong stomach. I'm not talking about colour here; that is a matter of individual taste; but about education, I mean, a stall-holder . . . not all that highly educated, I suspect, apart from knowing his mangoes and his bananas.'

'Most African men are natural athletes, aren't they?'

'True. Let's get out of here and go for a swim while the family are enjoying their tea-break; the professor said we could use the pool at any time. I'm badly in need of proper exercise.'

'I can't, Sinclair, not in broad daylight; I'm pale all over.'

'Come on, don't be such a spoilsport!'

'Can't we wait until dark? It'll be more cooling.'

'All right then, but it's on your head.'

'What do you mean? We're armed, aren't we?'

'What, in our swimming trunks? Once we're in the water, we're sitting ducks.'

They left the house as discreetly as they could, through the verandah where the family were still enjoying their tea in a distinctly cordial mood. The professor had either just cracked a joke. or reported a clever repartee of his to a fellow archaeologist; all the ladies were exchanging appraising glances and tittering to their hearts' content. Mrs. Murray acknowledged their leaving with a nod of the head of perfect timing, neither too curt nor too friendly; she was obviously a lady of some standing, whose manners had not been breached by the informality of Africa; and finding herself in the company of close relatives from home, she beamed with congeniality.

'Solvitur ambulando', muttered Sinclair, as he found himself strolling through the garden once more with time to kill before dinner time, another ritualistic landmark in the Murray household's agenda.

'The problem with that, Barnard, is, if you're not 'ambulando', how can you be 'solvitur'?'

'You know, all this is double Dutch to me, don't you?'

'I do, and I won't harp on it. Let me ask you another question. When, alledgedly according to you, I was turning the thumbscrew on poor old Professor Murray earlier on, did you by any chance notice any sign of emotional disturbance, however slight, on his face when I mentioned Charlie's name?'

'No; he didn't twitch a muscle.'

'Are you sure?'

'Positive; I couldn't have missed it. I made a point of watching him very carefully all the time. He didn't react.'

'That was my feeling too.'

'So?'

'Surely, you can figure it out for yourself?'

'He's innocent of a suspicious involvement with Charlie!'

'Or a man with tremendous self-control, practised in the art of deception, who may begin to wonder if Charlie has done the dirty on him, behind his back. You know those chaps in the Diplomatic Service; they're suave with every one, but secretive with it. The professor does not know what Charlie told us about his discovery; Charlie may have magnified its importance in order to get us interested, thus securing a secret service of his own. Trouble is we're in the dark about what Charlie really knows about the professor's discovery, and we're not likely to find out either.'

'You have got a pessimistic view of human nature, haven't you?'

'That's the privilege of age, Barnard. You'll see when you grow up.'

More or less the same happy relaxed atmosphere prevailed at dinner time as it had previously during the other meals. The daughter who no longer lived in the house was present, though the reason why that particular gracious concession to appearances had been exacted from her was difficult to imagine; but she seemed relaxed and cheerful enough. At the end of the day, which may have been fraught with hidden dangers, the Murray family had saved its face, and all was lovely in the garden.

'So much so for man's infinite capacity for self-deception', thought Sinclair, as he watched them go through all the esoteric motions which procured them such fantastic salutary benefits around the dinner table. Well, if it worked for them, why not? There was no harm in it as far as the other person—the neighbour—was concerned; it was a kind of clannish policy which went well with their Scottish ancestry. As for the stranger who happened to stray into their midst unawares, well, he was expected to play the game in a likewise manner to return the compliment, so to speak, and the right to do so was arrogated to him on trust de facto for so long as he did not trespass, infringing the sacrosanct rights of the host.

At long last, with coffee and liqueurs, the hour of liberation came. The two detectives claiming fatigue under the testing conditions of the African climate asked to be excused, and everyone encouraged them. to have an early night. The daughter who had to take a friend to Kampala airport at crack of dawn, took advantage of the commotion, and the sound of her car was soon heard fading away down the drive, giving the two men the all-clear for their escape down to the pool through the humid atmosphere of the African night. Approaching it as they did through the pavilion with the changing rooms, they found themselves level with the shallow end where they could see pretty well while the deep end with its ornamental fountains was shrouded in darkness. From time to time, the sound of a wading bird which had strayed from the stream at the bottom of the garden was heard splashing about cautiously against the constant background noise of the jets controlling the water level. As they tip-toed into the pool at the shallow end, Sebastian got hold of Sinclair's arm.

`I think I can hear something up there, at the other end.'

`An animal maybe?'

`No. Crouch down. I can see a human shape stirring, in fact two human shapes, rolled into one.'

`You don't mean, copulating?'

`Yes, that's what it looks like. Now we can't move and my teeth are chattering.'

`Here, throw this towel over your shoulders and try and creep back up the steps out of the water.'

`No, I can't; they're getting up.'

`Can you see who it is from where you are?'

`Yes, it's Professor Murray's daughter, with a male escort. It looks as though they're stark naked.'

`Could it be the stall-holder?'

`How can I distinguish a black man in the darkness?'

`Look at me and look at yourself, for peace' sake; we both show white against the darkness. If you can't see him, he's got to be black.'

`All right! Let's say she's clasping a dark shadow. They're leaving! Thank God for that; I'm shivering all over. She has got a nerve coming back here at night, after having been thrown out of the house by her father!'

`How do you know he threw her out? She probably walked out of her own accord to escape from his puritanical control. She's a wage earner ; she can have her cake and eat it as and when she fancies ; money sanctifies everything nowadays; it makes sex respectable, part of fair trading. Hey-ho, the lolly!'

`Oh, stop moralizing!. I'm frozen standing still waiting for you to dive in.'

`I'll be glad to oblige, Barnard, I'm indebted to you.`

`How's that?'

`Suggesting we come here at night for a swim. It was most interesting, yes, indeed, as Poirot would say. It's given me a lead. In fact, maybe, several leads.'

`Oh, yes?'

`Yes, I think to-morrow morning, we'll start the day investigating the lady of the house.'

Neither of then spoke during breakfast the next day, their minds still full of the events of the night over the reconstruction of which they mulled compulsively, though following two very different courses. With Sinclair, the liberal almost fatalistic view he took of it—a case of laissez-faire—was part of the evolutionary law of the cycles of. Nature. which he accepted philosophically. With Sebastian, the righteous, outspoken sense of social disgrace came uppermost :—it was not right, meaning it was not decorous. It was his aestheticism that deplored the disgrace not his morality. Every fibre of his being which had gone into perfecting the Geisha act in order to make it an event that lingered pleasantly in the mind as a testimony to his artistic temperament rebelled against it, condemning it as an objectionable crease in the sublime fabric of life. While Sinclair kept his face down over his porridge, he cast surreptitious look in Mrs. Murray's direction, wondering what revelations Sinclair would manage to extract from her that would throw a light on the event of the night and make acceptable sense of it, at least so far as she and her husband were concerned, for the real meaning of it might remain out of their reach, being who they were.

Breakfast being over, Mrs. Murray gave her husband a glance and walked into the verandah where she sat down with a resigned look on her face. She had never been one for introspection; she was just too busy dealing with the minutiae of domestic life which she enjoyed immensely to think of herself worthy of self-scrutiny, and the thought of having to come up with factual answers to a detective's questions was not at all to her liking. Why did he have to bother with her? What did she have to do with the outside world such as it was in modern-day Africa. and what could she tell him about it? Her world was a restricted family circle, enlivened by visits from relatives from home; it had not changed much in the odd forty years she had spent there, being punctuated mostly by her husband's ground-breaking discoveries in the field of Anthropology, the symbolism of which he often discussed with her, testing their emblematic validity against her down-to-earth common sense.

'Thank you for waiting, Mrs. Murray. I had hoped to see your daughter here to-day so I could also ask her a few questions. Is she likely to come later on in the day?'

'No, not to-day.'

'It's not one of the days she works for your husband?'

'No, it isn't.'

'I thought your husband said the arrangement was flexible. It strikes me in fact as being very irregular.'

'Yes, my daughter pleases herself; she's very independent by nature and she has another job'

'At the moment, she seems to be visiting quite often . . .'

'Yes, we have relatives from Scotland staying; she enjoys her cousin's company never having had a sister.'

'I expect you know your daughter has a boyfriend, an African boyfriend?'

'Yes. As a child we wanted her to mix with native children; we didn't want her to have racial prejudices.'

'Was this out of a genuine feeling of compassion for humanity as a whole or a matter of policy, to keep up with the more permissive members of the white community?'

'My husband and I were practising Christians without reservations about creed or colour.'

'I see. Has your daughter perhaps overdone it a bit? Gone too far in her choice of playmates? I mean, your husband is well-connected; he has friends in the Foreign Service, and she is an attractive girl.'

'People make choices . . .'

'True. This, I take it, is not a cause of tension in the household, of friction perhaps between your husband and yourself?'

'Oh, no, not at all; we've always seen eye to eye about everything.'

'Commendable, truly commendable Well, thank you, Mrs. Murray, that is all I wanted to know. I'd like a word with your husband now, if I may. Oh, just one last thing. What does your daughter do for a living?'

'She runs an export-import company.'

'Fruit and vegetables?'

'Yes.'

'I thought so.'

Sinclair signified to Sebastian by a nod of the head that he wanted the professor brought in.

Oh, dear, thought Sebastian, who had no trouble recognizing Sinclair's mood, he's gone into his imperious mode. Wondering what had induced it, he gathered that it must have been something Mrs. Murray said or something Sinclair inferred from her pious statement, being the shrewd judge of character that he was. Anyway, it was an indication that he was on to something, like an eagle which has just brought home a catch between his talons and stands grimly defying the world to come and snatch it from them in the empyrean region in which it lives. And Sebastian could only express the hope that it was so because at the moment, they were floundering and badly needed a lead.

As Mrs. Murray walked out of the verandah and her husband walked in, Sebastian thought they exchanged a meaningful glance, though the meaning of it eluded him. 'Beware of interpretation, Barnard', Sinclair was wont to say, 'nine times out of ten it's the mother of deception. Only once in a blue moon does one get it right, and so more often than not one is tossed about on murky waters between the evidence, which could have been planted, and the blinding light of a revelation about something reviled by the mob, which clamours for a sign so it can have its pound of flesh,' It was in moments such as these that Sebastian regretted having left the Geisha attire behind; donning it at the end of a long day in Central Africa would have acted as a salve.

There was little hope of anything approaching that with Professor Murray already on the bench of the accused, in the occurrence a comfortable wicker arm-chair in the verandah. One bully pitting his brains against another's? wondered Sebastian in a fit of cynical discouragement with the whole business for which Sinclair usually recommended a glass of Epsom salts 'to tickle the liver'. Maybe not; Sinclair was harping on about the way the professor had descended on them literally out of the blue. in a chartered plane to stop them from dawdling in the bush.

'I am sorry to keep on about it, Professor, but it was an odd thing for a Scotsman to do, totally out of character with the proverbial parsimony of the clans. To charter a private aircraft is not a cheap affair; you must have been under a lot of pressure to do so at your expense. When I was a child, my father had a friend in Glasgow who had seven children; his name was Macpherson. Every morning, after breakfast he would line up his children in front of him, toothbrush in hand at the ready, to squeeze out on each one of them the correct amount of toothpaste in order to avoid waste; and to this day I remember my father's large guffaws as he described the hilarious scene.'

'Your father must have had a peculiar sense of humour.'

'Maybe he did, but, generally speaking, there is a consensus of opinion about that particular national character trait of the Scottish people. And I can only reiterate what I said before, that you must have been under a lot of pressure to put your hand in your pocket in such an extravagant manner. What else would justify such an outlay? You can't be earning that much with your anthropological studies. What was the last time you published a major work about the emblematic ways of African tribes? Now, as tourists, my colleague and I may have behaved like a couple of idiots, overwhelmed by the colour, the mystery and whatever else you'd like to call it which normally bowls over Europeans when they first set foot on the African continent, but as detectives, I must tell you, we're all there. Let him who as ears hear. As detectives, it is our conviction that you did so because you felt threatened after seeking advice from your friend Charlie Davenport, the British consul in Kampala, who suggested a bodyguard, probably out of self-interest because he did not want to end up with a dead body on his patch. It would tarnish the scutcheon. People in the Foreign Service are good at opening the proverbial umbrella that they carry about with such dash'

'You're a very cynical man, Mr. Sinclair; Years of working among native Africans have induced in me a totally different mentality. Their ways are spontaneous and innocent.'

'Ah, the white man's burden! Premeditation and guilt and the ability to conceal both! Right, since you have invested such a large sum of money in getting yourself a bodyguard, it behoves us to perform our office as hired by you on the recommendation of a consular officer I happen to be friendly with ; the integrity of the standards of our profession demands it. So, from now on, you will not go out unescorted. Don't worry, we shall be inconspicuous at all times. Talking of money, incidentally as a matter of curiosity, how much do you pay your daughter for casual work?'

'Very little. Fuel to get here and on occasion repairs on her car. As you know, I have my own mechanic to maintain the vehicles on the estate. It's convenient for her while she works here in the office. My daughter does not need money; she earns a very good living with her company.'

'So your wife hinted. One last word before we let you go. If you were at all tempted to give us the slip for any reason, we would fly back home immediately and Charlie Davenport would be the first one to hear about it. Good day to you, professor. Barnard?'

'Yes, sir?'

'See the professor out, will you?'.'

Bemused, Sebastian stood in the doorway, not knowing whether or not he ought to give the poor man a friendly pat on the back to counteract the ferocity of Sinclair's onslaught.

'My God, Sinclair, you have got a way of turning on the thumbscrew! Talk about primitive methods! I don't know that I want to be associated with any of it. What can the poor man do now?'

'I had to precipitate a crisis, you know the way they do in classical Greek drama . . .'

'No, I don't, lacking a classical education Really, Sinclair, I don't think it was right for you to badger the old man.'

'For Christ's sake, Barnard, I had to do something. I can't hold them all indefinitely as guilty parties presumed innocent. It doesn't make good legal sense, does it?

'No, it doesn't. But, please, do not invoke the name of Christ. As I said before, I find it offensive. Well, perhaps, the time is ripe for you to reverse your policy. I sincerely hope so, because the tedium of the whole thing is beginning to get me down too.'

'Amen.'

A wave of tender concern swept over Sinclair's heart for the boy whom he had involved willy-nilly in the African adventure. Despite his assurances he personally had no lead, no clues and no hunches to offer as beacons to guide him through it; he was stumbling about in the dark, clinging to a spurious policy of considering all parties guilty until proven innocent, conscious of being an amateur not worth his salt . . . In his innermost self, he knew that he was over-faced, cowed by the powerful and mysterious presence of the African continent which loomed large like some ubiquitous potentate from a by-gone age. Confronted by it at every twist of the road, one felt beaten in advance. Only the most rigorous form of rationalisation, using a lexicon which did not exist, would help one convert the esoteric writing on the wall into a script accessible to all; but for that one needed co-ordinated elements. and at the moment there were none. Relying on fragmentary evidence to justify launching a major attack was wrong. Africa anyway had always been the source of bitter conflicts, not simply between nations but also between individuals who, striving for self-conquest, represented those nations; the very thought of the magnitude of the challenges they faced turned one's knees to jelly. Now, a different type of conflict took place between millions of native Africans who coming to grips with the basics of their religio-political identity, made the continent a dangerous place, where suspicion was rife. For an immature and fragile individual like Sebastian Barnard, it was fit and proper to be impressed by the exploits of a juvenile reporter like Tintin; his self-reliance before the challenges of a hazardous job in terra incognita was enough to make any adult feel inadequate. The Belgian boy relied primarily on his ability to solve problems in order to overcome obstacles; that was what made him so endearing and worthy of emulation; he could get out of any scrapes, thus putting chance, which favours the bold, on his side . . .

Casting about in his mind what to do next in order to redeem himself in Sebastian's eyes and boost up the boy's morale, Sinclair suggested they should take a walk in the direction of the garages with a view of investigating Professor Murray's mechanic. When they got there, they found the workshop was empty. There were printed sheets pinned round the walls, some giving details of jobs in hand and others containing instructions for repairs which had been booked, with duplicates of orders for parts, as well as descriptions of various safety standards. In a garage adjoining the workshop, a lot of underwater swimming equipment was stacked against the walls around an old car,—wet suits, scuba tubes and masks. In a corner, on the back of a dilapidated car seat, a pair of swimming trunks had been hung to drip dry.

'What's the matter?', asked Sinclair, looking at Sebastian, 'aren't you feeling well? You look as though you've just seen a ghost.'

'I've just had an aura.'

'Don't tell me you're epileptic as well as . . .'

'No, I meant a déjà vu, literally. That's him! That's the one who was with the Murray girl last night at the pool!'

'Don't be ridiculous! It was pitch dark; one couldn't see a thing.'

'It was him, I know it! Watch out, here he comes!'

Astounded, Sinclair wheeled round to come face to face with a smiling African. The young man was of average height, slim-built, with a clean-shaven head.

'Looking for me?'

'Yes, Detective Stewart Sinclair, and this is my assistant, Sebastian Barnard. Your name appears on the list of personnel supplied by Professor Murray.'

'That's right. I'm responsible for the maintenance of all the cars and vehicles on the estate. Did you want a job done on yours?'

'No . . . Fond of water sports, I see?'

'Yes, I am.'

'Would those swimming-trunks be yours by any chance?'

'Yes, I do wear them sometimes.'

'On special occasions, maybe?'

The young man gave a hearty laugh :

'Yes, when I want to impress the ladies; they're rather slick and show my figure to advantage. I'm a keen body-builder.'

'Nice set-up you've got here. I see you also take on jobs for outsiders?'

'Yes, professor Murray has always been very generous to me; ever since I left primary school; helped me get through my apprenticeship.'

'You were his protégé? I mean, he sponsored you.'

'Yes, I used to come here as a child with my mother who cooked for the Murrays. I used to play with their little girl.'

'Did you sometimes go swimming with her?'

'Yes, sometimes, when it was very hot, if she felt like it.'

'And are you still friends with her? Miss Murray has grown into a very attractive, successful young woman, running her own company . . .'

The mechanic opened up the bonnet of the old car and started unscrewing the battery.

'What Miss Murray does is none of my business, I work for her father.'

'You still look him in the face, do you?'

'Of course, I do! We're all equal, aren't we?'

'Yes, we are. One last question before we leave you to get on with your work. Do you also maintain the pumping system for the swimming-pool?'

'No, another chap comes in from a specialist firm.'

'I see. Well, good-day; it's been nice talking to you.'

'I was right, wasn't I?', Sebastian asked as soon as they were out of earshot. 'He was the one.'

'Just because he stuck his head under the bonnet of that clapped-out Ford Mondeo does not mean to say he wanted to avoid showing guilty or embarrassed feelings about his childhood sweetheart. He might have resented our prying into his private affairs.'

'I don't think there was anything particularly reminiscent of the style of childhood sweethearts about what they were doing by the pool last night . . .'

'You're jumping to conclusions.'

'I thought the policy was, they were all presumed guilty until proved innocent?'

'But the evidence Barnard! To my mind, the evidence is not strong enough to declare him guilty, and of what exactly? Becoming a threat to his benefactor justifying the hire of a bodyguard, in which case he would join all the others who are potentially guilty of the same crime, suggesting a conspiracy. Is that what you're hinting at?'

'Why not?'

'It's very far-fetched. Oh, I know, conspiracy theories have become popular. Whenever the FBI or Scotland Yard fail to make the arrest of a single culprit, a conspiracy theory is invoked—to save their face. Mind you, I am not ruling it out altogether, but it would have to be a massive one, with global ramifications. All those people strike me as being parochial . . . It sounds as though the Murray protégé was submitted to a lot of pious white democratic mouthwash during his childhood which he may have grown out of under the influence of persons unknown such as Muslims fundamentalists. However, as a sexual partner; he was now Miss Murray's equal though in deference to their past relationship as childhood sweethearts, as the cook's son, he still waited for her to give him the nod. She was popular with Alpha males in the business world—the company directors—and very much in demand.'

'Oh, dear, Sinclair, you sound mildly envious!'

'We can't win them all, can we?'

'If you say so.'

'To sum up, I think we've landed in a steamier atmosphere than previously intimated. What we must do now is engage in some intensive physical training of our own in readiness for the day when we have to trudge miles on Professor Murray's tail, which may not be far off.'

'You don't think he is likely to make a sudden dash?'

'No, I don't think so. He must be casting about in his mind what to do. The man's in a quandary. Put yourself in his place. By hiring us as bodyguards, he is sending out clear signals to those, whoever they are, who supposedly threatened him in the first place, provoking them to come out in the open ; and, by the same token, he is laying us open to being targeted by those who wish him harm on account of a discovery he has made in the course of his anthropological investigations It is not a pleasant situation to be in. As far as we're concerned, up to now, we've behaved like a couple of bland policemen going about their business more in the laconic style of Dickson of Dock Green than that of an Irish cop in New York. Once we start tailing Murray on a daily basis wherever he goes into uncharted territory, we become sitting ducks. I want you to know that.'

'You couldn't have put it in a more succinct way, Sinclair. And I am grateful to you for being so honest. Do you remember saying to me in the very beginning that in Africa we would be on to something big, very big? Well, I suppose, this is what you meant. You're almost clairvoyant, aren't you?'

'Oh, I don't know about that. I try and follow some very simple guidelines, like men's evil instincts lying dormant, till an opportunity reawakens them which they can't resist.'

'We're all potentially guilty then?'

'I'm afraid so. Nobody is immune.'

'Would you say that there is a kind of covert device inside each one of us which makes us harmless so long as it is not reactivated?'

'Yes, something like that.'

'By the devil?'

'Oh, no, I don't believe in a personal devil. That's a notion dating from Antiquity. To-day, the devil's is multiform and likely to become more so as Time makes the World Wide Web expand, causing natural frontiers to recede.'

Although Sebastian followed Sinclair's drift perfectly well, there was still a question mark in his mind,—what, if anything, was Charlie Davenport's role in all that? What criminal offence might he be presumed guilty of? Unless the professor was lying about it, to whitewash himself of cowardice, Charlie was the one who had suggested the invidious bodyguard in the first place, thus exposing the professor and the bodyguard to retaliation by the professor's secret enemies. What if Charlie wanted the professor out of the way because he was in league with his enemies? That sort of thing often happened in the secret services of the Diplomatic Corps. Or had Charlie merely tried to brush off the old man whose fears were probably irrational and the result of age and overwork? Sinclair had not conjured up Charlie's name during his otherwise comprehensive review of the facts, remembering perhaps what a sensitive issue the idea of the old school tie had proved to be for Sebastian, who had been educated at the French Lycée in London. Another participant whose spectre Sinclair had not raised was Professor Murray's daughter. He had only lightly touched upon the subject in relation to the mechanic, but not independently in any depth, as was his wont. It was as though an interdict hung over both Charlie and the Murray girl. Was it because he considered them birds of a feather on account of their sexual promiscuity, and the reticence to enlarge was a puritanical one? Plucking up courage, Sebastian thought he would hazard a risky question about Miss Murray's profile.

`Ah, now you're talking!' exclaimed Sinclair, as though he welcomed the opportunity to get it all off his chest, `Self-indulgent, permissive, a two-timer without any sense of loyalty to any one, money-grabbing, an adept of the motto "never let your right hand know what your left hand is doing', thus having the best of both worlds without acknowledging indebtedness to either . . . Her pragmatic response to her situation mid-way between two poles, the African and the European, is astounding, as is the ease with which she gravitates between the two as a megastar to the consternation of her parent whose motto in retrospect must be `The way to hell is paved with good intentions', for there is no doubt at all in my mind that they did mean to bring her up devoid of racial prejudices, in the spirit of Christian charity. It all misfired, horribly. And poor old Murray, who had been brought up in a mission house, in a station on the upper Congo, must entertain some melancholy thoughts when he looks back on the strife caused by the missionaries' intention to snatch natives both from the clutches of witch-doctors and Arab slave traders to open up Jesus' kingdom of heaven to them. Those prints round his study walls depicting various episodes of the battle of Massindi say it all.'

`She's guilty as hell, then?'

`No, she's irresponsible, and I don't mean of diminished responsibility, but fully compos mentis with it and enjoying every minute of it in a state of blessed immunity from even an awareness of danger such as animals are endowed with.'

'Good grief, Sinclair, you are full of doom and gloom. Do you think she and Charlie Davenport would hit it off well?'

'Yes, I dare say, except she lacks the arrogance of Charlie's class. She wouldn't be able to relish an on-going relationship with him such as the one she has with the mechanic on her own terms; a riotous one-night stand, maybe. You see, she has to dominate and bestow her largesse; Charlie would have no time for that. He's the super Alpha male, the "Who do you think you are? type" with all the inbred haughtiness that it requires.'

'I tell you what, Sinclair . . .'

'What?'

'On your trade card, you should have : *Stewart Sinclair, Psychologist Detective* . . . You're good at it.'

The next day, Mrs. Murray took the professor's breakfast into his study; he had spent the night puzzling over the reason why some native African cultures had progressed so as to be in advance on some others and seem sophisticated by comparison while remaining almost barbarous by European standards, a social phenomenon for which as a Christian anthropologist he saw a metaphor with the nucleus in which God and the Cherubims,`us', (v.22, ch.3) in *Genesis* lived in the midst of plenty as a superlative society, surrounded by plant food with amazing properties, a society which possessed the well-guarded secret of how to survive its own success, while beyond its boundaries, the soil was arid and only bore thorns and thistles, suggesting it co-existed as a parallel world with less advanced cultures which seemingly had not been so successful. That was how he liked to see things anyway, convinced that the Bible was primarily a record of the social history of man on earth from which people could draw valuable lessons with useful existentialist guidelines.

Mrs. Murray expressed concern for her husband's welfare; it was not sensible to pore over papers to the detriment of one's health, especially when they were going through anxious days. She reminded her husband that she would soon be leaving the house to go to market with her daughter, upon which he asked her to shut the door, much to the embarrassment of the two detectives who had sat all night outside the professor's study waiting for him to come out. It was not long before, hearing her daughter's car outside, Mrs. Murray came out of the study and made her way to the back door where she picked up her shopping bags.

About thirty minutes after his wife's departure, Professor Murray came out of the study and, after having had a shower, walked out of the house.

The two men sprang to their feet, checked their firearms and rushed down the front steps in time to see the professor disappear down the drive in his car. Jumping into their own vehicle, they soon caught up with him. Much to their surprise, they realized that the itinerary he was following was the one which led to the market-place, the very same one over which they had followed Mrs. Murray and their daughter.

'Oh, my God, no, not the market place! It's not a good place for a showdown . . .'

'Oh, stop crying like an old woman and keep your wits about you. Maybe, Murray feels guilty about not helping his wife with the shopping; devoting too much time to his work.'

'It's more likely he has come to breaking-point. All those interrogations, all those interviews . . . You went at him hammer and tongs, Sinclair.'

'Oh, yes? Maybe he needs to let his wife know that he is behind her all the way. She's been under a lot of stress lately, with a house full of guests, and two detectives in the bargain.'

They parked the car where they had left it before and took hurried steps towards the market; it was packed. Thinking the professor would make his way through the crowd to the last stall at the top end of the market where presumably he would find his wife and daughter engaged in conversation with the native Adonis who kept the fruit and vegetable stall, they launched themselves into the seething mass of people and animals that jostled against one another, hampering their progress. But when they got there, the professor was nowhere to be seen. Mrs. Murray sat on a stool behind the barrow, eyes cast down, while her daughter stood chatting to the owner with a leg cocked up against a crate of mangoes in a seductive pose. A movement behind a curtain on the opposite side of the alleyway attracted Sinclair's attention.

'Look out, Sebastian!. We're about to be shot at!'

Almost simultaneously, they dived downwards into the stall to shield Mrs. Murray and her daughter, while the stall holder, who had been wounded in the arm, jumped into a mini-van which was parked behind the stall and drove off, smashing rows of empty crates on the way. Leaving Sebastian to protect the ladies, Sinclair rushed across the way and tore the curtain down, thinking he would uncover Professor Murray, but at that precise moment, the professor appeared coming from the opposite direction, mopping his brow, in a visible state of shock. The whole place was in an uproar; people were rushing about in opposite directions, exchanging alarming comments about an attack on infidels by Islamic extremists which, according to some gloom merchants, had been long in coming.

'Quick', said Sinclair, 'out of here before the police arrive!' Putting their arms round the two ladies, the detectives guided them through the crowds back to the car park with the professor in tow, leaving him to fend for himself. At one point, he fell so far behind that Mrs. Murray, who kept looking back to make sure he was all right, refused to take another step until one of the detectives had brought him to the fore.

In the car park, Miss Murray said she had to go to work and could not take her parents home; it was important to show those people, whoever they were, that they could not disrupt every-day life. Sinclair said that was not a problem; Sebastian would drive her father's car back to the house, and he would take both her parents home in his car. However, he needed to ask her a few questions ; he had meant to do so for several days, but somehow he had had to attend to other more pressing matters. Sebastian thought there was nobody like Sinclair to put in the thin end of the wedge, though the innuendo about 'more pressing things' did not escape him :—if the little Madam thought everybody had to bow and scrape before her and give her precedence, when it came to Sinclair she had something coming.

At the house, professor Murray lost no time in making himself secure in his study, claiming that he had been badly shaken by the events of the morning and needed to recover his self-composure as soon as possible in order to resume his studies; at his age, it was not a good idea to leave stones unturned for long in case they became too heavy to lift. Sinclair told Sebastian to give Mrs. Murray a cup of herb tea with a couple of sedatives and bring her out on to the porch before the other ladies in the house fell upon her for news.

'You're not intending to question her now, are you?'

'Why not, while everything is fresh in her mind? You know how it is with elderly people; they tend to embroider as time goes by.'

Sebastian thought Sinclair's position was a bit extreme, but who was he to judge? The events of the morning had been exceptional enough to warrant what seemed like sharp practices in someone as principled as Sinclair, and it was not long before he appeared on the porch leading Mrs. Murray by the arm. As he had intimated, Sinclair's first question to her was:

'Did you know your husband was coming to the market?'

'Oh, yes' she answered with the unmistakable spontaneity of sincerity.

'Why?'

'Because I asked him to.'

'And why did you?'

'Because I could no longer face it without him at my side.'

'Face what, Mrs. Murray?'

'Going to that stall week in, week out, and having to be polite to the man . . .'

'You mean, the greengrocer?'

'Yes, he behaved in a familiar way which was embarrassing.'

'You mean, he was unduly intimate?'

'Yes; we're very private people, my husband and I.'

'Were you under any obligation to put up with it?'

'My daughter said I had to take it in my stride and make a joke of it; it was good for the business, you know, the export business. She said I was making a mountain out of a molehill, She also said I was two-faced, paying lip service to Christian notions about the brotherhood of man. What really bothered me, was the unguarded way I which she behaved with the man in public, in a busy market-place. I thought she showed too great a willingness to go along with a native who had embraced the ways of European culture. I thought she was playing with fire.'

'And you were right, of course, as was demonstrated to us earlier on to-day; things backfired on her. Obviously, your daughter thinks times have changed, and there is nothing to worry about; but you and I know better. There are agitators about. Tell me, was your husband willing to help you out when you opened your heart to him earlier on to-day?'

'Oh yes, he responded quite spontaneously. In fact, he reprimanded me for not telling him sooner.'

'Did he appear at all nervous at the prospect?'

'Not at all. There was a reassuring smile on his face.'

'I see. Well, thank you very much. That will be all.'

A chorus of Ho's! and Ha's! went up as Mrs. Murray joined her relatives who had been sitting in the verandah waiting for her to give them her personal account of the events of the morning which were just breaking news. A group of Islamic extremists had claimed the disturbance. Apparently, there had been numerous casualties, all coloured men, some of whom had been accidentally injured in the crossfire with the local Militia following their appearance on the scene. The other victims looked as though they had been individually targeted in a fanatical purge of Muslim renegades, a kind of holy genocide, some being chased over long distances before being executed. By all accounts, the greengrocer had been lucky to escape with his life.

What puzzled Sinclair was the indifference with which Miss Murray had reacted to the shooting; either she was capable of great self-control, which seemed to contradict what her mother said about her free and easy manner with the local men, or she expected a different turn of events—but what exactly?—and was taken aback by surprise and as a result had no alternative but to keep her counsel. She certainly struck one as being a cool customer. Sinclair accepted the notion that a question mark would remain in his mind until such time as he had questioned the Professor and heard what the latter had to say about the scrape in which his family had been involved through misadventure,—or did something else just as sinister other than ill-luck lie behind it all?

Sebastian could tell that Sinclair had something on his mind, but he felt reluctant to ask him what it was. The events in the market-place had been so extraordinary (not that he personally did not expect trouble, having been warned by Sinclair that tailing a client was an occupational hazard which lay the sleuth open to all sorts of dangers), that puzzlement, even in such sharp a mind, seemed inevitable. Achieving a moderately discreet cough, in order not to detract to the great maestro's attention from a constructive train of thought, Sebastian asked whether he ought to bring in the professor for questioning ; the man was still closeted in his study.

'About what, Sebastian, for God's sake? I am completely at sea.'

'Oh! I am sorry to hear it. Is there any way in which I can help?'

'No! I fear I have lost touch with my rational self.'

The very fact that Sinclair had called him by his Christian name, something which he had not done for a very long time, longer in fact than Sebastian cared to remember, encouraged him to press on.

'Could you tell me more?'

'Judge for yourself. This morning, in the market-place, when the first shot rang out and I dashed across the way because I had noticed a movement behind a curtain, guess whom I expected to find, concealed behind it?'

'A black militant?'

Sinclair gave a hideous laugh.

'Professor Murray!'

'You don't mean it?'

'Oh, but I do!'

'But why?'

'I don't know; that's the problem. If I knew, I wouldn't find myself in this quandary, would I?'

'No, and that's a fact.'

'And the terrible thing is, even now I know his presence in the market at the time of the outrage was perfectly legitimate and chivalrous—he was there to give his wife the moral support she had appealed for in a difficult family matter—even so, I am haunted by that vision which is contradicted by a material fact :—we both saw him with our own eyes coming from the opposite direction, from the car park. I am losing my grip.'

Sebastian pondered for a while.

'I know you won't like what I am about to say . . .'

'What now? What crime have I committed, unwittingly, of course, while the balance of my mind was affected?'

Sebastian could see that Sinclair was upset.

'To be honest, I think the trouble comes from that inverted basic principle you chose as a premiss about them all being guilty until proved innocent. That, I feel, can only lead to confusion, unfairness and abuse.'

'Oh, you do, do you?'

'Yes, I'm afraid so. So, the solution is simple,—revert to the correct guide-line, and sanity will be restored.'

Sinclair smiled.

'Out of the mouths of babes! Famous last words! Do you remember that phoney friar we met outside Cadiz, Father Ignatius? He used those very words about something or other you said. He saw your potential as an under-developed guru.'

'I don't think that is a particularly flattering comment, Sinclair; but I won't hold it against you. You're not your usual self.'

'No; I still think that the professor is guilty. He is hiding! He is hiding behind a curtain, but what kind of a curtain, a metaphoric one? He is concealing something, I know it, but what? And, if he is hiding and concealing, why the bodyguard which would draw attention to himself? None of it makes sense, and I am at my wits' end to figure it out.'

It was obvious that Sinclair's negative mood was nowhere near abating. All those great detectives were afflicted at times by the same temperamental defect. Sherlock Holmes had been the first to admit that he often fell a prey to it, but only because he had the good fortune of having a medical man in a supporting role who could legally prescribe cocaine or morphine on demand, as the case might be. Perhaps Sinclair had been short-sighted in not turning to the same profession for a suitable assistant, but that did not constitute an excuse for Sebastian not to try and rise to the occasion whenever compassion demanded the milk of human kindness as a soothing potion.

'Lets say, for argument's sake, if it can help you in any way to feel better about yourself, that we're all guilty of something or other at some particular time; nobody's perfect all the time. Why don't you confront the professor and have it out with him?'

'What now, this minute, in his study?'

'Why not? You didn't spare his wife earlier on, did you? And she was innocent, caught between the devil and the deep blue sea, poor lady. Come to think of it, I don't think the professor is behaving in a very sporting way towards his wife at the moment.'

'No, you're right. He ought to be comforting her instead of being closeted in his study poring over bloody archaeological records.'

Sinclair leapt to his feet and having knocked on the professor's door burst into the study, intent on putting an end to a humiliating deadlock. The professor had fallen asleep over a heap of papers, and Sinclair lost no time in dispatching Sebastian to the kitchen to make coffee, while he walked round the room, checking if the bugging devices were still in place, but they had gone. Unable to contain his frustration, Sinclair took hold of the professor by the shoulders and shook him until he opened his eyes.

'Wake up, professor! We've brought you a cup of coffee. Drink it, now, this minute!'

At the tone of Sinclair's voice, Sebastian cringed; he did not like what he was hearing nor what he was seeing. Maybe, the professor was the victim of blackmail, and Sinclair was treating him like a devious master criminal; but there was no stopping him now; he was intent on having his pound of flesh.

'Professor, I'll not beat about the bush; I'll come straight to the point. Did you intend to take a pot shot at the barrow-boy yourself in the market to put an end to your wife's unhappiness? She had confessed to you that very morning before leaving the house that she could no longer put up with the indelicate way in which he and your daughter carried on openly.'

'I would call the occurrence a coincidence.'

'Would you, now? A shooting incident that had been masterminded, by one of the most ruthlessly ingenious organizations in the world, involving a secret task force of sharpshooters hell-bent on carrying out orders from above? I am afraid I personally find it impossible to call that a coincidence.'

'It does happen. It was my misfortune. I had never ever gone to market with my wife before; that's a woman's job. I don't know that I ought not to ask for an apology from you people . . .'

Sinclair felt like putting his hands round the professor's throat. 'Oh, so now, we have misogynic feelings as well, have we, on top of puritanical ones with possibly a racist twist for good measure! You know, professor, I am beginning to understand why you get on well with Charlie Davenport. Charlie has a very clear idea of what a woman's job should be,—to get on with the chores and keep quiet, no matter what. Only your wife didn't keep quiet; she eventually broke down under the strain of all the missionary zeal in favour of the natives that you inherited half-heartedly from your father with which you conditioned your daughter and which has been backfiring on you for a number of years, to your embarrassment. Not that anybody gives a damn in this day and age about who has sex with whom, and where, and how, so long as they do have it in order to feel good about themselves. It's just a matter of perspective. In the old days, people liked to feel good about their souls.'

'" It must needs be that offences come, but woe to that man by whom the offence cometh!" Matthew, chapter 18 verse 7. It was bound to happen sooner or later.'

'Enough of this rhetoric. We're leaving. As a matter of policy, we don't get involved in other people's religio-political quarrels. Have our wages ready in half-an-hour, cash. Barnard?'

'Yes, sir?'

'Be so kind as to inform our hostess that we shall not be in for dinner to-night and pack your bags.'

'Right away, Sir!'

Sebastian felt a weight lifting off his shoulders. Since the affray in the market-place, he had felt very unhappy about the way things had turned out. Sinclair was not getting anywhere with the case and his frustration was beginning to tell on their relationship, which was fast becoming strained, causing Sebastian to fear for its future. What would he do, stranded in Africa, without Sinclair' s broad shoulders to lean on? The chances of his meeting up with some errant drag queens, wondering about in the African bush with all their gear, whom he could join in whatever capacity was remote. Perhaps, on the next job—if there was to be a next one—he would be well advised to travel with the Geisha outfit, in case of need. Having delivered the ominous message to Mrs. Murray, Sebastian went straight to the bedroom to pack his bags. Sinclair was already there, sorting out their travelling documents. He looked worn out. Words of comfort were in the order of the day, but Sebastian did not know where to begin applying the salve, whether to Sinclair's self-respect as a professional detective, or to the private person who had become a friend, without breaching the trust between them and creating an awkwardness. In the end, he plucked up courage and tentatively broached the subject.

'Would it be at all possible that, at a certain point, you suspected Professor Murray of being a voyeur? He would have been hiding behind that curtain in the alleyway opposite the greengrocer's stall, as you said he was, watching his daughter behaving in a suggestive way with the coloured vendor? Would that be anything that you might envisage, I mean, in the style of the great Sherlock?'

'Meaning?'

'It would not be incompatible with the powers of the imagination required by a good detective to sound hearts and minds in order to assess them fairly; it takes all sorts to make a world, if you see what I mean.'

'It is kind of you to suggest it, Barnard, to save my face; but I don't think so. The man's too much of an activist himself. You heard what he said quoting Matthew's gospel :—'Woe to the man by whom the offence cometh!' He meant business, impending business, retribution in the offing, and, as we know, it came, swift as hellfire from heaven.'

'So, you don't reckon the professor is guilty of voyeurism?'

'No; he's not.'

'What is he guilty of, in your opinion, apart from being a prig?'

'A sado-masochist, perhaps . . . Oh, I don't know, but I intend to find out.'

'But you've thrown up the sponge!'

'No, I haven't. We're not really leaving. That's just a stratagem.'

Sebastian did not know whether to rejoice over Sinclair's decision or to deplore it.

'This is what we do. We take the money and go under cover somewhere where we can safely keep the professor under surveillance. This is not really being dishonest; we are still discharging the duties we were hired for. I don't think the professor will be foolish enough to complain to Charlie about us giving up on him; it might start rumours circulating among expats about him being a temperamental employer; he won't want to tarnish the image, not now when he claims he is on the brink of a ground-breaking discovery and might need more sponsorship.'

Sebastian felt like clapping enthusiastically; Sinclair had regained his self-composure, his zest for the truth, his wonderful acumen and his swiftness of execution, all without having recourse to drugs. He had seen his course clearly. Great things were afoot!

In the pandemonium that followed the terrorist attack in the marketplace, a favourite haunt with tourists, nobody would notice that they had gone from professor Murray's house, and Mrs. Murray was unlikely to talk about it in case it reflected on their reputation. She was a woman who attached a great deal of importance to outward signs of respectability. The Police were busy appealing to eyewitnesses to come forward and help them in their enquiries. In view of the urgency of the matter, Sinclair and Sebastian would volunteer forfeiting all private commitments in order to assist them. They would hire a camping car which would present the dual advantage of mobility and anonymity as tourists . . . Again, Sebastian felt like giving way to jubilation, dancing like a child and bursting into a song of praise in celebration of the detective who so daringly and without false modesty dared follow in Holmes' footsteps; but he thought better of it in case he embarrassed the man.

Their first port of call after leaving the house was the agglomerate of sheds, workshops and garages where the mechanic operated. He must have been warned of their coming because he stood on the look-out on the threshold of one of them, wiping his hands on an old rag full of oil stains.

'Giving up on the old Susuki?' he asked with a grin on his face.

'That's right, mate', replied Sinclair, who knew how to deal with all manners of people, 'tell me, how much would you charge for the rental of that old Ford Mondeo next door?'

'Well, that would depend on what you wanted it for; I'm working on it at the moment. She's mine. I got her at auction.'

'Not long; but don't worry; we won't trash it seeing it's yours.'

'Smooth talker, aren't you? All right, then, fifty pounds a day in American dollars on condition you keep quiet about it.'

'Deal', said Sinclair pulling out the notes from his breast pocket. 'I'll sit at the wheel and you help my colleague to push her gently down the drive.'

It was not long before the vision of the mechanic standing in the middle of the drive still holding that oily rag vanished from the rear mirror, and Sinclair and Sebastian found themselves cruising into town. Road blocks had been erected way back into scrub land and when Sebastian caught sight of the first one, he asked Sinclair to stop, claiming he was feeling sick and was about to throw up.

Sinclair jammed on the brakes.

'What is the matter now? Pull yourself together; cant you?'

'I don't know; I think the whole thing has been too much for me. I can't take any more.'

'Nonsense! The minute we hit the town and the action begins, you'll feel your old self again and be game for anything. I grant you, it's been a bit of a roller-coaster up to now, but we're free now; we're our own masters. You'll be fine. You don't want to turn into an old archaeologist before your time, do you? digging fragments of pots and pans and sticking labels on them; or doing workmen's clubs in the north of England as a drag queen in your Geisha outfit?'

'I don't think that's a very sympathetic remark to make in the circumstances . . .'

'You don't need sympathy, Barnard. What you need is a kick in the pants. You're full of self-pity.'

Sebastian kept silent as Sinclair took his foot off the break and the old car resumed its course in the direction of the first road block.

'Now, I don't profess to have the ability to alter the course of events, but the reality is that at the moment your sitting beside me looking like death warmed up is not likely to put chance on our side. So, please, make an effort; pull yourself together; the future of our enquiry, our raison d'être, depends on it. Why would those chaps in the Militia want help from a private eye with a sidekick that looks like a ghost? Look at them, armed to the eyeballs by illegal arms traders! Encounters with reality are generally brutal and preferably to be avoided unless manipulated in advance to serve one's own ends, Sinclair sayeth so. I hope I make myself clear.'

'Yes', whispered Sebastian, 'quite clear, You do the talking while I try and memorize the maxim.'

Sinclair's story sounded like such a sumptuous treat in the ears of the militia that the sergeant in charge of the check-point fell for it and fetched the captain, who loved it, and telephoned headquarters in Masindi for permission to issue a pass, which was granted immediately on condition that the two detectives report to the proper authorities as soon as they got into town. Sebastian attempted a sketchy smile as he was handed the pass for safe keeping. All he hoped for was a bed in a decent hotel away from it all.

Although Sinclair did not feel too good himself, he managed to sit up late into the night, evolving a strategy which would ensure that he and Sebastian navigated safely between the devil—the local body in charge of arresting fanatics who had had a hand in the recent outbreak of violence—and the deep blue sea, the area where professor Murray claimed that he had discovered a 'lost' world.

If and when the professor did appear on what could hypothetically be called 'the crime scene', he and Sebastian would have to slink away from the official party in order to go in pursuit of their own suspect before he disappeared down some secret passage-way to enter the site which had of late taken up all his time, confirming his most advanced anthropological theories. So bold were those allegedly that they warranted the hire of a bodyguard to protect the man who had conceived them, leading Sinclair to suspect that if revealed they would be likely to create an uproar in academic circles as well as in the professor's entourage.

Sinclair's secret fear was that should the Militia vacate the crime scene before the professor put in an appearance, he and Sebastian would no longer be in a position to justify their own presence there; but, as luck would have it, they caught sight of him early one morning coming across the area, waving to the investigators, and they immediately took up the trail to track him down. The man seemed relaxed; he was taking great strides as though he were out for a constitutional with the confidence acquired through custom. At a certain point, he left the path which he had been following in a straight line to enter an area of scrub land which rose into a hillock, and there mysteriously he disappeared from sight as though he had fallen into a disused tiger trap. Both men darted forward. Could the professor have climbed up the hill-side in such a short time? They had not seen him negotiating the rise; there was no short cut by-passing the hill; the way ahead just fizzled out.

Suddenly, Sebastian cried out :

'Look, Sinclair, down there! I can see a neon sign flashing in the dark.'

'My God!', exclaimed Sinclair as he drew closer to investigate, 'It's an underground station!'

'What? Like Piccadilly Circus or Leicester Square?'

'Yes.'

'Any idea where we are?'

'None; we could be anywhere. Quick, there's a tube coming! We can't let our man get away.'

'Where? I can't hear anything.'

'You're not likely to.'

The absence of any sound as the tube approached was awesome; it was only when it came down to rest on the electro-magnetic track at the station stop that a faint whirr was heard as its metallic wings, which had been retracted during its passage through the underground, opened up to take on more passengers, as a giant bee gathering pollen.

'Welcome on the Equatorial Express, Barnard', said Sinclair with a grin on his face, as he watched mesmerized an army of exotic-looking hostesses help people get on board. Their long, sun-tanned, well muscled legs were displayed to advantage by the very short, tightly-belted tunics they wore as a uniform made out of multi-coloured floral ethnic cloth. At the sight of them, Sinclair felt sweat beading his temple and he hoped to goodness that he would not come into close contact with any of them accidentally before the journey ended.

'Where the hell is the professor, Barnard?' asked Sinclair, sobering up as the train began elevating itself above the track. 'We can't afford to lose our quarry, not now'

'There he is up there, smiling at us. Please, don't look.'

'Oh, I know what you're thinking, that I am likely to go off the deep end, to lose my rag as they say, and create an affray in front of all those charming people. But that would not be in keeping with my office as a bodyguard; men like us move discreetly; they know how to behave. Ever heard the expression 'the soul of discretion'? I think that describes us and our profession very well.'

Sebastian gave a polite cough. It seemed the events of the last few days were taking their toll. The great Sherlock would have reached for something potent or asked Watson to minister unto him, but Sebastian felt helpless as Sinclair rambled on.

'We still have to do what we came to do, Barnard; the profession demands it. Let us not forget it, no matter what life throws in our way to distract us from our course.'

To Sebastian's relief, Professor Murray was waiting for them at the terminus. He looked just as relaxed as when they had first set eyes on him earlier on that morning.

'Welcome to the City With No Name'. he announced, 'I always knew that sooner or later you two would manage to follow me down here. I very much doubt Charlie would have recommended you had you been useless at your job; Charlie is a connoisseur.'

'Excuse me interrupting your panegyric, professor; but why 'the city with no name'?

'Ah, well! A name would have invited comparisons with other great cities like Las Vegas, or Hollywood, or Dubai. This city is incomparable.'

'So, what exactly are you up to down here apart from verifying anthropological theories which will one day be invalidated by more sensational ones?'

'No, no; mine is the ultimate vision, the highest attainment beyond which the human psyche cannot aspire because there is nothing left for it to desire; it will have embraced it all in abundance, beyond its wildest dreams. There is nothing we cannot offer here to those who seek to enhance their ego under the guidance of masters and reach the ultimate beatific vision of themselves. We shall partake of a little light luncheon and then it will be my pleasure to take you on a conducted tour of the City Without a Name. knowing I have nothing to fear with you two acting as my bodyguard, which is more than a lot of people in antiquity could claim when they descended into the underground.'

'Why, this is outrageous! You're reversing the roles! We're not here to protect you. You're here to protect us against whatever or whoever lies down there, and I have a feeling it could be quite obnoxious.'

Once again Sebastian thought fit to intervene in favour of the boss's reputation.

'Sinclair's a classical scholar; he knows a lot about Greek mythology.'

'Ah', replied professor Murray, 'there is nothing mythological about the City Without a Name or its inhabitants. What we are dealing with is the ultimate reality to abolish all myths.'

At the entrance to the town, in a glass cage, an elderly man sat in front of a computer screen endless scrolling through images while watching the world go past in the High Street. He had straw-coloured hair, the shade of which was too vivid to be natural and only served to emphasize the flamboyance of the burgundy velvet jacket which he sported, probably a relic from the days when well-to-do gentlemen wore smoking jackets at home, after dinner.

'What is he looking at?', asked Sinclair, impressed by the way the old man concentrated on the screen in spite of the flux of people passing by.

'All the Art in the world', said Murray.

'What do you mean "all the art in the world"? Do you mean all the famous art in the world like the Gioconda?'

'And the rest.'

'Which is?'

'Whatever is produced in the City Without a Name.'

'Good or bad?', asked Sinclair.

'Yes, so long as it sells. That's about it.'

'But why?'

'Why not, if that's what the public wants.'

'Are commercial sales the only criteria then? Surely, it is the art dealer's role to educate the public, to create a taste for the genuine article and nurture it.'

'Not in this city. It is what catches the eye, what pleases it, good or bad, at a moment in time, that matters here.'

A strange feeling came over Sinclair. He felt he had seen the like of the old man before, but he could not remember where, and then the notion came to him:—the old man in the glass cage reminded him of a character in *Alice in Wonderland* though in actual fact there was no resemblance whatsoever between the two, and that character was the walrus, but not just the walrus as himself idiosyncratically, but a kind of composite figure made up of the walrus and the mock turtle, and Sinclair could not tell whether the effect created by the man's isolation inside the glass cage, which suggested that of a deep sea denizen, had fetched the metaphor with its marine environment, or something else on which he could not put his finger, until the analogy vanished, leaving behind an immense sense of pity for the old man in his alienation from the main stream of Art. The figure which he cut (almost a caricature of himself) was a pathetic one. As an art dealer, he was redundant. Like the mock turtle, who once upon a time had been a real turtle; he could exert no more influence. All art looked the same to him, good or bad, and he spent his time flicking through thousands of pictures, unable to discriminate between them.

Sinclair felt like tapping on the glass cage and reaching for the man, but professor Murray kept waving him on and he had to hurry away . . .

The professor was walking very fast and both Sinclair and Sebastian had trouble keeping up with him. The streets were narrow and they felt dwarfed by the colossal buildings that towered above them as well as afflicted by a sense of claustrophobia, which was enhanced by the very hot and stifling atmosphere dispensed at street level by buildings the tallness of which rarefied the air. At one point, the professor vanished into a dark alley where a neon sign advertized a basement luncheon place, and they both managed just in time to squeeze after him into a lift which was packed with people on their way to lunch. The descent seemed to last an awfully long time When the lift finally touched down, the clank of the heavy iron gates opening out to let people out coincided with another fast-approaching, chain-like, sound, like the clatter of wheels.

'Quick, jump in', shouted the professor, as he somersaulted into a small wagon which slowed down in front of him just long enough to enable all three to hop on, before moving away at breakneck speed down a line where hatches opened and shut in quick succession dispensing the various items on the menu of the day with clockwork precision.

'Did I hear you say something?', asked Sinclair as he and Sebastian obeyed the professor's command.

'Yes', replied Sebastian, "Like bats out of hell".

'Apt simile, Barnard. There's no turning back now.'

'No, we're in for it, good and proper.'

Before they could say "Jack Robinson", they had been deposited with their food at a table which carried the ominous number 13, and were looking round at their surroundings which at first sight did not look unfamiliar. Echoing across the marble-pillared hall, above the patrons' chatter, the sound of the shutters of the food dispensing windows could be heard slamming down one after the other with a finality which was chilling.

'Eat', said the professor, 'this is the best joint in town where all the food is produced by the ablest dieticians there are, world experts in inner cleanliness some of them.'

'Actually', Sinclair replied, 'speaking for myself, I am not very hungry, but a drink of water would be appreciated. It is very hot in here. What about you, Barnard?'

'That would be very nice, thank you, sir.'

'Water!' exclaimed the professor, 'Why, we have the purest water there is; the whole city rests on water which is stored underground in massive tanks and wells up everywhere as fountain heads for people to bathe in. Mr. M is very keen on ablutions, especially for new entrants.'

'Mr. M?', queried Sinclair.

'Yes, M for Maestro or Grand Master of Ceremony. He's the heart and soul behind the city; the instigator of all its initiatives, a real professional. He is the one to whom the city owes its relentless tempo, its dynamism.'

Shall we get to meet Mr. M during our tour of the city?'.asked Sinclair.

'Of course! Mr. M is the city.'

'What about my drink?', asked Sebastian who was getting more and more dehydrated by the minute and feared that Mr. M's fiery presence might make the condition worse.

'Be my guest', replied the professor. 'Have your fill at this fountain, or the next ; they all dispense water for the renewal of life. And follow me.'

It was not long before they found themselves in the High Street again, walking past endless rows of fashion shops. The professor kept peering inside all of them till at long last he found what he was looking for.

'Ah, there he is! I knew I would find him here sooner or later, at work on one of his protégées; the man's indefatigable in the pursuit of the sublimation of the female ego.'

.A tall man with a pointed chin and a dark head of hair shaven close to the skull which emphasized the pointedness of the chin was walking arm in arm between rows of fashion clothes with a somewhat plain, middle-aged woman with mousy hair. The lady had obviously lost a lot of weight; her features looked drawn as a result of the deprivation she had endured, and her clothes hung loosely about her, and Mr M's was on a mission to get her into the type of glamorous, tight-fitting clothes that would display her new figure to the best advantage, transforming her from a rather drab looking housewife into a fashion icon.

'It's not all blood and sweat here, Darling', Mr M was saying as he steered her round and round the shop floor of the High Street store which he had selected as being the most appropriate for her new look, commenting on every item of clothing which he deemed suitable for her with the expert eye of a connoisseur.

'It's not all drudgery. I have got a wonderful surprise in store for you', he was saying while hugging her. 'We do like to bestow on our charges a little something special from time to time to reward them for their dedication in the pursuit of the beloved image, especially when they are as dedicated as you are, Darling. Where there is a will, there is a way, and don't forget I am here to support that frail, ailing will from flagging till the beloved image has been achieved to your satisfaction and mine.'

'Shall we go and see what the great Maestro has in store for his protégée? asked the professor.

All three walked down a long passage by the side of the fashion store at the end of which there was a small door that gave access to a shooting studio which was in actual fact a hangar where the prototype of a passenger space craft was on display, its sleek silver exterior highlighted by crimson stripes artistically displayed by a shroud which had been draped round it to great effect. Soon the woman whom Mr. M had been mentoring came in wearing a bathrobe to conceal her nudity. Gingerly at first, casting nervous glances at the film crew, then more confidently as their comments egged her on, she began climbing up the scaffolding and disrobing herself as she went along till she stood almost stark naked against the cockpit in an explosion of flash photography celebrating her pristine nakedness which had all the allure and dash of the Victory of Samothrace in the Louvre.

The parallels were not lost on Sinclair, specious as they were. The Greeks held Technique in contempt; only representational Art could celebrate truth as far as they were concerned. All he could do to give the scene some kind of contemporary tenor was to exclaim :

'Per ardua ad astra! The motto of the Royal Air Force!', but that sounded like a cheap metaphor, almost a slur.

The woman had succeeded in projecting into the outside world a picture of herself that she cherished in an inner sanctum, aided and abetted by Mr. M. and her example would inspire others to do the same . . .

Speaking for himself, Sebastian was not particularly impressed by the on-going process. What puzzled him was Mr. M's absence from the apotheosis; after all, he was the inspiration behind it.

'Is Mr. M. not coming to ratify this?', he asked, turning towards professor Murray?

'Oh, no. As a Supremo, he does not have to endure the trip of another ego. He is not a role model; he is in a class of his own as a trend setter and an inspiration.'

A shiver went down Sebastian's spine; he felt exposed to the invisible presence of the great artificer and edged closer to Sinclair for protection. What if Mr. M. sensing his vulnerability suddenly took an interest in him? That would be the end of his partnership with Sinclair as a leader, all to be left high and dry at the end of it?

'Well', said Sinclair, 'I imagine there is a lot more to Mr. M. than meets the eye . . .'

'Oh, definitely, 'replied the professor. 'nobody as yet has fathomed his potential. He is indefatigable. He sits on all the committees in the town, advising, suggesting, instigating; his dynamic zest for new enterprises is unbelievable and he has the knack of communicating it to others. Though his presence on the panels of literary circles may surprise some people at first sight, in particular those which deal with creative writing, when one takes the trouble of listening attentively to what he has to say, one is struck by the relevancy of his insights into the writer's mind.'

'In other words, he has a finger in every pie, whether pork or custard', Sebastian concluded in a loud voice, earning a filthy look from Stewart who had been listening to the professor's panegyric with an open mind, though he did think that there was a degree of exaggeration in it created by fear of the man,—if Mr. M. could be called that without reservation. Sinclair had noticed a certain fullness about his hips, on one occasion when he had been seated, which suggested the morphology of a woman rather than that of a man, but maybe that was due to his having to sit down often to cogitate. That Mr. M. had a lot to think about no one could deny. The hedonistic age in which he lived, aided and abetted by scientific technology, offered him opportunities such as had never been available to him before. A person like Professor Murray, for instance, was just a puppet for him to manipulate at will; the man had no power of resistance to contrary impulses, having paved his own way to hell with good intentions . . .

To all intents and purposes, the photographic session had been a success, probably beyond the wildest dreams of Mr. M.'s candidate.

'Do you never encounter failures?', asked Sinclair, inquisitive as ever.

'Occasionally, yes, we do', replied the professor.

'And what becomes of the poor wretches?'

'They get relegated to the Club of Mediocrity,—Mr. M. calls it :¬ the Kingdom of the Dead. Would you like me to show you how the process of relegation is carried out, officially, of course?'

'Why not?', asked Sinclair jovially, 'we might as well while we're here.'

The professor led the way to a spacious hall, which was more like a reading-room in a museum, where examiners sat at trestle tables interviewing those whose applications to the Club of Mediocrity had to be checked.

'Please, don't misunderstand the spirit of the process', said professor Murray. 'Many have been called to the City Without a Name, but few have been elected as suitable Citizens. Mr. M.'s standards are very high.'

'What you say confirms the evidence before our eyes; there are an awful lot of failures filing past those tables out of the Hall. How do you constitute their private dossiers?'

'Well, it's quite simple, really. It depends on how quickly such people become ignored, you know, dropped by other citizens into isolation. There comes a time when they stick out like sore thumbs, sitting idly on park benches without company. Usually, a single call on a mobile phone suffices to locate them and fish them out for questioning. They're only too eager to respond and talk about themselves.'

'The ultimate citizen's spy ring, Heh?', asked Sinclair.

'You can call it that, if you like. We prefer to call it responsible citizenship. There are studies going on at the moment to determine why such people are not suitable material and need to be weeded out. But entry to the Club of Mediocrity is not all that easy, you know. Some of the questions regarding worthiness are quite tricky to answer.'

'So, some of those people are quite articulate?'

'Oh, yes; they're just misguided about their aims, that's all. The trouble is Mr. M. is the king of the living, not of the dead.'

'What happens to those poor wretches once they qualify for entry into the Club of Mediocrity, or should I say relegation to the kingdom of the dead?'

'We don't know for sure.'

For some time, Sinclair had been conscious of Sebastian nudging his elbow. It was an irritating habit the boy had of calling attention to himself in moments of stress.

'What is it, Barnard?'

'You see that man down there in the Hall of Judgment?'

'Yes. Well, what about him?'

'From time to time, he waves a piece of paper above his head, as if to call attention to it. Should I go down and find out what it's all about?'

'Yes, do; but make it snappy.'

The thought of having a mission gave Sebastian wings. He negotiated row after row of trestle tables with the agility of a gazelle and was soon back holding the precious piece of paper in his clenched fist while professor Murray looked on with a quizzical smile on his face.

'Well, what does it say?', he asked passing it on to Sinclair.

Reading, Sinclair replied : "The M in Mr. M. stands for Mephisto."

'Well, I'm damned! Who would ever have suspected such a thing?'

'Did it never occur to you', said the professor, 'that the 'M might stand for Murray?'

'Not in a million years, Professor. You lack a certain inborn subtlety; you've worked for too long in close contact with so-called 'primitive' people with simple minds who confuse the material with the immaterial, and the physical with the spiritual. Mr. Mephisto is a widely-travelled man.'

The sight of those queues of outcasts winding their way out of the hall at a slow. weary pace was unimaginable in such a vibrant city as the City Without a Name, and the pathos of it went straight to Sinclair's heart, but, seeing that his assistant was similarly affected, he quickly counteracted the melancholy and pity of it by bringing up a witty and less poignant similitude.

'Does it not remind you of something?', he asked Sebastian. 'You know, the tail of the mouse in *Alice in Wonderland*?'

'About it getting thinner and thinner as it goes on?'

'Yes! By the time these people reach the exit at the other end of the Hall their tale of woe as recorded in the dossiers will be very slender and carry no weight at all.'

'You mean, the body of evidence against them will be non-existent?'

'Precisely; but justice will have been seen to be done.'

By and by, the sound of chatter which had been mixed with that of footsteps died out as people shuffled out of the Hall to disappear out of the City Without a Name for good. Perhaps they were the lucky ones, escaping with their dreams intact . . . Sensing that the visit was drawing to a close, and it was time for him to attempt a parting shot to get Murray to open up about his latest archaeological discovery, Sinclair said :

'As I see it, Mr. Mephisto is conducting a salvationist mission like your father. The question is, Why do you support it? Come on, professor; be honest. What are your motives?'

Sebastian could tell from the urgency in his voice that Sinclair liked nothing better than to extract a confession from a suspect; when it came to the depravities of the human psyche, his curiosity was insatiable.

'Oh, I don't know. It seemed the thing to do at a time when the old morality that held society together brought its boundaries right up to the last frontier of acceptance. It appeared consistent with some of the theories I was putting forward concerning the survival of the ancestral mentality of African tribal leaders in this modern age . . .'

'An expedient to justify your own personal views? Oh, how could you, professor?'

'One was sick to death of the slipshod philanthropy of the times, the compromission in the name of Christianity when Jesus himself as a teacher of religious morality had been intransigent, lashing out at offenders right, left and centre, sparing no one, his tongue as sharp as a sword. The morality that my father taught the natives in his mission house on the Congo river was strictly evangelical.'

'And you brought up your daughter in the same spirit, but when she grew up she got mixed-up over some of the more practical issues of contemporary living in Africa, much to your and your wife's embarrassment?'

'She is not very bright', whispered the professor.

'So, you took revenge on the whole world, extolling your very own, newly-discovered 'city of sin' as a 'lost world' in order to condemn them into conforming with its ultimate hedonism?'

'As an anthropologist brought up in the Christian faith, I knew it wouldn't last; it couldn't last. Such successful societies never outlive their material success; sooner or later they succumb to it. Luke makes this quite clear in his gospel : 'And as it was in the days of Noe, so shall it be also in the days of the Son of man. They did eat, they drank, they married wives, they were given in marriage, until the day that Noe entered into the ark, and the flood came, and destroyed them all. Likewise also as it was in the days of Lot; they did eat, they drank, they bought, they sold, they planted, they builded; But the same day that Lot went out of Sodom it rained fire and brimstone from heaven, and destroyed them all.' Food for thought, don't you think, detective, in this day and age of global warming and environmental pollution?'

'So you didn't have to do anything? Your responsibility was not engaged? Given time, the fruit ripens on the tree and then falls to the ground where it rots,—from an excess of sucrose?'

'Yes; don't you see? It was all done for me, by the powers that be; you know, those dark market forces we intellectuals whisper about among ourselves during secret meetings in out-of-the-way places unable to identify them with any precision.'

'So, we're all manipulated indirectly by demons made to our own likeness? That includes your daughter as a sacrificial victim, does it? You never imagined she could practise with such abandon what you preached, I mean about mixing with native children and having no racial prejudice?'

'No, I thought there would be some natural sexual reticence in her, a kind of tasteful modesty when she grew up . . .'

'But she transcended all that, didn't she? Didn't she? She disappointed you.'

Sebastian erupted :

'That's enough, Sir! You're overstepping the mark! Your indignation is unwarranted; it does you no credit. Book him and have done with it.'

Sinclair felt like exploding.

'You mind your own business. Who are you to talk?'

'Ah!' exclaimed the professor, quick on the mark 'Another young offender?'

Sinclair shrugged his shoulders.

'I haven't finished with you, professor. Now, we all know what keeps Las Vegas going as a 'city of sin' in the middle of the Nevada desert—sex and gambling, two sound investments. What exactly keeps the 'City

Without a name' prosperous in Central Africa amid the religio-political turmoil of the time which the media keep us informed about?'

The professor remained silent.

'Come on, professor! It's not the arms trade, is it, though I suppose that comes into it. If you needed a bodyguard, your life was in some sort of danger; that much we could gather without taxing our brains too much. The question was, Who were the powers who threatened you, and why was Charlie Davenport involved? Charlie being the indiscriminate reveller that he is . . .'

'Ah, yes, Charlie! His bouts of debauchery are no secret. His wife is an angel of mercy.'

'Quite so. As a libertine, Charlie must have had a vested interest in your remaining alive other than as a consular officer whose duty it is to protect Her Majesty's subjects abroad. Could it have been one of these, by any chance?'

Sinclair had pulled a large diamond out of a velvet pouch which had been concealed in his breast pocket.

'Charlie needed one of those from time to time. didn't he? to appease and keep the wife he revered when he came back from his drunken orgies; he knew who supplied them to you and why, putting your life in jeopardy.'

'Who gave it to you?', cried the professor.

'Oh, don't worry; it wasn't Charlie, you haven't been betrayed. I found it in one of the incinerators at the back of your house when I was searching for clues. You see, I happen to read the local press; you'd be surprised to hear how useful it is; one picks up all sorts of useful snippets of information. The other day, Eleanor Davenport, Charlie's beautiful and adored wife, was the guest of honour at a charity fund raiser organised by the United Nations in aid of the victims of violence among rival gangs of diamond miners in the Congo, most of whom are in the pay of Al Quaida. Round her neck she wore a sizeable diamond. It was a fake; the real diamond was in a safety deposit box in the vaults of a bank in Kampala. It wouldn't have been safe for her to wear it. Charlie told me so himself when I queried it, out of curiosity.'

'You! You, traitor!' shouted the professor, 'I took you and your assistant into the privacy of my house, introduced you to my closest relatives. You lived among us as one of the family, and all the while I thought you were my minder, protecting me, you were raking up cinders at the back of our house to expose me!'

'You took a chance on it, Professor. You played a dangerous game in extremely dangerous times. You know what they say :—if you can't beat them, join them, and that is what you did. Your daughter was a linch-pin in your decision; you knew you could not stop her shaming you having a string of affairs with members of the black community. I'll come straight to the point. You are in the pay of Al Quaida who are investing a lot of diamond money in Africa into their crusades against Westerners as well as their renegade blood brothers. You had the right contacts in the Congo where you grew up as the son of a missionary who was undermining the power of local tribal chiefs by withdrawing their subjects from their savage authority. As seditious leaders, many of your connections were only too pleased to invest diamond money into the City Without a Name in order to keep it going as a den of iniquity, fomenting political tension between races as well as dissension between fundamentalists and the less radical members of the muslim community. My suspicions were first aroused the day of the terrorist attack on the market-place when I thought I espied you hiding behind a curtain opposite the allocated space where one of your daughter's coloured boyfriends kept a fruit and vegetable stall. Either you knew that the market was one of the places targeted for a terrorist attack and you were concerned for the safety of your wife, who went to market with her daughter on a regular basis, hoping to warn her in time, or from that vantage post across the way you could gloat on the distressing spectacle of your daughter throwing herself away on a local man, extremists would eventually deal with.'

Sebastian wondered what Sinclair would come up with next. The events of the day had taken their toll and he felt exhausted. What was the point of carrying on, rubbing it in so? The professor was guilty,—guilty as hell, and Sinclair was beside himself. Sebastian had never seen him in such an exultant mood. His psychological intuition had been confirmed, demonstrating the soundness of his intimations. Then, suddenly, Sebastian felt reprieve approaching—like the wings of a dove. Sinclair seemed to have run out of steam; he was talking about leaving the professor to his own devices, right there in the City Without a Name. Was that possible? Were they really on the verge of getting out of that infernal metropolis? He heard the professor repeating over and over again 'What? Without an escort? You can't do that! You're on my payroll. You followed me in here as my bodyguards!' That last remark seemed to re-kindle Sinclair's indignation.

'You have got a nerve, professor! As if anybody in their right mind would wish to save you from the wrath to come for filthy lucre! Here, take your diamond. It's blood money. It would be unsound for me to keep it.'

Sebastian could bear it no longer. . . .

'Excuse me, Sir. I am about to throw up. I need to get out into the fresh air.'

Sinclair wheeled around :

'Have I been carrying on?', he asked, sobered up. 'How very inconsiderate of me!'

'That you have, Sir. But who am I to say?'

Sinclair felt a surge of pity for the boy. He took hold of his assistant by the arm and guided him through the funnel-like exit that led out of Professor Murray's 'lost world' into the region where the ancient kingdom of Bunyoro had once prospered as an advanced culture under the iron fist of a king who was so enamoured of his sovereignty over his own subjects that he declared war on the whites whose mission it was to save them from Arab slave traders. Once he reached the open, Sinclair, supporting Sebastian as best he could, made his way towards a Banyan-tree, the branches of which had dropped to the ground and taken roots, thus covering a lot of ground and providing shelter like a pagoda.

The searching parties of the local militia had left. The air was quiet and balmy; the scene serene. The drum beating, the horn blowing and the yells of savages whipping up an appetite for war and white human flesh around Masindi, in the decayed kingdom of Bunyoro, had long ceased to disturb the peace. Seated under that Indian Fig Tree, they might have been back in England, anywhere in the Southern Counties, except here, in a peaceful garden, there would have been a display of cucumbers, melons, pumpkins and cotton seeds . . . Whatever drama Nature would unfold in days to come was no longer any concern of theirs. They were well and truly out of it for good.

FINIS

THE CHILEAN CASE

THE CHILEAN CASE

Sinclair had not been back long when he felt he ought to find out how Sebastian was faring. The adventure which they had just shared had raised doubts in his mind about the boy's ability to sustain spells of exceptional hardships without suffering deleterious effects. Not surprisingly, he found him where he thought he might, in Docklands, giving the usual performance. He looked pinched, a little thinner perhaps, which made him look taller, but apart from that nothing much had changed. The cramped space that served as dressing-room was still built of cardboard boxes, perched precariously on top of one another, the only unusual thing which caught Sinclair's attention being a copy of *Sherlock Holmes, Long Stories* by Conan Doyle which lay in a corner beside *Tintin au Congo*.

'Well, what news? I see you've reverted to your evil ways, impersonating a Geisha and reading about the Belgian boy's adventures in Africa. I suppose it helps going through familiar motions . . .'

'What do you mean?'

'T get back to normal after the trauma of our tout of Professor Murray's lost city. It wasn't exactly a tourist treat, was it?'

'No. I sometimes wonder if it really happened.'

'Oh, it happened all right; don't delude yourself. You may be living in a world of your own here but out there the City Without a Name is just as real as Dubai or Las Vegas. It might help if you were to stop being infatuated with Tintin, the junior reporter. As will be recalled in the Congo story, Tintin causes distress to an elephant. Though he is not responsible for firing the bullet that kills the animal, he is seen walking away from the dead elephant carrying a pair of tusks which graphically suggests the evil ivory trade of poachers.'

'Ah, yes, but the book does mention the illegal diamond trade in the Belgian Congo controlled by a ruthless gang of Chicago mobsters; investigating will be Tintin's next assignment as junior reporter. That shows he was aware of the presence of evil in the modern world and he wanted other young people to know about it.'

'Trouble is, diamonds are forever, Sebastian. They will always be symbolic of eternal love and beauty, two very rare things in the world. Men who are often enslaved by ruthless political regimes endure terrible hardships to mine them in extreme climates.'

Sebastian cast a sidelong glance at Sinclair.

'Incidentally, since you mention reading material, there is a question I would like to ask you. It concerns one of Conan Doyle's long stories about Sherlock Holmes, *The Sign of Four.*'

'Yes, I see you've been reading Doyle. Well, what is it?'

'Did it ever occur to you when we were investigating the case in Masindi that there were similarities between it and *The Sign of Four* where much of the action takes place in India around the Agra treasure, which contained one hundred and forty-three diamonds of the first water, the possession of which cost many people their lives?'

Sinclair gave Sebastian a searching glance,

'Maybe; but I've got the feeling that you are asking me a leading question, or even possibly a couple of leading questions, and I can't say I am too happy about that. There are areas of my life which I wish to keep private, just like Holmes. However, since you were involved in the case I am prepared exceptionally to satisfy your curiosity.'

'Well, in *The Sign of Four*, is it possible that Sherlock Holmes is drawn to Mary Morstan to whom Dr. Watson loses his heart at first sight? She is such an attractive young woman, blonde with large blue eyes, dressed in the most exquisite taste, and in the end, through Holmes's instrumentality she makes an ideal wife for Dr. Watson.'

'Maybe; but remember in the story she is the wronged party, more grievously than any other victim of crime on whose behalf Sherlock has had to take up the cudgels. Now, to Sherlock a client, any client, is 'a mere factor in a problem' which has to be resolved by means of the science of deduction, emotions being, as he says, 'antagonistic to clear reasoning'. Does that answer your question? Sherlock is not put off by Dr. Watson's aspersions on his character regarding his 'inhuman attitude'.

Sebastian remained silent for a while searching for signs of pent-up emotion on Sinclair's face.

'Well, what now?' he asked seeing that Sinclair remained unperturbed.

'I have been advertising my services again in a woman's magazine whose readership is mostly of the genteel type; you know the type of advertisement that claims extreme discretion and understanding nationwide. I thought a sedate job at home would make a welcome change after Uganda . . .'

'Yes, you have been gadding about abroad quite a lot lately.'

'The trouble is, when I get bored with a humdrum life, I am unable to pick up a violin like the great Sherlock, and play a few soothing arpeggios, or reach for an hypodermic syringe filled with a seven-per-cent solution of cocaine under the watchful eye of a benevolent doctor. Neither am I like you willing to perform a drag act for the sake of taking a short-lived, exotic trip a few times a week. How many hours does it take to put on all that Japanese make-up?'

'A few.'

'It hardly seems worth the trouble for such a short trip. Quite honestly, I prefer the sensation of actually moving through great distances on a trans-continental railway. I like the feeling one gets of being able to settle down for days and indulge in an orgy of random cogitation.'

'Well, you'll let me know, won't you, if anything comes from the advertisement?'

Sinclair gave the boy a searching glance.

'You know, I can't understand why you don't join a drama school, become a professional actor instead of an archaeologist? Look at you, kicking your heels in tis awful joint. It's a waste of time. Of course, they won't let you play Ophelia . . . I can't promise you that my next assignment will not again throw you into disreputable company, of the kind you disapprove of . . .'

'Well, so long as they don't belong to the Old School Tie Brigade like Charlie Davenport.'

'You didn't approve of Charlie, did you?'

'I found him insufferable. I'm sure he's a double agent.'

'Why not? It's not a bad way of serving one's country, especially nowadays when the threat is greater, from collective Terrorism. Speaking of spying, Sherlock Holmes was lucky with his 'Baker Street irregulars', a gang of dirty, ragged, little street Arabs, as he called them who for a shilling each would execute undercover missions of great importance to the success of his enquiries . . .'

'Meaning you are not so lucky?'

'Oh, no! I consider myself very lucky; it's just that I worry about you doing that kind of work when you could be learning more congenial skills, conducive to a more congenial future. I can't guarantee . . .'

'Well, we'll have to see, won't we?'

'Yes, that's right. Solvitur ambulando.'

'To be or not to be', whispered Sebastian, swinging round to face the mirror in his dressing-room as son as Sinclair had left. 'Whether 'tis nobler in the mind to suffer the stings and arrows of outrageous fortune . . . 'God knows, they had been outrageous enough out there in Uganda; and, after listening to Sinclair's praise of long-distance travelling one was entitled to have doubts about the wording of his new advertisement:—it was likely to include 'International Coverage' in small print. Not that Sinclair proved uncongenial as a travelling companion, far from it, but his admiration for Sherlock Holmes was embarrassing, almost child-like, in a man who had had a classical education and could exercise himself quite formidable powers of deduction. Such a tone of nostalgia had imbued Sinclair's voice when he had evoked the 'Baker Street irregulars', one would have to be thick-skinned not to notice it. The urchins in the Baker Street spy ring could in Holmes's words 'go anywhere, see everything, overhear every one' for a shilling each,—and a guinea for the one 'who found the boat'. Emulating those ubiquitous, dextrous brats was beyond Sebastian's ability, though he might occasionally notice a few helpful things.

The night that followed Sinclair's visit reflected his worst fears. He dreamt that he was on a cross-channel steamer, in a high sea, leaning over the side to throw up when a wave came over and swept him overboard. As he was about to drown along came Sinclair in a lifeboat, who putting out an arm lifted him clean out of the water to safety. The precision with which he executed the movement was unimaginable; he might have been picking out a winner at a funfair when the targets came round on the automatic belt . . .

To chase away the discomfort left behind by the dream, Sebastian took himself for a walk along the embankment. Since performing the Geisha act at the Sailors' Club, he had come to love that part of London. Out of the early morning mist the angles of buildings did not seem so sharp, nor the waters so menacing. By the time he turned round to go home, he felt in a more complacent mood, which was just as well, as Sinclair was standing in the doorway.

'What's the matter? You look peaky.'

'I've had a bad dream.'

'Oh, I'm sorry to hear it.'

'I was on a cross-channel steamer when a wave swept me overboard and I would have drowned had you not appeared in a lifeboat as if by magic and rescued me.'

'Highly improbable, Sebastian. You would not be travelling by sea, not if you were working alongside me; it would either be by rail in the Channel tunnel, or a flight on a well-known airline. You seem to be looking on me as a kind of saviour when I am just an ordinary guy trying to earn an honest living as a private eye, with a novice assistant at my side who happens to be a student in a gap year. I am sorry if I sound down-to-earth. I am, however, the bringer of good news that should put a smile on your face. I have had an answer to my advertisement, and guess what? We are not going overseas. My next case is at home, a wife gone missing.'

'How do you know she hasn't gone abroad?'

'The lady in question is disabled.'

'Oh!'

'She wears an orthopædic aid.'

'What kind of an orthopædic aid?'

'An artificial leg. The husband is beside himself. He wants to see us to-night.'

'But surely nowadays an artificial leg wouldn't stop anyone from going abroad? The mobility technology is very advanced . . .'

'No, but just the same it is a handicap both for the kidnappers and the victim.'

'Kidnappers! How do you know she's been kidnapped?'

'I don't.'

'She could have left the country out of her own free will . . .'

'Sebastian, what is the matter with you? You seem to have developed a phobia for foreign travel. You were game when we first joined forces.'

'True, but that was once upon a time. Between you and I, the trip we took to Professor Murray's Lost City was to hell and back as far as I am concerned.'

'Yes, the whole thing was surreal; you've made a point; but I have agreed to see a new client to-night. Are you game or not?'

'Oh, all right then.'

'Good. I'll pick you up at the Sailors' Club and make sure you apply make-up skimpily to get an early start.'

There was nothing surreal about the place in Holland Park at which they were looking at from inside the car. Situated in a quiet cul-de-sac, it was more or less as Sinclair imagined it when the address was given him over the telephone by the owner.

'Now', said Sinclair, switching off the engine a few yards away from the front door, 'remember when we're inside the house, let me do the talking. Keep your eyes peeled; do not touch anything; it may be a crime scene.'

'Oh, no! We're not starting on that wrong-footed caper again, are we? Assuming them all guilty until proved innocent?'

'Why not? It may be unorthodox but it worked perfectly well in the Murray case. The husband may have arranged for the wife to be kidnapped for all we know. He may have got sick of the sight of the prosthetic leg propped up at the bottom of the bed.'

'You know the trouble with you? You're thirsty for confessions.'

'Like a leech, Barnard; like a leech . . .'

The man who came to the door to let them in was more or less as Sinclair imagined him after listening to him over the telephone. He was of middle height, excessively nimble and athletic-looking with grey, close-cropped hair. The overall impression was one of pent-up nervous energy and extreme agility. He wore a classic business suit, fitted very close to the body, the colour of which matched that of his hair, a white shirt and surprisingly a red nondescript tie. He took dynamic strides across the entrance hall as he led them into the study. He might have been a dancer or an entertainer of some sort.

On the way to the study, on an occasional table, Sebastian espied a copy of the Woman's Magazine in which Sinclair advertised his services and he was sorely tempted to pick it up and check the small print at the bottom of the copy, but remembering Sinclair's recommendation he thought better of it.

'Gentlemen, please, sit down. I apologize for receiving you in this rather untidy den, but the reception rooms have been closed since the accident.'

'What accident, Mr. Allenby?'

'The car accident I told you about over the telephone in which my wife lost a leg. You see, I was at the wheel.'

'Oh, I thought we were called in to investigate a missing person's case . . .'

'Correct, but I feel I ought to acquaint you with as many of the facts as possible'.

'Fair enough. Please, go ahead; my assistant here will take notes.'

'About a year ago, Vivian (that's my wife) and I were invited to a celebrity party at the Tate Gallery. It was a glittering occasion and we were looking forward to it, though Vivian was always a rather shy and retiring person. On the way there, round a bend, as we got close to the embankment, I lost control of the car . . .'

'Did you incur a burst tyre by any chance, getting too close to the kerb?'

'It's possible, though unlikely in a new Bentley. As the car went on careering like a crazy meteor, I realized our only chance of surviving a crash was to jump out. Leaning over Vivian, who was terrified, I managed to open her door, ordering her to jump clear before it was too late, then I opened the door on my side and baled out. When Vivian saw the tarmac whizzing past, she panicked and decided to stay put . . . Eventually, the car hit the embankment, turned somersault and landed upside down, trapping Vivian . . . The rescue team worked solidly throughout the night to release her from the wreckage. She was conscious for most of the time, but lost a lot of blood.'

'A leg had to be amputated?'

'Yes.'

'I see. I wonder if I might have a look at some photographs of your wife, before and after the accident'.

'She didn't really look any different after the accident.'

'Just the same, it would be helpful. When your wife disappeared, did you go to the Police and report her as a missing person?'

'No, because I didn't want her to go on the Missing Persons Register.'

'Why not?'

'In case she was having an affair on the quiet, somewhere nice. I felt I owed it to her to keep quiet about it. She had gone through such a lot, by my fault; if she could find solace in another man's arms, someone who did not remind her of the accident, then all well and good.'

'That was very noble of you, sir, if I may say so. Were you married long?'

'Three years exactly.'

'Any children?'

'No.'

'Were there any signs of disturbance in the house after your wife vanished,—in your wife's bedroom, for instance?'

No, none whatsoever; she could have walked out of the house for a nice walk. Vivian was an outdoor girl; she didn't like exercizing in the gym.'

Do you know what clothes your wife wore on the day she disappeared?'

'Yes. She wore a pair of navy blue trousers, a blue and white anorak and a white woolly hat.'

'You're sure about that?'

'Yes, the cleaner told me so. You see, my wife normally waited for the cleaner to finish her chores before going out in case she needed help with the limb.'

'Would it be possible for us to have a quick word with the cleaner?'

'I am afraid she no longer works here; there's no need now most of the rooms have been closed. I am away a lot. Whenever I feel the house begins to look drab, I call in a specialist firm who blitz the place from top to bottom.'

'What did you tell the cleaner when you dismissed her?'

'I told her my wife had gone to a mobility clinic in Switzerland for an indefinite period to be reassessed.'

Sinclair paused for a minute to glance at Sebastian's notes over his shoulder, then focusing his eyes on his client again he asked in a more solemn tone of voice:

'Mr. Allenby, has it ever occurred to you that your wife might be suffering from amnesia as a result of the accident? Sometimes symptoms take time to appear. You said the accident happened about a year ago . . .'

'Vivian is monitored by a team of specialists; soundness of mind has never been an issue.'

'Maybe she suffered an upset recently, and that might have affected the balance of her mind, causing her to do something rash.'

'Not that I know of. Vivian was never a volatile person; she was quiet and stable.'

106

'Very well, Mr. Allenby. We'll start making enquiries first thing in the morning and report to you as soon as we have any thing of significance. Only you must understand, cases of missing persons are very complex and difficult to solve; people have a right to their personal freedom. Oh, by the way, one last thing. Is there a back door to your property?'

'Only the usual area in the basement, at the front of the house, where the dustbins are kept.'

'That's good. Now, it is important to keep on the bright side of things. Who knows, as we speak, Mrs. Allenby may very well be enjoying the sunshine in Florida.'

Sinclair thought he noticed a glint in his client's eyes, something he felt he ought to note mentally for future reference, though what exactly he did not know; quite often such flashes of intuitive insight only revealed their significance at the end of a case when a solution was found.

Back in the car, Sinclair suggested driving round the corner and stopping there for a quick preliminary assessment of the data they had obtained, wile the facts were fresh in their minds.

'Affluent area?' asked Sebastian, looking up at the impressive facades around them.

'I'd say.'

'Shrewd businessman?'

'Very, with an interest in the entertainment world and the Arts.'

'Yes, I did feel there was something showbiz about the man. You know, the sprightliness and the verve.'

'From the moment I stepped into that house, I felt there was something faintly disturbing about his presence, but it wasn't until we sat down that I noticed he had very small eyes and there was a cruel glint in them. He didn't seem to be crippled by guilt about the car accident, did he? But he wanted us to know right away that he was at the wheel when it happened.'

'I must say it's odd.'

'Somebody he knew, one of his associates maybe, might have provoked the accident by firing shots into the tyres. The wife may have heard them and that was what stopped her from baling out; she felt safer from bullets inside the car. Tyres don't suddenly go off on new Bentleys.'

'Do you think that might have been a first attempt at kidnaping masterminded by Allenby, who is as fit as a fiddle?'

'It's possible, one that went horribly wrong because the intended victim was trapped underneath the car and could not be snatched. Had it succeeded, the kidnappers would have thrown a blanket over Mrs. Allenby's head as she jumped clear of her husband's car and bundled her up inside their car where Allenby was probably waiting with just a few grazes.'

'You're a cynic, Sinclair.'

'No, a realist.'

'But why would he want her out of the way? She sounds harmless enough?'

'Sometimes, people who are inoffensive prove to be a nuisance to those who are aren't.'

'Is there a chance that the second time around the wife was waylaid out-of-doors, in some secluded spot where the kidnappers had easy access?'

'But where, Barnard? The woman couldn't get all that far on foot; she couldn't run. I know some disabled people are very fit and capable of sustaining strenuous exercise, but judging from the photographs Allenby gave us she doesn't strike me as being the type. Remember what Allenby said about her distaste for the gym in the house? What I can't understand is why we keep harping on kidnapping; Allenby didn't even mention it; I'm not even sure that he suggested it. From the beginning, he put the emphasis on the car accident, the blame for which he attributed to himself.'

'A smokescreen maybe to conceal the real motive behind his calling you? As you said, there is something devious about the man. Is there any chance that he killed his wife and liquefied her body in an acid bath somewhere in the basement of the house?'

'Not a chance; we wouldn't be here now. Such people go to the Police right away offering their services in the enquiry. They want to remain right at the heart of the action they have instigated themselves to see how successful they've been at outwitting inspectors from Scotland Yard; that's the thrill. They don't call in private investigators that advertise their services in a woman's magazine; that's not their style. This is not saying that Allenby didn't have a hand in his wife's disappearance.'

'What do you think about her having an affair?'

'Problematic, in her condition, with her physical handicap, married to a rich and popular man like Allenby. Don't forget she is supposed to be a shrinking violet. No, my feeling is, either she is dead, and Allenby knows it, and this is why he has called us in rather than the Police to put out feelers and to be seen doing something (he can dismiss us at any time; we're small fry), or she is held somewhere against her will, unable to get out owing to her disability. It's obvious that in his profession, successful as he is, she has become a real burden to him now the honeymoon is over and she is a cripple for the rest of her life, apart from the fact that they didn't seem too well suited. Allenby is not short of money; he could spend a fortune publicizing the case; people of lesser means do to keep the public interest alive when someone dear to them has been kidnapped.'

'How do you think he made his money?'

'I don't know but I intend to find out. I'll contact you at the Club. Don't try and get in touch.'

Getting through to Sebastian's cardboard boudoir at the rear of the Sailors' Club was not easy. One had to negociate hordes of leering Lascars vying with one another to catch a glimpse of their 'lady artist' in scant clothing, but it was well worth the effort when Sinclair happened to be 'on the scent', affording him anonymity as it was hardly the sort of night spot that Phillip Allenby was likely to visit.

Sinclair was quite pleased with himself. He had, he felt, done his homework well and in record time, as there was a measure of urgency attached to the case, and was in a better position to answer most of the questions which had puzzled him and Sebastian following their initial interview with Phillip Allenby. Lifting the shabby lace curtain that provided Sebastian with a modicum of privacy, he walked in and announced:

'Have I got news for you!'

The words uttered with petulance fell on Sebastian's ears with the force of an anti-climax.

'What now?' asked the boy. 'I've just given two performances on the trot. I'm fagged.'

'Listen to this, just for a minute. Phillip Allenby is the son of a Cornish mining engineer of some repute who made a pile in Chile.'

The word 'Chile' struck dismay in Sebastian's heart; it sounded outlandish.

'What is there in Chile to make men stinking rich?'

'Copper, Sebastian, copper! Think of the millions of copper filaments that are used worldwide by the electrical trade. Not to mention gold and silver mines.'

'I can't take in that sort of data at this time of night.'

'Of course, you can. God grants us strength we don't know we possess.'

'Who said that?'

'Good, isn't it? I've just made it up. Listen, Allenby's wife Vivian was born in Chile where there is a large British colony on account of the mines which attract engineers from the UK, the best in the world. She was privately educated in England at an exclusive Roman Catholic boarding school where she excelled as a model pupil, winning all the ribbons for good behaviour She was also very pretty and a gifted dancer. She met Phillip Allenby in Chile at a polo match. He used to fly out there regularly with his teams of ponies to take part in championships, competing against the best polo players in South America. I suppose Allenby had had his bellyful of sex kittens and gold diggers. Vivian was a paragon of virtue and she came from a wealthy background. Like most British business men in Chile, her father entertained visitors on a lavish scale at his hacienda where he bred cattle and horses; his daughter was elegant and refined. Allenby had always been in the driving seat where women were concerned and he thought he would have no problem continuing to do so with such a young and demure wife . . . They say opposites attract; in their case, it was to catastrophic effects. For all her social accomplishments, Vivian Allenby was a child of nature; she liked going for long walks alone, rather than long rides although she had her own ponies. She was very religious and did not care much for the fashionable and sometimes dissipated rounds of frivolities she had to take part in on a regular basis as Allenby's wife. She was also stubborn and bigoted.'

Sebastian could hear Sinclair's voice droning on and on in a kind of distant nirvana made denser by the fumes which had accumulated inside the Club during the evening until the word 'flight' followed by the name 'Chile' jolted him out of lethargy.

'No, Sinclair! You can't possibly mean it, not at this time of night. Wild horses wouldn't drag me.'

'I'm afraid we've got to go, Barnard. You'll love Chile! Miles and miles of beaches; it's a littoral country along the Pacific, between the ocean and the Cordillera of the Andes with a wonderful climate and delightful scenery, and a people who are by far the most hospitable in South America.'

'All those miles of beaches suggest to me 'a sea of troubles' to be 'opposed' and 'ended'. What exactly do you hope to find in Chile,—a ghost?'

'Hopefully, a marked grave; Vivian Allenby would have gone home to die for a reason better known to herself.'

'How do you know she is dead?'

'You know how in the case of a missing person, especially if it's a child, when one discusses it with other people, they are wont to make the same comment "Oh, she or it must be dead by now". It puts closure on the tragic event; it gives them peace of mind and they can get on with their lives.'

'You haven't excluded the idea of kidnap then? Vivian Allenby would still be alive at the mercy of her captors?'

'It wouldn't do to walk away from such a possibility for the sake of one's own moral comfort, would it? An investigator investigates . . . That is the onus that is laid on him. Besides, Vivian Allenby was too staunch a catholic not to show fortitude in adversity. Think of al the sashes she won a school as awards of merit for piety and decorum.'

'All right; I'll go with you; but first you must tell me how you came by all this amazing information about the Allenbys,'

'The night we went to Phillip Allenby's house in Holland Park, as he ushered us into his study, I noticed a cabinet full of trophies. With them was a photograph of him in polo gear being presented with a championship cup by royalty. An old school friend of mine happens to be a dedicated polo player; nothing extravagant; he just keeps a couple of teams of polo ponies and he has an Argentinian groom to look after them. All those grooms from Argentina know one another's business. My friend's groom knew Allenby's groom and the connection with Chile being an ally of Argentina made him forthcoming, so he was quite happy to chat to me informally. You know the rest.'

'I suppose the old school tie has its uses . . .'

'Yes, it does despite what you may think about it. I'll pick you up to-morrow night at the time you normally leave your digs to come here. Keep the Geisha outfit at home and fill your bag with clothes for travelling instead, including sweaters in case we have to flee up one of those steep mountain passes in the Andes where the weather can be treacherous.'

'So much for those 'pleasant valleys'. I knew there must be a catch in it.'

'I'll have you know that the main sea port of Chile is called Valparaiso, and that means 'Valley of Paradise'.

`So was that part of Uganda where the Massindi massacre took place called the `Vales of Paradise' . . . `A sea of trouble'; I saw it coming when I had that bad dream.'

`One last thing; when you leave here to-night, do not put up the sign which says `No performance to-night'.

`Why not?'

`Work it out for yourself, Barnard.'

Sebastian woke up to the memory of a disappointing night which had brought little respite to his apprehension about the trip to Chile. The day ahead promised to be an anti-climax without the Geisha act to look forward to at the end of it when he was used to stepping into a comfort zone that erased the memory of the monotony of the hours leading up to it. It was all right for Sinclair to feel full of zest; he was about to test his skills doing the job that he liked best, according to a rule he had devised himself, i.e.to consider each man guilty until proved innocent. Mercifully, perhaps in Chile the new job would spare him too many allusions to Sherlock Holmes, though he found them less irritating since he had began to read Conan Doyle and become familiar with the universe that Sherlock shared with Dr. Watson. It sounded as though a new star was in the ascendant in the person of Charles Darwin who sang the praises of Chile and all its natural wonders. Holmes had never shown any enthusiasm for the great outdoor. The purpose of his getting on Dartmoor was to empty the barrel of his gun into the hound of the Baskervilles.

Pacified by what seemed to him a reasonably orderly sequence of thoughts, Sebastian got up and started packing the clothes recommended by Sinclair. Few of them did anything for him being of the sensible kind to protect oneself against the hazards of the Chilean journey which could in some places throw almost anything at travellers, from experiencing mountain sickness on vertiginous passes to being worried by flights of condors. He just hoped that eventually he would warm up to Vivian Allenby's case sufficiently to come to appreciate Chile's natural beauty.

At London Airport where he arrived sagging under the weight of his travel bag, he was met by a impeccably dressed and self-composed Sinclair who scoffed at the sight of him.

`Had another one of your bad dreams?'

`Yes; I'll tell you all about it on the aircraft.'

`Just as well. See that man over there?'

'Yes . . .'

'That's Phillip Allenby's minder, an ex-policeman. They all do it when they retire from the Force. They existed in Sherlock Holmes' days.'

'Is he getting on the plane as well?'

'No; he's just checking on what we're up to. Allenby probably has other cronies waiting for us at the other end, and they will be a lot more difficult to shake off than an old copper with arthritic knees. By the way, we're flying to Santiago; from there we'll travel to the Atacama region where the mines are, staying at a place called Copiapò. I've brought you a copy of Darwin's journey through that particular area. He has some interesting comments to make about some British mining engineers, most of them from Cornwall, who took advantage of the local miners' ignorance to get hold of the mines cheap and earn colossal dividends for ever after.'

On the plane, Sinclair waited for Sebastian to settle down and for the aircraft to gain altitude before saying:

'Tell me about your dream'.

When silence ensued, he leant over; the boy was fast asleep.

When they reached the valley of Copiapò, the sight of it did nothing to raise Sebastian's spirits; it looked bleak even with the sun shining on it; and whatever Sinclair could say in defence of the town did nothing to alter Sebastian's view that the place was 'a waste of sunshine'. Sinclair took it all in his stride. The boy was nervous, and rightly so. He did not feel particularly happy himself in a town where everything centred round the mines and the money that could be made out of them. It was a place where people came and went, but never settled down. It was Sinclair's intention to stay there just long enough to find out the address of the hacienda of Vivian's Allenby's father—Vivian's birthplace—on the assumption that she had gone there when she disappeared from the house in Holland Park. That was Obtained quite quickly from the local post office where the presence of two 'Brits' was not likely to attract undue attention since the majority of mines had Cornish managers.

Sinclair had toyed with the idea of hiring a couple of horses from the local livery stables in order to enjoy a good ride through the countryside and revive Sebastian's flagging spirit, but on second thought he decided against it in case it attracted too much attention on their movements, and in the end they took the local bus, walking the rest of the way off the main road to the entrance of the hacienda.

The place looked deserted. In the keeper's lodge, there was an old man who made out that he had not seen them as he sat stroking the dog in his lap while staring into space. Sinclair thought he would try his halting Spanish on him :

'Donde Mr. MacGregor?'

The old man shook his head. 'MacGrego?' he muttered.

'Si, MacGrego, the boss. We need to speak to him urgently.'

The old man who must have known some English having been in the employ of an Englishman probably all his life, put the dog down and came out of the lodge to point a finger at some far-distant spot up in the hills.

'MacGrego gone up there in the hill country?', enquired Sinclair.

'Si, senor.Vache, cavallos, vacheros . . .'

'I get you. He's gone to the place on the hillside where his cattle and horses graze during the drought?'

'Si, senor.'

'Well, thank you very much. Nice dog', said Sinclair, patting the animal.

'What now?' asked Sebastian as they walked back to the bus stop.

'There's nothing we can do except go back into town and enquire from the local veterinary practice whereabout in the hills Mr. MacGregor keeps his livestock. Once we know the exact location, we can go and visit him.'

'You're still hoping Vivian will be there with her father?'

'You know what they say about hope rising eternal in the human heart?'

'Yes. In the Catholic Church it is deemed a virtue. And Vivian was a staunch believer and on top of that she was of Scottish descent . . .'

'What's that supposed to mean?'

'I've often wondered what were the mysterious affinities between you and her . . .'

'My ancestors may have been Catholics but I am an agnostic'.

'But you still have Scottish roots.'

'I think you're presuming and embroidering because you're at a loss to understand certain things. One may not be a practising whatever and still accept the existence of certain metaphysical phenomena. I hope that satisfies your curiosity.'

By a stroke of luck, the local vet had to go and inject some animals at their summer quarters including those that came from the MacGregor hacienda and he offered to give Sinclair and his assistant a lift. Like most vets, according to the ethics of the profession, he did not ask any questions about the why and wherefore of their visit, and dropped them outside what looked like a log cabin, saying they would find Mr.MacGregor there, before going on his errand further on down the track.

The cabin looked more substantial than the conventional one; it had a bigger, more stylish frontage and seemed to extend further at the back. On the threshold they saw a nurse in uniform saying goodbye to another nurse. At the sight of them both Sinclair's heart beat faster; perhaps Vivian was there,-sick.

The in-coming nurse waited for them to approach before enquiring in English :

'Can I help you?'

'We'd like to speak to Mr. MacGregor.'

A puzzled look came over her face which was reminiscent of the one which Sinclair thought he had seen fleeting across the old keeper's face back at the hacienda.

'I am afraid the owner of this place is no fit state to speak to anyone at the moment. Is it about the mines, by any chance?'

'Oh no', replied Sinclair, 'it's about his daughter, Vivian. Surely that's of greater importance to him than the mines.'

'In the state my patient is in, I don't think anything is of importance to him. Come in and see for yourself.'

The nurse ushered them into the bedroom where her patient sat on the edge of the bed staring into space. She took hold of his hand and pressing it several times said:

'Mr.MacGregor, these gentlemen are from England and they'd like a word with you about Vivian. You remember your daughter Vivian, your little angel? You used to enjoy leading her round the estate on her pony.'

Not a muscle twitched, not an eyelid batted; there was no recollection of anything. Sebastian turned his head away and said he would rather wait outside.

'How long has your patient been in that condition?' asked Sinclair.

'Quite some time, but I don't really know all the details. There are two of us working here, a day nurse—that's me—and a night nurse. We're both from Britain; Mr.MacGrego insisted on it when he fell ill. As you probably know, money's no object. The night nurse could tell you more; she's been here longer than I have.'

'How come?' asked Sinclair.

'Because Vivian was here looking after her father during the day to start with, and then she had to return to London where her husband needed her. That's when I came in. Vivian was a very dedicated wife and daughter. It's unusual nowadays.'

Sinclair gave another look in Mr. MacGregor's direction.

'Is there any chance of an improvement?', he asked.

'None whatsoever. There was an aggravation about six weeks ago. I was here at the time.'

'What brought that on?'

Mr.MacGregor got into a heated argument with Vivian's husband about the American who manages the silver mines.'

'What silver mines?'

'Mr. Allenby's and Mr. MacGregor's. It's all about mines and mining rights here although at first sight it might appear to be about cattle and horses . . . Mr.MacGregor tried to get up from his wheel-chair, but he lost his balance and fell headlong against a coffee-table. Mr. Allenby called me and said I had better see to my patient because he looked as though he might need some help.'

'It's a wonder the shock didn't kill the old man . . .'

'It was an accident waiting to happen. That's the trouble when elderly people get handicapped; one disability tends to lead to another.'

'Well, thank you for your help.'

'You're welcome.'

'I had better make tracks.'

'Sinclair could not wait to get outside.

'Guess what? Vivian was here looking after her invalid father.'

'So, she wasn't kidnapped?'

'No, not initially; she came out here of her own freewill to care for him and then went back to London where her husband needed her. The second time round she also walked out of her own freewill but didn't return . . .'

'So, Allenby wasn't lying when he told us it looked as though she had walked out of their London home for a stroll in the park?'

'No; but that does not mean to say that she wasn't abducted at a later date, possibly from here. The problem lies in deciding what made her leave the house surreptitiously the second time. She must have had strong motives, and knowing her I am prepared to entertain the idea that they were of a religious nature to do with the dogmas of the Roman Catholic Church, she was such a devout Catholic, to the point of fanaticism. That probably came from having been a role model at school. It can't have been about money; she had private means. The question is, where is she? We may have to start investigating cemeteries in the neighbourhood . . .'

'For that hallowed grave?'

'Or the local mines.'

'Oh, no; not another descent in the underworld!'

'Nothing like, if you're thinking about Professor Murray's Lost City. Television cameras have been down there. Documentaries have been filmed; I've downloaded quite a few myself. Besides, when you listen to what people in Copiapò talk about at street corners you soon realize it's all about the miners and their way of life. Who hasn't got a son or a daughter or a father who works down the mines? The trouble with you is you go about with your head in the clouds instead of pricking your ears to pick up valuable information.'

'Such as?'

'The miners' routine . . .'

'You know it?'

'Yes. They leave the mines once every three weeks when they stay with their families for two days.'

'You're not thinking of going down a disused mine then?'

'No. The kidnappers would attract attention to their movements to and fro when going to feed Mrs. Allenby if she were held in a disused mine . . . No, I reckon she's in one of Allenby's silver mines, the ones that are managed by the American chap over whom Phillip Allenby had an argument with Vivian's father. We must be extremely cautious, Sebastian. I've got a feeling that there is more to this case than meets the eye. Some of those mines are vast, with lots of shafts, the faces of some of which are unworked. Here are refuges here and there with most of the commodities necessary to the miners, but the environment is not stable and Vivian could easily become a casualty without any involvement on the kidnappers' part.'

'It's a terrible situation for her to be in, but I don't see what we can do to stop it.'

'Maybe something outside our control will happen, providing us with an opportunity to make a move; but that does not mean to say we must stop practising our skills or relaxing our vigilance. As things stand at the moment, there are two days to go before the miners leave the mines for their three-day break at the surface. I think we ought to spend some of that time investigating the American and the silver mines under his management. We haven't seen him yet.'

All Sinclair's tentative questions about the 'Americano', as he was referred to by people in the streets of Copiapò, had failed to produce a distinctive portrayal of the man. Like a lot of other males in the town, he was reported as wearing a baseball cap, blue jeans and trainers by those who claimed pompously to know him as he was some sort of celebrity in the area. 'L'Americano?' Ah si, senor', and off they went describing a typical, nondescript American with no particular distinctive trait. Sebastian thought Sinclair was taking chances enquiring so freely about the man, but Sinclair retorted that a foreigner in that superior position in so prosperous a town was bound to be sought after by a great number of professional people in connection with the mining industry, and Sebastian had to concede the point, and leave it at that, despite the warning issued by Sinclair at London Airport about Allenby having spies in Copiapò.

The silver mine where the American was said to spend most of his time was the furthest away from the centre of town, and that was considered a disadvantage by Sebastian who had taken a dislike to the scenery around it, which he called 'apocalyptic' despite the fact that unlike most mining towns in England it had no chimneys, claiming that the lack of smoke made it look even grimmer. They had taken short exploratory trips up and down the track but never actually trudged all the way up to the entrance of the mine, a task which had become a priority.

As they plodded their way up, they thought they heard a siren in the distance and stopping to turn round in order to identify the vehicle they saw an ambulance racing up the track towards the entrance of the mine. Sinclair intimated that whatever accident had occurred down the mine must be extremely serious since the casualty could not wait to be evacuated till the next day when the miners' rest period was due to start anyway, and all the men would automatically come up to the surface. Making tracks as fast as they could, they found a recess behind a mound of soil where they could hide to observe what was going on. Within minutes of the ambulance arriving at the scene they heard the lift clanking its way up and saw the ambulance crew carrying out on a stretcher a young man in a distraught condition who kept shouting 'La pierna! La pierna!' between screams of agony. As the noise died down after they put him inside the vehicle, Sinclair concluded that a shot of morphine had been administered . . . The silence after the commotion was overpowering and they both crept slowly away, bending down to keep close to the track like fugitives.

'Do you know what he was saying?' asked Sebastian when they reached the bottom.

'Yes. 'La pierna' means the leg. It sounded as though the young miner's leg had been mangled. I think a visit to the local hospital is a must, don't you?'

Sebastian threw his hands up in the air.

'What on earth for? You're not a doctor; it's crazy. I'm not going.'

'All right, I'll go alone. I'll find a white coat somewhere, but mind you don't get kidnapped while my back is turned. There are evil forces at work out here.'

'What do you mean?'

'I wish I could tell exactly right now. How can I put it? Basically, danger apart, it is to do with grammar. The casualty was brought up from the mine yelling 'la' pierna; he didn't say 'my' leg, 'my' poor leg'; he said 'the' leg. You heard him as I did, loud and clear, and don't pretend you didn't.'

'I don't understand what you are getting at?'

'It's simple. I need to find out whether it was purely a matter of syntax, a slip of the tongue under the influence of intense pain coming from an illiterate miner, or a plain statement of fact with a sinister relevance to this case; in other words the casualty was not screaming about his own leg.'

I think I get your drift . . . All right, I'll come with you to the hospital, under sufferance.'

Sinclair cast a quizzical look at his young assistant. The boy was obviously out of his depths. What if his powers of endurance had reached breaking point?

'Let's forget it; I've got a better plan. Do you remember that nurse who looked after Vivian Allenby's father at the lodge up in the hills?'

'Vaguely. I waited outside. Remember?'

'Yes, you often do that.'

'Well, what about her?'

'She was the day nurse, and Phillip Allenby knew her because she was on duty the day he had a heated argument with Vivian's father. Now, she mentioned another nurse,—a night nurse, whom we also saw that morning as she knocked off. There is just a chance that Philip Allenby has never met the woman; Vivian would have dealt with her when she looked after her father during the day. If she were to sneak into the hospital at night in her uniform to check the injured miner's condition, nobody would be any the wiser for it and she could tell me what I want to know . . .'

'Which is?'

'Try and work it out for yourself, Barnard; it is not too taxing . . .'

'What makes you so sure she'll comply?'

'We're all law-abiding Brits abroad, aren't we? I'll lead her to believe that I suspect foul play.'

There was nothing in the morning press about the incident; not that Sinclair expected anything. The English night nurse, waylaid down a path as she came off duty, was game enough, but she thought the time limits were too constricting, and it was only when Sinclair hinted at some form of felony that she accepted to oblige :—after all this was Chile . . . The appointed day passed slowly. There was nothing for it but wait for the time when the day nurse would leave and the other one arrive according to a fixed ritual, with Sinclair and Sebastian in readiness to stand in for her till she returned from her errand, Mr.MacGregor being in no fit state to notice anything different.

If the day had seemed tedious, the night was even more so, waiting for the night nurse to return on account of the independent spirit she showed in dealing with her schedule in those exceptional circumstances; her time was her own. When she did return from her secret mission, the way she launched herself into an orgy of extraneous details about it exasperated Sinclair, who was all agog. Finally, flopping down on a chair in the kitchen before a cup of tea she said that it had been a waste of time; regretfully, she had failed to find the victim.

'What do you mean?'

'He wasn't in the ward.'

'Well, did you look for him elsewhere?'

'Yes . . .'

'And?'

'I found him in an isolation room . . . I hesitated to go inside. You must understand I have a responsibility towards my patient. The risk of infection is a very real one for elderly people. I didn't want to take the risk of contaminating him.'

'Couldn't you have put a handkerchief over your mouth?'

'I did think of it, but then I couldn't find any rubber gloves; there weren't any lying around.'

'So, you sneaked out again?'

'I'm afraid so, but I'm willing to try again, properly equipped this time.'

'Very well. Same place to-morrow night. Time is of the essence.'

'A dreadful, dreadful delay', muttered Sinclair as they started stumbling in the dark down a mule track to return to the valley. It was hardly the sort of terrain to help Sebastian 'work things out for himself', as suggested by Sinclair. The business of the rubber gloves, for instance, was a real stumbling block. Some intelligence must have passed between Sinclair and the nurse about the purpose of her mission inside the hospital of which he had no knowledge . . .

Their second climb to Mr. MacGregor's hillside retreat did not feel as strenuous as the first one, nor did the waiting for the return of the night nurse from her secret errand seem so long. As soon as she appeared making her way back across the garden with a torch waving her arms jubilantly, they knew her mission had been successful.

'Amputation has not been carried out on the young man, I am glad to report' she announced beaming, 'I pulled back the bedclothes and saw both his legs were still intact. He was however heavily sedated; but that, I suppose, is to do with his head injuries; his head was bandaged all round.'

'Head injury? What head injury? You never mentioned a head injury.'

'I didn't think it was relevant. Your chief concern seemed to be the leg . . .'

'All right, all right; forget the head; we must dash. A million thanks'.

As they wended their way back down the track, Sebastian tugged at Sinclair's sleeve.

'I know what you wanted the nurse to find out . . .'

'You do, do you? And what was that?"

'Whether one of the young miner's legs had required amputation after the accident. That's why she needed rubber gloves,—to avoid contamination as well as not leaving finger prints behind when she lifted the bedclothes to take a look underneath. The leg that had sent him berserk was somebody else's leg he'd seen down the mine.'

`Go on . . .'

`It was Vivian's Allenby's artificial leg. You were right about her having been abducted here and not in London as Phillip Allenby gave us to understand.'

`Bravo, Barnard! You'll make a detective yet. But you know what all this means, don't you?'

`Going down the dreaded mine?'

`I am afraid so. God only knows what we shall find down there; and then, there is the additional problem of the poor bastard in that hospital bed; he may become a total imbecile, unable to remember anything.'

`Fancy the nurse not mentioning the head injury! That's women for you, I suppose.'

`Now, now, young man! She was doing us a favour, remember, at dead of night, taking a chance with her own patient, leaving him in the hands of two unknown investigators from the UK. The woman showed guts, entering the hospital surreptitiously not once but twice, at dead of night.'

`All the same . . .'

Sinclair smiled. It sounded as though his assistant was suffering from an attack of pique from having been upstaged by a female performing a task he had turned down to Sinclair's satisfaction.

`Now, to-morrow being the day the miners come up to the surface for their rest period, this is what we do. We post ourselves not too close to the exit to be noticed but close enough to be in a vantage point where we can observe the men as they file out—if they show any signs of injury in case a fight broke out down there the day before yesterday. They all seem pretty tame but one never knows, if there is a woman down there . . . Those men live in unusual conditions. One would imagine she's kept in solitary confinement, but mines are an unstable environment,—I am just thinking aloud. The American who manages the mine will be there and that'll give us a chance to see what he looks like; up to now he has proved pretty elusive. I need not remind you that he was the cause of an argument between Phillip Allenby and Vivian's father which had tragic consequences. As for the motive, please bear in mind that of all the human emotions, the desire for revenge is one of the most tenacious among them.'

`I think I get your drift.'

Having found their way back to the valley in darkness, they were relieved to see the lights of Copiapò which signalled food and rest.

Coming out of the hotel the next morning, at the start of a day that promised to be eventful, Sinclair cast a sidelong glance at Sebastian; the boy looked morose.

'What's the matter? Had too much to eat too late last night?'

'I guess so; those foreign diets don't agree with me. I haven't got a cast iron stomach like yours.'

'Well, you'd better pull yourself together because to-day you may get a dose of something far more indigestible than cold Chile beans.'

'Always encouraging and cheerful, aren't you? It's all right for you; you've had a soft spot for Vivian Allenby all along, haven't you?'

'It would be wrong of me to deny it. But, as you know, I am an adept of Sherlock's philosophy "The emotional qualities are antagonistic to clear reasoning". At this precise moment, clear reasoning imposes on me the following train of thought. The mine we are going to is four hundred and fifty feet deep. The men who are coming up for their scheduled rest will probably look pale, but that's not what we have come to verify. Watch for bruises, or signs of them having been involved in a fight, or other signs, such as embarrassment or awkwardness. Observe their faces and their body language. Anything and everything in that domain is relevant to our case, but more especially so when they file past the American mine manager. We've never seen the man before; to-day we can't miss him. Keep your eyes peeled and your ears open; we must be absolutely sure everybody's gone home before we enter the mine.'

'Do you think the accident that happened yesterday to that young man had something to do with the miners going home to-day? It seems a bit of a coincidence.'

'Could be. However, coincidences are often what criminals aver to plead innocence.'

When they arrived within vicinity of the mine, they took a side track which petered out not far from the entrance into a kind of hollow mound where they crouched. It afforded a propitious vantage-point in the sense that it was elevated in relation to the mine, and that was what they needed in order to dominate the scene rather than be level with it.

Here and there, isolated groups of on-lookers stood idly waiting for the miners to file out. The bus which was to take the men back to town was already there, parked in a corner. Again, Sebastian was struck by the absence of smoke which lent the place a kind of static look of barrenness.

He was bout to pull his cap over his eyes and settle down for a nap when Sinclair tugged at his sleeve.

'Here they come!' Startled by the ominous ring of Sinclair's words, Sebastian sat bolt upright, soon to relax. As far as he could see, the men looked relaxed and self-composed. None of them showed signs of injury. As was to be expected, some of the older miners looked pale and thin, but that was to be expected after three weeks below the surface.

'They look all right to me', he whispered.

'Too much so', retorted Sinclair whose attention had been aroused by the lack of diversity in the men's behaviour, as though they had been drilled. That was particularly noticeable when they filed past the American manager wearing a sheepish look and staring straight ahead as though to avoid eye contact. An air of unreality hung over the scene. And then the American's appearance had come as a bit of a surprise,—not at all what they imagined. He was a tall, burly, thick-set man with a bit of a paunch and looked much older than Philip Allenby . . .

The last man to come out of the mine looked the oldest. He went straight up to the American, said a few words nodding his head while the American listened to him intently, before sending him on his way with a pat on the back. Casting a last look round, the manager signalled to the bus driver to move off; he then got into his own car and followed the bus down the track. Sinclair was amazed at the man's nimbleness; despite his bulk, he moved with the agility of a ballet dancer. Perhaps he had trained as one, once upon a time?

'What do you think?' asked Sebastian, puzzled by Sinclair's reserve.

'I don't know . . . I thought there was something odd about the miners' behaviour,—too subdued; too much the same, as though they'd been briefed to present a united front, perhaps on account of the accident yesterday. I can't put my finger on it. But this is hardly the time to carry out post-mortems. We've got to get down the mine right away while all is quiet. If Vivian Allenby is down there, it is likely somebody will be back later to feed her.'

Both men leapt into a waggon with the vigour of toboggan runners on an Olympic track. The clatter of the rusty vehicle as it pursued its cranky course down the rails reverberated down the mine, loosening clumps of ore which occasionally pelted their unprotected heads, and then suddenly its run came to a stop with a dismal thud.

'Torch?', enquired Sebastian.

'Of course, though for the moment we must proceed very cautiously by the lights that show the way down the tunnel not to scare Mrs. Allenby in case she is able to move around now the men have gone home.'

'And why would she want to do that?'

'To look for food. She must know what she is up against.'

By and by, they came to a semi-circular opening in the rock face which looked like a store. There were shelves and niches all round the cavity wall on which various items of food had been stacked along with first-aid kits.

'A health bar?' asked Sebastian, picking up an empty packet of dehydrated soup. I can see NASA printed on the sachet—at four hundred and fifty feet below ground level? How come?'

'The American mine manager has a brother who works for NASA in their research laboratory. Actually, we ought to be looking for traces of blood instead of picking up recyclable litter. As for your question-: yes, there is a connection between astronauts who are stranded in space thousands of miles from Earth and miners trapped down a collapsed mine. In either case, to feed them carbo-hydrates would kill them; what they need to keep going is glucose and vitamins. And I strongly suspect that Vivian Allenby has been kept on such a diet . . .'

'Which means she ought to be in pretty good shape?'

'Indeed, Barnard, at least one hopes so.'

They left the refuge and resumed their crawl along the tunnel, their eyes glued to the floor for signs of bleeding till they came to another recess similar to the first one only deeper like an alcove across which a makeshift door had been fitted to conceal the interior, and there, at that very spot they saw a pool of blood which seemed to have trickled under the door from inside the alcove.

Sinclair knocked on the door several times.

'Ms. Allenby? Vivian? Are you there? We're private detectives from England come to get you out. Please, knock on the door to let us know you're in there . . . Mrs. Allenby?'

Sinclair quickly put his hand over Sebastian's mouth when he heard a faint stirring on the other side of the door.

'Mrs. Allenby? Vivian? You are Vivian Allenby, aren't you? Please, knock on the door once if you are able to move . . . All right, it's no problem; my colleague and I will break the door down. Get away from it as far as you can. At the count of three . . .'

125

The door gave way so easily that the two men were projected almost instantly by the very kinetic force of their combined effort. The scene inside the improvised chamber stunned them momentarily and they stood stock-still unable to take it in.

Blood had squirted everywhere and even the woman who was staring at them was covered in it. Sinclair ordered Sebastian to turn his face to the wall and promptly threw a blanket over the victim who was naked from the waist down and look as though she had been submitted to a horrendous sexual attack. Her prosthetic leg lay beside her on the floor also covered in blood.

'I bludgeoned him with it', she said when Sinclair picked up the limb to wipe the blood off it so she could put it on. 'I did it in self-defence. It was self-defence, wasn't it? And I will be acquitted, won't I?'

'Of course you will, Vivian, I mean, Mrs. Allenby. You are Vivian Allenby, aren't you? Well, let me tell you the good news. Your attacker is still alive, safe and sound in hospital, and I am sure no charges will be brought against you. He was a very young man, wasn't he?'

'Yes.'

'We're getting you out of here, now, this minute, Vivian.'

'They've all gone, you know; for three weeks.'

'Yes, I know; we watched them leave, but one of them may be back to feed you.'

'No; they said I would die of starvation as I couldn't get to the refuge.'

'That you won't; you'll live to see your father again.'

'My father?'

'Yes. We spent some time with him yesterday up at the lodge. There's a day nurse in attendance now as well as a night nurse, so he's well looked after.'

Sinclair attempted a sketchy smile; he had no idea where all this bogus cheerfulness came from. The stench from the mobile toilet was overpowering.

'They haven't been very generous with air fresheners, have they? Still, they will have to clear up the mess after you've gone.'

It was all very well trying to keep up the mock humorous banter that took the edge off the desperate situation in which they found themselves; the problem was how to get out of it, and by what means. If Vivian Allenby had managed to keep a slim figure in the past despite her handicap, at the present time through lack of exercise due to her confinement at the bottom of the mine she had put on a lot of weight and looked ungainly. In addition, that part of her amputated leg which Sinclair had been able to see when they first burst into the alcove looked inflamed as though she had tried to crawl on it, and it seemed unlikely that she would tolerate having the prosthetic limb fitted back on in order to achieve mobility, if only over a short distance, to spare the men having to carry her. Then, there was the problem of the wagon—how to get her into it despite her condition. All those were impediments likely to hinder a quick getaway. Sebastian was still standing with his face to the wall; he was probably too traumatized to come up with any suggestion, however impractical.

Even supposing they did manage to bring Vivian Allenby to the surface, what then? They had no transport waiting for them. They had come on foot round the back way to avoid being seen. It had been their policy anyway not to hire a car. Getting about on foot enabled them to mingle with the people in the streets of Copiapò and pick up snippets of useful gossip . . . Sinclair walked over to Sebastian's side.

'Go and get the night nurse, now, this minute; she has a car. She lives not far from here.'

'The night nurse? Are you crazy? She must be sleeping!'

'Wake her up and bring her here. There's no danger now we know they're not coming back to feed Mrs. Allenby. Go on, shift!'

Sebastian flew out of the refuge and started running. He could see the lights in the tunnel flashing past him, fast at first and then at increasing intervals, and he soon realised that he was losing speed. Something was bothering him, impeding his forward movement.

What if Mrs. Allenby had got it wrong about being left to starve on her own and by running he suddenly ran across someone in the tunnel? Walking would be safer because, should the need arise, he would have time to conceal his presence in a cavity in the rock face. On the other hand, walking was too slow as the victim was in a critical condition.

It seemed he had no choice and run he did, slowly at first just in case he had to duck, and then, as he began to see chinks of daylight ahead of him, faster and faster till he emerged from the mine. Down in the valley lights were beginning to go up. He dreaded the thought of waking up the nurse; she was a garrulous, demonstrative woman. He would have to impress on her the need for speed and efficiency, as well as discretion and he felt he lacked the authority.

As he expected, her first reaction in her excitement was to call the day nurse up at Mr. Macgregor's to tell her the news, 'not that it will make any difference to the old man, but one would want him to know just the same, don't you think?'

Sebastian confessed he had no views in the matter. Sinclair was waiting down a four hundred and fifty feet deep mine, probably with a delirious woman on his hands, they had to hurry . . .

Just as she was dressed and ready to go, she went round the house 'one last time' looking for more tranquillisers, despite Sebastian's assurances that the refuge lacked nothing in medical supplies The plan was to remove Vivian Allenby from the mine right away while conditions were propitious. There was not a minute to lose. The way she kept casting sidelong glances at him to size him up as a subaltern made Sebastian uncomfortable; she was obviously trying to find out how much more he knew about Sinclair's intentions regarding Vivian Allenby's aftercare. By a stroke of luck, he remembered one of Sinclair's foreign mottoes and blurted out 'solvitur ambulando'.

'Oh', she said, 'he hasn't got a plan then?'

'It was all very sudden, our finding her at the bottom of the mine . . .'

'Yes, I must say! Of all people! A woman with her disability. What a surprise! You weren't expecting it then?'

'Well, yes and no . . .'

'I see.'

In the car, he sat in the back, hoping he would be less conspicuous. When they arrived, Sinclair was waiting for them outside the refuge. Mrs. Allenby had lapsed into unconsciousness and was lying slumped across the chair. The nurse promptly propped her up and took her pulse.

'Coffee', she said 'strong black coffee, with glucose; there must be glucose in here in the miners' survival kits. Everybody in Copiapò knows that.'

While Sinclair prepared coffee, the nurse began wiping the blood off Vivian Allenby's face and neck. Then, when coffee was ready, she parted Vivian Allenby's lips with a small spoon and began pouring small amounts of coffee in her mouth till the casualty began showing signs of revival.

'Vivian? It's me, your father's night nurse. Do you remember me? It wasn't all that long ago, was it, when I used to take over from you to watch over him at night, so you could rest your leg? You're in safe hands now.'

Walking over to the men who stood in a corner, she asked for warm water.

'I cannot leave her like this; I need to clean her all over. The mess is awful. Such a good woman, a regular churchgoer; it's a disgrace. She was raped, wasn't she? That's what it looks like.'

'We don't know the circumstances,' replied Sinclair. 'At the present moment, my chief concern is to bring Mrs. Allenby up to the surface as quickly as possible. You will have to finish tidying her up later.'

While the nurse quickly ran a comb through Mrs. Allenby's hair, Sinclair signalled to Sebastian to meet him outside the refuge.

'Do you think she's established a connection between her errand to the hospital that night to check the miner's injuries and Mrs. Allenby's present condition?'

'Oh, I don't think so, not yet, but she is fishing. She started asking questions almost as soon as I got to her house, trying to worm things out of me, thinking I was a rookie.'

'You didn't let up about anything?'

'Of course not! What do you think?'

'All right. Keep it up.'

When it came to deciding by what method they would remove Mrs. Allenby from the mine, they agreed not to waste too much time casting about in their minds about the best ways of doing it, but to go for the most natural one, with Mrs. Allenby being supported by the two men with the night nurse relaying one of them at intervals till they found the wagon and somehow, between the three of them, managed to lift her safely into it, the prosthetic leg having previously been wrapped up in newspaper. Sebastian earned himself a withering look from Sinclair when he suggested wrapping up Mrs. Allenby in a carpet, like Cleopatra, to carry her into the car; the allusion was indelicate considering the Egyptian queen was known to have been a woman of indiscriminate sexual taste when it came to men . . . They also agreed not to act suspiciously when they got to the surface but simply and calmly to lead Vivian Allenby where the car was parked, in order to avoid panicking her as she had not seen daylight for months, damning the consequences. The matter anyway had sooner or later to become public knowledge.

Casting a look at the place for what he hoped to be the last time, its desolate look put Sebastian in mind of a disused miners' town in the Yukon after the Gold Rush in an old American movie.

'Where to?' asked the nurse, as she put her hand over the ignition.

'The last place we want to take Mrs. Allenby to,' replied Sinclair, 'is her father's house, not that the poor devil would be any the wiser for it, but because it is the most likely place where the kidnappers will go when they discover she's no longer in the mine.'

'You're not suggesting we take her to my place?' asked the night nurse.

'Why not?' asked Sinclair.

'Well, it's quite simple really when you think about it. I'm not there at night which means you would have to stand guard over her.'

'And what about the day?' asked Sinclair.

'You must be joking! I need my beauty sleep.'

'All right, you win; take us to Mr. MacGregor's place. You have to go anyway.'

'You've thought of everything, haven't you? But first I must warn my colleague. It's only fair.'

'You'll do no such thing.'

Cowed by the detective's authoritarian tone of voice, the night nurse turned on the ignition. Up at the lodge, everything was quiet. The day nurse was probably finishing to tidy up the place before completing her round of duties. The isolation of the place struck Sinclair as never before as he crossed the garden to knock on the door.

'Why, I remember you! You were here not long ago enquiring about Mr. MacGregor's daughter. Are you not making headway with the investigation, whatever it is?'

'As a matter of fact, I've come to ask a favour of you. It's kind of confidential. I've got Vivian Allenby in the car; she's in a bad way and I need to find somewhere where she'll be in safe hands. She's in need of urgent medical attention and I though between the two of you . . .'

The day nurse was craning her neck to see who was in the car.

'Why, that's my colleague, Sharon; she's early! I thought I recognised her car.'

'Yes, she's been a great help. If it's not too much trouble—I know you've finished for the day—if you could give her a hand to bring in the casualty?'

'Of course it's no problem'

'You've never met Mrs. Allenby before?'

'No. Oh my God, she does look in a bad way. What happened, Sharon?'

'She fell down her husband's silver mine . . .'

'You mean she's been lying down there on her own, a woman of her disability?'

'Well, obviously, no one thought of looking down there,' replied the night nurse.

'We don't know,' Sinclair said in a peremptory tone of voice, anxious to stop the night nurse from speaking out of turn. 'Anyway, Miss?'

'Jenkins, Pamela . . .'

'Miss Jenkins, this investigation has moved forward since the time we spoke to you. We are now treating it as a police matter, and I must ask you to be both vigilant and discreet from now on. I'll require statements from both of you and Mrs. Allenby as well. Please make sure that she is comfortable enough to comply when the time comes. As for letting her see your elderly patient, I leave that to your discretion.'

An enormous sense of relief came over Sebastian. Sinclair's calm manner and his authoritative way of addressing those two females had worked wonders; he had now regained control over the situation; the two nurses went about their business quietly and efficiently, keeping the shop talk to a minimum as they attended to Vivian Allenby's immediate needs till the time came from the switch-over, and the day nurse disappeared down the hill.

Having made sure the night nurse had retired to the kitchen to have her evening meal, Sinclair called Sebastian over.

'I think it would be a good thing if we managed to locate the nurse's car keys, don't you? Just in case.'

'You're not thinking of going for a ride in the moonlight, are you?'

'Well, maybe not tonight, but some time soon—while you chat her up.'

'Yes, all right, What for?'

'Only to make sure she doesn't go out, leaving us with two vulnerable people on our hands. She does go out sometimes, remember?'

Sebastian cast a quizzical look in Sinclair's direction.

'I think you worry unduly about Mrs. Allenby's condition.'

'Oh, yes?'

'Vivian Allenby is not as vulnerable as you think she is . . .'

'Oh, no?'

'No, she put up a good fight in the refuge, didn't she, battering that boy nearly to death with that leg of hers . . .'

'Oh, I'm sure she is resilient enough, but rape from one of the miners, and a young one at that . . . there are mental scars as well as physical ones in the aftermath of cases such as hers.'

'She responded in an equally brutal way . . .'

'Her faith gave her strength . . .'

'A tooth for a tooth? That's hardly a Christian way.'

'All right! What are you trying to say?'

'It's too quiet here; the place gives me the creeps. I don't think we ought to let the atmosphere grab us; it could be fatal.'

'I don't like it any more than you do, but I need a statement from Mrs. Allenby and I don't want to rush her and end up with a statement that is not exact. Some details may be too painful or shocking for her to recall yet.'

Sinclair pondered in silence. 'You can be sure there'll be nothing about it in the local papers . . . We've become the prisoners of a situation I've partially created myself and it us up to me to rectify it, but first we must address certain aspects of the case as it stands today. Either nurse may be in touch with Phillip Allenby regarding wages, expenses, etc.—we don't know. The day nurse had been in the house the day that he had the fatal argument with Vivian's elderly father, after Vivian supposedly had gone back to England to look after him. The night nurse to my mind represents the greater danger on account of the errand she ran for me down to the local hospital at dead of night to check on the young miner's condition. She is loose-tongued and curiosity may in the end get the better of her; she'll establish a connection between the miner's condition and Mrs. Allenby's and then we'll all be accountable . . . There's only one thing for it and that is to take a statement from Mrs. Allenby at the earliest possible opportunity, much as I dislike the idea for many reasons, and to do it when the day nurse is on duty because of the two she is the more discreet and therefore the one less likely to upset Mrs. Allenby with irrelevant comments.'

'What about the old man?' asked Sebastian whose diffident mood had not been allayed by Sinclair's arguments.

'What about him?'

'Is it your intention to let Mrs. Allenby see him before you take a statement from her?'

'Yes and no.'

'What's that supposed to mean?'

'I'm leaving it to chance. At the moment she is too weak to go wandering round the house on her own.'

'You could ask one of the nurses to take her to see him while he's having a nap . . . She won't know the difference, I mean about her father being away with the fairies all the time.'

'Yes, that's true. I'll think about it.'

Much to Sebastian's satisfaction, Mrs. Allenby welcomed the idea of a statement, which was put to her tactfully by the night nurse when she offered her an extra dose of sleeping pills on the eve of the day appointed by Sinclair so she would wake up feeling self-composed. She was, she said, anxious to get the whole thing over and done with so as to enable those two wonderful detectives to wind up the case and go home. Sinclair, however, still had qualms about having made a rash decision in bringing the date of her statement forward. What puzzled Sebastian was Sinclair's air of confidence about the potential power of good inherent in Vivian Allenby's statement; there seemed not the slightest doubt in his mind that whoever heard it would immediately be won over by the woman's candour and feel for her as the victim of a despicable attack, made on a disabled member of the weaker sex. And where in all this was Sinclair's philosophy—about all the people involved in a case being guilty until proved innocent? Did he still adhere to it as a guiding principle, like a clew in a labyrinth, or had this case thrown it by the board, raising unusual issues, like some two-headed monster casting a frightening shadow? So far, Sinclair, who was a courageous man, had been reticent about ascribing guilt; he seemed to fight shy of the concept altogether. The atmosphere of suspense in the house had a lot to do with it, caught as they were between two incapacitated people and two nurses, who were unknown quantities; but then they had been in a similarly invidious position when staying with Professor Murray and his relatives at their house in Uganda . . . Here Sebastian stopped. The case in Uganda was simple and straight-forward compared to this one where there were two parties, not one deserving of guilt at first sight, each for a separate offence—the party that had abducted Mrs. Allenby and the one that had conducted the attempted rape, and somehow the guilt of each party reflected on the other, and it was that 'somehow' which mystified, preventing the adjudication of personal guilt at first sight. Yet there had been no conspiracy between the two; they had happened as two separate 'acts of God', each generating its own momentum . . .

Mrs Allenby insisted on giving her statement properly seated at a table. The day nurse had found a discarded dress of hers from the old days which did not look too outmoded, and Sinclair was pleased to see that on that particularly unsavoury occasion some effort had gone into making it as dignified as possible; and so, with an air of confidence, he switched on the tape recorder.

Mrs. Allenby began by making the sign of the cross and then she took off a holy medal she wore round her neck and put it on the table before her. She gave her name, her date of birth as well as details of her education as a boarder at an exclusive convent school in England. She looked fairly relaxed and it wasn't until she gave the date of her marriage to Phillip Allenby that her lips began to quiver.

At school, she had been a devout Catholic, she said, and it was assumed by the other pupils and the nuns who taught her at the convent that she would eventually take the veil and become part of the teaching establishment, instead of which, under pressure from her father who considered she would throw her life away becoming a nun, she surprised everybody and got married to Phillip Allenby. There were financial links between the two families whose fortunes in Chile had been made out of precious metals and were accrued through Phillip having acquired copper mines, copper filaments for the electrical trade being much in demand . . . Here tears began running down Mrs. Allenby's face.

'After our wedding, we led an idyllic life on two continents, doing all the things fashionable newly-married couples do. I was young and ignorant about sexual matters. Although in the sixth form at school, the nuns had held classes in human reproduction, those were taught from a purely biological point of view to enlighten us about pregnancy and childbirth . . . whereas other women, like fashion models and aspiring starlets of stage and screen, during their one-night stands with Phillip, had complied with his requests for unusual sexual practices, which seemed a small price to pay to be seen in the company of such a popular playboy, I considered them anathema and after a while became determined to ban them from the marital bed.'

'Here, Mrs. Allenby broke down and Sinclair asked her if she wanted to stop. She shook her head in the negative and after the nurse handed her a glass of water she resumed:

'After a while, Phillip told me he wanted a divorce. I reminded him that there was no possibility of divorce in the Catholic Church. He raved and ranted but still I did not give in. At about that time, the car accident in which I lost my leg occurred and I began to suspect that my life was in danger; Phillip wanted me dead.'

'Did you then quit the house of your own free will to go and live with your father in Chile?'

'Yes. In the meantime, Father had had a stroke; he needed looking after. Phillip thought I had gone home temporarily to seek advice from Father about a divorce, and when he heard I was nursing him and had no intention of going back or giving him a divorce, he was furious. One day, while I went out shopping, he came here and told my father to put pressure on me to agree to a divorce as he wanted to go through a gay marriage with the American who managed all the silver mines belonging to the family. The shock nearly killed Father who fell headlong against the corner of a coffee table, narrowly avoiding death; he was never the same after that. The day nurse will confirm it; Phillip went and got her to assist Father. She was already in our employ at the time because I had been overdoing it, standing on my feet for long periods at a time and there were side effects with my sectioned limb. Prior to that, I had managed with only a night nurse.'

The nurse nodded her head in assent.

'Mrs. Allenby, I need you to clarify one thing. From whom did you head about the purpose of your husband's visit to your father?'

'From Father himself. He made a tremendous effort despite his injury to tell me when I got home after Phillip called and that seemed to finish him off. He must have though of my grief, of my shame; maybe he felt responsible and it broke his heart.'

Here Mrs. Allenby could contain her sorrow no longer; she bent down and gave way to sobs.

'I don't see why,' promptly retorted Sinclair to try and pacify her. 'It was such a perfect marriage for his only daughter. He couldn't have wished for anything better.'

Comforted, Mrs. Allenby dabbed her eyes and went on.

'Soon, the news of my father's deterioration went round the Anglo-Chilean community and there was a wave of sympathy. The hacienda down in the valley had been put on the market and I had lost a leg. For a while nothing happened. I went on looking after Father with the help of the two nurses and life went on. Then an old friend of Father's suggested I learnt to ride again at a hacienda not far from here where a lot was being done for disabled children thanks to the generosity of the owner whose own child was handicapped. It cheered me up a lot. One day, when I was returning from a riding lesson across the fields where Father used to lead me on my pony when I was a child, Phillip and the mine manager waylaid me. They said they wanted to talk to me about selling our shares in the silver mines—Father's and mine. When I refused, they pushed me into a car and took me to the mine where you found me. Phillip said they would let me out only on one condition, that I sold the shares to offer the Vatican a large sum of money with a view of getting our marriage annulled. I replied I didn't care about being confined as long as they kept both nurses to look after Father.'

Sinclair turned towards the nurse:

'How did Mr. Allenby account for his wife's sudden departure?'

'He told us he had at long last managed to persuade Mrs. Allenby to go back to England with him for a much-needed break.'

'I see.'

Sinclair, perceiving that Mrs. Allenby had come to the most sensitive part of her statement asked her if she wished for an intermission. She declined and picking up the holy medal that lay in front of her on the table she kissed it and crossed herself with it before putting it back on the table; and then went on.

'The mine was empty at the time; the men had gone home for their usual period of rest. Every day, I would say my prayers, especially to our Lady of Fatima in Portugal where I had gone on a pilgrimage with my parents to pray for a relative's recovery. Every day, at the same time, the foreman came and fed me.'

'On astronaut's rations?' asked Sinclair?

'Yes, the mine manager had a brother in the States who worked for NASA in their research laboratory.'

Sebastian smiled. That was one up on Sinclair's scutcheon . . .

'He would knock on the makeshift door of the confined space where I was held and leave the rations outside on the floor.'

'Did you ever see him face to face?'

'No. I waited till he'd gone to open the door just enough to pick up the rations, but I knew he was an elderly man because of the way he used to slouch back up the tunnel. After a few weeks, I became used to the sounds in the mine and I was able to identify them. There were long periods when everything down there was dead quiet, and I knew the miners had gone back up to the surface to spend time with their families. When they were working the mine, they often used to stand outside my door, cracking stupid jokes and calling me silly names. I knew they were ignorant, illiterate men and just ignored them. The banter usually got worse just before they left the mine for their rest period when the younger ones among them often got over-excited, and I fretted. On such an occasion, more recently, I sensed the men were in an unusual state of euphoria; they were egging on one another outside my cell, banging on the door, daring me to come out and wish them a happy holiday, so much that I began to fear for my safety. Finally, what I dreaded happened. The door of my cell, which was a shoddy affair, as you know, caved in and I was faced by a horde of men of all ages. At first, the men just stood there stupidly staring at me, too stunned to do anything. I recognised the foreman at the front. Beside him stood a very young man who was trying to get back into the tunnel, but the men wouldn't loosen their ranks to let him through; they kept pushing him forward instead, laughing and joking about him still being a virgin. The men began chanting and clapping to encourage him, throwing him back inside the cell like a manikin till be obliged them by removing his trousers . . . I didn't have my prosthetic limb on at the time; it was lying on the floor beside me and as he lunged forward to jump on me, I picked it up and hit him with it thinking it would keep him at bay. But the miners had other ideas; they weren't going to let him off the hook until he had done what he came to do—lose his virginity. So I hit him again. That seemed to drive him mad and he stood back ready for the final lunge. I don't know what possessed me. It seemed God had granted me strength I didn't know I possessed. I hit him. First on his private parts to incapacitate him and then over and over again on the head. Blood squirted everywhere. Still, I went on bashing till the foreman rushed in and pulled him away screaming . . .'

'La pierna! La pierna!' said Sinclair.

'How did you know?'

'My assistant and I heard him. He was still screaming those very words when the ambulance men brought him out of the mine on a stretcher. We were there by chance for a reconnaissance of the place the day before the miners were due to go home for their routine break. The reconnaissance was part of an on-going private investigation regarding a missing person—you, Mrs. Allenby—initiated by your husband. I don't know why; the wiles of the human mind will always remain a source of mystery to me . . . He said he didn't want your name to appear on the Police's list of missing persons, which made sense; a man in his position.

Maybe he was trying to give himself an alibi thinking we were amateurs and would never find you.'

'Phillip had no conscience. He thought money could buy everything, including alibis. While you were investigating my disappearance in your amateurish way, he felt safe.'

'Ah!' chimed in Sebastian. 'What he didn't know was that Mr. Sinclair had a classical education; he probably thought he was an average detective with a rookie in tow . . .'

'Barnard, I would be obliged if you didn't speak out of turn. Please pack up the equipment.'

'Yes, Sir.'

'Mrs. Allenby, thank you for your co-operation; it was much appreciated. I leave you in good hands; I am sure Miss Jenkins will see you're comfortable for the rest of the day. I'll speak to you tomorrow. I have rather a lot of thinking to do.'

To Sebastian, that sounded like the understatement of the day; the disclosures contained in Mrs. Allenby's declaration were mind-boggling, and although he felt peeved by Sinclair's personal remark made in front of the ladies, he understood that the poor man had a lot on his plate and allowances were in the order of the day. The boss was such a brilliant observer of manners! In the smallest detail of a person's behaviour, which perhaps to other people might seem insignificant, Sinclair read a meaningful sign of some essential trait that summed up a person's character and even sometimes gave an inkling of their sexual orientation. On that fateful day when the minders went home for their break, he had deciphered correctly the body language between the American mine manager and the foreman which suggested some form of connivance between the two. The foreman looked sheepish and apologetic while the American displayed an attitude for supercilious forbearance, patting the old man on the back and telling him not to worry:—it had been an accident; everything would be taken care of; the young man was secure in hospital and he would soon be transferred to another safe haven where his screams wouldn't disturb anyone because everybody in there screamed. His parents, who were poor Chilean farmers, would be compensated; accidents happened in mines all the time all over the world. And the foreman had walked away pacified. Sebastian could see it all.

A strange quietness fell over the house in the days that followed Mrs. Allenby making her statement. The nurses came and went, attending to their business with the calm efficiency characteristic of their profession. Mrs. Allenby started moving around the house on crutches until eventually her prosthetic limb was fitted back on her and she was able to enjoy unrestricted movement. She saw her father while he slept and said how well he looked and what a good job the nurses had done while she was incarcerated . . .

Then one morning, after taking over from her colleague, the day nurse asked is she might have a word with Sinclair.

'Sharon and I have been thinking that maybe we ought to start looking for another job, either together or separately.'

'Really, and why is that?'

'Well, the way we see it, Mrs. Allenby may not be here for very much longer and her father will go into a home.'

'Oh, yes,' said Sinclair, 'that's an interesting theory . . . and on what premises does it rest?'

'Well, chances are, after hearing her statement, that Mrs. Allenby will be charged with assault and battery, and if the young miner dies, with attempted murder. Sharon saw him in hospital and she thought he was in a very bad way.'

'I see. Well, thank you very much for being so open. Will you leave the matter with me for a few days?'

'Of course there's no hurry. It was just something that occurred to us. As you know, we've come all the way from Britain to work here.'

'Quite. And what a wonderful job you've made of it, both of you!'

'Sinclair knew at once that he had postponed for too long what he had to do. He called Sebastian; the boy was nowhere to be seen; he was probably in the garden reciting Hamlet, perched on a rock as if it were a battlement at Elsinore. And sure enough he suddenly appeared with a copy of the bard's play.

'Why don't you read Darwin's accounts of Chile and Chilean people instead? They're wonderful. There's a copy of Darwin's voyage on *The Beagle* in the lounge.'

'You were looking for me?'

'Yes, I need to speak to Mrs. Allenby urgently and in private. Where is she?'

'Having breakfast in bed.'

'Are you sure?'

'Positive; I've just seen the nurse go in there with a tray.'

'Right. Stand outside the door and make sure nobody disturbs us.'

'Mrs. Allenby? It's Sinclair. May I come in?'

'Of course! What can I do for you? You're such a hardworking man . . .'

'Mrs. Allenby, at the risk of exceeding my professional duties, I feel I must enlighten you about the invidious situation in which you find yourself.'

'Invidious situation, what invidious situation?'

'Mrs. Allenby, has it ever occurred to you that on the night of the attempted rape you might have behaved in a different way, a way—how shall I put it?—more fitting for a person with your religious convictions?'

'I acted in self-defence, for God's sake!'

'Please, allow me to explain. You might have made the sign of the Cross, kissed the holy medal you wear round your neck, gone down on your knees and begged for mercy. The miners are devout Roman Catholics; they have wives, daughters, mothers. You could have tried to touch their hearts instead of which you seized your prosthetic limb and battered an ignorant young man nearly to death . . . That young man is still in a critical condition. Should he die, Mrs. Allenby, you will be charged with homicide . . . make no mistake about that, your husband will see to it.'

'But Phillip's a criminal! He made an attempt on my life in which I lost a leg. He kidnapped me and imprisoned me at the bottom of a mine, exposing me to the lechery of sex-starved miners . . .'

'Mrs. Allenby. I need not remind you that your husband is a very wealthy man. He'll hire the best lawyers . . . the Prosecution will make a meal of the fact you behaved—shall we say "out of character" on the night; the jury will be divided. What will you do? Plead temporary insanity? You may end up in a psychiatric prison.'

Mrs. Allenby put down the breakfast tray on the side-table and, pushing back the bedclothes, made as though she would get up.

'Where are you going?' asked Sinclair.

'I must seek advice from Father, he'll tell me what to do.'

'Mrs. Allenby, you know as well as I do that your father is in no fit state to advise you; he has been a vegetable for years and he may end his life in an old people's home through your obstinacy. How do you feel about that?'

A sullen look came over her face as she retreated back into bed.

'What do you want me to do?' she asked.

'"Vengeance is mine, saith the Lord." Now, you understand that, don't you, as a church-going person. Please, I beg of you, do not bring charges for kidnapping and attempted rape against your husband, Mrs. Allenby.'

'Not bring charges against a criminal like Phillip?'

'Forgive and forget! You know your husband and the American mine manager are lovers; what difference does it make their living together in a civil partnership? Live and let live, Mrs. Allenby. Resume your riding lessons. Become a Dressage rider. Compete in the next Paralympics. Your father would have liked that . . .'

'Do you think so? Do you really think so?'

'Of course I do; and so do you in your heart of hearts.'

She smiled through her tears as she waved goodbye.

Sebastian stepped aside to let Sinclair through the bedroom door.

'Job done?' he asked.

'Job done.' Let's get out of here before she changes her mind.

FINIS

THE LAST WALTZ

The Last Waltz

It was always a matter of conscience for Stewart when he received an enquiry about a new investigation whether or not to ask Sebastian to join him as his assistant; the boy needed to find his feet and being driven from pillar to post, from one job to another, did not necessarily assist the process. To appease his conscience, Sinclair liked to hope that in some way the new job as an unusual experience would as far as Sebastian was concerned contain aspects which might prove instrumental, whether overtly or covertly, to the acquisition of some further degree of self-knowledge; perhaps, it was a better alternative to being left to one's own devices, Sebastian being inclined to being uncommunicative.

Having a reason which had little or nothing to do with the job helped, of course, to renew ties in a casual way, and such a piece of luck came Sinclair's way when he saw an advertisement for a football match, and on the spur of the moment bought two tickets,—one for him and one for Sebastian It was such an exceptional occasion, he had to go and tell Sebastian right away.

'I've got a surprise for you!'

Sebastian eyed Sinclair with dismay. It was not often that the great man burst on one with such petulance; normally his approach was more of the laconic kind, especially if he had a favour to ask of one.

'Yes, and what is it?'

'Tickets for a football match!'

'You must be joking! I never watch football!'

'Not even on Television?'

'No! It's always the same old jazz with fans behaving badly, the umpires making mistakes and the players over-reacting . . .'

'Ah, but this one is special!'

`How special?'

Sinclair wondered if the moment for indulging in a little personal vanity had come, but then he thought it would be mean.

`Well, special to us in an uncommon way, a way the other spectators can't share with us.'

`You do like talking in riddles, don't you?'

`This match will be watched not just by the fans but by a team of miners from Chile,—twelve of them, all wearing football shirts. Brilliant, isn't it?'

Sebastian stared at Sinclair : `You can't mean it?'

`Oh, but I do! They're not our miners, of course. They come from another mining district in Chile where a mine collapsed trapping the men underground for several weeks. Surely, you must have watched the rescue operations on Television; they went on for weeks and, at a point, when one more delay occurred, hope of getting the miners back to the surface began to fade. You can imagine the enthusiasm of the fans when they appear on the pitch, can't you?'

`Oh, it's a brilliant idea. Yes, I'll come.'

`Good. I hoped you would . . . Of course, you know, any personal feelings we harbour must be swept aside, I mean, about Chile and its miners and all that . . .'

`That goes without saying.'

Sebastian looked at Sinclair who was staring at the floor and wondered if his thoughts had strayed back to Copiapò.

`Do you know if . . . ?'

`The Chilean case is closed, Barnard. You understand me,—closed. I don't want to hear another word about it.'

`All right. Let's talk about the next one then.'

`What next one?'

`You haven't come here to talk to me about a football match; that was only an excuse, a good one as it happens, I must admit . . .'

`Well, I have had an enquiry, but I am in two minds about it.'

`I'm afraid I can't',

`You can't what?'

`Help you; I've just joined an amateur repertory company.'

`Oh! They're giving you a part?'

`Yes. It's only a walk-on one as a flunkey, but it's a start. I might end up giving up archaeology altogether.'

146

`I see, and what have you got to say when you walk on stage? I mean, what are your lines? They're usually brief for a beginner.'

`Oh, not even. I don't have to say anything.'

`Not say anything, not even `Dinner is served, My Lady'?'

`No. I just walk on; it's the major-domo who says "Dinner is served."'

`You would turn down another opportunity to work alongside me for the chance of not saying `Dinner is served'? You need to think about this very carefully, Barnard. You could be throwing away valuable experience which might one day help you to portray a really memorable Hamlet. You can't say it's a chance for you to broaden your repertoire; you haven't got a repertoire. Why don't you leave it for a while? You'll only be a jack-of-all trades in the company; they'll have you running round in circles. With me, you stand a good chance of developing at your own pace.'

Sebastian picked up a towel and made as though he was heading for the shower.

`All right; but be brief. What's the new job about so I have an element of comparison? You haven't come here to talk to me about football or give me fatherly advice, not at this time of night . . .'

`I don't know enough yet to tell you in any detail. In fact, I have serious misgivings about it'

`How's that going to help me make a decision?'

`You don't want to rush things. I'll contact you as soon as I have found out more. See you at the football stadium!'

The main interest in a case for Sinclair had always been the motives,-what drove people to infringe a moral code of conduct widely accepted by all-, rather than the practical way in which those were implemented more or less craftily, according to the degree of cunning and ingenuity the criminal was able to display. Though there was a medieval ring to them, the seven deadly sins had always been good purveyors of motives. They had a vivid pictorial quality which still struck the imagination, and going back further in time, more or less the same could be said about the excesses the gods of the Greek and Roman pantheons were guilty of, all of them relating to instincts which were typical of the human race. However, since he had been approached by a new client with a very unusual enquiry, Sinclair had begun to wonder if in the electronic age `malice aforesaid' did not assume a less picturesque appearance, of no theatrical appeal, lurking about in the hardware unbeknown to us as it was wont to, and while the technician responsible for tempering with the microchips in a factory may be said to be theoretically speaking guilty of malicious intent, in actual fact whatever dreadful consequences arose from his act it could not be imputed to him as a crime for which he would, in the normal course of events, have had specific motives and been held accountable. Furthermore, the potential, long term felony might lie in limbo uncommitted for decades and even outlive the perpetrator, raising a guffaw from the Olympian Gods who would hugely enjoy such a prank being played on unsuspecting humans . . . All that could be said about the type of criminal activity thus electronically engineered was that it was well beyond the scope of any common garden detective to investigate and maybe beyond that of criminal justice to adjudicate as well, raising quite a few knotty issues.

How to explain all this to Sebastian would not be an easy task, not that the boy would not grasp the problems that might confront him as a detective of the old school should he take up the new inquiry which included a few unusual aspects. So, when both of them were comfortably seated in his flat, this is how he began :

'A young girl has seen one of my advertisements in a woman's magazine. She works alongside her brother in a firm of undertakers, a family business of long standing. Other relatives help occasionally when they are hard pressed for time, but in the main the two of them are in full charge of the business, the brother who is a qualified accountant keeping the books. Apart from the shock of discovering that such a pretty, intelligent, well-spoken girl could perform such a task day in, day out, what she said sounded so plausible that I could not help becoming interested; and it was not until she mentioned that her brother had gone to America to investigate an unusual type of funeral, thinking it might open up a new market in the United Kingdom, that I began to feel uneasy. To start with, a location abroad had cropped up once again. I knew you were not keen and I would have to put pressure on you, invoking some more or less valid arguments in favour of a job away from home despite the fact that I myself would have preferred an investigation on home-ground, for a change.'

Sinclair could see he had Sebastian's ear.

'Then the girl then went on to say that while in the States her brother had struck a deal with a firm of undertakers who offered the new-fangled type of funeral he was interested in, and he needed more money. Would she send him her share of last year's benefits which he would invest in the new venture in her name/'

'And did she?'

'Well, no; so far she hasn't sent anything, She wanted to consult me first.'

'What's her problem? I thought the two were joint partners in a family concern?'

'The brother has been away some time, leaving her in full charge, to do everything, including applying make-up to the dead, at which she excels. She calls it 'pampering the dead, poor things, some of them have never been pampered before' (her feelings are quite refreshing, really) The other members of the family do what they can to relieve her, but she is Chief Mourner and when the time comes, she has to get into her uniform and go, no matter what. She has a boyfriend, who's keen on ballroom dancing; they have won quite a few dance contests together, but she fears he will soon be looking for another partner if she has to carry on overworking due to her brother lingering in America. At that point, I saw tears welling up in her eyes. Naturally, I asked her if she knew why her brother was staying so long in America. The question seemed to unsettle her. 'I am afraid', she said, 'he has picked up some bad company'. 'What in the undertakers' business?', I asked, surprised.

'No', she replied, 'with men who sound undesirable company for people like us.'

I couldn't help wondering whether she was sore because her brother was having a good time abroad while she slaved at home to keep the family business going; she is very young to shoulder such responsibility. And then I thought about her earnings . . .'

'Well, yes', said Sebastian, 'she has a right to know about that; she's earned the money. The brother can't embezzle it or gamble it all away. It seems to me she is appealing for help. What are you going to do?'

'I don't know,. I've thought about it and not been any the wiser for it. Of course, the thing to do would be to ask her I she wants her brother put under surveillance in America. I mean, we could organise that for her over there without having to go ourselves. What do you think?'

'It sounds like a good idea to me considering I've had my bellyful of travelling.'

Sebastian could see that at that juncture there were still areas in Sinclair's mind that remained in semi-darkness.

'Anything else?', he asked.

Sinclair took his time to answer.

'Well, yes, there is, and that's where the hitch occurs. When I asked the girl—by the way her name is Laura Knight—what she meant by 'undesirable company for people like them' thinking she had gamblers and drinkers in mind, she replied :

'Electronic engineers, Space enthusiasts, and people interested in cybernetics.'

'Why!', I exclaimed, 'you never told me your brother was a computer expert!'

She cast down her eyes out of embarrassment:

'It's unusual in our family and in the profession as a whole', she whispered as though it were a dirty secret 'Usually, the boys take up extreme sports like abseiling. my brother did for a while, and then he became hooked on the computer and gave it up. He just goes jogging now.'

'Oh', I said with a sense of relief, 'Well, in that case what you need is a cyber security expert, not a common garden investigator like me' and guess what? When I thought I had got out of the woods, she said :

'Please; I'd be happier with someone like you.'

'Holy mackerel!'

'I felt devastated. She was throwing herself on my mercy; I couldn't believe it. Someone like her who handled dead bodies, washed their hair and trimmed it and set it, she couldn't handle a relatively easy task,—engage a specialist. I didn't know what to say. She is so pretty and a dancer too! Then . . .'

'Don't tell me! You thought of your mentor! What would the great Sherlock advise in such a case, bearing in mind that the client was attractive, well-dressed. etc., recalling Mary Morstan in *The Sign of Four* or Maud Bellamy in *The Lion's Mane's* perhaps? Or even, maybe, Flora Millar in *The Noble Bachelor*?'

'Yes. I remembered what the great man had said precisely in *The Sign of Four* 'Detection is, or ought to be, an exact science, and should be treated in the same cold and unemotional manner.' He also said : 'The motives of women are so inscrutable.' Now you can understand why I hesitated before telling you what the new enquiry was all about. I know absolutely nothing about electronics, but since I have met the new prospective client who goes by the name of Laura Knight, I have spent many a sleepless night agonizing over the inevitability of horrific breaches of the law which remain undetectable thanks to advanced computer technology; of lethal bugs lying dormant along complicated, integrated circuits until activated by some trigger, all due to the vulnerability of microchips through their being manufactured all over the world, out of any kind of control. It is perfectly frightening. And let me tell you, Barnard, that they do evoke in my mind some of the legendary monsters in Antiquity, like the Minotaur who lived in a labyrinth and was fed young men and women on a daily basis, as well as the dragons of medieval romance that interfered with the progress of genteel knights from castle to castle. Oh, I know what you think about my having had a classical education; that it is detrimental to me in my job as a run-of-the-mill, common-garden detective because it stirs up my imagination too much, contrary to the guidelines laid down by the great maestro. But I tell you. it is not so, Barnard; quite the opposite. Now, you have nothing to say, have you? Because in your heart of hearts you know I am right, Barnard, downright right!'

Sebastian let the storm ride over his head; it was obvious the poor man was temporarily out of his depths.

'I think you are influenced by the fact that Laura Knight, pretty as she looks, is a funeral director; the nature of the thoughts that keep you awake at night seem to indicate it, anyway; they sound morbid to me. But I take the point about the analogy with the Minotaur [a hacker or somebody who uses their technical skills with malice aforesaid] not giving any indication of its presence in its labyrinth [a complex integrated circuit of microchips] and the resultant havoc when things go wrong [a covert attack] and thousands of people die or something to that effect, but I am not quite sure what, as I am not really interested in electronics though I, like millions of other people, make use of microprocessors, night and day.'

'All right, all right! Enough of that. Who am I to know anyway?'

Sinclair looked as though he were floundering. Sebastian thought for a minute and then he asked tentatively :

'The question is, Where do we go from here?

'We?', asked Sinclair, 'I thought you had joined an amateur Rep?'

'I did . . .'

'And?'

'You were right about it. I'm just a Jack-of-all-trade. I'm thinking that maybe I ought to put my time to better use, like helping you with the Laura Knight case, even temporarily; it sounds a stinker.'

'Well, that's very decent of you, Sebastian. I feel at my wits' end.'

'The only thing is, there is something I would rather you did yourself . . .'

'Yes . . . What's that?'

'Call at the funeral parlour; I couldn't do it.'

'Don't worry; I've already been. It's not as bad as one might expect. When you walk through the door to go into the shop at the front of the premises, no one comes out to greet you; a tape recorded message invites you to look around at the different options according to the amount of money you want to spend on the funeral rites.'

'Just the same, that sort of place gives me the creeps. I remember when my grandmother died . . .'

'All right, all right, Sebastian, there's no need to enlarge. Just now, you asked a very pertinent question, Where do we go from here? For my part, I am prepared to give Laura Knight the moral support she desires. As her chosen advisor, I must protect her financial assets against her brother's demands. You won't believe this when I tell you that when I called at the funeral parlour earlier on to-day, having sneaked round the back to find her hard at work 'pampering' an old lady, she told me she had sent her brother the funds he asked for. She said she felt quite safe to do so since I was there to protect her interests! I was dumbfounded. She's either terribly candid and innocent or the greatest actress you ever saw. Talk about women's motives being inscrutable.'

The evening had been a long and arduous one with so many diverse issues to review and the two men agreed to meet the next day to devise some much needed measures to try and establish some kind of logic into Laura Knight's affairs. One thing was clear to Sinclair; he would in future have to show a firm hand.

Whatever course of action each man had considered independently from the other during the night came to nothing in the morning and had to be wiped off the slate :—a signal had come through from the American detective agency responsible for putting a tail on Laura's bother to the effect that he had left New York and was now in Florida. 'Silly girl!' muttered Sinclair. 'Serves her right', commented Sebastian 'Sending him all that money when she knew he had fallen into bad company.'

Sinclair immediately sent a signal back asking where exactly in Florida was Jacob Knight staying to which the reply was `Cocoa Beach, at the famous La Quinta Inn.' `Famous for what?'asked Sinclair exasperated, and the immediate response was `cookies'. Sinclair fumed. Laura Knight was taking him for a ride; the boy was a harmless wastrel. Sebastian seeing the state of unrest Sinclair was in immediately began investigating Jacob Knight's destination in Florida.

The La Qinta motel was the most famous of all the Cocoa Beach hotels near Cape Kennedy Space Centre at which the astronauts had stayed at the time of the Apollo missions. Now that made sense for a Space enthusiast, especially one that had developed an interest in the conquest of Space at a time when a feeling of nostalgia pervaded the sphere of Space exploration, due to a change of policy by the Obama administration curtailing the programme for a planned return to the moon and a landing on Mars, instilling in the aficionados the spirit of pilgrims wending their way. from shrine to shrine in Florida, on the trail of the heroes of the Apollo missions. And to consolidate the feeling that Laura Knight's brother, under the influence of his new friends, had become one of those devotees, came another signal saying that, after having toured Florida, Jacob Knight in the company of a gang of other people had moved to a causeway over the Indian river, near to Cape Canaveral, to watch the night launch of a Delta IV rocket carrying a satellite which had been delayed.

When Sinclair passed on the news, Laura Knight greeted it with mixed feelings. She looked, he thought, pale and wan. Due to the current 'Flu epidemic, she had been overworking and it was plain to see that she could have done with some Florida sunshine herself.

`Well, it won't be long now before your brother returns home. From what I understand about his movements, it looks as though he has achieved his gaol in the States, don't you? and he'll be back full of new ideas and projects to take some of the load off your shoulders.'

`Oh, I don't carry coffins', she said;`the men do that.'

`What I meant was, share the brunt of the burden with you.'

`Maybe', she said wistfully.

`You fear his new enthusiasm for Space science may take up much of his time?'

She nodded her head in assent and Sinclair could see that she was near to tears.

'Is it your intention to introduce me to your brother?' he asked

She said she might, She had up to now never kept a secret from him.

'I think you ought to contemplate it. It would clear the air. I wouldn't like your brother to think I was coming between the two of you, interfering with the running of the business. That way, you'll feel happier reporting to me if there is the slightest thing that bothers you . . .'

'Like what?', she asked, perking up suddenly.

'Oh, I don't know . . . Like paying you back the money you sent him. If that money goes towards further investments, and extra benefits accrue from them, then it is only fair that you should recoup some, if not all of it, especially if the new venture is profitable.'

'Yes, I see what you mean. But you're not interested in Space science, are you? Not like him . . .'

'No, that's true. But I have contacts in the States, and I am sure we would find plenty of other things to talk about. I have travelled a lot, you know.'

As she walked to the back door with him, she asked :

'Are you worried about the money?'

'What money, Laura?'

'The money I owe you for the investigation in America and all that, seeing I've sent all my savings to my brother?'

'Of course not, Laura! I never ask for a fee until the investigation is over. Don't you worry about that side of things.'

That seemed to cheer her up and she said how much she was looking forward to resuming her ballroom dancing when her brother returned home; she had really missed it and it had made her morose. By a happy coincidence, her boy friend had been in touch with her again about taking part in a dance contest; he was not keen on looking around for another dancing partner seeing they performed so well together, winning most of the competitions they entered.

'Will you come and watch me dance on the night?', she asked with a far-distant look on her face, as though she had already taken to the dance floor in her partner's arms.

'Of course! I'd love to. To what tune will you be dancing?'

'The Blue Danube. The Viennese waltz is our best dance.'

'Wonderful! And who knows, maybe it will be a new beginning for you and your partner; at least, I hope so.'

To Sebastian, the whole thing, as Sinclair reported it, sounded unreal. Not in so far as Laura Knight was concerned (coming from arch women anything was possible. and this one sounded like a real treasure), but in relation to Sinclair as a matter of personal perplexity. Inexplicably, the boss had allowed the objective spirit of chivalry which had been so very characteristic of Sherlock Holmes's attitude to women to acquire a distinct medieval flavour, allowing for a certain magnanimous closeness to creep into his relationship with Laura Knight, which struck him personally as being fraught with danger. Admittedly, the girl looked frail and delicate like a medieval maiden. She may have been doing a job which required a strong stomach or the skin of a rhino, or both, but in Sebastian's view she was not unaware of the appeal that such a character as herself had on men outside her profession, and possibly she made the most of it when the occasion presented itself; not omitting the fact that in this particular case she had initiated the relationship by answering Sinclair's advertisement, which gave her a certain edge . . . Those were not thoughts one could share with the boss; one had to bear their silent burden as they trailed past and hope there was a technical reason behind them, and all would be revealed in good time.

Once again, as it had happened so often in the past in the case of a new investigation, a period of tedious inactivity followed the initial excitement created by its novelty and the brain-storming sessions that ensued. Sinclair waited for a signal from Laura Knight, inviting him to meet her brother, and he knew it would take time, considering the young man planned to transform the business from an old-fashioned firm of undertakers following traditional methods of dispatch into an agent of the ultimate modern funeral rite, sending people's ashes spinning off into orbit round the earth in funerary satellites, which had become popular in the States. It was a huge project, requiring a complete overhaul of the premises, as Laura explained excitingly over the telephone, and one that was bound to take time, plus the fact that she and her dancing partner were busy rehearsing for the dance contest, the date for which was not far-off,. but she had not forgotten their last conversation and would arrange a meeting with her brother as soon as his own schedule for abseiling permitted;—he had taken to the sport again in a big way for relaxation purposes, and was away every week-end.

Sebastian hated those interim period when one was torn by contrary impulses, whether to go back to the Amateur Rep, even as principal tea-maker or rubbish collector, just for the chance of treading the boards once more and let the adrenaline flow, or simply kick one's heels for the sake of remaining available to Sinclair out of loyalty in case there were developments with Laura Knight which required speedy action, possibly to protect her against her brother's demands for more funds now he was expanding the business in such a spectacular manner. Every day, people flocked to the funeral parlour to collect information about the new procedure; it was the next best thing to ascending to heaven. Sinclair was lucky; although he could not like his mentor the great Sherlock play the violin to soothe his nerves, he could walk round museums and galleries and stimulate his brain cells while titillating his taste for culture and the Arts.

Every day, in the evening, at the same time, Sebastian would go to the Sailors' Club and give the usual performance. He had thought of making changes to the act, and had started putting out feelers, but the men failed to respond. Their interest seemed to be entirely concentrated on the latest crime wave to grip the imagination of people in London and the speculation surrounding it about a serial killer being on the loose on its streets from which people vanished mysteriously, linked by an age factor, all of them being under twenty-five. When Sebastian casually mentioned his difficulty with the sailors and the reason for it, Sinclair shrugged his shoulders. Since all the victims were Londoners, it was fitting to recall what Sherlock Holmes, who lived on one of London's busiest thoroughfares, had to say about theories in *A Scandal in Bohemia* 'It is a capital mistake to theorize before one has data. Insensibly, one begins to twist facts to suit theories instead of theories to suit facts.' As far as he knew no evidence of such a criminal stalking likely victims within a certain age group had as yet been produced to prove his existence.

'That's all very well' retorted Sebastian, 'but what about intuition, insight, especially insight into female psychology? Holmes had it and he used it to advantage?'

Sinclair smiled.

'I am well aware that you are asking me a leading question, Sebastian, inspired perhaps by the way I behave with a certain client of the female sex, and I'll reserve my right to remain silent, but beware of jumping to conclusions. Although I may not have Holmes's wide range of experience, I do benefit from belonging to an age that has crossed many boundaries, other than the sound barrier. Documentaries about air crashes on mountain ranges have accustomed us to such practices as cannibalism.

being admissible as a means of ensuring survival, which would have horrified Holmes. My range of experience, restricted as it is, is therefore of an entirely different nature from his, and it is likely that in an age to come all the books will have to be re-written, from a different standpoint, due to the progress of Science. You have nothing to say, have you?'

'Well, talking of progress, since you challenge me, it would be a help for me to know where we stand in the case of the female funeral director. Any development?'

'As we speak, she is probably practising the Viennese Waltz with a view to taking part in a dance competition to be held at the Palais on Saturday night. Now her brother is back in the saddle, she can enjoy herself to her heart's content. Does that satisfy your curiosity? I hardly think so.'

'What about her brother? Has she introduced him to you yet? He's been back a while.'

'No, not yet; he works flat out during the week refurbishing the business and, at week-ends, he abseils, and there's nothing we can do about it. That's life. Any comment?'

'Oh, none! Absolutely none; everything's lovely in the garden.'

'I tell you what . . . Why don't we stroll down to the Palais and watch Laura Knight rehearsing with her boyfriend in one of the dance studios? That might refresh her memory.'

'Yes, all right.'

Most of the lights outside the soundproof studios were turned on and it was not until they had peered into most of them that on hearing the strains of the Viennese Waltz coming through the door of the last one, they made bold and walked in.

'Have you seen her dance before?'. asked Sebastian.

'No, never', whispered Sinclair, mesmerized by the vision of Laura Knight whirling round to the enchanting lilt of Johan Strauss's waltz. She was a picture to watch. All traces of anxiety had vanished from her face; she danced with complete abandon, no longer burdened by worldly cares. The spectacle took Sinclair's breath away. He did not know whether to laugh or cry; suddenly the tune the young girl was waltzing to had jogged his memory.

'What's the matter?' asked Sebastian. 'You look as though you've seen a ghost.'

Grabbing Sebastian by the arm, Sinclair pushed him through the studio door into the passage.

'Tell me I'm dreaming. Pinch me, punch me, do something.'

'Why, what's up?'

'Do you remember how in Stanley Kubrick's film *2001: a Space Odyssey* when the space travellers board the spaceship at the start of their journey they do so to the tune of *The Blue Danube*?'

'Yes . . .'

'That's the tune to which Laura Knight is dancing all her cares away . . .'

'So what?'

'Why couldn't I see it before? While she waltzes spellbound in her boyfriend's arms, and her brother is abseiling somewhere in Wales, the funerary satellites he has sent off into orbit to the tune of the *Blue Danube* spin round the earth carrying not people's ashes, Barnard, but body parts. No wonder she looks ecstatic. Thanks to her brother's newfangled venture, she no longer has to overwork; there are fewer bodies to wash and groom, and the money keeps flowing in to the tune of a Viennese waltz: How *he* does it, I haven't the foggiest; that's for the Police to find out when they arrest him on suspicion of mutilating the dead. Did you know the Greeks mutilated the slain?'

'So much for their great culture. Do you think she knows what her brother is up to?'

'Maybe not in absolute terms. She may have had suspicions about his sadistic instincts for some time, and that may be the reason why she felt impelled to contact me in the first place; she sounded like a person who hankered after advice, but, as Sherlock Holmes said of one of his female clients 'she was not sure that the matter was not too delicate for communication'; it would appear that way. Her brother may have dropped hints now and then, and perhaps she began to fear for her own life, if she didn't go along with it.'

'Is it your intention to find out?'

'No; the Police will question her. Right now, I must dash to the funeral parlour before the waltz practice comes to an end.'

'In that case, I'll wait here.'

'Oh, no, you don't, Barnard! I need you over there to stand guard outside the back door. This is no time for namby-pamby nerves.'

As far as Sinclair could see in the semi-darkness, nothing much had changed in the external aspect of the building; it was more or less as Sinclair remembered it. Not until he stepped into the grooming parlour where he had seen Laura Knight practising her cosmetic skills on the dead did differences become perceptible to him. From a kind of modest, nondescript set-up designed not to offend the dead, the place had acquired a clinical look reminiscent of that of a surgery. The deep, earthenware butler's sink from Scotland that had lent the place a homely feeling had been replaced by a plugged-in metal bath, and from the middle of the room the table on which the dead used to rest in their coffins prior to being groomed that had gone too, leaving an empty space which made Sinclair feel suddenly vulnerable. Walking through to the next room, which was much smaller, he noticed a hanging rail with zip-up body bags hanging from it. Behind it, through the aperture he made by carefully sliding them along to one side, there was a cupboard which contained an assortment of surgical tools of various uses with one exception :—there was no saw among them. Retrieving his steps, he then went over to the bath and pulling out the plug, inserted a cotton wool bud into the plug-hole, and twisting it all round its sides as a smear waited for a second before retrieving it, hoping it would prove to be evidence enough for Scotland Yard to launch an enquiry.

'Quick back to the Palais', he whispered as he rejoined Sebastian who stood huddled up in the shadow of the back door.

At the dance hall, most of the studio lights had gone out. The two men rushed down the corridor and burst on to Laura Knight and her partner just in time to see them executing the last movement of their rehearsal with perfect harmony.

'Bravo! Bravo!' shouted Sinclair, unable to resist clapping.

Laura Knight was not impressed.

'You have got a nerve to come barging in here uninvited at this time of night. I said I would contact you. The piper calls the tune.I've been on my feet for hours and I am exhausted.'

The boyfriend, sensing trouble, picked up his jacket and waving goodbye made for the exit.

'Just answer this one question, Laura. Where is your brother's hacksaw?'

'Oh', she said sounding relieved, 'if that's what you want to know, he takes it with him every time he goes abseiling in case he gets trapped inside a crevice and has to hack his way out.'

'You'll have to tell that to the Police, won't you? It cuts no ice with me.'

'Ah, that's a good one!', exclaimed Sebastian. 'It cuts no ice! When you think about it, the bodies don't get the chance to turn icy cold; he has to dismember them quickly while they're still warm.'

'I'll have you containing yourself, Barnard!'

'Yes, Sir. Sorry.'

Sinclair turned once more to face Laura.

'Are you aware that world space launches of satellites are regularly listed in Satellite digests? It makes no difference where the launching site is, in New Mexico or French Guiana; they're all listed with relevant details of cargo, and the listings are available from the United States Strategic Command Space Track website. Satellites may also be relocated to a decaying orbit, eventually crashing into the sea where they can be retrieved.'

'Why are you telling me all that? I'm just a girl who loves to dance.'

'The Police will be the best judge of that. You're on your own, Laura. I know! It makes no difference; you've always been on your own—with the dead, pampering them. But those days are over; you're with the living now, and you may not find them quite so amenable.'

'Don' t you think you were a bit hard on her?', asked Sebastian, as he sat in the car waiting for Sinclair to start the engine. 'She looked pathetic in the middle of the dance floor in her regalia . . .'

'Hard, did you say? She was not on the level with me; that made it harder for me. What's worse, it raises the question, When are women intelligible when even the suspicion of mutilating the dead does not sober them up enough to render them intelligible?'

FINIS

THE MISSING LINK

The Missing Link

The case of Laura Knight had shaken Sebastian. The way Sinclair had treated the poor girl whose soul had become a battleground for conflicts of interest, some of them of a subterranean nature, had in the main been harsh, and perhaps even tainted with wounded vanity, but who was he to judge? Now that on Sinclair's advice he had taken to reading Conan Doyle, occasionally immersing himself into the adventures of Sherlock Holmes rather than those of Tintin, the junior reporter, he could see that regarding women, although Sinclair often resorted to quoting Holmes in that area, he did not possess his mentor's wide range of experience and perhaps the lacuna called for a more lenient view of Sinclair's attitude.

Sherlock had known a variety of women, of all shapes and sizes and from all classes of society and of different nationalities as well. There was Irene Adler, an operatic contralto from New Jersey, 'the daintiest thing under a bonnet on this planet', according to Holmes. in *A Scandal in Bohemia*; Anna, a Russian member of a Nihilist party 'at best she could never have been handsome' remarked Watson, who was a lady's man', in *The Golden Pince-nez* ; Maud Bellamy, the daughter of a boat and bathing-cot proprietor at a seaside resort in Sussex, a local beauty of whom Holmes said she 'will always remain in my memory as a most complete and remarkable woman', in *The Lion's Mane*; Lady Brackenstall of Adelaide in *The Abbey Grange*; Miss Burnet, a governess who was a drug addict in *Wisteria Lodge*; Lady Frances Carfax, a beautiful woman who was kidnapped in *The Disappearance of Lady Frances Fairfax*, (shades of Vivian Allenby in Sinclair's own casebook *The Chilean Case*!); there were the three Cushing sisters, one of whom received a severed ear in a parcel through the post in *The Cardboard Box* ; Mrs. Ferguson, a Peruvian lady in *The Sussex Vampire*; Hope, Lady Hilda Trelawney, 'the most lovely woman in London' in *The Second Stain* ; Isadora Klein, a celebrated beauty, 'the richest as well as the most lovely widow upon earth', whom Holmes called the *"Belle dame sans merci"* of fiction in *The Three Gables* ; Laura Lyons, the perfect beauty whose face was marred by something subtly wrong with it in *The Hound of the Baskervilles* ; Violet de Merville, who was 'beautiful, but with the ethereal other-world beauty of some fanatic whose thoughts are set on high' in *The Illustrious Client* ; Mary Morstan in *The Sign of Four* of whom Holmes said 'I think she is one of the most charming young ladies I have ever met' while adopting a patronizing attitude towards her after she became Dr. Watson's bride. To this list must be added the typical Swedish beauty Ettie Shafter 'blonde and fair-haired, with the piquant contrast of a pair of beautiful dark eyes' in *The Valley of Fear* and Alice Turner, the charming daughter of a landowner in *The Boscombe Valley Mystery*.

Not that Sherlock Holmes refrained from making unmitigated remarks when it came to pointing out the physical or moral defects of women, but on the whole, whether or not by calculation to save himself the opprobrium of being called a misogynist, he always managed to give the impression that he was on the whole an admirer of women, which could not be said of Sinclair with any certainty. One simply did not know because there was precious little to go by one way or another, all leading questions being aborted by Sinclair with a kind of defensive gruffness that bordered at times on ferocity, depending on the mood he was in; and he was currently in a foul one.

Not that Sebastian minded. He had a lot to think about. The Sailors' Club was being refurbished, and a more sedate personal comportment required of all its members by the new management under threat of eviction. As a result, Sebastian whose standards of performance complied with the new criteria was offered a proper, more secure space of his own as a dressing-room to do whatever he wanted with it.

He knew of a second-hand furniture store in the Holloway Road where the owner had a large collection of pieces in the 'oriental' style which would be in harmony with the Club's premises since the majority of its members were of Chinese origin, and he thought he would invite Sinclair to go along with him and help him select a few items, in the hope it might distract his mind from whatever was troubling it.

Sinclair was not keen.

'Why do you want to go to all that expense? It's only a gap year arrangement, for God's sake!'

'Why not? I like it there.'

'Personally, I've made a decision . . .'

'What's that?'

'We will be going abroad, should the next case demand it. No more footling at home; it just isn't worth the trouble. Besides, it is not advisable to curtail experience in foreign lands, not when it's offered on a plate; it can only induce professional stagnation in the end.'

'Holmes never went abroad', remarked Sebastian.

'That's a silly remark to make. If people had flown in his time, Holmes would have jumped on a plane at Heathrow with the same enthusiasm as he hopped on a train at Charing Cross station. Don't forget, his age was the age of the Railway.'

It was obvious that Sinclair had not put closure on the Laura Knight case and it was time Sebastian gave him a piece of his mind.

'I think deep down you're unhappy about the way you treated Jacob's Knight sister. It was harsh, if you don't mind my saying so, and I can only hope that going abroad will help to modify your attitude to women . . .'

'Holmes never changed his. He was a good professional detective because he never allowed his heart to govern his brain. I am too sensitive to the softness of women, Barnard, and some of them may be evil personified. Remember what Holmes said about the woman who poisoned three little children? She was and I quote 'the most winning woman' he ever saw. There is a kind of magnanimous pity in men which is aroused by the sight of a woman who has fallen from grace. And the worst type to my mind is the little woman who closes her eyes to evil out of self-interest. The beauty of the ball gown Laura Knight wore to dance *The Blue Danube* still haunts me.'

It was clear the thought that such a radiant creature had been able to compromise with her conscience over the nature of her brother's commercial Space presence still rankled. Another enquiry might help to take Sinclair's mind off the case.

'I've just had a thought . . . Work is a kind of narcotic, isn't it? I know when I do my Geisha act, I get transported into another world. Why don't you offer to help the Police in their search for the shoe that is missing from the body of the strangled Works Manager now they've found it? Her murder is causing a great deal of concern among young career women; some of them are afraid of going to work.'

165

'The Police don't need us, Sebastian! They've got a squad of something like eighteen freelance detectives working on the case and the inspector in charge of the enquiry is one of the ablest at the Yard.'

'The shoe is a fetish, isn't it?'

'Everybody knows that, Sebastian! Actually, come to think of it, it might send them barking up the wrong tree. It's such an obvious sexual symbol. The girl was not sexually assaulted, was she?'

'No, only strangled, with a shoe lace.'

'Yes . . . that's what makes it such an interesting case . . . unusual nowadays as far as motives are concerned. Mind you, it takes all sorts ; it might have been a stalker . . .'

Sebastian could see he had managed to engage Sinclair's attention. To get him to pit his brains against a baffling combination of unusual aspects in a case that kept the media buzzing was just the thing to take his mind off the Laura Knight case, especially as the Police were making no headway. Following the discovery of the body, so anxiously awaited by the girl's parents as well as the public who feared there might be a sex maniac in the neighbourhood—a nice, quiet residential area—the enquiry had reached a stalemate.

'So, you have been following the case . . .'

'Difficult not to when the media are so keen to keep the public informed about the latest developments in the enquiry. Every time one switches on the Television to hear a news bulletin, pictures of the murdered girl appear with a summary of the features of the case. It is a way for the Police to appeal to the public for information.'

Sinclair paused and Sebastian hung on his lips.

'Right', declared Sinclair, 'this is what we do.'

Sebastian managed to refrain from clapping; Sinclair seemed well and truly hooked.

'I want you to put on DVD all the news programmes that come up, whether or not they include information about the murder victim . . .'

'All of them?'

'Yes, all of them as footage to constitute an archive so we can play them back over and over again, and see what others can't see that makes sense, remembering the great Sherlock's saying in *The Dancing Men* 'Every problem becomes very childish when once it is explained to you.' The grammar sounds atrocious, but the aphorism is true, meaning the explanation is so evident that the Police can't or won't see it . . . I think the Police have been blinded by the simplicity of the case; there are some facts in a murder case that are too simple to be noted and worse still acknowledged as potential motives for murder.'

Sinclair stopped, staring ahead of him as though he were looking at some invisible blackboard and then he turned his head once more towards Sebastian :

'I know it sounds a tedious task but having this database will save us from having to collaborate with the Police as we had to in Uganda when we were tracking down Professor Murray. By the way, talking of Professor Murray, do you remember the large diamond I handed back to him claiming I had found it in the incinerator at the back of his house?'

'Yes . . . ?'

'It was a fake.'

'You gave the professor a fake diamond! What happened to the real one?'

'I handed it over to the local police as proof of his involvement with Al Quaida.'

'You have got a nerve, Sinclair!'

'I knew all along the man was guilty of conniving with militant extremists out of sado-masochism, but I had to prove it. I tell you, his daughter was lucky not to end up with a shoe lace round her neck. Of course, no African Muslim would 'have gone into her' either as the biblical expression goes, but that would have been evident . . .'

'You mean, as evident as it is in this case?'

'Yes, Barnard! Yes! Can't you see? Oh, never mind; it's early days yet; the penny will drop, I'm sure. Now, while you deal with the data base, I shall walk round building sites with a tin hat on, of course, and carry out a few futile enquiries of my own.'

'Why futile?'

'My dear boy, it'll be like looking for a needle in a haystack! Do you realize how many thousands of men are employed on a building-site, men of all shapes and sizes, and of all ages? The strangled works manager worked for a top firm of builders; she was no wallflower. She had caught the attention of her bosses very quickly, collecting many awards on the way. To get from one building site to another she rode a Harley-Davidson or drove a second-hand red Ferrari. She spent most of her holidays in Japan with her best girl friend who worked as an hostess in a businessmen's bar in Tokyo. Free and easy, you'd say, but fresh-looking, like a daisy, or rather

167

the typical English rose. For all we know, she may have been spotted by a talent scout in a rival firm who made her an offer she couldn't resist.'

'She had a boyfriend', remarked Sebastian, shocked at the clinical way Sinclair spoke of the dead.

'Who hasn't these days? It goes with the lifestyle, like the ipad and the mobile phone, mere accoutrements or perhaps even amulets. to protect them against being non-entities. What smart girl would be seen without them? Besides, in our culture a girl's entitled to making choices. All this is very sensitive stuff for the Police to handle; they've got to weigh every word they say. Officially, they must be seen to uphold puritanical standards.'

'Why bother to visit building sites at all then?'

'To prove a point, Barnard. It's as simple as that.'

'Like what?'

'Like having to look for the murderer much closer to home than that. The Police keep harping on about the victim having known her killer, or killers. I would prefer to put it another way,—about her killers having known her extremely well; it narrows down the field right away. The question I ask myself is, What is there left for those girls to do to create a perfect world?'

Sinclair sank into a depressing silence.

'What shall I do about furnishing my new dressing-room?', asked Sebastian feeling suddenly dispirited.

'All right; you win; I'll visit the furniture store with you as soon as you have started the database, that is when I am not traipsing round building sites uselessly. By the way, did you know that in Constantinople work on the underground tunnel across the Bosphorus has come to a complete standstill because workmen have uncovered the remains of the old city built by Alexander the Great? Archaeologists are having a field-day down there.'

'Why are you asking me this?'

'There is such a thing as the archaeology of crime. Deeds, however insignificant, become vestiges in a person's past which attach themselves to it like barnacles on an antique pontoon, eventually becoming potential motives for murder. Think about it.'

It was all very well for Sinclair to advise Sebastian to cogitate, but deliberate mental exertion had never been Sebastian's forte; that was one of the reasons why he wanted to become an actor. He would learn lines that had been written by somebody else; say them in a manner indicated by the director who had given a lot of thought to the characteristic way he wanted the script handled. Constituting a database was not taxing. What Sebastian felt apprehensive about was being closeted for hours on end with Sinclair who would go from one brilliant extempore comment to another about whatever came up on the screen, adding another leaf to the Book on the Anatomy of Crime which pivoted round the missing shoe; according to him, it was the sine qua non of the case and he kept harping on it. This was not a crime of passion with a conventional sexual motive because the girl had been a bit indiscreet, but rather a crime where the morbid emotional energy required to commit the act had been induced in the murderer or murderers (since a witness claimed he had seen the victim in the company of two people on the night of the murder) by the sight of some sort of footwear to which no erotic meaning was attached since the girl had not been sexually interfered with. That to Sinclair sent out a very clear message, and he would no doubt dwell on it ad nauseam every time they watched the DVD just as he was wont to out of the blue, for no reason at all.

For Sebastian, the acquisition of furniture in the oriental style was a priority. He intended to stay on good terms with the new management having felt uncomfortable with the previous one whose standards were poor. His Geisha act was good of its kind and, as Sinclair kept saying it deserved better than the rough and tumble of a rundown Sailors' Club in the East End full of rowdy mariners . . .

Having slipped out surreptitiously early one afternoon to pay another visit to the junk shop in Holloway Road, Sebastian came back to find Sinclair where he had left him, glued to the Television screen where diverse items of the archive were being flicked over fast and then played back and held over one by one long enough to provide scope for Sinclair's commentaries about those aspects of the case which he considered worthier of scrutiny than others and regarding which he blamed Sebastian for not paying enough attention, claiming as an excuse that they were too intensely emotional to watch.

`That's just the point I'm trying to make, compared to other appeals to the public made by victims' parents in similar cases, this one is totally devoid of any attempt at self-control on either part; the two of them are in the throes of unbridled sorrow and it is, I agree, shockingly painful to watch. Normally, the one who is the more capable of self-control takes on the task of reading the statement live on Television to spare the other one the trauma of breaking down during the appeal; in most cases it's the husband, but in this instance, it is the mother who delivers the heartrending message and that in a way made it all the more poignant, as she kept breaking down while the father lay slumped across her breast, weeping his heart out while holding on to her hand. It's unusual.'

'One shouldn't judge people on appearances . . . 'hazarded Sebastian.

'I know! He's a big, burly man on the obese side while she seems by comparison the frailer one of the two; but these are elderly people who may have had a child late in life, a child who did them proud career-wise, probably beyond their expectations (don't forget the victim was high-flying)., and they haven't got many years left to savour her success. Remember how the father blurted out during the initial interview, after the girl first went missing, 'We want her back.' If that isn't a heartrending cry, expressing regret for what can never be again, I don't know what is. What I am saying is, there is such a thing as body language. You can't deny that the father looks the more devastated parent of the two in a kind of helpless way, unseemly in a man of his size; he certainly can't handle his grief. It's inordinate. She tries to do better. I mean, look at this shot where the camera focuses on their hands; he's clasping her fingers for dear life and he keeps pummeling them spasmodically as she speaks to proffer encouragement and hang on to her at the same time.'

'Maybe she was not as emotionally involved with the daughter as he was', retorted Sebastian. 'People vary in their attitude to offspring. They react in different ways.'

'Yes, but the mother does not really do very much better, does she? I mean the difference is marginal. They're in it together; their sense of loss is immense but somehow he bears the brunt of the burden of their grief for whatever reason . . .'

'That's true. They don't appear to try and put a brave face on it for appearance's sake. They don't seem to care about sparing the public's feelings.'

'I have to agree with you ; it is upsetting to watch, in an almost obscene way, turning the public into peeping toms . . .'

'Why do you think Inspector Blakeney let it go out live, in the raw, so to speak?'

'Good question, Sebastian. He could have had a female member of staff, a social worker, read out the statement in front of the Television cameras, but the dramatic impact of the appeal on the public at large would have been much less. Who can blame him? Here's a man at the end of his career, near retirement age, who gets given the chance to end on a good note. He has to make a quick arrest; that is vitally important to him It is undeniable that the spectacle of such devastating grief as that displayed by the parents during their television interview will induce people to come forward more promptly with whatever information they think they may have about the murder. I imagine that Inspector Blakeney knows what an unsensitive bully he's been, and that's why he paid tribute not to the courage and self-control of the victim's mother in delivering the appeal, which would have been more to the point, but to the 'self-respect' of both of them, of which the public saw hardly anything at all; they were both hysterical most of the time; one never saw them attempting to pull themselves together in order to carry on in a more acceptable sedate manner . . . That's the way it goes, Sebastian. Blakeney is also deploying a large posse of private investigators. Judging by the number of them, I'd say that he is in a hurry to make an arrest, and it wouldn't surprise me if he didn't break news soon with one, only to release the suspect without charge after holding him in custody for the maximum amount of time allowed by the Law, just to fool the real murderer.'

'Any ideas as to what type of person that might be? A stalker perhaps?'

'It's possible. This would support the Police's theory that the victim knew her killer, or killers. Stalkers generally harass people who have been in a relationship with them.'

'What about the current boyfriend?'

'What about him?'

'Isn't it odd that she never mentioned that potential stalker to him? He looks like a decent sort of chap . . .'

Sinclair nodded his head in silence and began flicking through photographs of the murder victim, focusing on the ones which had been released on News bulletins.

'Look at those rosy, chubby cheeks; all that long, loose blond hair in no particular style, this is not really the picture of your typical career girl, is it? There's something immature about the face; the thing that strikes me most about it is the impish, almost mischievous smile; it is not the smile of a coquette. Here's somebody who enjoys playing pranks on other people . . . A party girl, yes, but a rather juvenile one.'

'What the French call an 'allumeuse'?'

'No, Barnard, no! More of a female Puck, 'a playful sprite' in contemporary office garb, if that's at all possible. Puck had a very mischievous disposition. Now, that the murder victim did tease somebody unwittingly to distraction, beyond their endurance, without malice aforesaid because such was her nature that I am prepared to accept, somebody who in the end put a garrotte round her throat.'

'I don't think you should talk of the dead like that, comparing them to prankish spirits from the world of comedy; it sounds frivolous.'

Sinclair switched off the Television and started looking round the room while talking :

'Puck was an honest sprite; he never meant to hurt anyone; it was in his nature to be prankish—that could be an epitaph.'

'If you're looking for the car keys,' said Sebastian, 'I've got them. I borrowed the car to pick up some furniture.'

'Oh, good! I was toying with the idea of driving round to the neighbourhood where the victim's parents live.'

'Are you crazy? The place will be crawling with Police.'

'Not necessarily. They're probably inundated with calls from the public responding to the parents' emotional appeal for information on the News. Some telephone lines will be jammed for hours . . . Here's our chance. It'll make a welcome change from traipsing round building sites with a tin hat that feels too tight on me.'

'You mean, you've got so swollen-headed, it doesn't fit you any more?'

'You know, Barnard, one of the things I appreciate about you is your devastating sense of humour. It never fails to warm up the cockles of my heart.'

In the approach to the residential area where the victim's parents lived Sinclair slowed the engine right down and on seeing there were no bobbies on duty anywhere he parked the car close by, so they could keep their eyes focused on the house.

All the curtains on the ground floor were drawn. Upstairs, a single light shone in one of the bedrooms. The garage door was closed. The place looked deserted.

Briskly, Sinclair got out of the car and motioning Sebastian to follow him strode up to the front door and rang the bell.

A hand appeared round a curtain in one of the ground-floor rooms but it was too dark inside for Sinclair to see who was standing there, peering at them. After he rang the bell several times, the door opened and in the half light of the embrasure he recognized the burly figure of the victim's father, and held up his ID.

'Stewart Sinclair, private eye, currently on Inspector Blakeney's supplementary task force, and this is my assistant, Sebastian Barnard.'

'What do you want?'

'We'd like to take another look at your daughter's Ferrari. We understand it was driven back here after the body was found?'

'Forensics have already been over it.'

'I know; but new information has just come in regarding it which needs to be checked ; it'll only take a minute.'

'Very well, if you must, but please, make as little noise as possible; my wife is resting.'

Sebastian walked gingerly into the house in Stewart's wake, unsure of his own steps. He had not got the faintest idea what Sinclair was talking about, and thought that to be on the safe side he would take up the conventionally sturdy stance of a policeman on picket duty outside the garage door in the hall while Sinclair ostensibly checked out the mysterious information which most likely he had invented, while searching inside the car for the exceptional clue on which his solution of the murder probably rested. It was an anxious moment; there was very little he could do other than stare straight ahead past the victim's father's sullen gaze, taking comfort in the thought that Sinclair could not afford to linger for long on a lame excuse in such a place. And sure enough, about a couple of minutes later, he reappeared and made for the front door in a business-like manner, bidding the host goodbye.

'Well, thank you, sir. You'll be informed if anything transpires; often such tips come from time wasters.'

'Any luck?' asked Sebastian as soon as they got into the car.

Sinclair pulled out his mobile 'phone and handed it over to his assistant.

'What is it? The photograph's not very clear. I can't really perceive the objects on the garage shelf.'

'Yes, you can, Sebastian, look again! They're plainly visible though covered in dust.'

'They look vaguely like baby shoes.'

'They are baby shoes! And guess what, there's another one just like them inside the Ferrari, hanging from the rear mirror, a red one in pristine condition.'

'A baby's bootee as some sort of fetish! How sick is that?'

'No, no! Up the wrong pole. In this case, the bootee is not an object held in reverential awe irrationally like a fetish, but almost the opposite as a lucky charm to protect the owner against some form of devilment associated with early childhood,—the victim's own, I'd say. Now, as you've probably gathered, there were no pairs of bootees either on the shelf in the garage or inside the car . . .'

'The missing link! The murderer knew about the missing baby shoe!'

'Not so fast, Barnard! You're jumping to conclusions. Though the missing shoe may be an essential part of the anatomy of this murder, I think the case is much more involved than that and probably a lot simpler as well, linked to some pattern of infant behaviour in early childhood when bootees are put on babies' feet, rather than to a phase in later life when the shoe becomes known to an adult as the ultimate sexual symbol.'

'But that raises problems in this case, doesn't it?'

'It certainly does, Barnard; but the central clue to this murder must remain the singular fact that although one shoe was taken from the murder victim, she was not sexually assaulted, indicating that the motive was not strictly speaking sexual and referring us back to the early part of the victim's life when she wore bootees which eventually ended up constituting a peculiar collection from which one bootee per pair was missing. And I can't say that I am thrilled at having been dumped into it. I know! I know! You meant well, but please don't do it again. I don't particularly enjoy this case.'

Sinclair started the engine. As the car moved away, Sebastian casting a look at the house thought he saw a curtain being drawn back in one of the upstairs bedrooms.

'It looks as though your visit to the garage may have been worth waking up the wife . . .'

'I think he very much depends on her as a staunch helpmate, don't you?'

Sebastian could see that Sinclair's mind was engaged elsewhere and there was little point in elaborating on the relationship just for the sake of making polite conversation because the atmosphere had become somewhat tense. Perhaps Sinclair was sore at having to play second fiddle to Inspector Blakeney who was in a hurry to make an arrest and end his career on a good note.? Perhaps he did genuinely dislike the case; Sinclair was not without his pet aversions as a detective, nor without quirks, such as considering everybody guilty until proven innocent and probably this case aroused too many of his secret antipathies, such as they were. He was on the whole a very secretive man despite being voluble whenever people's psychological motives excited his curiosity about the criminal mind. Whatever chafed him in this case, he kept it close to his chest.

Two questions about the murder were currently on everybody's lips. One was, had the missing shoe been found, and the other, why had the murderer removed it from the body? The question Sebastian was itching to ask Sinclair was, What did he think about the discovery he had just made in the garage at the victim's parents' house? It seemed impossible he did not feel inclined to comment about it. He had got quite excited on the spur of the moment, and yet, as he drove along, he kept silent looking thoroughly disenchanted with the case.

'I know this case is not your cup of tea, Sinclair, but would you mind very much telling me what you think has happened to the missing bootees? Why are you keeping mum? Surely, their disappearance is primordial to the solution of this case?'

'I suppose one way of answering your question would be to say, only the murderer knows that, or someone close to the murderer, but that would be presuming a lot. I would prefer to say provisionally that they were mislaid or rather never retrieved in the normal way. Has it never happened to you to lose a glove on a bus or a train? I know the missing shoe has greatly excited the public's imagination because there appears to have been no sexual motive to the strangulation; and now I have given you that prosaic explanation, your own imagination may stop running away with you, for a little while anyway. Sorry to have disappointed you.'

Back at Sinclair's lodgings, Sebastian thought it expedient to compose himself right away for another session in front of the Television examining photographs on the DVD. It would have to be a quick one as he had to be back at the club for its grand reopening under the new management when he would be performing extended versions of the Geisha act in front of a larger audience. But, no sooner had they settled down that news broke through about Inspector Blakeney having arrested a man and keeping him in custody for questioning following an anonymous call from a woman whose conscience had been nudging her ever since she watched the distressing appeal to the public made by the murdered girl's parents on Television. An ex-boy friend of hers, who was a night-watchman at a book store near the property where the murdered girl lived, was a self-confessed voyeur and lately, before she broke up with him, he had boasted about keeping his binoculars trained on a `saucy' girl, who did a striptease for her boyfriend in front of a window.'

Sinclair threw his hands up in the air. `First a stalker, and now a voyeur! A stalker is never a voyeur and vice-versa! Come on, Barnard! There's not a moment to lose. Back to the parents' house!'

`Are you mad? To-night is the grand re-opening of the Sailors' Club. I'm due there in two hours' time; my make-up's got to be flawless.'

`Is that all you ever think about? How great you look? What about the naked truth? Because you're about to get a dose of that, plain and unadulterated, and it won't be pretty. A minute ago, you were miffed because I held out on you; here's your chance to hear all about it. Get set!'

`Oh, no, please, Sinclair! They're plain, ordinary people. Your sophisticated tirades will be lost on them!'

`I don't think so, `Buddy'. Move it!'

The drive through the early evening rush hour was hair-raising. Sebastian's hands kept flying to his face in a protective gesture which exasperated Sinclair. Back at the house, noticing that there were still no policemen on duty, Sinclair parked right outside the front door and jumping out of the car put his finger on the buzzer, and kept it there until the victim's father answered the call, whereupon he rushed in, brandishing his ID like a scimitar, with Sebastian in tow.

`You knew your daughter's killer many years ago. He was in your employ as a caretaker over a long period of time. That's how well you knew him, and he knew you, and your daughter.'

The old man flinched and for a moment staggered on the threshold before regaining his composure and letting them in.

`He knew your daughter was a mischievous sprite almost from the cradle, and how much that used to upset you. Deny it.'

The victim's father made as though he wanted to sit down on a near by-chair in the hall when a noise upstairs attracted his attention. His wife was slowly coming down the stairs in her dressing-gown.

`Don't tell him anything, Gerry; he's a nobody. Let Inspector Blakeney handle it; he knows what he is doing.'

Sebastian felt his own knees buckling up as Sinclair proceeded, ignoring the woman:

'He was more like a friend, wasn't he? You trusted him and you chatted to him about all sorts of things like those niggardly vexations that test parents' patience when they have a child late in life and are perhaps not as resilient as people in their twenties or even thirties. He understood and he sympathized, and perhaps even offered advice, and you were grateful. Isn't that so?'

'Yes', whispered the victim's father before bursting into tears as his wife put her arms around him. 'Please Gerry, calm down. I told you not to tell him anything. He hasn't got a clue; he's just fishing.'

'Oh'. retorted Sinclair, 'talking of fishing, where are your daughter's bootees, the ones that matched those on the garage shelf? Did the dog bury them in the garden?'

'Dog? What dog?'. asked the wife. 'We've never had a dog. My husband is allergic to them.'

'I know, that's why he was dosed up to the eyeballs with anti-histamine tablets on the day of the Television interview just in case he came across a police dog by chance.'

'My daughter dropped them over the side of the pram', whispered the father. 'It was a tiresome habit she had. There was nothing I could do to stop it. We were only trying to keep her feet warm, for God's sake.'

'And you never tried to recover any of them?'

'What was the point? She had an infuriating way of doing it when I least expected it, as though she were watching me to pick the right moment when my attention was engaged elsewhere. In Winter, when it got dark early, I didn't have the time to retrieve my steps and go in search of the missing bootee . . .'

'And when you arrived back home, the caretaker was there to commiserate with you and tell you not to worry; it was only a phase and the child would grow out of it. He'd take the remaining bootee and store it in the garage along with all the other odd ones, like a relic. But, she didn't grow out of it, did she? Despite all those prestigious achievement awards, the high-flying works manager went on being mischievous; she couldn't help it; it was in her genes. So you hung a red bootee on the rear mirror of the Ferrari you gave her for her twenty-seventh birthday as a talisman to protect her against her prankish nature. Then one day, suddenly out of the blue, someone enacted your own worst nightmare; they put their fingers round your daughter's neck and squeezed it a little too hard to make her understand she had to stop teasing men for fun, out of mischief.'

`Preposterous!', exclaimed the victim's mother,`Sheer conjecture! I'm calling the Police.'

`You'll do nothing of the kind, Madam. I am, we are, with the Police. Besides, at the moment, they have their work cut out for them. Where was I? Ah, yes! To explain fatality, some people are fond of saying `What goes around, comes around.' Possibly. there is some truth in that and the inordinate grief you showed on Television seemed to confirm that you at least accepted the idea that Nemesis, the goddess of retributive justice, had struck, and you would have given anything to have your daughter back as she was in her pram with all her playful mischieviousness so you could shrug your shoulders and make light of it wholeheartedly. People who are religious also say that the tears of repentance and regret for past misdemeanours bring a renewal of spiritual life. I sincerely hope they're right so that when you see sitting in the dock across the courtroom the man you confided in all those years ago you'll keep a steady gaze. Remember, he didn't rape your daughter ; he had his dignity; he just left his signature on an accident that was waiting to happen by removing a shoe. I'll convey congratulations from you both to Inspector Blakeney. Good day. Thank you for your time.'

Back in the car, Sinclair looked as though he were searching for something in his pocket.

`Don't tell me you've nicked a baby boot from the basket in the hall? There were heaps!'

`Of course not, Barnard! I was looking for a handkerchief to mop up my brow.'

`Yes, things were rather hectic in there, weren't they? Here, use mine.'

FINIS

THE DAY
THE PYRAMIDS
CLOSED DOWN

The Day The Pyramids Closed Down

The day had started well for Sebastian, with time on his hands to savour his personal situation. Sinclair was away on holiday in Egypt; furthermore, following the huge success of the extended Geisha act at the refurbished Sailors' Club, offers from club managers in other parts of London were coming in, promising a more prosperous future and confirming his belief that the Geisha act was not just any old drag act. There was an added quality to it, as Sinclair, tight-lipped though he was, admitted in his more loquacious moments when his natural nobility of feelings was not denied by a flow of invectives against the frailties of his fellow creatures, from which Sebastian was spared at present for a lull which promised to stretch ahead into an appreciable period of time.

If travel brochures and commercials on Television were anything to go by, there was plenty in the land of the Pharaohs to keep Sinclair interested, not to mention the unusual quests that his own erudition would undoubtedly suggest to lure him far and wide across the region; and he would come back full of quaint anecdotes illustrating the ancient Egyptians' genius as builders and promoters of lofty religious ideas, such as the after-life. Already Sebastian had received a collection of postcards with enthusiastic comments, confirming his feeling that Sinclair was enjoying Egypt so much that he was in no hurry to return; and he personally could relish the moment.

A message which his father had left on his answer 'phone did not succeed in spoiling his mood, though he did wonder why the old man suddenly bothered to contact him. Was he in for another homily about the way he was wasting his gap year, hanging around seedy night clubs and making an exhibition of himself in female clothes in front of a lot of grinning nincompoops from the sub-continent?

'Why aren't you in Egypt with your mate, the detective? As a future archaeologist, it would be an invaluable experience', said the message when he had the courage to listen to it. The answer was swift and to the point: 'Because I didn't enjoy being shown mummies in the British Museum that looked like death warmed up when I was a child.'

That seemed to settle the matter; his father did not bother to reply, and everything looked rosy again, except, at lunch-time, there were disturbing news on Television about unrest in Egypt; protesters against the regime of the dictator who had governed the country for the past twenty-five years had taken to the streets in Cairo, destabilizing the region. 'Well, that's that, Father!' thought Sebastian. Then came a message from Sinclair, saying 'Need you here. Law and order breaking down; riot police out.' followed by another which confirmed the first one : 'crime rampant; they've closed the pyramids. Hurry.'

Sebastian flopped down on a chair. Outside, the London traffic flowed past the window with the regularity of a sequence in a film; it didn't seem fair he had to be wrenched from its normality at a moment's notice to be plunged into political turmoil abroad. What on earth had possessed the Egyptian people suddenly to erupt against a dictatorship which they had tolerated for decades? Some cynics said the Muslim brotherhood was fomenting the revolt; others the Americans who had put the dictator in office in the first place to safeguard their interests in the Middle East, and others still hinted at some even more machiavellian machination, involving the Egyptian army which was in the pay of the United Nations! It sounded like a messy deadlock.

Why Sinclair couldn't recruit help on the spot, emulating Sherlock Holmes who on a number of occasions used a gang of little 'street arabs' to assist him, was difficult to understand; the streets of Cairo must have been crawling with them.

Looking round the room dispiritedly Sebastian espied the Geisha outfit which was hanging from the top of the wardrobe. It had been to the cleaners in preparation for the next series of performances and looked beautiful in its pristine condition. Without wasting any more time, Sebastian sent Sinclair a text message which said : 'Deal. Geisha in luggage. Catching first flight out.' to which he got an immediate response : 'Customs officials open to decent size bribe. See you at the hotel'.

That last sentence sent a chill down Sebastian's spine. Either Sinclair was on to something which had the hotel as its theatre of war and he couldn't leave, or the streets of Cairo were jammed full of protestors, and there was no point in both of them risking to be pulled out of a taxi and molested. Even some BBC camera crew and reporters had been submitted to such treatment by angry crowds, hinting at some obscure grievance against the British, or simply collective, mass hysteria.

At Cairo airport, a man holding a placard with Sebastian's name on it was waiting outside the arrival gate. He took Sebastian's luggage without saying a word, and carried it to a near-by car. The blinds of the car were pulled down and Sebastian couldn't see who was in the car till he climbed inside and heard a voice say 'Hello, I believe you know my nephew, Stewart Sinclair? Any friend of Stewart's is a friend of mine. I work in one the museums of antiquity in Cairo. Welcome to Egypt!'

Sebastian heaved a sigh of relief. It was nice to know that the man who greeted him did not belong to the old school tie brigade like Charlie Davenport.

'What you are about to see on the way to the hotel is not very nice, but please do not judge the Egyptian people too harshly. They are not religious fanatics and the middle classes are politically educated and some of the working class as well. They're a great people.'

'They certainly have a great past', hazarded Sebastian who felt out of his depths.

'Yes, and their past does show that still to-day they're guided by commendable human aspirations about the kind of society they want to live in, which are not unlike those of their dynastic ancestors regarding the pleasures they wished for themselves in the after-life, avoiding servitude and being in authority. It's quite remarkable, really.'

'I am afraid I don't know enough to be in a position to comment, but I'm sure you're right; you've probably been here some years . . .'

'Yes, I have, most of my life. It was a kind of tradition in the family, Stewart's grandfather being an eminent Egyptologist, but I won't bore you with family history; your mind's probably on other things in the circumstances.'

The driver must have known the back streets of Cairo exceptionally well and much to Sebastian's relief the dreaded journey from the airport seemed shorter and less hectic than he anticipated.

'You, not coming in?' he asked.

'No', replied Sinclair's uncle, 'I'll let you two have a happy reunion considering you practically risked your neck to get over here.'

Sebastian was relieved to hear it. His main concern was to unpack the Geisha outfit as promptly as possible. He had folded it very tightly and compactly to make it fit in his travel bad along with his other articles of clothing so as not to arouse the curiosity of the Egyptian custom officials and avoid questions of the embarrassing kind.

'Welcome to the land of the Pharaohs!', exclaimed Sinclair, who was pacing in front of the hotel swing door. 'Have I got news for you!'

Sebastian looked nervously around him; the foyer of the hotel was packed with people; there weren't enough armchairs in the lounge to accommodate them all; some sat on their luggage while others lay sprawled out on the floor.

'What are all those people doing in the foyer? Is that a welcome committee?'

'No! Don't worry about them. They're stranded British tourists, waiting to be repatriated. The British Vice Consul will be here any minute to give them their marching orders. Nice chap, a bit overbearing . . .'

'Like Charlie Davenport? Heaven helps us!'

'You never did take to Charlie in Uganda, did you?'

'No; I found him insufferable. By the way, you never told me you had an uncle in Egypt . . .'

'Should I tell you everything? You're pretty cagey yourself when it comes to family relationships . . . Go and freshen up. I'll see you in the snack bar.'

'Actually, I'd like to go to my room to unpack before we eat . . .'

'Don't tell me the customs men didn't confiscate the geisha outfit! You surprise me . . .'

'I didn't give them the chance, Sinclair.'

'And now you need Room Service to have it pressed! What do you think you're going to do with it anyway? Play a posh night club full of sophisticated Egyptians to take their minds off things?'

'Well, you never know; it might come in handy.'

The snack bar was empty. Those of the stranded tourists who were not in the foyer waiting for their marching orders had gone to the cinema in the hotel, where they were showing 'Death on the Nile', for lack of something better to do. Sinclair made his way to a table in a corner away from the bar where two waiters were preparing sandwiches—round the clock. Apart from cakes and bananas, there was nothing much else to be had as the hotel was overrun, not simply by unscheduled airline passengers but also by foreign correspondents who had to seek refuge indoors from the chaos outside and were watching events concealed behind curtains, like furtive double agents.

Sinclair felt he owed Sebastian an explanation.

'Let me tell you why you're here. There's obviously a lot more going on than meets the eye and one can only hope that soon all will be revealed, because at the moment one only has the wildest speculations to go by, fuelled by shock and dismay. It is as though the whole world were holding its breath, waiting on events while Egypt descends into chaos, which leads one to believe that the corridors of international diplomacy must be buzzing as to who will make the first move to stop it without compromising its political influence in the region.'

'Please, come straight to the point, Sinclair. You know I am not interested in international politics. Why am I here and not the street arabs you could recruit at any street corner?'

'Well, yes; I would normally recruit the type,—if I were working here, which I'm not, I mean on a case. I have been caught by events, Sebastian, and find myself in a quandary.'

'How's that?'

'All the jail birds or ex-cons I would normally employ in this country to solve a case have been released from prison to create a party of fanatic supporters agitating in favour of the hated dictator the Egyptian people want to oust; it's obviously a desperate measure for him and his government to stay in power. Those men are thugs; they will stop at nothing, and there's every chance that scuffles will turn into bloody clashes, but you see my predicament; it's created a shortage of man power.'

'I love the way you put it! And, if you don't mind my asking, how would you have recruited those thugs in the first place?'

'Oh, that's easy; through my uncle who knows all the prison governors in the land.'

'What exactly does your uncle do in the Cairo museum?'

185

'He's the head of the papyrus department. Some of the papyri go back as far as the XIth dynasty when they were first introduced into funerary rites out of compassion for the not so rich. Inscribed pyramids, sarcophagi and coffins were expensive and only wealthy people could afford them, but a roll of papyrus from the papyrus swamps round the Nile did not cost much, and if a man could not afford the services of a professional scribe, he could write his own copy of *The Book of the Dead* on the papyrus to be put in his coffin, as required by religious custom. My uncle is an expert; he knows what he is talking about, and he is much respected in the international community in Cairo. Some of the papyri in his keeping are outstandingly beautiful, describing the funeral service of mummified persons according to the rites prescribed in *The Book of The Dead* in a colourful way which is as pictorially brilliant as anything one sees in burial chambers inside Pyramids.'

'Good for you!'

'I don't see what you have to be peeved about . . .'

'Where do I fit in is what I'd like to know.'

'It's not possible for me to answer that question with any precision precisely at this very minute. It is feared that some of those thugs which have been either paroled or pardoned by the regime will take advantage of the disturbance and sneak away to some underground hiding-place such as the Pyramids to resume their criminal activities.'

'But the Pyramids have been closed! You said so yourself, to put pressure on me, I suppose . . .'

'My dear boy, tomb raiders have been getting in and out of pyramids from times immemorial; it's become a national institution and most antique dealers know where to find their contacts.'

'I know. Even Tutankhamen's tomb was broken into.'

'That's not in a pyramid, Sebastian. Tut was buried in the Valley of Kings, near the ancient city of Thebes, miles away from here. Why are you sniggering?'

'It reminds me of something. When I was at school at the French Lycée in London—under sufferance, I might add—we would joke about 'Où-Quand-Comment', la célèbre momie égyptiennne'. Do you get it?'

'Ya, ya, I do! Don't you dare come out with such silly jokes in my uncle's presence; I'd lose all credibility. Well, think about what I've just said and give me one good reason why I should walk away whistling down the wind.'

Sinclair moved closer to Sebastian as people started drifting back into the snackbar.

'Actually, to put you fully in the picture, I have been approached by an unknown source whom I suspect is a friend of my uncle's to keep an eye on the Antique market, without seeming to, you know, as a tourist, with a view of spotting any object, however small, likely to be a national treasure recently stolen from a royal grave, officials from the Egyptian Antiquities Service being too conspicuous. I thought this might be the sort of thing you would enjoy . . .'

'What, in the midst of a bloody revolution?'

'You're very young to get set in your ways . . .'

Sebastian scrambled to his feet and claiming that bananas gave him a headache made for his room. The weight of Sinclair's erudition and that of his uncle, combined with the lethal combination of sugar and starch in the banana, was proving a little too much for his delicate stomach. Fortunately after lying down on the bed a while, the sight of the Geisha garment hanging from the top of the wardrobe brought its own brand of medicinal relief. He promptly removed it from its polythene cover and slipped it on and was thinking that it was as delightfully elegant and seductive as any Tutankhamen might have worn when the light went out. Thinking there was a power cut as a result of the political mayhem at the centre of Cairo, he went outside to check, but the lights were still on in the passage and over the stairs, and in the semi-darkness he thought he saw a figure slinking away into the shadows. Returning to his bedroom, where the light had come back, he looked up at the bulb overhead and shrugged his shoulders; the revolutionary situation was obviously affecting every aspect of daily life in the Egyptian capital, including standards of hotel management. He then went over to the window to draw the curtains in case his donning the Geisha outfit had attracted the attention of some local peeping-tom without political conviction, and looking down casually at the pavement below, he thought he saw the car belonging to the chauffeur of Sinclair's uncle parked on the corner, but he was not sure as in the semi-darkness one car looked pretty much like another, especially in a foreign country where one feels out of one's depths. Maybe, some affluent patrons of the hotel were being evacuated on unscheduled, chartered flights, friends of Sinclair's uncle who seemed to have contacts all over the world. By then, he felt jaded; the light-hearted mood that had possessed him all and truly gone in a flash, extinguished like the light in a faulty bulb, and, putting the Geisha garment back in its protective cover, he went to bed.

He did not sleep well and Sinclair who was his usual boisterous self first thing in the morning marvelled at it.

'I would have thought after all the excitement of the journey to a place that had the eyes of the world glued to Television screens round the clock, you would have gone out like a light.'

'Ah, ah! very funny, Sinclair, but let me tell you that your peculiar sense of humour does not go down well at this time of morning. The power cut at the hotel last night upset me.'

'Power cut? What power cut? I stayed up chatting to journalists and never noticed.'

'What was your uncle's chauffeur doing parked outside the hotel last night? Was he spying on me?'

'How do I know? Maybe he was picking up a late fare to take them to the airport. Travel arrangements are pretty chaotic at the moment, as you know.'

'Does he not work full time for your uncle?'

'No, of course not! My uncle couldn't afford it; he's a man of modest means. You know what those scholars are like; so long as they can keep their heads buried in valuable documents, they're happy; they don't need all the perks business people are after.'

'Did you by any chance come up to my room late last night to check if I was all right?'

'No, Sebastian! I've just told you! I got involved in discussions with chaps from the News Agency. I don't know what's come over you. I think you have been reading too much rubbish about the vengeance of the Pharaohs that was associated at one time in the popular mind with the discovery of Tutankhamen's tomb, such as all the lights going out in the Continental Hotel in Cairo at the precise moment Lord Carnarvon died there from a mosquito bite turned septic, a result of the curse of the Pharaohs. Next you'll be telling me that you heard a dog howling to death in the distance just as Lord Carnarvon's dog did thousands of miles away, in England, at the exact moment his master died, dying immediately after. It is enough to give anybody bad dreams.'

'As a matter of fact, I did hear a dog barking in the distance, if you must know everything; it sounded as though it had been tied to a post and abandoned . . . I suppose I feel out of my depths here. I've never been

188

interested in politics; and my father put me off Egyptian mummies at an early age; he just could not wait to take me to the British Museum so I could share his kind of thrills as an archaeologist. I'd rather he had taken me to see *Cinderella* or *Puss in Boots* or even *A Midsummer's Night Dream.*:

"What angel wakes me from my flowery bed?"
"I pray thee, gentle mortal, sing again :
"Mine ear is much enamoured of thy note
"So is mine eye enthralled to thy shape."

`It's lovely, don't you think?'

`Come on, Titania! Don't be an ass! Pull yourself together; there's work to be done, and wipe that mournful expression from your face. No tourist in search of souvenirs goes about looking as dyspeptic as you do.'

According to the latest news bulletin, the bulk of the protesters remained firmly entrenched in Tahir square, shoulder to shoulder; the rest of the town seemed relatively quiet. That was considered an advantage by Sinclair who had been given a list of antique dealers with shops mostly in back streets to permit discreet enquiries. Out of sympathy for Sebastian, he decided to start with the one nearest to the hotel.

The owner was just opening shop and as soon as he espied the two men, he pulled down the blind again, went back indoors, and then let them in by the side door, and there made a sign for them to follow him into a room at the rear.

`Ii does not do these days to be seen dealing with American tourists', he said by way of an apology

`We're British, not American.'

`It's all the same unfortunately at the moment. Were you looking for anything in particular?'

`What my friend had in mind', said Sinclair, `was something like an unguent jar in the form of an ibex; he's fond of animals.'

`Oh, I've got nothing like that at the moment. I've had to send a lot of my most valuable stuff away in case of looting. though I don't think my compatriots would ever descend to such depths of depravity. It's the others that worry me.'

`What others?'

`You know, the jail birds the hated dictator has let out of prison to agitate on his behalf. They're hardened criminals; they'll go on the rampage.'

`Do you think they're likely to rob burial chambers?'

`They'll stop at nothing, and then they'll plant the stolen goods on us honest dealers for us to harbour them while they deal in illegal trafficking from some secret hiding-place. That's what happens when law and order break down. Many of my colleagues live in fear and trembling of such a thing happening, We daren't join the demonstrations and show our faces.'

`But, if they are ruffians, how can they possibly gauge the value of the objects they steal?'

The dealer looked nervously in the direction of the shop front and bending down he whispered :

`There are plenty of experts in high places willing to enlighten them and put a price on those objects to get their cut. Here, take this reproduction in glass paste of a winged scarab, symbol of resurrection. That what Egypt needs.—rebirth under a new independent government, not sold out to any foreign power. Take care how you go. A lot of money is being made out of foreign tourists nowadays as hostages.'

After they had walked down the street a few yards, they looked over their shoulders to see what the dealer was doing, but the blind was still down.

`What do you think?', asked Sebastian.

`The man looked nervous; I think he has good reasons to. It seems to me there's wide scale corruption; always has been in that line of business. Quite honestly, I don't see the point of carrying on with this enquiry; they'll all say more or less the same thing. I think we had better go back to the hotel and wait on events; the situation must evolve. You can't have a country held at ransom by its people for an indefinite period of time, no matter how well-meaning they are and how legitimate their motives; supplies will run short; diseases will be rampant One has the awful feeling that the Great Powers are watching from the corridors of international diplomacy like actors in the wings waiting for their queues.'

No sooner had they reached the hotel than scenes of violence appeared on Television for the first time. The newly-released convicts mounted on horses and camels were caught on camera charging the peaceful demonstrators and hitting them right left and centre with batons and other blunt instruments, followed by groups of the dictator's supporters, marching locked together arm in arm. People were running away screaming,—men, women and children. And still the world held its breath, as though that was some sort of a play with a cryptic plot that had to be watched to the end in complete silence for lack of clues. The dead were immediately dubbed martyrs and the next day appointed for their funeral, regardless as to whether they were Moslems, Christians or Jews, though no one knew what the next day would bring; and Sinclair, like many of the foreign correspondents who were sheltering inside the hotel, abstained from making predictions.

The following days brought very little change in the behaviour of the protesters' crowds ; if anything they seemed bigger and louder. Photographs of the martyrs who had died for Democracy were held high over the crowds' heads as relatives paraded them on placards decorated with wreaths through Tahir square, which remained the epicentre of the political storm. The talk was all about brutality, how the Police had joined the ex-convicts and bludgeoned those who kept clamouring for the dictator's immediate departure from the country.

When Sebastian was not glued to a Television set in the hotel lounge, he spent time in his room striking pretty positions in front of the mirror to see how he could improve the Geisha act, still clinging to the hope that he would do a Cabaret number in a smart night-club in Cairo. Sinclair was not happy. Every time he suggested to Sebastian that he should come out with him to a safe vantage point near the hotel, where a Chemist's shop had been converted into an emergency first-aid post, he made the same lame excuse about the sight of blood making him faint. Fearing that things might get suddenly worse, and they would be unable to go out at all for fresh air, he told Sebastian over breakfast that he was no longer willing to take `no' for an answer; immediately they finished eating, they were going out together to watch the demonstrators.

`I know of a good vantage point where there are families with young children; you can chat to them.'

They had not been watching the crowds for long when Sebastian cried out :

`Look, it's the antique dealer!'

`Where?'

191

'On that photograph over there coming our way. He's been killed! He's among the martyrs!'

'You're right! But how come? He was never a political activist. He said he daren't show his face among the demonstrators, neither did his colleagues . . . He's been assassinated! This is one easy way of accounting for dead bodies, is it not? I mean who's going to notice?'

'I'd say! Do you think he knew his life was in danger, and that's why he gave me the scarab as a symbol of resurrection?'

'It's very likely. He must have left instructions to his relatives of how to attract attention to his death since he couldn't take part in the uprising . . . I'm off to the Morgue just in case his killers dumped him there, where nobody is likely to claim his body. You can go back to the hotel, if you like. The Morgue is not for the squeamish.'

'No, I'll come with you but I'll wait in the entrance hall.'

At the Morgue, the Senior pathologist was not available. The junior pathologist claimed he knew just as much and could answer all queries adequately. Who wanted to know?

'Stewart Sinclair, private eye, investigating on behalf of the Egyptian Antiquities Service', announced Sinclair, pulling a notebook out of his breast pocket.

'What name?'

'Ahmed Hamad, antique dealer, suspected of the misappropriation of antiquities through the agency of necropolis thieves, depleting the national treasure'

'Did you know this man?', asked the pathologist, standing in front of the drawer that bore Hamad's name.

'We had occasion to investigate him recently regarding the illegal trafficking of Egyptian antiquities.'

'Well, whoever dealt with him did not do it the way they used to in the old days, with a few chops of the cane on his hands and feet . . .'

'What do you mean? The man was not a thief . . .'

'Take a look for yourself; it's not a pretty sight.'

Sinclair waited for the pathologist to slide the drawer outward and remove the sheet from the man's body; what was disclosed to his eyes then made him flinch. The whole of the abdominal cavity had been scooped out; the heart, the lungs, the kidneys—all of the soft tissue organs—had been removed. There were still traces of caked blood around the nostrils which led Sinclair to suspect that the brains had been scooped out through the nose and the convulsed grin on the victim's face suggested that he had seen the surgeon's knife coming before the anaesthetic had time to work.

'Thank you; that'll do', said Sinclair. 'There's no need to turn him over.'

'It's a wonder they left the head on', remarked the pathologist, sliding back the body.

'Actually, no. This is not a ritualistic murder, nor the work of a cannibal taking advantage of the social upheaval to give way to his depraved appetite. This is something else.'

'Gang warfare among robbers under cover of the revolution?'

'I doubt it. Would it be possible for me to take a quick look at the senior pathologist's report?'

'Of course. It's upstairs in my office. You can have see it on the way out'

'By the way, has anybody been to identify the body? Relatives, colleagues?'

'No, no one, not to my knowledge. But you have, haven't you? You gave me his name as Ahmed Hamad. He is Ahmed Hamad, is he not?'

'Oh, yes, most definitely. But how did you know his name?'

'A piece of linen was found lodged at the back of his throat with his name on it. Skilfully done, all of it, wouldn't you say?'

'Yes. Whoever did the surgery on the poor bastard knew what they were doing.'

After casting a glance at the senior pathologist's report, Sinclair joined Sebastian who was sitting bolt upright on a bench in the hall watching the entrance.

'Found him?', he asked.

'Yes. It wasn't a pretty sight; just as well you didn't come. Shall I tell you what I think? I think we've been barking up the wrong tree; worse still, I think somebody has sent us up the wrong path—with the sniffer dogs! because they need to act swiftly while the revolution is on and take advantage of the exceptional opportunities it offers to carry out their deadly trade, which is not the pilfering of royal tombs, is it?'

'No?'

'No; it's something else requiring far greater skills, and speed. I'm thinking aloud, you understand . . .'

'What you need is a strong cup of black coffee with plenty of sugar in it, over which you can sit quietly in the hotel lounge and collect your thoughts. I could do with one myself, actually.'

Back at the hotel, Sinclair tried to describe what he had seen at the Morgue in a slightly modified way so as not to discourage Sebastian; the shock of seeing the face of the antique dealer—a sincere, gentle and generous man—being paraded among the dead had been bad enough for him, especially as he had been put off mummies at an early age. Another factor of restraint was the fact that Sebastian had no real in-depth knowledge of the ethos of the ancient Egyptians other than that preserved in legendary anecdotes, and he was not sure that the boy would perceive the sense behind his own scientific deductions, which were founded on a sound knowledge of Egypt's historical past; and yet the rationality of it all was staring him personally in the face!

'You see, Sebastian, what finished to convince me that we had been barking up the wrong tree was the condition of Hamad's penis. According to the senior pathologist's report, it had not been tempered with at all at any time, and that was inconsistent with the other mummifying rites practised by the ancient Egyptians to which the poor man had been submitted to while still partly conscious.'

'Really?'

'In other words, the penis was useless; it had no market value. Are you receiving me?'

'I am trying . . . Wait a minute! The penis was worthless compared to all the other vital organs removed from Ahmed Hamad which fetched a lot of money on the black market for donors' organs! How about that?'

'Pretty close for an adjunct . . .'

'You would never have found out had you not gone to the Morgue, would you?"

'Oh, I don't know about that. It certainly would have taken a lot longer. The question is, Where do we go from here?'

'Why don't you have a chat about it with your uncle? He struck me as being an upright man, a great admirer of the Egyptian people's democratic aspirations. After all, he was instrumental to the enquiry.'

'That's the snag. My uncle is getting old. He's been under a lot of stress lately worrying about the safety of the invaluable documents he has in his custody at the museum. I wouldn't want to add to his worries by hinting that some Egyptians are not as upright as he thinks they are.'

'You could say you're concerned about his welfare in these anxious days . . .'

`Yes, I think I will pay him a visit and you must come with me and get him to show you some of the beautiful papyri he has in his custody.'

Sinclair kept stirring sugar in his cup while gazing in the far distance and Sebastian could see he was dithering.

`When I was a child, whenever something I couldn't understand worried me, my mother would pick me up and say a nursery rhyme, always the same one :

`Pussy cat, pussy cat, where have you been?

I've been to London to see the queen . . . .'

`Pussy cat, pussy cat', that's me. `Where have you been? I've been to Cairo to see my uncle Bill.

`Pussy cat, pussy cat, what did you see there?

`I saw a mouse hiding under a chair.'

`A mouse? Something small and insignificant as compared to a larger rodent, something grey . . . Under a chair? What kind of chair? A royal chair, a seat of authority, the seat of a university professor, or a judgment-seat? I don't like the parallels, Barnard . . .'

`You mean, your anxiety may relate to somebody humble with grey hair, who is in a position of authority, hiding under a professorial chair?'

`Or a throne in the Judgment Hall where people's hearts were weighed in the balance before they were admitted into the presence of Osiris, king of the dead . . . Oh, Sebastian, I can't bear the thought of it!'

`Come on! Let's go and see your uncle. You cannot let your fears undermine you just now; you must confront them. Maybe you're sickening for something. It wouldn't surprise me in this polluted atmosphere; I haven't seen a sanitary vehicle since I joined you here.'

`Oh, I know! A cat must do what a cat must do,—chase a mouse hiding under a chair with a view of catching it. Please, don't rub it in."

Sebastian thought Sinclair's uncle looked a lot older and thinner than when he had first met him. He dragged his feet as he moved along between rows of showcases and his hands on which he wore white gloves shook as he pointed to the colourful papyri inside them, most of which described the judgment of the dead by Osiris, king of the dead, that took place soon after death, when those who were not condemned were depicted entering Osiris's kingdom where they led a life of everlasting happiness which was a replica of the one they had known on earth by the banks of the Nile. Presently, Sebastian watched him shuffle back towards the entrance of the room where Sinclair waited, and he hoped that his own position by the last rows of exhibits was close enough for him to overhear if not all their conversation at least the best part of it.

'Well, how are you keeping, Uncle Bill, in the midst of this commotion?'

'These are anxious days but I am managing all right. I've been here pretty well all my life, you know.'

'Yes, I know.'

'And you two, boys?.'

'We're doing fine uncle. Now about the enquiry I was entrusted with. I've got bad news for you. One of the antique dealers whose name was on the list of suspects I was given has been murdered.'

'Murdered! Isn't that a strange word to use during a political uprising when people take their lives into their own hands? I have been watching the events in Tahir Square on Television and seen acts of police brutality that resulted in people's accidental death.'

Without seeming to, Sebastian began edging his way back between showcases till he came within earshot; Sinclair was on the warpath.

'No, uncle, Ahmed Hamad was not killed accidentally in a scuffle with the Police. His death was due to something else, utterly repugnant to any civilized person of any political party. You see, uncle Bill, everything about the condition of Hamad's body when I saw it at the Morgue tallied with that of a dynastic Egyptian after the disembowelment process required to ensure rebirth in Osiris's kingdom had been carried out by the embalmers, except for one thing'

'Oh, yes, and what was that?'

'His penis had not been treated so as to make it stand up in the erect position as a symbol of fertility as was the custom in those days. Why don't you come to the Morgue with me and see for yourself? And why the Morgue, anyway? Ahmed Hamad was a muslim; he should have been buried within twenty-four hours as required by Islamic law along all the other victims of acts of brutality committed either by the Police or the thugs the hated dictator let out of prison to form a posse of supporters. You could find out who the jail birds are since you are on friendly terms with most prison governors in the land, if you wanted to, uncle Bill.'

'Why, this is scandalous! Fancy taking advantage of a people's revolutionary zeal to commit such atrocities! Have you spoken to the Police about it?'

'No, not yet. I wanted to have a word with you first.'

'Well, I would advise caution. The role of the Police in this uprising has not been clearly defined. If I were you, I would wait on events to see which way the wind blows. Who knows? The Moslem Brotherhood may still make a move, backed by the people's army. Do we really know what goes on behind the scene? The Arab world seems to be on the move, first Tunisia, then this; one wonders who's next. It'll be interesting to see how the Syrians react. There was a time when people thought that Lebanon held the key to peace in the Middle-East.'

'All right, uncle Bill; I'll take your advice, but only because it comes from you, a blood relative.'

'I am so sorry it has turned out that way., Stewart. You see, initially I thought the enquiry would put a feather in your cap and ingratiate you with the authorities. Well, I was wrong. Never mind!'

As he rejoined the two men, Sebastian averted Sinclair's eyes; he looked devastated.

Outside the museum, they walked in silence and then Sebastian could contain himself no longer.

'What do you think? The old man may look frail and tottery, but he's as sharp as ever. I mean, look at the way he summed up the political situation!'

'I don't particularly want to think, Sebastian.'

'Well, if it's any help to you, let me remind you that according to your rule of thumb 'they're all guilty till proved innocent'.

'I presume you are referring to my uncle . . .'

'Isn't that what you hinted earlier on, which led us to visit your uncle?'

'Yes, Barnard, yes!'

'That he may have had something to do with Ahmed's horrific murder? Well, you're the detective.'

'It's not as simple as you think, even admitting I'd brush my own family feelings aside, it is in fact damned complicated. For instance, having noted a ritual anomaly with the condition of the victim's penis, ruling out some kind of macabre re-enactment of the embalmment process carried out in ancient Egypt, we find that Ahmed Hamad arrived at the Morgue with his name printed on a piece of linen which had been stuck at the back of his throat so he did not lose it. Now according to *The Book of The Dead* the most extraordinary precautions were to be taken to preserve the name of a person; unless the name of a person was preserved he ceased to exist. And the same thing happened if you forgot the name of the things around you, which seem to indicate that the ancient Egyptians knew a thing or two about dementia. Like the name of a man, the preservation of the heart of a man was held to be of the greatest importance. Chapters of *The Book of the Dead* were composed to prevent the heart of a man from being carried off in the underworld by 'stealers of hearts'. You must have seen vignettes depicting such dreadful hazards in the papyri my uncle showed you . . .'

'Yes I did, and some of them were pretty scary like the one where the deceased is depicted clasping his heart to his breast while kneeling before a monster in human form who holds a knife in his right hand.'

'So, you see, the journey to the Elysean Fields through the underworld was far from trouble-free even though a man had walked through the Judgment Hall, having passed all the necessary tests of worthiness.'

Sinclair paused and looked at Sebastian :

'When we came out of the museum, you made a remark about my uncle having all his faculties . . . I would like to qualify that by saying that the faculty of reason in him has become distorted partly through age and partly through isolation from the real world. Thus, Ahmed Hamad's heart was taken from him, an awful thing to do to a man, but this terrible loss was compensated by the fact that his name was preserved in such a way that he could not lose it in the underworld.'

'You mean, your uncle's mind is deranged?'

'I can find no other explanation. It was an aberration, of course, but in his troubled mind, as a scholar, it made perfect sense, obsessed as he was with the rationale of the ideological after-life of the ancient Egyptians . . . His being party to the illegal trading of body parts, carried out under cover of the revolution, which he knows to be wrong, becomes sanctified by the performance of some of the most important rites in the ancient Egyptians' funeral cult, ensuring the victim eternal life in

Osiris's kingdom to compensate him. I am afraid my uncle can no longer distinguish between phantasy and reality.'

'What are you going to do?'

'I don't know. I need time to think. I just want him to go quietly when the Police come for him. I may have to enlist the help of the British Consul. It's a terrible business. And I feel guilty for having neglected him, my own flesh and blood . . .'

'Do you plan on going back to the Morgue, to see if any more bodies turn up in the same condition as Ahmed's? Would that make it easier for you?'

'There won't be any. I bet you the word is out and they will be dumping them somewhere else, probably in one of the Pyramids that have been closed down.'

'You don't mean to say we shall be tracking down your uncle the way we did Professor Murray in Uganda, another old fogey?'

'No, Barnard, stop fretting; this is a totally different case and I know what I have to do. As I said, I just want him to go quietly when the Police arrest him, and I think I can organize this, if my surmise about what goes on at the scene of the removal of the organs is correct. Now, for all his political predictions, my uncle has no idea when this revolution is likely to fizzle out. What he may know is that I am, we are, on the warpath and time may be short . . .'

'Meaning there'll be an increase of executions?'

'Correct; the thugs in the dictator's party will round up another lot of victims in scuffles with protesters, and the surgeons, whoever they are, will have their work cut out for them. Now, if my hunch is anything to go by, my uncle is the grand master of ceremony who presides over the whole ghastly performance. I believe the French have a word for it . . .'

'Yes, they call it Grand Guignol. Funny sort of Punch and Judy, if you ask me.'

'So, we must put him on twenty-four hour surveillance and the minute we see him leaving the museum with a heavy bag, we must follow him. He'll be on his own; the others, the crew, will already be at the venue, wherever that is. Obviously, the fact that law and order have broken down, that nearly all of Cairo's population is now concentrating in Tahir Square makes things a lot easier for those people to carry out their evil trade.'

`Why would your uncle be carrying a bag? Surely, with his shaky hands he wouldn't be able to handle surgical tools?'

`Oh, no; the bag would be full of clothes, Egyptian clothes like the ones worn by some of the characters depicted in the papyri my uncle showed you at the museum; he would don them to enact a part and if my surmise is right about him being a megalomaniac, it would be a very important one. What we need to do now is to call at the British Consulate; I expect there'll be queues outside . . .'

`But you will only have to whisper the magic word, Harrow, or Westminster, or whatever, and hey, presto! somebody will be along to help you.'

`You can jeer as much as you like, but what I have at heart here is my uncle's welfare. I want an assurance from the British Consul that as an eminent Egyptologist the old man will be treated with dignity when the Police raid the premises, and he'll walked straight into the arms of a psychiatric nurse. Do you read me?'

`Perfectly.'

Time was passing slowly for Sebastian. From where he sat at the British Consulate, he could see Sinclair in conference with the consul and two Egyptian Police officers; presently a fourth man joined them, who gave his name as Zaky Zayed, a tank commander whose appearance did nothing to allay Sebastian's discomfort with the whole scheme. Was it right that in the tense political circumstances the time of all those officials should concentrate on devising a plan to save the face of a potential criminal in an unbalanced state of mind, just because he happened to be a relative of Stewart Sinclair's as well as an eminent Egyptologist? The answer was a dubious one . . . Furthermore, it showed that Sinclair's poise was indecorously affected by a guilt complex when in fact he had nothing to reproach himself with regarding his responsibility for his uncle's welfare since the two of them were not close; in fact, Sinclair had never mentioned that he had a close relative in Egypt; and the more Sebastian thought about it, the more he was tempted to suspect that Sinclair was ashamed of his uncle and that the whole scenario he had concocted to save his uncle the shame of being arrested like a common criminal was in fact destined to save his own face. Was the old man as crazy as Sinclair had led him to believe, even if he were obsessed with the embalming rites of the ancient Egyptians? The whole ideology of the after-life was pretty fascinating anyway with its colourful cortège of priests and musicians, both male and female, artists, dancers, scribes and architects, not to mention the lofty principles which had pervaded the moral life of the people of Egypt from times immemorial. The death industry had provided employment over generations,. contributing to the peace and stability of the social life of all manners of class. Of course, the British Consul had ethically speaking no alternative but to comply to Sinclair's request for an humanitarian, face-saving raid on the premises wherever to save his uncle's face; William Sinclair was probably the oldest resident in the British colony in Cairo, as well as the most cultured and erudite, maintaining invaluable links between the two nations.

Suddenly, there was a clatter of chairs. The consul was the first one to rise; he shook hands with the Police officials; the tank officer put his beret back on his head and walked out. It was all over, except Sinclair was the last one to leave. He was probably reminiscing about the good old days and Sebastian thought he had better wait outside where people were still queuing up, anxious to find out about their prospects.

`Well?', asked Sebastian when Sinclair appeared.

`Spot on! Harry couldn't have been more co-operative. It's all arranged. The Police will drill their men not to start raiding the place till I have enacted my scenario and my uncle is well and truly out of harm's way; the tanks will surround the place but they won't fire on anyone trying to escape. I can't tell you what a relief it all is! All we need to do right now is to initiate the twenty-four hour surveillance; but my feeling is we shan't have to hang around long.'

`And why is that?'

`Ever heard of the theory of the perfectibility of man, Barnard? Well, I don't believe in it.'

`Fingers crossed, then?'

`Fingers crossed.'

At dusk, the two men watched the lights go up one by one in Sinclair's uncle's house.

`Why so many?', asked Sebastian.

`My uncle's eyesight is not what it used to be; small wonder really when you consider he's pored over hieroglyphics all his life. It won't be long before they go out again; my uncle goes to bed early, so he says.'

`In that case, I had better steal a quick nap now.'

'Yes, things may hot up later on.'

Sebastian fell into an awkward slumber in which an old scurfy-looking cat played a prominent part. The cat had had an operation and though it spent most of its time perched on a garden wall, it was still very much part of family life, being present in most situations, including rides in the car. On one occasions, he was sitting on Sebastian's lap outside a night club full of Egyptian playboys where Sinclair was dancing with a beautiful girl.

A jolt on his arm brought him back to earth.

'What's up?'

'Nothing; that's the snag; it's well past my uncle's bedtime and the lights are still on. I smell a rat.'

Sebastian started looking for his torch which had fallen under the seat.

'Hang on! I think there's a signal coming through on my mobile phone. It's from Zaky Zayed, the tank commander I met earlier on. Stop fidgeting! Right! According to a colleague of his on duty in the pyramid area an unusual amount of traffic has been spotted on the road from Cairo to Giza, which is odd considering the Pyramids were closed to the public almost since the day the unrest started in the capital. Bingo! If they can't be loads of tourists, they can only be the organ robbers out to redouble their gains in one last desperate scoop. The question is, Where in such a vast area? I know tank commanders can, when they stand up in their turrets, survey the terrain far ahead of them, and all around. This line of traffic has to turn off somewhere. Send Zayed a signal asking 'What junction?' It's worth a try; the Army is with the people, against the dictator and his party. Go on, what are you waiting for? I'll drive.'

'Why don't you contact your old school friend, the British consul? I mean go through the proper channel. Surely he is keen to help with your uncle's 'diplomatic' arrest?'

'Leave Harry out of this, will you? My relationships are none of your business. Just do as you're told.'

They had covered about half the distance on the Cairo-Giza road when a message came back on Sinclair's answer phone saying 'Party report having veered at twenty-first pylon. No Army intelligence available.'

Sinclair slammed on the brakes.

'There are no long spans of electrical cables straddling this road. What's he on about?', asked Sebastian.

Sinclair did not reply; he just kept staring ahead in a daze.

'I'll tell you what he alluded to without the help of Army Intelligence . . .'

'Yes?'

'Yes, Barnard, and make a note of it for future reference in your archaeological note-book. A pylon, in recent use, is not just a gate tower; what is meant by it is a monumental gateway to an Egyptian temple. Having dealt with it as an architectural landmark, let me deal with it as a mystical object symbolizing one of the twenty-one secret gateways a dead Egyptian had to go through before entering Osiris's kingdom.

According to *The Book of the Dead*, the deceased had to stand by the side of each of the twenty-one pylons to justify his being worthy of going through to the next one. and the pylon would say 'Pass on, then, thou art pure.'

'A form of primitive audio-visual system to make up for the lack of electricity, I suppose?'

'Barnard, why is it that whenever I try and explain to you how lofty the spiritual conceptions of the dynastic Egyptians were, you have to come up with some inept comment of your own. I find this very discouraging at times.'

'This is obviously one of those times?'

'Yes, I am afraid, it is. Has it dawned on you that that message about the party having turned off the main Cairo-Giza road at the twenty-first pylon could only have come from my uncle? Nobody but him knew what it meant. Zaky Zahed couldn't work it out, not without the help of Army Intelligence which happened to be unavailable at the time. But my uncle knew I was likely to understand its esoteric meaning. He also knew I was coming after him, and perhaps in his heart of hearts he was relieved.'

'Oh, yes, I see. Sorry. Yes, it is upsetting; but what can you do? I mean, he is guilty, isn't he? And you are going after him, aren't you? I mean, there's no turning back now, not after having got the British Consul and the Egyptian Police and the Army to co-operate. and all that during a bloody revolution . . .'

Sinclair took his foot off the brake and let the car roll on.

'Well, let me tell you that to me that last message from my uncle is further proof of his derangement, and I am more than ever determined to go through the scenario which was elaborated earlier on to-day under the consul's aegis in order to save him from public disgrace. Let's put our heads together and try and de-code the message to find out at what junction we must turn off the main road in order to locate the site where the organ robbers will be perpetrating their atrocities.'

'What we could do with now is a gang of those 'little street arabs', you know, like Sherlock Holmes's 'Baker Street Irregulars' who could "go everywhere, and hear everything."'

'We're on the wrong stretch of the Nile here. You would have to be in the area west of Thebes to find urchins at the helm of a *felucca* waiting to ferry you across the river, or offering to take you to some secret spot bareback on a donkey to show you a souvenir pilfered from a royal grave which would be a forgery. But let's get back to our pylons. They were, of course, monumental stone structures, but what sometimes made them stand out even more in the landscape was the fact that some of them were gilt and they glittered in the sun or the moonlight.'

'They were covered with gold!'

'No, not exactly. They were painted over with electron which was an alloy of 75% gold, 22% silver and 3% copper, if my memory serves me right. Now, whether here my uncle has incorporated a material clue in his cryptic message to the tank commander, or he is, in fact, trying to mislead us as we are not in the right region of Egypt for monumental temple structures, I do not know, not omitting the fact, of course, that he is disturbed in his mind. Due to that factor, he may be referring to the twenty-first pylon as the last secret gateway a dead Egyptian had to walk through in ancient Egypt before entering the kingdom of the dead.'

The gruesome metaphor sent a shiver down Sebastian's back. He thought of all the victims which the ex-convicts had rounded up in recent clashes who were at the present moment awaiting the Ahmed Hamad treatment.

'Do you think your uncle anticipates being caught and getting killed?'

'It's possible. He has gone into a decline lately; he may be aspiring to eternal rest . . . Whether we shall at some point on the road see a glittering object telling us we're on the right track, is a remote possibility; all I hope is it becomes visible soon so we can advise the Police and the tank brigade where to take up their positions. As I have said before, my main concern is to secrete my uncle away before all hell breaks loose, wherever. Just keep your eyes peeled, Barnard. Think of all those poor bastards.'.

'Oh, I do, though I didn't see Ahmed's body at the morgue. It's difficult to imagine how all that could assume the appearance of a phantasy in an old man's brain, and one with a religious background to boot.'

It was now getting quite dark and Sinclair reduced speed to give Sebastian a better chance of spotting a likely clue among the desert sand, but the slower motion made him drowsy and he started nodding.

'All right, you drive and I'll run alongside the vehicle, but keep the lights dimmed.'

As he tried to work up a rhythm, Sinclair realized how unfit he had become through lack of regular exercise, and after a few yards he had to relapse into a fast walk, turning his head from right to left as he progressed in order to keep the prospect covered, which meant Sebastian kept getting ahead of him, leaving him in a kind of rearguard twilight zone. He was in the process of catching up when suddenly Sebastian slammed on the brakes.

'Look, over there! On top of that heap of sand, there are some objects glittering in the dark, all in a row.'

"With silver bells and cockle shells", sang Sinclair. 'Come on, Copycat! Don't just sit there gaping. Time's of the essence.'

Right beneath the camber of the road, there were deep tyre marks showing vehicles had turned off at that spot, and a little way onwards the two men came upon a substantial heap of sand crowned with twenty-one stones which had been dabbed over with gold paint.

'Look! The twenty-one pylons in miniature!', exclaimed Sinclair. 'Quick, send directions to the rescue squad while I walk on ahead to reconnoitre.'

To Sinclair, the sand mound looked suspiciously like the one which rested on the top of pit graves in pre-dynastic times, where bodies were buried in the contracted position, and he did not want Sebastian to see him worrying over its significance if indeed it were merely the clumsy simulacrum of a temple gateway. Beside it, Sinclair could see tyre marks stretching ahead into the darkness; they were all deep indicating that several vehicles had passed over them. The sense of isolation conveyed to him by the openness of the desert scene was overwhelming, as was. the feeling of his own vulnerability in such a location, which made him wish he had been near a necropolis sheltered by rocky peaks. Here, the spirits of all the hereditary enemies of ancient Egypt, not just the African and the Asian, seemed to have foregathered to plot revenge on the intruder.

'Spooky?', asked Sebastian as he rejoined the boss.

'I'd say! Let's get moving!'

The sound of tanks getting nearer sounded like that of magic flutes in Sinclair's ears. During the meeting at the Consulate, it was agreed that the tanks would scatter far and wide round the area in a kind of pincer movement to make it impossible for the criminals to escape. He and Sebastian had now got to a dip in the track where the tyre marks suddenly dived down a steep slope to come to an abrupt end in front of what looked like a door made of two corrugated iron sheets stood upright side by side. The police vehicles unable to carry on any further parked round the spot where the track took a downward dip. Looking overhead, Sinclair noticed that the roof which extended over the doorway at the entrance of what looked like an underground chamber of a primitive *mastala* type was also made of corrugated iron—all in all a shoddy affair. Seizing a piece of timber which lay around, Sinclair motioned the police to come down and all together they started using it as a battering ram to break down the door.

As the Chief of the Police prepared to use his loudhailer, Sinclair said:

'Let me handle this' and. grabbing the instrument he called out:

'Osiris William, I know thou art pure. Pass on through the twenty-first pylon into my everlasting kingdom. I am Osiris, king of the dead, and thou art an Osiris too. I know thee and I know thy name; pass on. Thou hast not fallen a prey to the devourer of the impure; thou shalt not become worms. Thou shalt not fall into rottenness; pass on, Osiris William. Thy name shall live for ever.'

A hush fell over the posse assembled outside the organ robbers' den. 'You could have heard a pin drop', was Sebastian's pedestrian comment as he stood ears pricked waiting for all hell to break loose. For a while nothing happened; then, all of a sudden, ending the ominous silence on the other side of the door, a metallic sound was heard like the tap-tapping of a walking-stick over a hard floor surface. The makeshift door opened and a slight bent figure appeared through what looked like an opening in a painted coffin chest stood upright to make an embrasure. Over a large white wig, the old man was wearing the *Aftef* crown of Osiris, and the stick which he used to steady himself under the weight of the apparel was a crook, one of the two traditional sceptres of Osiris, while in his other hand he held the other sceptre, the flail, all three insignias being emblematic of authority, dominion and sovereignty. Again, Sinclair picked up the loudhailer :

'Welcome to thee, Osiris William. I have sent Thoth and Anubis, to greet thee.'

At that precise moment, two psychiatric male nurses wearing respectively a falcon mask and the mask of a jackal came forward with extended arms, ready to enfold Sinclair's uncle into their embrace.

The old man kept advancing, leaning on the improvised stick, oblivious to the outside world. As the ambulance crew bent his head to get him into the vehicle, the *Aftef* crown fell off, causing the voluminous white wig to come adrift.

'Look, sir!', cried Sebastian, 'that's not your uncle; that's just an old man!'

The impersonator looked bewildered by the attention he was getting as two policemen handcuffed him and began interrogating him, there and then.

'I might have known!', cried Sinclair, 'Had he been my uncle he would have been wearing a large linen hairnet. A white wig is something of an anomaly to an erudite Egyptologist. The dynastic Egyptians worshipped youth, beauty, sex.'

As the Chief of Police shouted through the loudhailer 'You are surrounded. Come out with your hands above your head', pandemonium ensued. The men inside the building, frantic to get out, attempted to break down the opening where victims and would-be criminals alike were getting jammed in a horrendous mêlée. The sight of a tank appearing at the top of the slope stopped them just in time as casualties were about to get trampled underfoot by the stampede. Soon most of them had been sorted out into two groups :—those whose organs were about to be removed (the innocent casualties of Tahir Square) and those who meant to carry out the infamous deed for profit, under cover of the people's revolution.

Dazed, Sinclair walked about among the first group. Most of them had no idea what hideous fate they had just escaped. As they were pulled out of an affray in Tahir Square, some of them badly hurt, they were told that an impecunious, old, foreign film-maker needed extras to shoot a film near the pyramids. They were then loaded into trucks and driven away out of town under cover of darkness.

'The old man was obviously erudite', said one of them. 'though to most of us, what he said was double Dutch, but the pay we were promised was good, and we went along with it in good faith. We had a good laugh when he put on his costume for the main part,—that of Osiris, king of the dead. At that point we realized he was a bit cranky. It was all a lark, you understand, during a very dark, uncertain time. We had no reason to query any of it. Every time something happened, the old boy would say it was in the script and we accepted what he said. We just wanted to get the whole thing over and done with as quickly as possible, get paid and go back home to our families.'

'Is that what my uncle said when he heard me calling him on the loudhailer, that it was part of the script?'

'Yes.'

'And when he took off his costume and got one of you to put it on, and enact the part of Osiris?'

'Same again; we had no reason to doubt him.'

'Did he by any chance say where he was going?'

'He said he had to go outside to place himself behind the camera, in front of the set, and the costume was too cumbersome. Isn't that what they do in Hollywood, those actor/directors? People like Charlton Heston and Mel Gibson. Run backwards and forwards like lunatics, acting and shooting? We didn't think anything of it.'

'And when mayhem ensued?'

'We were convinced that it was all part of the script and he was out there in front with the camera rolling.'

Sebastian thought he had never seen such an expression of discouragement on Sinclair's face. The poor man could be heard repeating 'Unbelievable!Unbelievable!' as he walked about among the 'extras' questioning them.

'Excuse me butting in, Sir, the chief of Police wants a word.'

Reluctantly, Sinclair broke away from the rescued prisoners.

As far as he was concerned personally, the chief of Police considered his job done. All the potential murderers and illegal traffickers had been arrested; the wolves had been sorted out from the lambs, and he was taking the sacrificial victims back to Cairo in trucks under Police escort. He had liaised with the officer commanding the tank unit . . .'

'Zachy Zayed?' asked Sinclair.

'Yes; Zachy Zayed, that's our man. He agrees with me that our combined roles are over and he is pulling back. It is now up to the British Consul to deal with one of her Britannic Majesty's subjects who has lived in Egypt among us for many years. I hope you'll soon have news of your uncle. Good night.'

'Good night', said Sinclair, muttering 'God-damn-you' under his breath.

'Is there anything I can do to help, Sir?', asked Sebastian concerned at the unexpected bout of swearing coming from a man who seldom swore.

'No! My uncle's got away.'

'He can't have got very far in the desert . . .'

'How do you know? He had friends; he had influence. Why couldn't I see it?'

'See what?'

'That he would get away with murder, and make a fool of me?'

'You had his best interest at heart; he was not of a sound mind. I'll vouch to that.'

'And what weight do you think your testimony will carry, I ask you? Please, come to your senses, Remember where we are.'

Sebastian turned round and looked about him as the sound of the last truck died away in the distance and silence fell once more over the desert, broken now and then by the surge of traffic on the main road. The stars shone above the Pyramids evoking mystery and superstitious beliefs about their lay-out which, some said, had been inspired by three stars in the constellation of Orion, the hunter, considered to be the most magnificent in the sky.

'Do you think somebody did the dirty on you?' whispered Sebastian, alerted by Sinclair's reminder of their insignificance in such a place. 'I mean tipped your uncle and helped him to escape?'

'It's possible. Anything is possible during a revolution when both men's evil instincts and their more noble ones come uppermost.'

'The tank commander or perhaps the Chief of Police?'

'Why not Harry Battenberg, the British consul, while you're at it? You don't like public schoolboys, do you?'

'Well, if you ask me, all three of them had covert vested interests in the William Sinclair affair.'

'True, too true' replied Sinclair, nodding his head.

The sad expression on the boss's face prompted Sebastian to ask once more:

'Is there anything I can do to help?'

'Yes. Start the engine; we're going back to town. At first lights, I'll ask Harry to evacuate us on the next 'diplomatic' flight home. The cat does not always catch the mouse hiding under the chair.'

Having got the car on to the tarmac again, Sebastian was anxious to engage in small talk.

'Have you by any chance read a story by Conan Doyle called *The Ring of Thoth*? It's about an Egyptian mummy in a museum; it's quite a good story, though it has not got Sherlock Holmes in it.'

FINIS

CHARITY BEGINS AT HOME

Charity Begins At Home

'For a dream cometh through the multitude of business' (Ecclesiastes 5,3)

It was a beautiful quiet Spring evening in early March when Sinclair took advantage of the lingering light and the lack of wind to walk along the embankment with Sebastian on the way to the Sailors' Club. The two had not met since their hurried return from Cairo in the thick of the Egyptian people's revolution, and Sebastian felt loath to evoke those days in case the memory of his discomfiture still smarted in Sinclair's memory.

'Do you remember the young man I spoke to at the airport when we were flown home from Cairo with the other British evacuees?'

'Vaguely,' replied Sebastian relieved that Sinclair had no compunction about broaching the subject.

'He had a shock of curly hair like a lion's mane held together by a bandanna. Quite a striking sort of chap. Tall and athletic-looking. Swims a lot.'

'Yes, now you mention it. When you said a lion's mane I thought for a moment that perhaps you had temporary retirement in mind and you were making a subtle allusion to it by evoking *The Lion's Mane*, you know the Conan Doyle story in which Holmes comes out of retirement to investigate a horrible murder.'

Sinclair cast a quizzical look in Sebastian's direction.

'You're really into Doyle now, aren't you? Well, I'm very glad to hear it; one grade up on *Tintin* and his adventures. But why this idea of retirement? How did that come about?'

'I don't know. The disappointment over your uncle, I suppose. After all the trouble you put yourself through to ensure a dignified exit for him, I thought maybe you had become discouraged.'

'Are you, by any chance, trying to tell me obliquely that *you* have lost heart?'

'Oh, no, not at all.'

'Well, in that case, let me tell you a bit more about Daniel Blacker, the chap with the lion's mane. He's a humanitarian aid worker. He was in Haiti at the time of the earthquake. He's been all over the place in disaster areas as a volunteer tourist.'

'Good for him!'

'What's that supposed to mean?'

'You always know such amazing people, Sinclair. It makes one feel so small.'

.'Actually, I'm not so sure that Daniel Blacker qualifies as one of those 'amazing' people . . .'

'He can't be a public school boy then?'

'You have a bee in your bonnet about those, haven't you? Just because you've been to the French Lycée where everybody is equal according to the great principles of the Republic. Well, let me tell you that Daniel Blacker was a day boy; he attended a 'round the corner' school. There is something that puzzles me about him. He doesn't have to work; he can dedicate himself to his voluntary relief work, yet he always sounds so flush. Maybe, it's just talk. In the short time I spoke to him at the airport, he managed to tell me he had just bought a Lamborghini; he said I ought to go and try it some time . . .'

'You must be joking! A relief worker?'

'His father is a multi-millionaire; he owns a yacht; the boat's moored in Santa Lucia, in the Caribbean.'

'Handy for him in between natural disasters. He can sun-bathe stark-naked on the top deck. Tax free?'

'Probably. It makes me feel uneasy. Most charity workers look overworked and underpaid.'

'And will you?'

'What?'

'Put the Lamborghini through its paces?'

'I might. Just to draw him out. You know, out of curiosity. It is interesting to find out how the other half comes to terms with their conscience about being so exclusively affluent in the welfare society. It's like a protectorate.'

'All the same, you've got to hand it to him; he does give something back, other than in the shape of hand-outs and donations.'

'That's true . . . About the Lamborghini, when would he find the opportunity to use it is one of the questions I ask myself. I mean nowadays natural disasters occur at a faster rate. The tsunami in Shri-Lanka at the time it happened took everybody by surprise; it looked like an exceptional event. Few people even in the scientific community foresaw the kind of crescendo that has overtaken Natural occurrences since.'

'Maybe the Lamborghini is just a status symbol. He wants to know he still belongs to the Club despite his unusual occupation. Some social bonds are very compelling.'

'Listen, if I seduced a beautiful woman, would I want to keep her under a dust sheet?'

'Well, you would if you were a Muslim. I can see you're not prepared to deliver him a clean bill of health?'

'No, not really. I don't know what it is . . .'

'Could it be the hair? The abundance of it, compared to yours which is, I won't say thin, but just barely adequate, or the bandanna, maybe, to give that romantic South American guerrilla look? Should Charity workers look morose and emaciated?'

'Are you, by any chance, trying to tell me that I am getting disgruntled and crotchety and envious?'

'No, not exactly, but I think your self-confidence has been undermined by the events which surrounded your uncle's escape, and the thought of the people you trusted who winked an eye to make it possible. It must be hard to bear.'

'Setbacks are good for one; they strengthen one's determination to do better next time.'

The two men had arrived at the Club where the doorman was beginning to let people in sanctimoniously one at a time. Amused, Sinclair paused to watch for a moment and then, turning to Sebastian, he said :

'If I were to contemplate taking another holiday, considering the last one was such a fiasco, in the Caribbean, for instance, would you consider joining me? Your knowledge of French would be invaluable to me. Most islands out there like Haiti were French colonies initially and the natives still speak French among themselves, a kind of patois.'

'Ah, yes, like Baby Doc Duvalier, I've heard of him. After the earthquake, he went back to Port au Prince to be among his people, didn't he? Well, if I knew I could do a run of the yachts that are moored round the islands performing the Geisha act, I might consider investing in a pair of swimming trunks.'

'It would be a chance for you to find out the truth about *Vodou*. It's been misinterpreted in the West by the popular media, and vilified as a result. Personally, I find it connects well with some of the spiritual conceptions that the ancient Egyptians inherited from their African ancestors in pre-dynastic times. Furthermore, it upholds the fundamental tenet of Christian monotheism.'

'Oh, I don't know about that. It might induce some rogue voodoo priest who sticks pins through the hearts of little dolls made of bread dough to fashion one in a Geisha outfit . . . Thanks anyway for the offer. I'll think about it and let you know. Be careful when you put the Lamborghini through its paces. Some people say it's not as reliable as a Ferrari or a Porsche. I know such comments are inspired by jealousy, but just the same, take care.'

The task of avoiding the over-enthusiastic response of Chinese seamen elbowing outside his dressing-room to catch a glimpse of him in his natural condition, 'as God made him', soon erased from Sebastian's mind the travel prospects that Sinclair had conjured up, and not until next morning did they re-emerge with their exotic appeal as well as their risks. Knowing what an acerbated state of mind. Sinclair was in Sebastian intimated that developments were afoot. Sinclair would throw caution to the wind, eager to test his reticent response to Daniel Blacker's eccentric lifestyle, and he would waste no time in accepting the latter's offer to take the Lamborghini for a lap round the old Dunsfold air strip.

Sinclair having admitted of his own accord that his driving skills had been tested to the full on only two occasions,—once when negotiating the traffic in the evening rush hour in Milan, and the second time whizzing round the Concorde *rond point* in Paris, Sebastian was bracing himself up for a possible fiasco when a laconic text message appeared on the screen of his mobile 'phone which read 'Great news. Call me.'

'Well, how was it?' asked Sebastian, puzzled by the sobriety of the text.

'All right. Guess what?'

'`You lost it round the first corner of the old air strip?'

'No, I didn't!'

'You hit a bollard then?'

'No!'

'One of the tyres burst?'

'No! I found the name of the dealer who sold Blacker the Lamborghini inside the car! I'm on my way to the showroom. Want to come?'

'No; I can't stand car salesmen.'

'Don't be such a ninny. I'll do the talking. They won't even bother to look at you.'

'You mean, you'll apply the usual Sinclair intimation tactics? I can't do aggressiveness this early in the morning.'

'Oh, come on! Repressed aggression is part of the bargain pleas of daily life; it's a skill we acquired in the cave age or we wouldn't be here. Be real.'

It dawned on Sebastian that there was a modicum of rationality in Sinclair's voice which had not been heard for some time and that it would be wrong to discourage it.

'Oh, all right, then!'

At the showroom, the sales manager came forward with the suave manner typical of a debonair Mayfair dealer, but the brusque Sinclair approach soon took the wind out of his sails.

'Stewart Sinclair, private eye, and this is my assistant, Sebastian Barnard. You had a Lamborghini here in the window not so long ago. I've got the registration number with me. I'd like to see the sales record of the past six months, please.'

The manager bit his lip.

'Actually, Sir, the sale of that particular model was not registered in the usual manner.'

'No?'

'No, Sir.'

'And why was that?'

'The gentleman who bought it paid for it cash.'

'Cash! Do you mean in wads of bank notes?'

'Yes, Sir, that is precisely what I mean. We didn't want to sell him the car in the first place.'

'No?'

'No; he didn't look the part.'

'No?'

'No, Sir; his style of dress was—what shall I say—unconventional; not the kind we are accustomed to in this salesroom . . .'

'But, when you saw the stacks of bank notes in the suitcase, you changed your minds?'

'That is correct, Sir. It was a difficult decision. You see, the gentleman in question was not Russian.'

'No?'

'No, Sir, he was an Englishman, like you and me, and young too.'

'Yes, I see your point. Well, thank you; you've been very helpful. Good day to you.'

As they stepped outside, the sales manager ran after them.

'Is the car all right?'

'Oh, yes perfectly. Never gone so well.'

Sebastian could not resist looking over his shoulder. The sales manager had got back into the showroom and was standing by the window staring at the floor.

'What do you make of it?', asked Sebastian.

'It looks as though you will be investing in a pair of swimming trunks after all, Barnard. Prepare yourself for life in the fast lane, in a danger zone, in the Caribbean. That's where the money is.'

'You can't mean it! I feel I'm driven from pillar to post . . .'

'And you fear this could be the Last Post or should I say the Last Pylon?'

'Very funny!', exclaimed Sebastian.

'Don't worry. I have friends in America amid the coloured community in the deep South who are also true descendants of African slaves like those on Haiti, and they would have no problem counteracting any spell cast on you through double-dealing witch doctors in the Caribbean.'

'I'm beginning to suspect that putting the Lamborghini through its paces has made you swollen-headed.'

'I didn't drive it; he did; he just could not resist showing off, I suppose. When he finished swanking, he let me take it up the road for a quiet spin round Dunsfold. That suited me; all I wanted was a chance to examine the car in my own time and listen to the messages it sent out.'

Sinclair paused before going on as though he needed to gather his thoughts.

'Even admitting he gets hands-out from his father, who, one supposes, is proud of him for the work he does in dangerous conditions when he could spend his time footling at home in the company of top models, the man is still a little too flush for a volunteer tourist; he is also too brazen.

To walk into a Mayfair car salesroom with enough money in a suitcase to buy a Lamborghini cash down like any glorified member of the Russian mafia requires nerves of a different kind from those needed to pull out the victims of an earthquake from a crumbling building while wearing a bandanna . . . I am afraid the vibrations I get are not very good. And here we must let the matter rest till we go out there and test the immaterial against the material.'

'What about the risk of Cholera?'

'What about it?'

'Didn't they have an outbreak in Port-au-Prince after the earthquake?'

'Ah, now you're talking! I agree that with an individual like you who goes for hours without wanting a pee, and feels lethargical at the best of time, the symptoms of Cholera would be difficult to detect.'

'Like what?'

'Low urine output, sleepiness; there are others, of course, like abdominal cramps, dry mucus membranes, excessive thirst . . .'

'You've been researching then?'

'What else? You'll be all right so long as you keep off shellfish and contaminated water.'

There were entire tracts of dialectical thinking that Sinclair had to keep to himself just as Sherlock Holmes had kept his private because Dr. Watson on account of his experiences as a surgeon both at sea and in Afghanistan would not have been able to apprehend them, let alone act on them spontaneously. To try and communicate to Sebastian the idea that the doubts which he personally entertained about Daniel Blacker's integrity were founded on intangible rather than tangible grounds, though the Lamborghini and the bandanna were both substantial enough, would have been a waste of breath. The image of the mad Englishman, of which Lord Byron remained the glamorous epitome, dashing across continents in exotic costume to embrace humanitarian causes, had long lost its appeal for the young. Their garb had become universal :—trainers, jeans, anoraks, sweatshirts and peak caps. Among all those nondescript items, conveying anonymity, who could deny that Daniel Blacker's bandanna struck an incongruous note; and the fast Italian car raised a few issues to boot, unless it could be seen as having served a therapeutic purpose,—disposed of an awful lot of money in one fell swoop rather than finance slow-release debauchery; but Sebastian had no comment to make about them. Similarly, the apparently senseless decision to go to Haiti when another earthquake in the south island of New Zealand in all likelihood claimed Daniel Blacker's presence there had not elicited a murmur from him. At best, Sebastian had palmed off an oblique objection to the scheme by expressing a fear of Voodoo and a dread of Cholera, both mantles for his anxiety about the boss's mental health, signifying his tacit acceptance that it should remain unquestioned for the time being, and the decision to proceed to Haiti unchallenged . . . Yet, the boy had put his finger on a really sensitive spot; it was a fact that he was still smarting under the blow to his self-esteem earned in Egypt in a rather theatrical way which did not contribute to enhance his reputation. Since his return home, most of the enquiries which had come his way through the agency of advertisements in various magazines had been run-of-the-mill ones and had done little to restore his morale, or allow the vivid impressions made by Daniel Blacker's accoutrement to fade. Those kept taunting him and at times the reproach they signified was so acute that he felt his own integrity challenged by it, not so much in a strictly personal sense as in a corporate one, as though the whole of decent humanity were involved; and in the end the pressure was so great that he had to respond. But this time, there would be no demeaning chase, no fiasco, no loss of face at the eleventh hour. He would be there lying in wait, when Daniel Blacker returned to the Caribbean after his exertions in New Zealand,—ready to pounce on him and pluck him like some great bird of paradise.

Landing in Haiti was like experiencing a *déjà vu* ; a year on, the devastation of the landscape made familiar by Television programmes after the earthquake struck looked the same. People were still walking about among rubble carrying over their heads chunks of slabs salvaged from collapsed government buildings where officials had died to take them somewhere else to rebuild Haiti's infrastructure; and Sinclair, almost knocked out by an influx of contrary responses to the apocalyptic effluvium, did not know whether to rejoice over his own good fortune at possessing the right flair for the chase which had led him to come to Haiti in the first place, or to grieve for the Haitian people who seemed no better off than they were twelve months earlier. It was as though Television cameras had been left running on for an indefinite period of time, in preparation for an unscheduled scenario, in a timeless zone . . . Far away over the horizon, as they picked their way haphazardly through a collection of debris, the lush island scenery which lay beyond the devastated areas opened up a tantalizing vista.

Sebastian struggling not to lose his footing due to sickness motion soon gave vent to discouragement. According to him, Tintin on the moon had found a better surface to walk on in the regolith that littered it than the terrain they had to cope with. Sinclair, who was anxious to establish contact with the UN and the Haitian Police at the earliest possible opportunity, suggested that, instead of moaning about the going, Sebastian ought to save his breath and try his skill at patois through engaging the local people in conversations of the useful kind.

'So long as you remember not to imitate the kind of primitive exchanges in broken French that Tintin had with the natives in the Belgian Congo. What did they call it?It wasn't patois . . .'

'No, *petit nègre*. A kind of infantile sub idiom which often raised laughs.'

'Oh, dear, no, that wouldn't do.'

As soon as one elderly man saw Sinclair and Sebastian approaching, he waved his arms up in the air, shouting :

'Yo ameriken! Ce sont des Américains!'

But when Sebastian said :

'Non, des Anglais' the poor man let his arms drop and he said :

'Mesye, kote ameriken? Messieurs, où sont les Américains?' and turning to his mate who was squatting in the dirt, he said:

'Ils sont repartis sur leurs grand bateaux. Bonnwit! Goodnight!'

'Quick', said Sinclair, 'ask him about the Charities and the volunteer aid workers. Tell him, there was a nice one, who always wore a red bandanna, a big chap . . .'

'Ah, wi', replied the old man, 'l'homme au bandeau rouge! Il aimait bien les dames . . .'

'What's this, about the ladies?'

'He says the one who wore a red bandanna was a bit of a ladies' man.'

'Ask him what kind of ladies?'

'Des dames agées comme sa maman', replied the old man.

'Elderly ladies, his mother's age.'

'Celles qui habitaient tout en haut dans de belles maisons.'

'Those that lived on the hillside in beautiful houses.'

`Il était trés fort et elles si légères, comme des plumes.'

`He was very strong and they were so light, like feathers . . .'

`That's enough!', cried Sinclair, `I don't have to listen to any more of this mush; the old man's embroidering! He's read Derek Walcott's long poem about Jamaican fishermen. Here, give the old boy these notes. and his mate too., US dollars; that should keep them happy for a while.'

By the time, Sebastian had distributed the money, a crowd of bystanders had gathered, and they offered to escort Sinclair, who had gone off ahead in a fuming temper, all the way to the UN and Haitian Police Headquarters because, they said, there were escaped convicts lurking about who might intercept him, criminals who had broken out of jail on the day of the earthquake and were still on the loose, though many of them had succeeded in infiltrating the camp in the Champ de Mars where persons who had been made homeless by the earthquake still lived under canvas.

`Tell them I don't need an escort. Tell them the man with the red bandanna is miles away, in New Zealand, and he is the devil incarnate.'

At the mention of the word `diable' relayed by Sebastian the Haytians took off and scrambled back downtown; and Sebastian had no option but to catch up with Sinclair over the awkward terrain, wondering where to look for purified water as he was feeling more and more parched by the minute. Once again, they had got off to a bad start, with Sinclair in a foul mood.

`Come on, Barnard! No, you haven't contracted Cholera; not yet. Cheer up; the fun's only just beginning.'

`If you say so' replied Sebastian, and to show goodwill he asked :

`What was that all about . . . A Jamaican epic?'

`Oh, absolutely brilliant; Derek Walcott's Nobel prize winner; a first for Poetry, about a Jamaican fisherman called Homer. Trouble is, they all fancy themselves as Homer now. He's been sublimated like a lot of other cretins in other parts of the world.'

It all went above Sebastian's head, but he felt he had to humour up the boss. Not only was he thirsty, which was unusual for him as having no thirst had always been a feature of his constitutional profile, but he felt clammy as well. Down below, the sea sparkled and a quick dip would have been welcome.

`Do you think there will be time for a swim soon?', he asked, `my sweatshirt' s too thick.'

'Not with all those criminals on the loose. Some of them may be living in rock caves.'

Sebastian stopped walking and looked at Sinclair straight in the eye :

'Has anybody ever told you you're a selfish brute?'

'Oh, yeah?'

'Yes; look at the way you behaved with those poor natives; they're traumatized. In the end, few of the nations who promised help delivered. There was so much sadness in the old man's voice when he said the Americans had gone away in their great, big ships. He and his people feel let down, but you didn't commiserate with him. Neither did you press the point about us being British, a real British presence on the island as caring individuals, not just onlookers out on a mission of their own. It was all about you, and your private quarrel with a voluntary aid worker who wore a red bandanna which you happened to object to. And the old man was forthcoming, but you disapproved of his style of delivery, for crying out loud!'

'Holier than thou, hey, Barnard? I tell you what. To celebrate that great caring British presence on the island, why don't you get into your Geisha outfit and give a charity performance for the displaced persons at their camp? Afraid of getting raped? I grant you it wouldn't be quite the sort of venue you had in mind initially, but 'charity seeketh not her own' as the apostle sayeth. Come on, Barnard! Pull yourself together. We can't take on the sins of the world just because nations defaulted on promises of aid. Let's be empirical, and that's British enough. We're investigating a suspicious individual who may have taken advantage of the plight of helpless victims to feather his cap. No one, do you hear me, no one is above temptation.'

The best part of the homily went straight over Sebastian's head. He felt just too hot and thirsty to pass from the world of physical sensations to that of highfalutin metaphysical conceptions.

At the UN post, the Police officer in charge, a Dutchman, was busy reporting on the radio to a colleague at the next check-point under the watchful eye of a heavily-armed Haitian policeman whose face was almost entirely concealed by a sanitary mask. As Sinclair presented his credentials, it took him no time at all to understand the sign language that the man from the Netherlands conveyed by waving his white gauntlets while the Haitian attempted some menacing shadow-boxing with his machine-gun. With something like five thousand escaped criminals to catch in a place where desperate people were tempted to turn to crime every day, he had little time for the futile pursuits of private investigators; Sinclair would have to do the best he could left to his own devices on an island that had acquired a bad name for criminality. Sebastian could see that the boss's common sense entreaties would cut no ice,—how they might through combined efforts sustain each other in a common task. The UN policeman kept waving his gauntlets in a manner that left no room for misunderstanding. All he was prepared to do was to recommend a safe haven for the night at a near-by orphanage where nuns did bed and breakfast to keep the place going as the number of orphans increased by the day. No, it wasn't the well-known St. Joseph's home for street boys Guest House in Rue La Plume; that had been flattened by the earthquake . . .

To Sebastian, it was music to his ears . . . Now Sinclair had been left out on a limb, he would have to show his assistant more consideration in order to be able to rely on him almost exclusively. He would have to take on board Sebastian's psychosomatic symptoms as well as his clinical ones and give them due attention. There would be secret bargain pleas galore, and Sebastian fully intended to make the most of them, swimming in the sea being one of them as he felt he had been arbitrarily deprived of a simple pleasure. After all, nobody knew when, or if, Daniel Blacker would return to the Caribbean to recover from his exertions in New Zealand; another earthquake might claim his presence somewhere else at a moment's notice; only Sinclair felt sure he would catch his man in the area around Port au Prince. Therefore, a pleasant routine had to be established without any further delay to make up for lost time and create a congenial ego space for the future.

The mother superior in charge of the orphanage fell over herself when she heard Sinclair was a criminal investigator from England. Novice nuns were sent scouring round the place for the softest pillows, and both Sinclair and Sebastian assured that their names would from then on be included in evening prayers. She and her girls lived in fear and trembling of being raped by escaped convicts and the children taken away for human trafficking. Divine providence had answered her prayers. It was said in the Bible :'Be not forgetful to entertain strangers : for thereby some have entertained angels unawares.' The trouble was in Haiti strangers were often wolves in sheep's clothing and one never knew. Sebastian held his breath, wondering if Sinclair would return the compliment and exchange personal views with the mother superior about wolves in sheep's clothing through alluding to a certain stranger who wore a bandanna and had worked in Haiti during the earthquake as a voluntary aid worker; but much to his relief Sinclair kept his counsel. He was obviously the man of the hour, keen to enjoy his providential status as a glorified stranger; and that Sebastian considered to his own advantage as the nuns there and then set about organising a session for Sinclair to enlighten the orphans about crime detection, thus creating an opportunity for Sebastian to disappear early and do his own thing, as well as snoop around lest Blacker returned 'unawares' and slipped through the noose. But Sinclair must have sensed the danger and he was on to it right away.

'I can't let the children down, not to-day. They really think I'm an angel in disguise. I trust you will keep your eyes and ears open when you go downtown; walk round the harbour quays; look for possible helicopter pads; listen to gossip . . . You know what to do and report back to me if you see anything suspicious.'

'Of course, I will.'

'Here, take those US dollar bills; they might come in handy. I'll join you as soon as I can. And, Barnard . . .'

'Yes?'

'Remember to take off that silly wide brimmed sun hat and those sunglasses; they made sitting-ducks of us when we landed. Rely on sunscreen with SPF to protect yourself against exposure to the sun.'

Sebastian took to his heels and made for the sea, letting himself be guided by glimpses of blue sparkling in gaps between collapsed buildings. He would have scrambled down to the water's edge quite quickly had his attention not been caught by a curious sight which he spotted below on a tiny stretch of sand. Supporting what looked like a frail elderly lady with a bandage round her head, he saw a man who looked like the spitting image of Daniel Blacker except for one thing :—he was completely bald; his skull shone in the sunlight like polished ivory; and he can't have been any older than thirty-four! Amazed, Sebastian kept staring at him as he prepared to go into the water while the old lady watched, sitting on a portable beach chair under a sun shade. 'Damn', Sebastian whispered to himself, and thinking the man could not possibly know him, even if he were Daniel Blacker after a course of chemotherapy, he gave himself up to the blessed coolness of the sea breeze and let himself slither down into the water. He attempted a few strokes but soon let the motion of the undertow toss him about in the shallows like flotsam under the Caribbean sky which conjured up quintessential visions of endless stretches of white sand with rows of coconut trees in the background and rollers breaking in . . . How long he lolled about in that desultory manner, he did not know. At times, his mind had been vacant and at other times it had been aware of snippets of conversation which he had overheard recently echoing over and over again through his dream-sodden consciousness . . .

When he came to with a start, the thought of the two people whom he had seen early on made him leap out of the water. Picking up his clothes, he hurried to the spot where he had first espied them, but they were gone. Conscious of a dereliction of duty, he willed himself to rememorate the snippets of conversation that had echoed through his mind in the water, evoking the rhyming jingle produced by the old fisherman when they first landed on the island about a Charity worker 'qui aimait bien les dames . . . des dames agées comme sa maman'. But the old boy's comments had been made in answer to a query about a rescuer who wore a red bandanna, not one whose head was completely bald! The whole thing was suspicious and needed clarification before reporting to Sinclair. Scrambling back into his clothes, Sebastian retraced his steps and wended his way in direction of the harbour where they had first met the old bard.

There was a great deal of activity on the quayside and at first Sebastian could not see the person he was seeking to help him out of his quandary, and then he spotted him standing in a group of bystanders in front of the moorings of the 'Margarita', Daniel Blacker's father's yacht, which was about to put out to sea. Parked a little way off the gangway, there was a Hertz chauffeur-driven, rented car waiting. Despite the absence of the sun hat and the dark glasses, the old boy must have recognized Sebastian because as soon as he espied him, he pointed in the direction of the well where Daniel Blacker, wearing the charismatic bandanna, suddenly appeared, shouting :

'Tell Mrs. Blacker to get her arse up on deck now, this minute.'

Bewildered, Sebastian turned to the old boy and whispered :

'Where's he going?'

'To Santa Lucia to get the boat refitted. They've been on their honeymoon, touring the islands in the Caribbean.'

'What about her? I mean, Mrs. Blacker. Where is she going?'

The old boy pointed to the rented car :

'Back to Laboule Garden Aparthotel, in the tranquillity of the hills, with Maman Brigitte. They haven't been married long, about a week, I think.'

Sebastian could feel sweat running down his back. He had a choice, either get on a taptap or a camionette and by hook or by crook follow Mrs. Blacker up to the luxury apartments in the hills, or go and get Sinclair, who so far had not showed up. He was dithering when Mrs. Blacker appeared on deck and began coming across the gangway like an ethereal apparition out of a medieval romance, and all he could do was to stand and gape, deprived of volition. She was very tall and thin, with long, fair hair which fell naturally about her face on which there was no trace of make-up. She wore a loose white dress in a light semi-transparent fabric and on her feet were gold sandals discreetly studded with crystal beads. Silence fell on the assembly as she stepped off the gangway and turning back blew a kiss in the direction of the boat which was sliding out of its moorings. Sebastian did not know which way to look, whether at the wake of the boat as it began to cut a swathe through the water or at that heavenly vision as it got driven away. And in that very instant he realized that he had lost the chance to turn himself into a man of action, capable of making split-second decisions. He could see himself going through the motions, hopping on to an overcrowded vehicle and pushing his way into the garden apartment to warn Mrs. Blacker that her life was in danger because she had married the wrong man . . . And now, all he could do was to go back to the orphanage and report to the man in charge . . .

'I thought you said you'd join me', he said as soon as he saw him, attack being the best policy against reproach.

'I couldn't get away. The children were all over me.'

'The children or the nuns?'

'All right, all right! I know they're a bunch of sex-starved females, but that does not mean to say they don't take their vow of chastity seriously. Well, what have you got to say for yourself?'

'Oh, man, have I got news for you! I've seen Mrs. Blacker.'

'Who the hell is Mrs. Blacker?'

'Daniel Blacker's wife of just a week.'

'Tarted up to the eyeball?'

'Not at all. A celestial being. I was gobsmacked, as they say.'

'And what would you know about such creatures?'

'I can tell an angel when I see one. She was very tall and slender . . .'

'All right! That'll do. What about him?'

'Ah, well, prepare yourself for a shock. He's gone, ostensibly to take the boat back to Santa Lucia for refitting.'

'You mean he just sailed in to put Mrs Blacker ashore?'

'Yes; they've been touring the islands on their honeymoon. Now prepare yourself for the bad news,—Blacker has a look-a-like who is completely bald; I've seen him with my own eyes; and there is a mystery lady, a very old one with a bandage on her head who looks like death warmed up.'

'Mrs. Blacker's mother?'

'Could be.'

'Barnard, I hope you realize you took an awful risk exposing yourself single-handed on the wharf. Did you speak to anyone?'

'Of course, I did. How else do you think I would have picked up all that information?'

'Who was it?'

'Homer, the old fisherman. Remember him? You discounted what he said about the man with the red bandanna; you thought it was poetic drivel at the time. Jolly handy, if you ask me. All we've got to do now is to hop into a taxi and pay Mrs. Blacker a visit in her luxury apartment on the hillside. That'll make a nice change from the orphanage, and the nuns.'

'It's as simple as that, is it, Barnard, with wide-scale corruption and debris from the earthquake everywhere? Suppose, just suppose for an instant that Mrs. Blacker is a she-devil in disguise and she is harbouring a criminal up there, not Daniel, he's in Santa Lucia, but the other one, the spitting image, the bald one. Suppose that she is implicated in a plot to do away with the old lady in order to inherit a fortune, any fortune. You have a very naïve way of looking at people, Barnard; their motives are never as simple as they seem, at least not in Haiti.'

'Why not?'

Sinclair laughed.

'Because, apart from any other factor, the Haitian infrastructure has collapsed, and the serpent is a subtle beast as it is written in *Genesis*,'more subtil than any beast of the field'. Now, if the serpent could infiltrate the most foolproof social infrastructure that ever existed in Eden, what couldn't he do here in Haiti where law and order have broken down following a natural disaster which could be seen as an 'act of God', and Vodou is guaranteed freedom of Religion under the Haitian constitution?'

'Your rational anthropology leaves me speechless.'

'Good. I rely on you to remain that way while I tackle Mrs. Blacker. All I would ask of you, should you see her reaching for her mobile phone, grab it.'

'Why? Can't you grab it yourself?'

'In case I get scorched touching that sex symbol of the Holy Grail who might be an enchantress of the same ilk as Morgan le Fay; she even managed to seduce her brother King Arthur through her wiles. Not everybody approved of the Knights of the Round Table in those days, you know.'

'What's that supposed to mean?'

'Oh, I don't know! I suppose that social values are ambivalent. I'm just speaking extempore. I guess I'm disheartened on the one hand by your impulsiveness and on the other hand by the duplicity of the devil's face in Haiti, which inclines me to look on Vodou ceremonials as therapeutic ways of cleansing the national psyche from time to time through song and dance. Why not believe in a merciful God who wants us to achieve salvation by whatever means possible? How's that for a sceptic?"

It seemed to Sebastian that there was a note of lassitude in Sinclair's voice, and he felt guilty for having been bent on achieving his own ends first and foremost, though his escapade had proved grist to the mill in the end.

'Shall I call a taxi, Sir?', he asked by way of an amend.

'Yes, do. I think the time has come for us to tackle our fears, don't you?'

A glance at the figure who answered the door of the apartment on the hillside, off the Route de Laboule, convinced Sinclair that Sebastian's description had been no exaggeration; the woman radiated an aura which was difficult to ignore; she was every bit as ethereal, with a kind of transcendental sex-appeal.

'Mrs. Blacker? Mrs. Daniel Blacker?', asked Sinclair.

'Yes.'

'Stewart Sinclair, private eye, and this is my assistant, Sebastian Barnard. We're in Haiti investing claims for life insurance policies taken out by people who went missing during the earthquake. May I see some ID, please?'

'Of course.'

She pulled a British passport out of a bag that Sebastian had seen her clutching when she walked off the *Margarita,* and that somehow jogged his memory.

'May I have a word with you, please, Sir?'

'Perhaps you'd like to take your assistant on to the terrace, through the French windows?', Mrs. Blacker asked, 'It is a bit stuffy in here.'

Yes, thank you; my assistant does find the climate taxing'

'What's the big idea, Barnard? Couldn't take the heat? I had only just got started.'

'Shouldn't you ask her where her mother is? Homer said that she was going back to the Laboule apartment to be with *Maman Brigitte.*'

'You fool! Why didn't you tell me before? According to the Vodou pantheon. Maman Brigitte is the wife of Baron, also known as Baron Samedi—figuratively the last day of the working week—who represents Death, and they are both masters of the dead and keepers of the cemeteries. Her counterpart in the Catholic hagiography is Saint Brigitte. I would need a warrant to search the apartment for a dead body . . .'

'Oh, my God!'

'Yes, well you might cry out loud! Follow me.'

Getting back into the hall, Sinclair started walking round the place sniffing.

'Is there anything wrong?', asked Mrs. Blacker.

'Yes', replied Sinclair, 'my assistant says he has been upset by a combination of the excessive heat with hospital smells. The air should feel quite balmy up here . . . I mean the apartment is spacious enough. Would you mind if I took a look round?'

'No, not at all'.

The spaciousness of the rooms Sinclair walked through was emphasized by the tidiness of the place and the plain style of the soft furnishings which though colourful in a very exotic way somehow did not create any vulgar disturbance for the eye. In the en suite bathroom of one of the master bedrooms the lid of a sanitary bin had been left ajar and Sinclair caught sight of some blood-stained gauze bandages lying at the bottom; using a back-brush he pulled one out and held ii up in the air to examine it.

'Oh, dear', said Mrs. Blacker, 'it looks as though the housekeeper forgot to empty this bin right out in the panic.'

'What panic, Mrs. Blacker?'

'My mother had to be rushed into hospital early this morning. Her head wounds had started bleeding again. That is the reason why we, Daniel and I, had to cut short our honeymoon.'

'Head wounds?, asked Sinclair, 'What kind of head wounds?'

'The ones she sustained during the earthquake. You see, it was Daniel who pulled her out from the rubble. At the time, we didn't think she would survive her injuries.'

'Is that how you met your husband, Mrs. Blacker?'

'Yes.'

'I see . . . and who looked after your mother while you were on honeymoon?'

'Daniel's brother, Jacob.'

'And where is he now?'

'He's gone to Curaçao on an urgent family errand.'

'To do with legal matters?'

'Yes. When my mother took a turn for the worse, she began to fret about her will, and asked Jacob to contact her lawyers to make known her last wishes. She did not want to spoil our honeymoon.'

'What is your mother's name, Mrs. Blacker?'

'Mrs. Vanderwelt.'

'Where did she come from?'

'From Curaçao, where her ancestors made the famous liqueur. It's still the best in the world, you know, though it's manufactured all over the place.'

'Oh, I wouldn't know about that, not being a connaisseur of liqueurs. Mrs. Blacker, I don't think there is any need for me to detain you any longer. There appears to have been some mistake. Obviously, your mother at no time in her life found herself in a position where she had to take out a life insurance policy with you as beneficiary; her name should not have appeared on my list. I am sorry we disturbed you at such an anxious time. I hope your mother soon feels better; she sounds very resilient, I mean, to survive such horrific head injuries all this time . . .'

'Yes, she is a very tough lady and there is a history of longevity in our family . . .'

'All that orange liqueur, hey? I remember my grandmother saying that if you wanted to live to a ripe old age, you had to eat the rind of an orange every day.'

'An apple a day is supposed to keep the doctor away, Sir,' piped in Sebastian, who was beginning to feel uneasy about the less than peremptory way Sinclair was conducting the interview, and wished to put the lid on it.

'Would your assistant like a glass of water before leaving? It's two miles from Laboule Garden residence to the heart of Petionville . . .'

'No, thank you', said Sinclair. 'It's getting late and we must make tracks. Good day, Mrs. Blacker.'

'What was the big idea stopping her from giving me a glass of water? I was supposed to be under the weather . . . ', asked Sebastian as soon as they had climbed down the stairs of the private terrace entrance.

'There is such a thing as leaving finger prints on glasses, Barnard.'

'You're not suspecting her, are you? You know, guilty until proven innocent according to your basic principle, and guilty of what exactly?'

'I don't know. By the way, don't turn round now; we're being followed. I first spotted them when Mrs. Blacker invited us to step on the terrace for a breath of fresh air.'

'What do they look like?'

'They're wearing wide-brimmed hats and sun glasses. My guess is they're from the Miami Vice squad.'

'I thought they weren't allowed to wear sunglasses on duty.'

'I didn't say they were from the Federal Bureau; I said Miami vice, Barnard. Do try and listen to what I say, and let me tackle them.'

When the two agents saw Sinclair and his assistant wheel around sharply, they stopped walking and standing by the roadside pointed seaward as though they were admiring the view.

'Hi, guys! Hope the beauty spot was worth the seven hour flight from Miami.'

One of the men took his sunglasses off and smiled.

'My colleague here is a sailing enthusiast. We were trying to spot out the *Margarita*. We were told the owner sometimes charters her out for short trips.'

'Ah, the *Margarita*! Now you're talking! Well, let me tell you the bad news; she's gone back to Santa Lucia for refitting; right out of your league. Why don't you go down to the harbour and see what else they can rig up for you in a hurry? They'll fall over themselves to help you out. And now, if you will excuse us, we have more Life Insurance policies to check out in the area . . .'

Noticing a cloud of dust that was fast approaching, signalling a taptap which he hoped had the letters PV painted on the side of the cab doors, Sinclair started running, with Sebastian in tow, and disregarding the usual protocol of banging on the side of the vehicle to stop the driver for a request stop in case he had no space for more travellers, both men jumped on to the running boards and were soon clinging for dear life to the sides of the vehicle, hoping the religious slogans painted on them about God's mercy would ensure their safe return to Petionville, where they would have a choice of three different routes to return to Port-au-Prince, thus increasing their chances of losing the men from the Miami vice squad. At the terminal, when Sebastian asked `*Konbyen?*' how much, the driver replied by pouring out a torrent of invectives against foreigners who frightened away their *ti-bonanj,* their guardian angel, and become suicidal as a result, but soon clamed down when Sinclair offered him a wad of American dollar bills instead of the usual ten Haitian gourdes for two fares.

As he paced the floor of the tiny makeshift bedroom he shared with Sebastian, unable to lie down for the multiple bruises he had collected on his wrists, elbows and knees during their hair-raising descent from the Laboule garden district, Sinclair had to concede that the sudden appearance on the scene of the men from Miami Vice had singularly compromised matters, and he spent the best part of the night elaborating hypotheses, and reviewing them over and over again while Sebastian nodded. It was the business of the *Margarita* that unsettled him most. Those guys from the Miami Vice Squad had not flown to Haiti without a reason. Daniel Blacker as a drug trafficker? Somehow, the idea upset him; he felt mortified by it, as though the Americans had stolen his thunder. He wanted the man for himself as a potential murderer who went from disaster scene to disaster scene as a volunteer tourist scavenging for likely victims to pull out of the rubble with multiple wounds, most of which he had, he would confess, inadvertently aggravated himself during the delicate rescue operations, his father's lifestyle around the Caribbean isles as part of the smart set giving him the chance to keep informed about the movements of the rich and famous. Daniel Blacker as a drug trafficker, using his father's yacht to run the stuff on the quiet, like a schoolboy escapade? It sounded too surreptitious for someone with such a flamboyant style of dress, but the chaps from the Miami vice squad were not to know that, were they? It was not within the scope of their duties to take into account such ostentatious sartorial vagaries in a suspect. Nor to ask about the beautiful wife whose retiring style begged the question, Why such a refined, discreet, sylph-like creature as the lawful wedded wife of a loud-mouthed swank like Daniel Blacker? It was an odd choice for an exhibitionist such as him . . .

She had been born in Curaçao—so her passport said—probably like her mother before her. That made her a `colonial', that is a person who lived in a closed community in a strange land, under a different sky, where the habits of the motherland were observed to the exclusion of local customs, and family relationships tight-knit on account of the remoteness of the ancestral roots. To go native was the worst misdemeanour any one could commit,—a kind of felony. She had probably been educated in Holland, learning at an early age what long homeward journeys meant at the end of term, and what tight-lipped decorum to observe throughout in order to avoid trouble while in transit. Her chances of meeting the brothers of schoolmates on home ground had for that reason been few and far between. Opposites attract, they say. . . . Daniel Blacker's humanitarian volunteerism, commendable in someone who had private means, must have conferred upon him an aura of dedicated heroism which was irresistible to a girl who had a close relationship with her mother due to the somewhat isolated circumstances attached to their colonial status . . . But the real burr in this equation with so many unknown quantities was the other one, the look-a-like, whose name, alas, recalled the story of the famous twins, Esau and Jacob, in a situation where biblical parallels were to be avoided at all costs lest they prejudiced the outcome. Was he a figment of Sebastian's imagination, distorted by the sudden heat on Haiti combined with the after-effects of jet lag? As far as he himself knew, Daniel Blacker had never had a twin brother. Could it have been a coincidence, somebody who looked like Daniel Blacker from a distance? Very little differentiated one athletic `beach boy' from another when wearing a cap over their hair. How much time had Sebastian benefited from at London Airport to take in and fix in his memory the physiognomy of the man as he moved forward among a crowd of passengers? Come to think of it Sebastian had used the expression 'look-alike' it was Mrs. Blacker who had mentioned the word `brother'. That was what in conjunction with an elderly lady suffering from head injuries, which might well continue plaguing her a year after she incurred them in the earthquake, due to age, brought in complexities too unwholesome to unravel when one bore in mind the old Haitian fisherman's allusion to *Maman Brigitte*. Those poor islanders were too sincere in their devotions to the Vodu pantheon to invoke the name of such a powerful spirit in vain. Taking into consideration the fact that Homer seemed to hold the British in higher esteem than the Americans, his revelations to Sebastian were not to be taken lightly. Foul play might well be in the offing, buttressing all Sinclair's own intimations about Daniel Blacker's expensive lifestyle. And here, it seemed Sinclair had in his restless review of the facts of the case gone back to square one in a game where a way ahead. might be better obtained through offering *Maman Brigitte* a bottle of Barbancourt rum as an offering for her curative powers.

'Wake up, Sebastian!'

'What's up? It's two o'clock in the morning, for peace sake!'

'We've got to move Mrs. Vanderwelt out of the hospital and bring her here. There's not a moment to lose. I fear an attack on her life.'

'And how do you propose to do that?'

'The nuns have a clapped-out camionette in which they collect children off the streets. We'll put the old lady in a coffin and load it on to the van. Come on, chuck some clothes on and get moving, now this minute.'

At the hospital, they found Mrs. Blacker sitting at her mother's bedside.

'Mrs. Blacker, I don't know if you've ever belonged to an amateur dramatic society; they say people who live in the colonies often do because it reminds them of home, but I need you to put up a convincing show of grief when we take your mother out of here on a trolley, in a coffin.'

'But, why? You said my mother didn't come within the scope of your enquiries . . .'

'I know, but since then information has come my way which leads me to believe that your mother's life is in danger. I need to move her to a safe house where I can organize twenty-four hour surveillance and she can have round the clock nursing as well. Ah, here comes my assistant with a trolley. Please, do your bit, look the part, for your mother's sake.'

Mrs. Blacker pulled a tissue out of her handbag and started dabbing her eyes as the men pushed the trolley down the corridor into a courtyard where rows of coffins were stacked up against the walls before loading the coffin into the nuns' camionette.

At the orphanage, with the space already stretched to capacity, Mrs. Vanderwelt and her daughter were put in the tiny attic room which the two men had shared while Sinclair and Sebastian were given sleeping bags to lie on the floor space outside the chapel where a round-the-clock prayer vigil was organized.

'What did you think of her as an actress?', asked Sebastian as soon as Mrs. Blacker had retired, 'her tears seemed genuine enough . . .'

'In the circumstances, yes, but don't jump to conclusions, Barnard. There is more to this case than meets the eye, and I don't think we've seen the half of it yet. You'll never make a good detective if you underestimate the power of evil.'

Sebastian stared woefully at the sleeping bags on the floor.

'Frankly, I don't understand. If I didn't know you better, I'd say you were acting out of self-interest.'

'What's that supposed to mean?'

'That you'd fallen for Daniel Blacker's wife and couldn't bear to let her out of your sight . . . I mean, Mrs. Vanderwelt is doomed to die anyway, sooner or later; with such slow-healing head injuries at her age, she has no life expectancy . . .'

'Well, since you seem to give credit to an old fisherman's Vodu beliefs, let me tell you that according to them *Maman Brigitte's* powers over the dying are ineffective until her husband, *Baron Samedi*, decides to start digging the grave. With two men, who may be rivals, ostensibly away on official errands, I still maintain I have good reason to think an attempt on Mrs. Vanderwelt's life is within the realm of possibilities. What I can't predict is the exact time of the attack.'

Sebastian shook his head.

'I hear what you say but I have trouble grasping the sense behind it . . .'

'That's because you let fortuitous events pass you by without bothering to extract clues from them. Those two men from the Miami Vice squad . . .'

'Yes. What about them?'

'They had been alerted to the movements of the *Margarita* in shipping channels the traffic of which they knew well. Why? Because she was not going to Santa Lucia in the usual way. She was heading in the opposite direction, for Curaçao.'

'What on earth for?'

'You don't get it, do you? For Daniel Blacker to find out what Mrs. Vanderwelt's last wishes were, for crying out loud! Try and recall what Mrs. Blacker told us when we called on her in the Laboule apartment, how when they were away on their honeymoon, her mother took a turn for the worse and commissioned Jacob, who was looking after her during their absence, to contact her lawyers in Curaçao about her last wishes. Obviously, she had changed her mind about certain things, and Daniel suspected Jacob of having disclosed to her how she really came by those terrible head injuries of hers when pulled out of the rubble by Daniel during the earthquake. And so, as soon as he had put Mrs. Blacker ashore, he set sail for Curaçao to challenge him. I leave you to imagine the rest. Now maybe, you'll understand my concern for Mrs. Vanderwelt's life. It's not over yet.'

'Do you think I ought to go and consult Homer?'

'Oh, I wouldn't do that if I were you! I need you on stand-by.'

'Do you think Mrs. Blacker knows?'

'No; she doesn't.'

'How can you be so sure?'

'She lives in a world of her own where that kind of sordid thing doesn't happen,—an ideal world. She has never known the world of all of us, its rough and tumble, the battle for life. Now, please listen carefully to what I say. In the event of Daniel waylaying Jacob in Curaçao to stop him from delivering Mrs. Vanderwelt's message to her lawyers, and killing him, he will put the body in the yacht and dump it somewhere in the Caribbean on the way to Santa Lucia, where the *Margarita* is due to go in dry docks. In the event of Jacob killing Daniel, he too will throw the body in the sea. Both men are due to fly back on local flights which means neither one of them will arrive at Toussaint Louverture international airport or Cap-Haïtien, which is a blessing. Whoever comes back out of the two will go straight to the hospital, either to wreak vengeance on Mrs. Vanderwelt if it's Daniel; or bring glad tidings to the old lady, if it's Jacob, and I have to be there to see who shows up . . .'

'In the hope it is Daniel? You have always considered him a dubious character in spite of his spontaneous charity work.'

'Well, of course.'

'It's a bee in your bonnet . . .'

'Or, to continue the animal allegory, I can smell a rat when I see one.'

'What if one twin assumed the identity of the other? I remember seeing a famous Hollywood movie about one twin deliberately letting her sister drown so as to assume her identity because she was the more popular of the two. Of course, it would not be so easy in the case of the Blacker brothers with one twin being hairy and the other bald.'

'Some would say it was in their genes, with hirsuteness being sex-linked to masculinity and more dominant to baldness according to Mendel's theory of heredity, but that's another story.'

A noise behind the door of the attic made them look up. Mrs. Blacker appeared in the embrasure and asked for the nursing sister on duty to come at once; her mother's breathing was getting shallower and, as she went back she cried out :

'Oh, my God, she's gone! Just like that, in the space of a second; her breast no longer moves. I can't believe it!.'

The mother superior came in followed by the nursing sister who pronounced Mrs. Vanderwelt dead.

'Come along, dear child,' said the mother superior putting her arms round Mrs. Blacker, 'there's nothing more you can do. You can use my office to call your relatives; it'll be more private in there.'

Then she turned towards Sinclair :

'Mr. Sinclair, we have no facilities for refrigerating bodies here, but we have got a coffin so we must prepare for an immediate burial. Now, whilst you and your assistant are very welcome here, you must understand that the very cramped conditions under which we operate on Haiti regretfully make it difficult for me to offer you both extended accommodation for an indefinite period of time.'

'I do understand, Reverend Mother, have no fear; we will not impose on you. As a matter of fact, it is possible that the matter which brought us here may not require our presence on the island for much longer.'

'Oh, I'm sorry to hear that. We did enjoy having you around. Please, feel free to join us in chapel for the liturgy of the dead.'

To Sinclair, it seemed that the convent bell which began to toll mourned the collapse of his scheme to catch a potential psychopath. The whole edifice had collapsed like a pack of cards; a carefully planned operation had been thwarted by Fate. Had he been an ancient Greek he would have been inclined to think that Nemesis had meted out his just deserts for wrongly accusing a potentially innocent man . . . But murder was essentially a matter of degree, and to prove murder by intent rather than manslaughter was not that easy, and he had had the chance to do just that; Daniel Blacker had the motive . . .

To Sebastian, the look of disappointment on Sinclair's face said it all.

'I've been thinking . . . Is it possible that while the newly-weds were away on their honeymoon and Jacob Blacker looked after Mrs. Vanderwelt that under the influence of his kind attention to her needs she relaxed and had flashes of memory about the way she came by her injuries, I mean about Daniel hitting her on the head just before pulling her out of the rubble, and she confided in Jacob, expressing fears for her daughter's future safety as the potential heiress of the Vanderwelt fortune now she was married to his brother?'

'It's possible. Memory works in mysterious ways especially after a trauma. Why?'

'Oh, I don't know. Maybe you shouldn't feel so guilty about harbouring suspicious thoughts about Daniel Blacker. Maybe he is a confirmed predator . . . Why don't we offer to take Mrs. Blacker back to the Laboule apartment? She may feel like a change of clothes before the funeral . . .'

'Yes, let's, and, who knows, we may meet our friends from the Miami Vice Squad up there, admiring the view, and they may have something interesting to say about the *Margarita*.'

'The *Margarita*?'

'Yes, the Blackers' yacht. The Miami Vice men alerted me to the possibility of her having changed course after she put out to sea again the day Daniel Blacker dropped his wife ashore . . .'

'Oh, my God! I've just remembered something about the *Margarita* that possibly the Miami Vice men didn't know. Daniel Blacker can't have been alone on the yacht when he dropped off his wife on the harbour quay . . .'

'No?'

'No, because, as he prepared to cast off moorings, he turned in the direction of the well and shouted : "Tell Mrs. Blacker to get her arse up on deck, now, this minute." I remember feeling shocked at the time by the gross way he referred to such a refined creature.'

'So, to start with, we had a look-alike and a mystery lady with a bandage round her head, and now we have an invisible man, supposedly used to rough language. Congratulations, Barnard! You've just knocked the stuffing out of my antecedent premisses!'

'I don't know what you mean . . .'

'Each case, Barnard, has a synchronic momentum and a syncretism all its own,—the attempted union of diverse facts. My speculation about Daniel Blacker putting Jacob's body on board the *Margarita* with a view of dumping it in the sea later was based on the assumption that he was alone on board; you have just destroyed that assumption through suggesting there was someone else down in the well. Congratulations!'

'Well, you just made a remark about memory working in mysterious ways.'

'For crying out loud, Barnard! When I made that remark about the way memory works, we were speculating about Mrs. Vanderwelt's head injury, how the memory trace of the trauma which has remained isolated from the rest of the mind suddenly re-enters it, causing a panic attack.'

'You also stopped me from consulting Homer, remember? There's nothing he doesn't know about what goes on in the harbour. You could have saved yourself the inconvenience of going off on the wrong foot.'

'You call that an inconvenience? It was a regretfully misleading oversight on my part which invalidated the rest of my reasoning. You know, Barnard, you sound full of petty grievances, and I'm beginning to wonder whether you've not gone too long without wearing the Geisha outfit, talking of which I suspect that the Mother Superior's decision to give us our marching orders may have been influenced by her catching sight of it hanging on the back of the attic door; I don't think much escapes her lynx eyes. Now, as I see it, there will still be time for us to consult Homer about the mystery man on board the *Margarita* after we've escorted Mrs. Blacker back to her apartment.'

'Why don't you ask her? She came up from below deck.'

'I'd rather not; the woman's mourning.'

When they spotted Homer, he was sitting in the usual place on the water front, by the edge, talking to cronies. One of them must have warned him company was approaching and he immediately broke away to greet Sinclair and Sebastian.

'Bonswa, Mesye. Ki jan ou ye? M pal pi mal? Good evening, gentlemen. How are you? Not bad?'

'Nou OK', replied Sebastian.

'Ask him if he can help us.'

'Eske ou kap ede nou?'

'Wi', he replied, without the slightest hesitation.

'Ask him who was on board the *Margarita* with the man with the red bandanna when she left Port au Prince bound for Santa Lucia.'

Sinclair noted the word 'silvouple' which sounded like 's'il vous plait' and immediately noted Homer's proud bearing as he replied :

'Mon fils' before launching into a lengthy explanation.

'He says his son was on board.'

'What's his son's name?'

'Aristide. Apparently, his son is a sailor who is also a cook, specializing in Creole cooking. Daniel Blacker hired him because he didn't want his wife to lift a finger during their honeymoon. Aristide has often worked for Daniel's father in Santa Lucia where the boat went back for refitting, staying away for long periods at a time doing odd jobs. around the island. Homer sometimes doesn't hear from his son for weeks on end but he doesn't worry; Aristide is a good son, who always comes home with good wages to help his father out.'

'All right. Thank him and give him those American dollars notes and ask him to let us know if he hears from his son in the near future.'

'There you are!', exclaimed Sebastian as they walked away.'What did I tell you? Homer is a wonderful source of information.'

Sinclair stopped and looked out over the horizon.

'What if it were all eye wash? or rather whitewash, to protect his son from a disreputable association with a criminal? He didn't mention Curaçao, did he?'

'No, that's true.'

'According to him, the *Margarita* went to Santa Lucia for refitting, a routine trip for her. A good alibi, I suppose. The *Margarita* has a powerful engine; she can put up speed whenever necessary; she could easily make up time after a detour to Curaçao to reach Santa Lucia on schedule for refurbishment, especially if Daniel Blacker had help on board. Then 'Mon fils' could resume his usual occupations, bumming round the island, before returning to Haiti to visit his father with plenty of cash in his pocket to dispense his largesse. I wonder how the old boy would have reacted had you asked him point blank if he thought 'Mon fils' could ever be accused of being an accessory to crime? I suppose he would have protested vehemently and started an uproar in the market place which he would have followed up by calling a Vodou service with a *mambo*, a female priest, as officiant to summon the spirits, and then we would have been in real trouble.'

'So, where do we go from here? I'm utterly worn out by lack of sleep. I need a good night's rest.'

'Well, we've got a choice, but it's not terribly promising.'

'Why not?'

'Because, between one thing and another, we've lost the time schedule which was tight enough. Either we split up and go and enquire independently from domestic airlines about in-coming flights to check if Daniel's or Jacob's name figure on their lists, but it could be too late; or we both go to Mrs. Vanderwelt's funeral and chat to Mrs. Blacker as humanely as we can in the circumstances to find out what she knows—if anything. Shall we toss for it?'

'Yes, let's; head for the airlines, tail for the funeral.'

As Sinclair prepared to toss the coin, he saw the two men from the Miami Vice squad heading in their direction with long, hurried strides.

'Oh, oh!' exclaimed Sinclair, 'Here comes trouble. What do you bet it's about the *Margarita*? Hello, guys, been sailing yet?'

The men shook their head in the negative and handed a copy of 'Le Monde' to Sebastian.

'Perhaps, you'd like to translate this for your boss.' And with that they were gone.

Sebastian read the copy which had a red circle around it, and then looking over the harbour at the sea, he said :

'The *Margarita* has been torched.'

'Where?', asked Sinclair.

'Over there, in the Caribbean.'

'Whereabouts in the Caribbean? It covers an area of seven-hundred-and-fifty miles, for heaven's sake!'

'It doesn't say. What a tragedy!'

'The insurance will pay. The tragedy is, with an average depth of 8,400 feet and the greatest depth at just over 23.000 feet, the chances of recovering the bodies are minimal. Besides, they would have been charred in the fire beyond recognition, leaving no physical evidence for identification, not to mention the undertow which would make inroads on the soft facial tissues through rolling them about in the shallows, and the fishes, and the birds.'

'Is that all you can do in the face of such a tragedy? Come up with statistics. What about poor Mrs. Blacker? She must know by now. I mean it must be all over the news and she must feel devastated, what with her mother and her husband and brother-in-law, all dead.'

'How do you know they're both dead? There was a third party on board,—Aristide, Homer's son. Perhaps, he helped them both men to safety and will come back bringing glad tidings.'

'You're not happy with that idea, are you?'

'What idea?'

Daniel Blacker's body lying at the bottom of the sea, out of reach, like a quarry that has slipped away quietly to die later in the undergrowth by accident.'

'You're right. By choice I would prefer a different kind of scenario, whereby Daniel Blacker would kill his brother, before he had a chance to speak to Mrs. Vanderwelt's lawyers about the changes she wanted to make to her last will and testament, and then killed Aristide on the off chance that he witnessed the murder.'

'And then?'

'He would set the *Margarita* alight and jump off the side. He was a strong swimmer.'

'So was Jacob; they both were.'

'He could swim away by stages between islands, from cove to cove. Besides, how do you know he didn't assume Jacob's identity? He was clean-shaven; therefore he owned a razor and could shave all his hair off to look like Jacob. It's likely we'll never know.'

'There will be photographs though on some people's websites, people lucky enough to be in the area to catch the burning wreck either from the air or some near-by landfall . . .'

'It's possible.'

'You are going to do the decent thing by Mrs. Blacker, aren't you?'

'You mean send her a sympathy card or take her in my arms and let her cry over my shoulder the way it happens in Hollywood movies? I somehow think that would not go down well with the mother superior. What I can't understand is why you don't run back to Homer to find out what happened to the *Margarita*. Cold feet about a possible Vodou ceremony by a mambo invoking the ancestral spirits to wreak vengeance on white employers? Aristide was a good son, and he's been wantonly killed. Come along; there's no need for us to linger on the island. Let's go back to the orphanage and pack our bags.'

An unusually quiet atmosphere hung over the place; the children were standing about aimlessly in the playground; the nuns were nowhere to be seen. Sebastian went into the kitchen to enquire about the chance of a meal, but it was deserted. Then the mother superior burst in, holding an empty jug of water followed by Sinclair who had gone to look for her.

'Come to finish packing, have you?'

'Yes, reverend mother, if that's all right with you.'

'Of course, it is.'

'Reverend mother, may I ask how Mrs. Blacker is taking it?'

'Taking what, Mr. Sinclair?'

'The news about the *Margarita*?'

'Oh, you know, do you? News travels fast nowadays. It's not just local gossip . . .'

'No, reverend mother; it's live and it's global.'

'Well, let me tell you that Mrs. Blacker has taken it very badly, so badly in fact that I had to get our doctor to put her under heavy sedation in my office, where she lost control. She's sleeping now. Her father-in-law will be collecting her later on to take her to Santa Lucia to live with him. She's going to need a lot of love from now on.'

The mother superior filled the jug from the water purifier and then turning round, she cast a searching look at both men.

'I don't suppose you people know anything about what happened out there?'

'No', replied Sinclair, 'accidents at sea occur very quickly and unexpectedly because of the amount of time that has to be spent attending to essential tasks in order to keep the vessel going, though to-day navigation is largely electronic. Once the trouble starts, there may not be enough time to deal with it.'

'I see. I am sorry there is nobody available in the kitchen; all my nuns are in chapel offering prayers for Mrs. Blacker's recovery. School has been suspended. Do feel free to join us in chapel and now, if you will excuse me, I must join my flock. Have a safe journey home.'

Sinclair ran after the mother superior as she walked through the door.

'Reverend mother . . .'

'Yes, what is it?'

'In your opinion, is there any likelihood of Mrs. Blacker ever joining your outfit, I mean as a nun, taking the veil and the vows?'

'Mr. Sinclair, I find your question somewhat indiscreet. God's wisdom works in mysterious ways, and who am I to presume on having an inkling into His designs? All I can say is I hope Mrs. Blacker will one day fulfil herself through finding a nice husband who will give her lovely children. She needs a lot of love. And now, I really must go; my nuns are waiting.'

'Amazing woman! You know, Sebastian, in the Middle Ages, there were nunneries full of women like her, who had had affairs with knights and knew all about romantic involvements. In those days, they had an amazing system for indulging their sexual desires more or less instantly, wherever. Each knight had an army of squires who at a moment's notice, and with extraordinary skill, could erect pavilions in the open countryside in between castles, in meadows full of flowers in Springtime, so they could lie with their ladies as and when.'

'You mean, it was the equivalent if the motel in our time?'

'Yes. The problem, of course, was the disarming of the knight; it was a procedure, almost a ritual, that took some time, as you can imagine, with all that armour, and mail shirt underneath . . .'

'It must have been a real nuisance for those who suffered from premature ejaculation . . .'

'Barnard, why is it that when I indulge a flight of romantic fancy once in a blue moon you feel obliged to make a trite remark that kills it?'

'Probably because I am embarrassed by it; you're such a down-to-earth person, Sinclair.'

Sinclair was puzzled another foolscap envelope had arrived in the mail. The envelopes had started coming through the post a few weeks after his return from Haiti. They contained 7x5 photographs of the *Margarita* as she sank on fire in the Caribbean. Neither the envelopes nor the prints inside them bore any mark to enlighten the recipient as to their origin or the identity of the sender. Sinclair had not seen nor heard from Sebastian since their return and thought that maybe the boy who had been such an integral part of the Haitian enquiry might be able to make some useful comments about the photographs.

The Sailors' Club was quiet when Sinclair walked into Sebastian's dressing-room.

'Nice', he said, 'very nice. Are you still pleased with it?'

`Yes, I am; it's restful and it's my own. What do you want?'

`Well, if it's not shattering the peace and tranquillity of your retreat too much, I'd like you to take a look at those photographs and tell me what you think; but before you handle them, please put on those gloves.'

`What are they printed on?', asked Sebastian as he opened the envelope.

`The usual photographic Kodak paper. Anybody could have downloaded them.'

`Any finger prints on them?'

`None. I keep getting them through the Woman's magazine where I advertise my services as a private eye.'

`Well, in that case, might not a woman be the sender?'

`Who, for instance?'

`The Mother Superior at the orphanage or Eleanor Blacker from her father-in-law's place in Santa Lucia.'

`What for? As far as they knew we were investigating claims for an insurance company about Life policies.'

`Well, from what I can see, I'd say the photographs were taken from close up with a mobile phone.'

`Yes. That rules out a plane flying overhead or a cruise ship sailing past, and a passenger with a proper camera taking the shots; no need to check with shipping companies or airlines for schedules . . .'

`Are you trying to tell me that Daniel Blacker himself took those photographs? How would he have dispatched them?'

`Maybe he has a courier. Don't forget he owns a bachelor pad somewhere off Canary Wharf.'

`To what purpose would he do such a thing? To fake his own death?'

`No; to taunt me.'

`It is sad to see how obsessional thoughts can overthrow a great mind . . .'

`I'll tell you what happened on the evidence of those photographs.'

`Daniel Blacker engineered the whole thing to make it look like an accident?'

`Yes. The day you saw him at Port au Prince putting out to sea, bound for Santa Lucia, he altered course and made for Wilhemstad in Curaçao where he killed Jacob to stop him from contacting Mrs. Vanderwelt's lawyers knowing the changes she wished to make to her last wishes were detrimental to him. He then gets Aristide, Homer's son, to help him carry the body on board, and they sail for Santa Lucia. When he gets close enough to the island, he drugs Aristide and when he is sure Aristide is unconscious, he lays him alongside Jacob's body. He waits until the fire develops, lowers the dinghy, fixes the gangway, then shaves his head, and, when the fire has gained control, climbs down into the dinghy and takes photographs of the blaze on his mobile phone. That, Sebastian, is a perfectly reasonable reconstruction of a rationally elaborated crime, not the product of a mind affected by an obsessional neurosis.'

`So, he sails away "for a year and a day, to the land where the Bongo tree grows", Santa Lucia, home and dry to Daddy?'

`I don't know about "a year and a day", but he can't go drifting from coast to coast for ever, can he? Besides, he's Jacob now, the good guy who may find favour with that bereaved lady, who may be craving for solace, having lost first a mother and then a husband. But, from his own endoscopic point of view, he's also Daniel and, as Daniel, he has marital rights over Eleanor, and she is still a potential heiress, despite Jacob's ill-fated intervention.'

`"Cherchez la femme", as the French say?'

`Yes, Barnard, but there's something else we have to "chercher"'.

`What's that?'

`The dinghy, Barnard, for crying out loud, the bloody dinghy as evidence! You can't nail a suspect without physical evidence.'

`No; that's true.'

`The dinghy must have washed up somewhere. I can't tell you how often that dinghy has haunted my dreams since those photographs started coming through the post! It wasn't one of those `cheap and cheerful' rubber contraptions, was it?'

`Oh, no, sirrah, that it wasn't! I saw it with my own eyes when the *Margarita* left Port au Prince; it was a beautifully crafted piece of carpentry that did not deter in any way from the class and elegance of the boat, a small vessel in its own rights.'

`As you've probably gathered by now, I had an ulterior motive in coming here with those prints. Arthur Blacker, the twins' father, has placed an advertisement in a sailing magazine calling for volunteers. He is commandeering a diving operation round the wreck of the *Margarita*.'

`She's been located then?'

Yes, and that leads me to believe that things must be happening up there at the villa which are puzzling him. I know it may be sheer surmise on my part but, as I said, Daniel Blacker can't go on beachcombing for ever . . . The old man probably hopes to find clues at the bottom of the Caribbean either to dispel or confirm his fears about a possible switch of identity.'

'I knew your coming here was a bad omen. I can't bear depths.'

'Oh, no, don't get me wrong; I'll be doing the diving. I have in fact already added my name to the list of volunteers. No, what I thought you could do was to keep the Blackers' villa under surveillance while I dive. You've done that sort of job before.'

'That sounds like a reasonable offer . . .'

'If you do take it up, there is one thing you must promise me not to do, and that is to contact Aristide's father in Haiti or we might be the victims of a cyber Vodu attack. There are malevolent spirits among the benevolent ones in the Vodu pantheon. What I mean is, Aristide was a good retainer, always doing his best to please his white masters; he didn't deserve to die in such a ghastly way . . .'

'All right; it's a deal. There is something that puzzles me though, I mean about Arthur Blacker going to all that trouble organizing a diving expedition when there is somebody up there at the villa who could clear up any doubt he may entertain about the identity of the son who's turned up at the villa . . .'

'Eleanor Blacker?'

'Yes—in the bedroom.'

'It may be too early for that, if Daniel, alias Jacob, is in poor shape depending on how long he spent getting back home; or she might be too terrified to say anything if she suspects Jacob is in fact Daniel with his hair shaved off. Women are very sensitive to atmosphere. Besides, we don't know what transpired between her and Jacob on the day she came back from her honeymoon. As far as we know, she went straight back to the Laboule apartment before visiting her mother in hospital where Jacob had taken the old lady in a critical condition before flying to Wilhemstad to see her lawyers at her behest. What if they met very briefly and Jacob disclosed to her what Mrs. Vanderwelt revealed to him about her head injury, and the changes she wanted made to her last will and testament as a result? The poor woman must be living in fear and tremble. This is why I need you to keep the villa under surveillance while I take part in the diving expedition.'

'You really have a bee in your bonnet about Daniel Blacker being a rogue volunteer tourist, haven't you?'

'That's not the point at issue, Barnard; a woman's life may be at stake.'

'What I can't understand is why you can't go up to the villa yourself and waylay Eleanor Blacker round the corner of some dimly-lit corridor, and ask her point blank who sleeps with her.'

'Because this is not James Bond, Barnard; this is real; forget James Bond. At the moment, I have to focus on locating the dinghy, and I am not likely to find it at the bottom of the sea, am I? That puts the ball in your quarter. Please make sure you bring a telescope as well as a pair of binoculars.'

To Sebastian, the prospect looked glum. With Sinclair gone off shore to join the other volunteers on the diving boat, he was left alone to get on with the tedious task of keeping Arthur Blacker's villa under surveillance; but it was not long before he realized it would not be the exacting job that he imagined at first.

Every morning, after breakfast, Arthur Blacker would lead his daughter-in-law on to the terrace and help her settle down in a recliner chair. Then, he would go back indoors and return carrying what looked like books and magazines which he would put on a table beside her. Then, he would sit next to her and hand her a glass of water to swallow medicines with. It went like clockwork, and while he watched the scenario unfold from a cramped position that made his knees and elbows sore, Sebastian could not help thinking of Sinclair describing fluid arabesques on the sea bed of the Caribbean. What unnerved him most was the lack of communication; there were no text messages; no signals; Arthur Blacker up at the house was in all likelihood the recipient of umpteen bulletins about the dives . . . Then, one day, as Sebastian's powers of endurance began to flag, something alerted his eyes and made him sit up with a sense of expectancy.

Behind the patio doors, as Arthur Blacker led his daughter-in-law on to the terrace, he thought he noticed a shadow moving and, as he peered more closely, he distinguished a figure moving on crutches. The figure waved to Mrs. Blacker and she waved back; then the routine unfolded in the usual humdrum way; Arthur Blacker brought out the books and the magazines, and a tray for refreshments.

The next day, again Sebastian observed the same shadowy figure moving on crutches behind the patio doors. Then Arthur Blacker did an unusual thing; he kissed his daughter-in-law on both cheeks and went back indoors to reappear a few minutes later in the courtyard where he got into his car. No sooner had he disappeared down the drive then the shadowy figure on crutches that Sebastian had noticed before came through the patio doors, threw his crutches down and bent over Eleanor Blacker to kiss her, then he settled down beside her on the couch and took her in his arms.

Sweat ran down Sebastian back. From what he could see Eleanor lay perfectly still and let herself be fondled. After a while, neither of them moved; it looked as though they had fallen asleep in each other's arms . . . Did they not expect Arthur Blacker to come back? Normally, he never went out in the morning; he and Eleanor had lunch on the terrace; after lunch, they went indoors for a siesta and did not reappear on the terrace till late in the afternoon, and then Arthur Blacker would go out, not returning till dinner time. Was Eleanor Blacker still officially married to Daniel Blacker having an affair with Jacob? The man who lay beside her looked bald. Perhaps she had come to realize that it was Jacob she loved because he was the worthier one of the two; or was she still too traumatized to care,—just needed comfort in someone's arms, someone she knew?

A text message from Sinclair on Sebastian's mobile phone explained the situation :—Arthur Blacker had gone down to the harbour master's office to make an announcement; he was calling off the marine survey of the *Magarita* ; the volunteers were free to go home at the end of the day. They had responded well to his appeal to try and salvage clues from the wreck which would help him and his daughter-in-law to come to terms with their losses. And he was enormously grateful.

Sebastian felt suddenly disappointed; perhaps not so much disappointed as let down. After all that,—the muscular discomfort, the loneliness, the climate (he had never been one for the heat, and the poor diet, just as he was on the brink of making a tremendous discovery about some of the inmates at the villa, Sinclair was coming back none the wiser for having been on a diving spree,—and he was not alone! As Sebastian hurried across the quay to welcome him back, he saw a young man still in a diving suit walking beside him.

'Sebastian, meet Tom! Tom, this is Sebastian, my assistant; he's studying to be an archaeologist. Tom's got nothing to do for a few days till he joins another marine exploration; he's volunteered to help us look for the dinghy.'

'That's all very well, but it'll have to wait. I have something to tell you.'

Tom patted Sinclair on the back. 'That's all right, mate. I'll see you on the beach to-morrow morning. Shall we take our wet suits just in case?'

'Yes, let's', replied Sinclair, and before he could say any more Sebastian dropped his bombshell :

'Eleanor Blacker has a boyfriend, a bald-headed man who walks on crutches. How's that for a discovery?'

'You could discern a bald-headed man on the end of a telescope?'

'Don't forget you pointed out Daniel Blacker to me at London Airport; he had amazing hair. Well, at least, I've come up with something, which is more than some people have.'

'What's that supposed to mean?'

'I've provided you with an independent lead, can't you see? Why on earth did you have to go on that diving jaunt? You knew before you started it would be a waste of time.'

'Barnard, a good detective must be seen to be doing what a good detective must do in order to confuse the enemy; it's an old warfare tactic.'

'Oh, by the way, I forgot to tell you. Your friends of Miami Vice asked to be remembered to you. They said they were sorry about the *Margarita*; they were so looking forward to go sailing in her.'

'Are you sure they were the same men?'

'Yes, with wide-brimmed hats and sun glasses.'

'First, you see a bald-headed man on the end of a telescope; then you meet the Miami men from the Vice squad close enough to recognize them. Are you sure you're not under the weather?'

'I never feel a hundred per cent in these tropical parts; you know that; the climate doesn't suit me,' and looking up at the sky which was getting dark, he said :

'So, the underwater search proved fruitless, which was to be expected if Daniel Blacker is the cunning criminal you rate him to be . . .'

'All criminals are ingenious; they want to show the world how clever they are.'

'Arthur Blacker didn't find what he was looking for to help him out of his quandary?'

'I'm afraid not; the boat is completely burnt out. There's not a shred of evidence down there to confirm or deny foul play.'

251

'Do you think he knows Eleanor is copulating with whoever?'

'Maybe Jacob was giving her a Thai massage. Did you know that in Thailand all the members of a family massage one another to counteract the stress of modern life?'

'It doesn't cost them anything then?'

'No, Barnard, it doesn't cost them anything.'

Sebastian pondered for a moment and then he asked :

'So, you're off beachcombing to-morrow with Tom Whoever?'

'No, Barnard, we're all going in search of the *Margarita's* dinghy to-morrow.'

'You're suspending the surveillance of the Blackers' villa?'

'Yes, I think you've seen enough to excite your imagination, don't you?'

'The dinghy must be reduced to smithereens by now . . .'

'Well, we'll see. Even a plank with a few nails in it would do. The forensic foray is now declared open.'

It was just like Sinclair to make an optimistic forecast when he had a bee in his bonnet. The surveillance of the Blackers' villa which had been a priority a few weeks ago all of a sudden had lost its urgency; the interest had switched to the dinghy. Yet, it was not outside the realm of possibilities that the dinghy—if it still existed—had been stored in some secure, out-of-the-way place inside the villa, and that an assiduous form of surveillance might in the end disclose its location, but who was he to question Sinclair's ability to make the right decision? There was a kind of frivolity in Sinclair' decision-making; he called it flair,—the flair of the well-bred sniffer dog which would have been too highly-strung for the average household, ensconced in a despotic domestic routine of its own making, to tolerate. Most detectives possessed it in some measure as an essential attribute and, where supported by the apparatus of modern forensic science, whatever case they worked on was destined to succeed. He would point out that often in the early stages of an enquiry a detective would put forward a theory which logically ensued from the circumstantial evidence, but it sometimes took years to find the physical evidence to corroborate it. Thus, a killer who had stored his victim's body parts in an old trunk of his, often used the top of it as a table to have a picnic on the beach when the bustle of city life got too much for him, and that's where it was found eventually by children playing 'Pirates of the Caribbean' . . . It was an ineluctable fact that the *Margarita* had at one time possessed a dinghy and that her dinghy was a substantial piece of carpentry able to stand being buffeted about. It was also an ineluctable fact that being made of wood, it would burn.

All the thoughts which had gone round and round in Sebastian's head during the night that followed Sinclair's return from his trip offshore returned to plague him next morning as he trudged across the beach a few strides behind Sinclair and his diving mate; and he realized then that he had no alternative in order to regain peace of mind but to go with the flow . . . Casting a backward glance at the Blacker's villa, he lunged forward, crying :

'Then heigh-ho! The holly! This life is most jolly.'

Both Sinclair and Tom turned round in time to see Sebastian cutting a series of silly capers across the sand like a hermit crab.

End of Part I

Part II

When Sinclair and Sebastian walked into the courtroom at the Old Baileys, it was packed, but that did not surprise them in the least. The story of a beautiful yacht which had gone up in flames in the Caribbean, a few nautical miles away from the island of Santa Lucia, with the loss of two lives on board had caught the public's imagination due to media interest. Already when Jacob Blacker had appeared at a Magistrate court in London after being remanded in custody, and he pleaded `not guilty' to the charges brought against him, i.e. arson and double murder, large crowds had gathered on the pavement outside the court on account of the amount of publicity given to the case.

For Sinclair personally it was a day of hope,—to see his theory vindicated (a theory which he had nurtured over months, and which had been fortified by a second visit to the Caribbean) and a criminal brought to justice.

Among the people in the courtroom, Sinclair recognized Arthur Blacker and, seated next to him, his daughter-in-law Eleanor Blacker, dressed in black. He had not set eyes on the unfortunate lady since the day her mother died at the orphanage in Haiti, and found her appearance much altered though she still possessed that distinctive and refined charm that set her apart from other beautiful women.

When Daniel (alias Jacob) Blacker was bought in, he looked round the courtroom, and when he saw Mrs. Blacker he stopped and let his eyes rest on her until moved on by the guards.

`All rise', announced the clerk of court as Judge Leo Ruddersfold Q.C. walked into the courtroom to take the bench. Sinclair looked at the judge with particular attention. There were rumours going round the courts that Judge Ruddersford was one of those legal authorities who wanted the jury system abolished, claiming that it was obsolete because life in the modern age had become too involved with Science and Technology for ten 'plain' honest men as jurors to sift through and assess all the specialist evidence put before them. Whereas other judges would have been adamant about not going ahead with a trial with only eight jurors, if two of them had been issued with a medical certificate exonerating them from jury service, claiming it would be a breach of civic liberty, Judge Ruddersford would have been happy to do without the lot of them and deal with the matter in camera with the help of a team of experts . . .

The jurors having been sworn in, and cautioned about the severity of the penalty they would be liable to if they were to discuss the court proceedings with people in the outside world, Mr. Mark Silversteen, counsel for the Defence, took the floor.

'Ladies and gentlemen of the jury, there have been many famous twins in History,—Romulus and Remus in ancient Rome, Castor and Pollux in Greek and Roman mythology, Esau and Jacob in the Bible. It is not my intention to bring a religious book like the Bible to he fore in a court of law as a source of fitting parallels, but, since I have it on the authority of Arthur Blacker, the father of the twins involved in this case, that his son Daniel was born first and he was very hairy at birth, and for that reason the twin that followed hard on his heels was called Jacob, I will continue to evoke the biblical parallel because in actual fact, in this case, it affords more than one analogy, extending to character traits as well as physical ones. Like Esau, Daniel Blacker was a man of action, 'a cunning hunter', whereas Jacob Blacker, like his biblical counterpart, preferred a more sedate way of life, within a community. Bearing in mind those distinctive temperamental traits as well as the outward ones, I ask you, members of the jury to take a long, hard look at the man sitting in the dock, whose name is Jacob, and to ask yourselves whether a man with such a meek and mild nature, whose bald-headedness differentiated him as a significant genetic feature from his brother Daniel, who sported a magnificent head of hair, so magnificent in fact that it had to be restrained by a bandanna, whether such a man would be capable of killing first his brother Daniel, an athletic type, then the deckhand, a seasoned Haitian mariner, employed on the *Margarita*, and having committed those two crimes, set the boat on fire and escaped unscathed to make his way back to his father's house in Santa Lucia. Thank you, ladies and gentlemen. That is all.'

Mr. John Harrison, counsel for the Prosecution, then took the floor.

'Ladies and gentlemen of the jury, my honoured colleague has gone to great lengths to depict the man who claims to be Jacob Blacker as a meek and mild individual who would be incapable of committing the crimes he stands accused of and to which he pleaded 'not guilty'. My purpose is far simpler and more straightforward. It is to prove to you 'beyond the shadow of a doubt' that the person you see now sitting on the bench of the accused is not the harmless one that he pretends to be, but a hardened criminal who posed as a philanthropic, humanitarian volunteer tourist operating in disaster areas alongside genuine air workers in order to satisfy his sadistic instincts to the detriment of helpless victims trapped under rubble. Not only is the accused a criminal but is he also an impostor whose real name is Daniel Blacker,—minus the flamboyant hirsuteness, shaved off to impersonate his bald-headed twin, Jacob. That is all, ladies and gentlemen of the jury.'

It was clear to Sinclair that the battle of wits between the two counsels was to be fought mainly on the issue of identity; that, in fact, was perhaps what constituted the major aspect of this courtroom drama for many of those sitting in the courtroom, as well as the public at large. Who was the man sitting in the dock? Was the case one of mistaken identity? Obviously a verdict could not be reached until the matter had been cleared up. That was what worried Sinclair because Sebastian was due to testify next morning as an independent witness and the Defence was likely to discredit his testimony; the boy was such an indolent, wool-gathering character. It was a real pity because, as it so happened, Sebastian was the only person who could claim to have seen both Jacob and Daniel Blacker on the same day in Haiti, a few hours apart. But, being who he was, his testimony was unlikely to be of advantage to the Prosecution, and Sinclair assumed philosophically that his assistant would end the day branded as an unreliable witness.

'Sebastian Barnard, to take the stand! Please, raise your right hand and repeat after me 'I swear to speak the truth, the whole truth and nothing but the truth., so help me God.'

'Mr. Barnard, you claim to have seen on a beach in Haiti, through a cleft in the rock, a male figure whom you thought was a 'look-a-like' of Daniel Blacker, a man who had been pointed out to you in a crowd of passengers at London Airport a few months earlier. Please, tell the court in your own words how you came to identify the swimmer as a 'look-alike' of Daniel Blacker.'

'Well, it was like this. We had just arrived in Haiti from London, via Miami, at Toussaint Louverture international airport, and we couldn't find lodgings because the place we originally wanted to stay at had been destroyed in the earthquake. Eventually, through the recommendation of a UN officer, we did find a place run by nuns who went out of their way to greet us in a proper manner. They and the orphans in their care fell over my boss who became tied up with them.'

'Please, come straight to the point, Mr. Barnard'.

'Well, it was very hot and I was at a loose end, and I could see the Caribbean sea sparkling down below, and I thought it would be nice to go for a dip. On my way down to the sea, through a chink in a rock, I saw a man on a strip of sand, getting ready to go into the water, and he was the spitting image of Daniel Blacker except for one thing.'

'What was that, Mr. Barnard?'

'As he put on a swim cap I noticed he had a clean-shaven head.'

'So, you were suffering from jet lag, and the extreme heat of the Caribbean, and possibly a sense of displacement as well due to the dereliction that lay all around as a result of the earthquake, and you thought you would go for a nice dip in the sea to refresh yourself, and it was then that, through a cleft in the rock face, you saw the accused down below by the water. How far away were you then? Fifteen, twenty, thirty yards?'

'I couldn't say with any precision. I was taken by surprise.'

'Please, tell the court in your own words what happened next.'

'I went into the water, and closed my eyes and let the undertow toss me about.'

'And how long did you stay in that state of suspended motion, Mr. Barnard? Fifteen minutes? Half an hour? An hour? The truth of the matter is, you don't know; you simply have no recollection of what happened, and when you came to, the man you identified as a 'look-a-like' of Daniel Blacker's had vanished, and you did not see him again until you saw him in Santa Lucia several months later on the end of a telescope while you were carrying out the surveillance of the Blackers' villa. Is that right?'

'Yes, it is.'

'Mr. Barnard, was that man the man you now see sitting in the dock?'

'Yes, it was.'

'No further question, your honour.'

'You may stand down, Mr. Barnard.'

Sinclair had to bow down to the inevitable. It had not taken the Defence long to throw discredit on Sebastian's testimony. It remained to be seen what the Prosecution could do with Arthur Blacker's own testimony in order to bring forward the process of identification which was a prime issue in the case.

The twins' father looked self-composed as he took the oath. Before rising, Sinclair noticed that he had patted his daughter-in-law's hand several times.

'Mr. Blacker', counsel for the defence began, 'you have two sons, twin sons as a matter of fact. Is it not common knowledge, Mr. Blacker, that parents of twins of the same gender claim they can tell which is which even when they're apart, and lovers who get married to twin sisters on the same day can tell their brides apart?'

'Yes, it is.'

'Now you, Mr. Blacker, are fortunate in the sense that your twin sons were born with distinctive outward signs which could not in the worst circumstances allow for any kind of confusion. One, Daniel, was hirsute, and the other had scanty hair, showing signs of baldness at an early age; and when he became prematurely bald as it happens in families due to the facts of heredity, no perplexity was at all possible from then on,—if ever.'

'No, it was never a problem', said the twins' father.

'So, now your son Daniel is missing, presumed dead, killed in a fire that broke out on your yacht, the *Margarita*, and caused it to sink, you should have no problem recognizing the person sitting in the dock as you son Jacob, Daniel's twin. Mr. Blacker, I ask you the question, is the man sitting in the dock your son Jacob? Mr. Blacker? Remember you're under oath.'

'Yes.'

'No further question, your honour.'

Counsel for the Prosecution asked for permission to cross-examine the witness.

'Permission granted', replied Judge Ruddersford.

'Mr, Blacker, when my honoured colleague questioned you about the identity of the person sitting in the dock, who, as far as the court knows to all intents and purposes is your son Jacob, you did not answer spontaneously right away; as a matter of fact you hesitated, whereas, in the light of what you said before, the question should have elicited from you a spontaneous and forthright answer. Isn't it true, Mr. Blacker, that some time after your son 'Jacob' turned up at your house in Santa Lucia claiming to have survived the fire on the *Margarita* where his brother Daniel and the Haitian deckhand Aristide both lost their lives, you thought fit to commandeer a diving survey of the boat where she lay?'

'Yes, I did.'

'Isn't it also true that you did so because you had doubts about the identity of the survivor who had turned up at your house, and you hoped that by having the wreck investigated by professional divers some clue would be brought uppermost to resolve your quandary one way or another?'

'Objection', shouted counsel for the Defence.

'Overruled', replied Judge Ruddersford, 'answer the question.'

'Yes, I did.'

'No further question, your honour.'

'You may step down, Mr. Blacker. This court will adjourn and reconvene to-morrow morning at nine a.m.'

Sinclair was not displeased with the way things were going. Mr. John Harrison, counsel for the prosecution, seemed determined to break down the wall of silence—or was it one of fear?—that had so far protected the anonymity of the man in the dock, who, to Sinclair's personal knowledge, operated under a despicable alias. In the morning, when the court reconvened, in all likelihood counsel for the Defence would try and delay proceedings by bringing up again the question of the hereditary factors which he had briefly touched upon during the twins' father's interrogation, the reason for that being that Eleanor Blacker was due to testify, and scientific date about the physical basis of personality might not come amiss since she had had close relationships with both the Blacker twins.

'There is no doubt at all', Mr. Mark Silversteen, counsel for the defence, began by saying, when he took the floor first thing, 'that personality is largely determined by physical endowment and physical endowment is inherited and therefore it behoves us to become acquainted with the modern view of inheritance based on Gregor Mendel's principles which show that our physical makeup is determined by our inheritance.'

'Please, come straight to the point, Mr. Silversteen', interrupted Judge Ruddersford.

'Your honour, I have here a genealogical sketch showing scanty hair and hirsuteness more compatible with hirsuteness being dominant to baldness according to Mendelian characteristics, and to be sex-linked to masculinity, as exemplified by the story of Samson in the Book of Judges.'

`Wouldn't it be simpler to say', interrupted counsel for the Prosecution, `in accordance with Darwin's principle of natural selection, that organisms have the property of copying themselves but with occasional inaccuracies?'

A few titters were heard coming from the gallery. Judge Ruddersford ordered the clerk to clear the court and then announced :

`This court will reconvene in half an hour. Mr. Harrison and Mr. Silversteen, I'll see you in my chamber in ten minutes.'

Once the two counsels stood before him, Judge Ruddersford lost no time in addressing them :

`I must caution you both against using your oratorical skills to engage in over-hasty generalisations about the Mendelian laws of heredity which at the best of times would require the guidance of an expert biologist on account of the ambiguity of certain terms like `dominant' and `recessive', not to mention Darwin's controversial views on evolution. Not only is this course digressive and time-wasting but is it also dangerous because it may mislead the jurors. Remember they are ten `plain' honest men, with the emphasis falling on the word `plain', and I personally do not recognize such highfalutin arguments as having any relevance to this case. That is all. I'll see you both in court in ten minutes.'

There was quite a lot of good-humoured banter bandied between the two parties as court reconvened and the two lawyers resumed their separate stance; Solomon had spoken.

Sinclair dreaded what lay ahead; not so much the examination as the cross-examination of a tender-hearted woman such as Eleanor Blacker. As she took the oath, a hush fell on the court.

`Mrs. Blacker, please tell the court the circumstances in which you met your husband, Daniel Blacker', said Mr. Silversteen.

`My mother, who lived in Curaçao, had gone to Port au Prince to visit some old friends who owned an ancient distillery. She had not been there long when the earthquake occurred and she happened to be in one the worst hit areas of the town. She did not know how long she remained trapped under rubble, but she remembered being pulled out by a young man who had a lot of hair under his tin hat, and being taken to a field hospital. It took me a long time to locate her, and, when I did, her rescuer stood at her bedside; his name was Daniel Blacker. He said he was a volunteer tourist whose vocation was to help victims in disaster areas. My mother was too frail to travel back to Wilhemstad, so we rented a furnished apartment in the Laboule district, which was nice and quiet for her. Soon after she asked me to let her lawyers know that she wished to endow Daniel Blacker with a substantial sum of money as a reward for rescuing her.'

'Do you know how much it was?'

'No; all I knew ultimately was that she wanted all the money left in trust for me personally with her bank in Wilhemstad as trustees.'

'You mean, she had second thoughts about endowing Daniel Blacker as her rescuer?'

'Yes.'

Mrs. Blacker took a handkerchief out of her handbag and dabbed her eyes.

'After Daniel and I got married, when the question of a honeymoon cropped up, Daniel said he had a twin brother who would bring their father's yacht over from Santa Lucia so we could spent our honeymoon sailing round the Caribbean, and he would stay in the apartment to look after my mother with the help of the housekeeper. Two days before we were due to come back from our honeymoon, we received a signal from Jacob saying my mother's condition had deteriorated and he was taking her back to hospital before flying to Wilhemstad to see her lawyers as she was fretting over her last wishes. Daniel had to take the boat back to Santa Lucia for refitting, so he dropped me off at Port au Prince, and soon after I went to see my mother in hospital. She was drifting in and out of consciousness; she told me certain areas of her memory had come back and she remembered being dealt a heavy blow on the head by her rescuer before being brought to the surface. She kept saying how kind and helpful Jacob had been and how spontaneously he had offered to go and see her lawyers about her last will.'

'Mrs. Blacker, did you see Jacob Blacker, your brother-in-law, before he left for

Wilhelmstad on his errand of mercy?'

No, there was no time in view of my mother's critical condition.'

'So, he left for Curaçao before your husband dropped you off at Port au Prince?'

'Yes'.

`And you never saw him again until he reappeared in Santa Lucia where you lived with your father-in-law, claiming to have escaped from the fire on the *Margarita*?'

`No, I didn't.'

`Did he say how he came to be on the *Margarita* in the first place, I mean before the fire?'

`He said Daniel had picked him up in Wilhenstad to take him back to Santa Lucia where he lived.'

`Mrs. Blacker, I am fully aware that the question I am about to ask you is one which any self-respecting woman would find indiscreet and even repugnant. Did you at any time during the intimate moments that you shared with the accused at your father-in-law's villa notice anything, anything at all that would lead you to believe that he was not the person he claimed to be? I mean that his lovemaking was not in keeping with his kind, gentle nature, and it reminded you of someone else, someone more virile and hirsute?'

`Objection!', cried counsel for the Prosecution.

`Overruled. Answer the question, Mrs. Blacker', said Judge Ruddersford.

`No', whispered Mrs. Blacker.

`Mrs. Blacker, please raise your voice so the court can hear you', said the Judge.

`No', repeated Mrs. Blacker.

`No further question, your honour.'

`You may step down, Mrs. Blacker . . . 'Judge Ruddersford's voice trailed and became barely audible; the courtroom was in an uproar; people were giving vent to indignation.; from the gallery women shouted `Shame! Disgrace!' In vain, the clerk of the court cried `Order! Order!' until told by the judge to clear the courtroom. Mrs. Blacker had been asked a leading question and an insidious one at that. Had she answered `yes' instead of `no', she risked unmasking the man in the dock as an impostor and, by the same token, laying herself open to retaliation, should he walk free.

The people's reaction heartened Sinclair. There was still a sense of decency, and compassion for the underdog in England among the common people whom he considered to be the backbone of the nation.

Following Mrs. Blacker's dramatic testimony Sinclair knew events would follow on very quickly, and he looked forward to the next hearing when Mr. Harrison, counsel for the Prosecution, would launch his offensive in order to enable the jury to reach a verdict.

'All rise', said the clerk of the court as Judge Ruddersford entered the courtroom and made his way to the bench. After sitting down and gathering a few papers in front of him, he let his eyes wander over the assembly with a quizzical look. So far, the voice of the accused had not been heard in court, and perhaps he wondered what lay in store in the way of disorderly behaviour of the kind that he had to put up with the day before when it was.

Jacob Blacker took the oath calmly, like someone who has nothing to fear from the law, and when counsel for the Defence invited him to tell the court in his own words what happened the day the *Margarita* went up in flames and sank in the Caribbean, he began speaking in a self-controlled and matter-of-fact way. He said his brother Daniel went to pick him up in Wilhemstad to save him having to fly back to Santa Lucia, as the boat had to go back there anyway for refitting. During the crossing, Daniel started drinking heavily and got Aristide to join him. He went to lie down in his bunk as they caroused and fell asleep to be woken up later by the smell of smoke. As he attempted to climb up the stairwell, the smell was so dense it drove him back several times causing him to fall and injure his hip and, when he finally managed to emerge up on deck, the fire had spread beyond control; all he could do was to grab a lifebuoy and jump overboard. Fortunately, the coastline of Santa Lucia was visible in the offing and he was able to swim the distance by fits and starts although his injured hip made his progress in the water painfully slow.

'And so, by and by, doggedly, you reached the shore and went to your father's house, where your sister-in-law was staying?'

'Yes.'

'No more questions.'

Counsel for the Prosecution wasted no time on preliminaries when his turn came to address the court. He signalled to the clerk of court who handed him a foolscap envelope which he put on a table in front of him, and launched his attack on the defendant.

'Mr. Blacker, Mr. Daniel Blacker, isn't it true that some time after you left Port au Prince, having first put ashore your bride of just a week, ostensibly to take the *Margarita* to Santa Lucia where she was due to be refitted, you changed course and sailed for Wilhemstad Curaçao where you waylaid your brother Jacob and challenged him to tell you the reason behind his visit to Mrs. Vanderwelt's lawyers, and, when he told you, you killed him in order to stop him from delivering her message?'

'No, I did not.'

'Isn't it also true that you got Aristide to help you carry Jacob's body on board the *Margarita* before you sailed for Santa Lucia?'

'No, I did not.'

'Isn't it also true that three quarters of the way across, close to the windward islands known as the Grenadines, in the lesser Antilles, between the 10th and 15th° of longitude but closer to the 15th, you drugged Aristide, and when you felt sure he was knocked out, you laid his body alongside Jacob's and set fire to the *Margarita*?'

'No, I did not.'

'You waited until the fire had developed, then lowered the dinghy, fixed the gangway, and shaved your head. When the fire had gained hold you climbed down into the dinghy and took photographs of the blaze on your mobile phone.'

M. Harrison picked up the envelope that had been passed on to him earlier on.

'I have here an envelope marked Exhibit A containing prints of the photographs you took on your mobile phone as the *Margarita* went up in flames, prints which you sent anonymously as a conundrum to tease him with to an old college friend of yours you considered 'staid and bookish', Mr. Stewart Sinclair, a private eye, who happened to be on your trail at the time on account of the suspiciously lavish lifestyle you enjoyed as a charity worker. All credit to him for suspecting foul play. As the jury will see, those photographs can only have been taken from close up on a mobile phone, and from a secure and dry position like a dinghy, not from the interior of a life-buoy. I will now ask for Exhibit B to be brought into the courtroom.'

All eyes turned toward the courtroom door as Sinclair and Sebastian walked in carrying a large object wrapped in a tarpaulin which they set down on a table in front

Of the bench, in full view of the jury.

'This is a large fragment of the dinghy of the *Margarita*, is it not, Daniel Blacker? The dinghy in which you made your getaway after setting the family yacht on fire with Jacob's body on board. As you can see, as everybody can see, although the name on it is partially erased, some of the letters that spelt it like I, T, A are still visible on the stern. Its discovery is owed to Mr. Stewart Sinclair's determination to uncover physical evidence in support of the circumstantial evidence. It was found on a beach in Santa Lucia where beachcombers had been using it as firewood. That is all.'

'This court will adjourn until to-morrow morning when it will reconvene at 9 a.m. for the jury to deliver its verdict', said Judge Ruddersford who seemed to be in a hurry to expedite the matter.

'What do you think?', Sebastian asked Sinclair as they left the court.

'I don't know. Lots of boats have feminine names ending in A, like 'Evita', 'Pepita'; there are no documents from a shipbuilding yard to prove that that particular dinghy came with the *Margarita*, and the Defence was able right at the beginning through adroitly questioning witnesses like yourself and Arthur Blacker to throw a doubt on their ability to formally identify the accused as Jacob; even their bullying of Eleanor Blacker failed to dispel the possibility that he might not be who he said he was. We have to wait and see.'

Next morning. When Judge Ruddersford asked if they had reached a verdict, the foreman said they had and handed the clerk of the court a piece of paper which he passed on to the judge. Putting on his spectacles, Judge Ruddersford addressed the accused ;

'Jacob Blacker, please rise. You have been found not guilty. You are free to go.'

Although the courtroom was filled to capacity, it seemed as though the sound of people leaving was muffled up by a kind of puzzled numbness. Again, a wave of sympathy flowed towards Eleanor Blacker as she left the courtroom supported by her father-in-law.

Jacob Blacker, who had got up to hear the verdict, had sat down again apparently dead to the world. The noise of officials and employees of the court going about their business did not seem to make an impression on him. In vain, the clerk of the court touched him on the shoulder to urge him to go, saying :

'Mr. Blacker, you must leave. Your relatives have gone ahead.' It made no impression.

Sinclair walked up to him. 'What's the matter, Samson? Lost your strength when you shaved off your hair? You'll have to be more careful next time.'

FINIS

265